PLAYLIST

Spread Your Love - Black Rebel Motorcycle Club
Rehab - Amy Winehouse
Anarchy in the U.K. - Sex Pistols
I Want A New Drug - Huey Lewis & The News
Sabotage - Beastie Boys
I'm On Fire - Bruce Springsteen
Eternal Life - Jeff Buckley
Here's To The Rest Of The World - Whiskeytown
Talk - beabadoobee
The Chain - Fleetwood Mac
cardigan - Taylor Swift
Maps - Yeah Yeah Yeahs
You're Gonna Make Me Lonesome When You Go - Bob Dylan
Gimme Something Good - Ryan Adams
In the Blood - John Mayer
Dear Prudence - The Beatles
Goodbye Yellow Brick Road - Elton John
Don't Look Back In Anger - Oasis

PLAYLIST

Fix It to Break It - Clinton Kane
Keep Me in Your Heart - Warren Zevon
All Your Favorite Bands - Dawes

Listen to the playlist on Spotify.

BROKEN LINES

A DARK ROMANCE

JAGGER COLE

Broken Lines
Jagger Cole © 2022
All rights reserved.
Cover and interior design by Emily Wittig Designs
Photography by Wander Aguiar

This is a literary work of fiction. Any names, places, or incidents are the product of the author's imagination. Similarities or resemblance to actual persons, living or dead, or events or establishments, are solely coincidental. No part of this book may be reproduced, scanned, or distributed in any printed or electronic form without prior written permission from the author, except for the use of brief quotations in a book review.
The unauthorized reproduction, transmission, or distribution of this copyrighted work is illegal and a violation of US copyright law.

❦ Created with Vellum

TRIGGER WARNING

This book contains darker themes and graphic depictions of past SA and trauma. While these scenes were written to create a more vivid, in-depth story, they may be triggering to some readers. Please read with that in mind.

PROLOGUE

Twenty years ago, New York City:

WE'RE COMING to you today live outside Madison Square Garden, just hours before the lights go down for the very first US concert by British rock sensation Velvet Guillotine.

Behind me, you can see the *thousands* of people who've been camped out on the streets of midtown Manhattan since last night, all here waiting for their chance to be the first inside the doors when they open. And I honestly don't think anyone's seen anything like this in a long time, maybe since Elvis, or Beatle-mania.

Like The Beatles, the four boys of Velvet Guillotine also hail from Liverpool. But where the Fab Four were all charming smiles and bowl haircuts, these new Brit sensations are all middle fingers, bottles of booze, and pure sex appeal.

The band has been causing a real stir amongst publications here in the US even before they landed last night—labeled too hot for public airways or television and too wild for a US market. But, in this reporter's opinion, the four members of Velvet Guillotine are nothing short of the revival of rock and roll in its most gritty, undiluted form. And I, for one, am here for it.

Velvet Guillotine exploded out of the scene just six months ago with their smash hit single *Wreck Me Gently*, which has been absolutely destroying chart records across the UK and the US. And here we are just six months after that debut release and the four of them are playing five—count them, *five*—sold-out shows at Madison Square Garden.

Additionally, if the rumors are true, the band has allegedly already been fielding collaboration requests from music icons like Jimmy Paige, Elton John, Eminem, Doctor Dre, and Madonna. Plans are already underway for a worldwide tour following this US circuit. But not before a brief layover here in New York where the band will start recording their follow-up record at the famous Electric Lady Studios.

Of course, the centerpiece of all this, which you can hear on the lips of the fans chanting his name behind me, is undeniably frontman Jackson Havoc, who's been branded the devil of rock 'n roll. But love him or hate him, the wild child *enfant terrible* lead singer and lead guitar player for Velvet Guillotine is the primary reason every single one of these people is standing outside right now.

The magnetic stage presence of David Bowie or Freddie Mercury, the allure of Mick Jagger, and the sex appeal of Prince. I daresay Jackson Havoc is going to be a busy man while he's in New York.

And judging by this crowd and the *state* of this crowd, crying and screaming for Velvet Guillotine and of course, Havoc himself, I can safely say it's time to hang onto your head.

Because Guillotine-mania is here, and it's not going anywhere.

Fifteen years ago, London:

WE'RE LIVE IN LONDON, standing outside of the Willesden Magistrate Court, where rock icon Jackson Havoc has just been arraigned on assault and narcotics charges stemming from an altercation at the Royal International Hotel in Knightsbridge.

Police were summoned to the hotel two nights ago after Velvet Guillotine's sold-out third show here in London, to a party allegedly taking up the entire top floor and roof of the famous hotel. Authorities were able to clear out what has been described as "orgiastic mayhem" by a hotel spokesman, who added that the hotel will be pressing charges for damages incurred.

But the story of the hour, of course, is that police allegedly discovered Velvet Guillotine frontman Jackson Havoc heavily intoxicated and running *naked* through the halls of the hotel. Havoc was allegedly banging on every door screaming the lyrics to Elton John's *Goodbye Yellow Brick Road*.

In true Velvet Guillotine form, Havoc did not go quietly. After allegedly throwing punches and taking out three officers, Mr. Havoc was eventually subdued by four police officers with the help of a tranquilizer.

While excessive, this newest altercation with law enforcement and flaunting of the law, in general, comes after a long string of similar incidents stretching back to essentially the band's formation. Velvet Guillotine has risen through the charts over the last five years to be one of, if not *the*, best-selling rock band of all time. And are currently on track to beat out Elvis Presley, The Eagles, Oasis, and The Beatles for that title. The band has built a reputation with their fan base on a culture of excess, mayhem, and as they've frequently referred to it in interviews, "pure rock 'n roll hedonism."

While this makes for a great show, multiple voices have been quite loud in condemning this "hedonism" for bleeding off the stage into the day-to-day lives of the four members. Mr. Havoc along with all three other members of the band have been publicly linked with not just leading ladies of Hollywood and fashion supermodels, but also the criminal elements of London, New York, Chicago, and elsewhere. Most recently, in Las Vegas, where rhythm guitarist Will Cates allegedly got into a brawl with mob prince Luca Carvelli at Caesars Palace three months ago.

While the band's—and mostly Mr. Havoc's—off-stage escapades seem to have done nothing but *increase* record and ticket sales, an insider in the Velvet Guillotine camp has told us that legal representation and management have begged the band, especially Havoc, to tone down the partying and to finish the rest of this tour without incident. Especially considering the wide range of civil and criminal legal battles that have been mounting against the band over the last five years.

And yet, the band seems to show no sign of slowing down or stopping. Hot on the heels of their fourth studio record in just five years, Velvet Guillotine has just announced plans for yet another U.S. tour of thirty cities. This, of course, flies directly in the face of the United States Justice Department issuing a statement apparently banning the group from even landing on US soil in light of unaddressed drug allegations from the last tour. Viewers may recall that drummer Iggy Watts was arrested by undercover agents for attempting to purchase large amounts of heroin, cocaine, and MDMA before the group's sold-out Miami show last summer.

Whether or not the might of even the United States Justice Department can stop a force of nature like Velvet Guillotine, has yet to be determined.

Twelve years ago, New York City:

IN SHOCKING NEWS TODAY—OR perhaps not so shocking news if you've ever even once *heard* of the band Velvet Guillotine—frontman Jackson Havoc is allegedly being questioned by police regarding an incident earlier in which he allegedly waved a loaded gun in the faces of paparazzi outside his hotel.

Mr. Havoc was seen leaving The Waldorf Astoria, seemingly extremely intoxicated, along with band members Will Cates, Iggy Watts, and Asher Sins. The four were accompanied by Victoria's Secret sensation Vanessa Hill, eighteen-year-old Hollywood starlet Elena Martins, infamous band groupie and one-time Playboy Playmate Judy Blue, and of course, Mr. Watt's wife of almost ten years, Alice Watts.

When confronted by paparazzi, Havoc allegedly shoved them back. When pressed, he allegedly pulled the firearm from his jacket and brandished it before firing once into the air.

Speculation has of course already run rampant that this will derail Velvet Guillotine's newest U.S. tour before it even begins. Fears that, in this reporter's mind, are completely unfounded if not utterly ridiculous.

Because, as it seems, *nothing* can stop Velvet Guillotine. Not the US Justice Department. Not the hurricane that almost took their plane out of the sky nine months ago. And certainly not any of the legendary antics of frontman Jackson Havoc.

Not with a forty-venue tour already sold out ahead of them. Not with the release of their fifth studio record, *Infinite Excess*, which has been sitting at the very top of the charts since it was released two months ago. And not with the band's new video for the hit single *Exorcise My Love* winning the distinction of being the first video on YouTube to break two *billion* plays...a record speculated to be at least partially due to frontman Havoc's costume—or perhaps lack thereof.

Mr. Havoc can be seen in the video cavorting suggestively on stage with his guitar, clad only in low slung leather pants. Pants slung *so* low, in fact, that the band's records have been pulled from shelves in more religiously conservative communities around the US and Europe. The smash hit video for *Exorcise My Love* is also allegedly responsible for the band's shows in Turkey and Russia being canceled, with local authorities citing "questionable morality".

But something tells me, this is just one more "setback" that will end up propelling this untouchable band even higher.

Because it would seem nothing on earth can stop the meteoric rise of Velvet Guillotine.

11 years ago, New York City:

IT IS WITH HEAVY, broken hearts that we interrupt this program to bring you breaking news from here in New York

City, where rock icon and Velvet Guillotine drummer Iggy Watts has just been pronounced dead from heroin overdose.

To repeat: Iggy Watts, drummer for the hit rock band Velvet Guillotine, is dead.

I...I don't actually know what to say. I have...There are no words for a loss like this.

Tragically, Mr. Watts has had a very public battle with his demons over the last ten years of his career, frequently in and out of rehab. He leaves behind his long-time partner and wife, Alice, who he frequently referred to as his rock and his tether to reality. In the hedonistic and frequently non-monogamous world of rock and roll, Iggy and Alice Watts carved a place for themselves in the hearts of many fans with their commitment to each other.

Making this loss even more tragic, however, is that Mr. Watts also leaves behind he and Alice's newborn daughter, Eleanor.

Mr. Watts's body was discovered by housekeepers at his residence at the iconic Dakota building here in New York...also the site of another music tragedy in 1980, when Mark David Chapman shot John Lennon dead outside the building's very front doors.

Already, if you can see behind me, crowds that may even rival the memorial to John Lennon are forming. Some are holding candles, or posters, or records. Many with tears on their face—

I'm sorry. I'm sorry. I can't. I can't. I'm sorry...

Good evening. That was Michelle on the ground in New York City, and we're now switching back to here in the main studio. And I think I speak for all of us here when I say we all feel the sense of loss and helplessness that Michelle and everyone else is feeling right now. There are no words. There are simply no words to describe this profound loss that the music world, and the world at large has experienced tonight.

Again, Iggy Watts, founding member and drummer for Velvet Guillotine, is dead.

Ten years ago, Los Angeles:

THIS IS Matt Carver with The Hollywood Reporter, comin' at you *live* from the Hollywood Bowl. We are seconds away from jumping into the live broadcast of the very special and very intimate "Concert for Iggy"—the memorial show being put on by some of music's greatest, including Robert Plant, Bono, Bob Dylan, Dave Grohl, Jay-Z, Kurt Harrison, and Mark Cooper.

And, of course, iconically, the very first public appearance and performance by Velvet Guillotine frontman Jackson Havoc since the loss of his long-time friend and musical collaborator one year ago to a heroin overdose.

Billed as a solo act for this show in light of Velvet Guillotine's unofficial breakup following Iggy Watts's passing, Havoc is here alone to open this live-streamed memorial show to his friend.

It's been a hard year for Havoc and the surviving members of Velvet Guillotine. Rhythm guitar player Will Cates has been dogged since last year by a series of legal battles as well as an apparently on-going public feud with Vegas mob prince Luca Carvelli. Bass player Asher Sins followed the loss of his friend Iggy Watts with the death of his father and mentor, the jazz great Leonard Sins, and has chosen to step out of the limelight.

And of course, just six months ago, we saw Jackson Havoc—voluntarily, it would seem, for the first time in his entire career despite his very public abuse of substances—checking *himself* into a Santa Monica rehabilitation center, where he lasted just two days before leaving of his own accord.

Speculation has run rampant as to the future of Velvet Guillotine. Will there be a new drummer? Will the band finish the allegedly *un*finished, highly anticipated new record? And what about the upcoming tour next year?

These are all questions many hope will be answered tonight with this first appearance by Havoc in almost six months.

And…there we are. We're getting the go-ahead, and the house lights are dimming behind me here on stage. This is *very* exciting, and you can tell the crowd is on their toes ready for their first dose in months of that dark magic only Jackson Havoc seems to be able to bring to a stage.

Okay, and we are going live to the stage where the backing band is starting to play. Of course, this is not the *actual* Velvet Guillotine, merely a house band backing Havoc tonight. They're playing what appears to be the intro to…wait, hang on. The band just stopped playing abruptly.

Folks, I'm not sure what we're seeing here. But the backing band has *stopped*, and there seems to be some confusion. Okay, the house lights are coming back on and there seems to be a flurry of activity happening in the wings of the stage. There is shouting and…

Oh my *God*. Ladies and gentlemen, a *fight* has just broken out on stage left between what appears to be the Hollywood

Bowl stage manager and Havoc's longtime manager, Cliff Jenkins.

And yet... there seems to be no sign of Havoc himself. I repeat, there is no sign of the legendary rock star....

Okay, okay, the stage manager has distanced himself from Cliff Jenkins and is walking out to center stage. The house lights are on and...Oh my God. Oh my *God*. We're being told...

I...I don't know what this means, but we're being told that Havoc will *not* be playing tonight, because he cannot be *found*.

I repeat; rock icon Jackson Havoc has apparently disappeared.

1

MELODY

Present, New York City:

"Pitch me."

I swallow, doing my absolute best to keep the easy smile on my face. Which is no easy feat when the executive editor for one of the biggest music publications in the world is leering across the desk at you with a smug smile, just waiting of you to fail so that he can kick you out and go on with his day.

But I've been expecting this question. Becca, a friend of a friend of mine, who already works here at Ignition Magazine—who also got me this interview—prepared me for senior editor Chuck Garver's legendarily smug, snide grin. Just like she prepared me for his favorite interview question: "pitch me", where he wants the candidate to literally sell him a front-page-worthy story on the spot.

She also prepared me for the way the leering editor has a fondness for talking to the *chests* of young woman…as he's doing right now, to me.

I swallow again, sinking a little more into the chair at my back as I roll my shoulders forward slightly, as if to hide my boobs a little.

But Chuck is in it to win it, it would seem.

"Well? Ain't got all fuckin' day, kid."

My teeth rake over my bottom lip.

Becca was right: I should have opened with who my mom is.

Should have. But won't. But can't. I spent my entire childhood living in the shadow of my mother's fame and narcissism. And *yeah*, it would probably help with getting a job at a famous rock music magazine like Ignition to mention the teeny, little fact that my mother is one of the most famous rock 'n roll groupies of the last thirty years.

But no. I want this, but I want this on my terms. I want it because I earned it. Not because Judy banged a bunch of famous musicians.

Chuck sighs, lacing his fingers together as he leans across his big desk.

"Elevator pitch. You've got thirty fucking seconds to grab me, Melody," he grunts at my tits. "So…*go*."

You've got this.

I take a deep breath.

"Okay, so, a piece about DJ Smash getting caught up in that e-cigarette company scandal—"

"Fucking boring. Twenty seconds. What else you got."

Fuck.

I thought that'd be a slam dunk of a story. A mix of current events, politics, and music, which is what Becca was telling me Chuck is obsessed with finding for the magazine these days. Luckily, I came armed with backups.

"Alright, well, Madonna—"

Chuckle laughs coldly.

"Whatever it is, with Madge, it's already been done to death. Fuck no. Ten seconds. Tick tock, kid."

The panic starts to rise.

"The return of eighties synth—"

"Already published."

"Cancel culture and nineties rap lyrics—"

"*Hard* fucking no."

"Okay, okay…what about—"

"Time's up."

The room goes still. My brow furrows.

Tell him! I can hear Becca slurring at me over drinks last night. *Just fucking tell him about your mom! It's your foot in the door!*

Chuck sighs, and his eyes actually drag up from my tits to my eyes.

"Well, Melody," he smiles thinly. "It's been fun. And look, good luck. But…" he lifts a shoulder. "I think we're good on—"

"My mother is Judy Blue."

I blurt the words out like it's one long word. Or one long swear. Chuck frowns.

"What?"

"Judy Blue," I repeat. "She's my mom."

He stares at me, his brow furrowed.

"*The* Judy Blue."

I nod. He grins widely, lightbulbs and perhaps dollar signs flashing in his eyes.

"Judy *fucking* Blue, like…like THE Judy Blue-Eyes? The groupie?"

I groan to myself.

"*Yep.*"

"Why on *earth* would you not tell people that?!" He grins, staring at me. "Holy shit, I had like three copies of her issue when she was a centerfold!"

Yeah, *that* would be why I don't tell people.

Hi, nice to meet you. There's a not zero percent chance that you've seen my mom's labia printed in high definition in a Playboy centerfold.

"This is huge!"

Suddenly, his eyes go wide.

"Oh, *fuck* yeah! That's our story!"

Fuck fuck fuck.

"I—I don't think a story on my mom—"

"Oh, fuck no."

His brow furrows.

"No, I'm not printing another whiney nostalgic cash grab from yet another star-fucker like your mom. No. Hell no."

I frown curiously.

"So…."

Chuck lifts a brow.

"You don't know where I'm going with this?"

"Not…really?"

"Do you fucking use the internet?"

"Uh, yeah—"

"Did you use the internet *today*?"

I'm confused.

"Yes?"

He laughs.

"Christ, kid. When's the last time you talked to your mother?"

Not as long ago as I'd have liked.

"Here."

He drags his laptop over, opens it, and bangs on the keyboard before spinning it so that we can both see the screen. Up on it is Rolling Stone Magazine's website. And there, front and center on the main page…

Is my mother.

Giving an interview in a video clip to Connor Newsome, a top Rolling Stone columnist.

"Ah, well, we used to have quite a time back then, Connor."

My mother chuckles a cigarette-ash laugh as she lights one. She exhales slowly, in what I'm sure she thinks is a glamorous way, before nodding at the interviewer.

"But you were saying?"

"Well, Judy, I was just commenting that you were publicly linked to quite a few infamous music legends back in the day."

She grins.

"Oh yes, oh yes. There was Mark Cooper. Leighton James from Soul Scream."

I grit my teeth. It all comes back. The relentless teasing in school about my mom fucking every rock star of the last twenty years. Not being able to walk into a single bar or coffee shop without hearing *someone* singing who's been romantically linked with Judy.

"Brian Cummings. Slade. Will Cates, from Velvet Guillotine, of course."

"Of course," Connor nods. "Which is detailed pretty extensively in your book, if I remember."

"That's right, Connor."

I roll my eyes, going numb.

"Her" book—her "tell all memoir". As in, the book that a team of four writers working for a publishing house wrote before putting her name on it in order to sell copies.

"And Jackson Havoc, too."

Connor blinks. So do I.

Wait, what?

"Sorry, did you just say Jackson Havoc?" Connor's brows lift as he leans closer to my mother.

"That's right, Connor."

"You dated *the* Jackson Havoc?"

"Well…" She grins. "We…spent time together."

"Until he disappeared, of course," Connor sighs.

"Oh, no, even after that."

Connors jaw drops as my mother keeps going.

"But, yeah, there was Tom Roberts, from Matchbook 30—"

"I'm sorry, Judy, could we go back for a sec?"

"Sure, Connor," she grins a Cheshire Cat grin as she drags on her cigarette.

"Did you just say you've kept in touch with *Jackson Havoc*?"

She shrugs. "A bit, sure."

Chuck hits the pause button as the office goes silent.

"You understand what this means, right?"

He sits, swiveling his gaze back to stab into me.

"Melody, Jackson Havoc, the biggest fuck-off rock god since Led Zeppelin, dis-a-fucking-pears off the face of the goddamn earth. Shit, some people think he's as dead as most of the rest of his band."

"Yeah…?"

"And *your mom* knows where he is?! Do you see how fucking huge that is?!"

I groan to myself.

Yeah, it'd be huge if it wasn't complete *bullshit*. Because I know my mother, and I know she's completely full of shit, as always.

"Look, Mr. Garver—"

"It's Chuck," he grins widely. "Just call me chuck, Mel."

He stands, rapping his knuckles on the desk before he turns to pace the floor behind his desk.

"There's our story."

"What, that my mom screwed—"

"No, I don't give a fuck whose dick your mom sucked, Melody."

He strolls the front of his desk and sits back against the edge of it, crossing his arms over his chest.

"But I give a huge fuck about landing the music story of the *decade*. Jackson. Goddamn. Havoc."

He grins hungrily at me.

"That's your story."

My jaw drops.

"Wait, *my* stor—"

"Your mom; your story," he shrugs. "You're hired. Effective immediately."

My heart thuds in my ears.

"Welcome to Ignition Magazine, Ms. Blue."

I blink, slowly shaking my head as I try and fight through the floating feeling humming in my chest.

"Look, Mr.—*Chuck*. You should know that my mom is full of shit—"

"Better hope she's not with this."

He glares at me.

"I'll be blunt. I don't need another puff writer hacking up stories about rap DJs and e-cigarettes, or Madonna, or anything like that. So, if you're not up for this, there's the fucking door, kid. But if you *do* want this?"

He raps his knuckles on the edge of the desk again.

"Opportunity knocks."

I swallow, nodding slowly.

"A bit of advice?" Chuck grunts.

I raise my gaze to his.

"If you do find him—Havoc, that is—" he frowns. "Are you a fan?"

"Of his?"

"Or of Velvet Guillotine."

My face heats. "Yeah, a *huge* one. I mean, I don't know if you know this, but Will Cates actually lived with my mom and I—"

"Yeah, great, I don't give a fuck." Chuck sighs. "But Havoc will. I mean, if he's even alive, which is still fifty-fifty odds, if you ask me."

He frowns.

"What I'm saying, Mel, is if you *do* find this prick? Don't mention being a fan. You don't *ever* mention being a fan to these vampires."

My brow furrows.

"Vampires?"

"Rock stars. Movie stars. Celebrities." Chuck lifts a shoulder. "As much as every publication on earth, us included, likes to pretend they're deities to be worshiped? Spoiler, they're not. But they're not 'just like us', either. They take and they take—like bloodsucking vampires. They're twisted, and they're all —and I do mean *all*—fucked up. It's the only way a person can possibly sustain being at the top like that and being worshiped by mere mortals like us on a daily basis. You get me?"

I smile wryly. "I've been around a fair number of famous musicians, Mr. Garver. I don't get starstruck."

He grins.

"Good. But I need you to do more than not ask for a goddamn autograph. I need you to not give him a fucking inch. If you find him, that is. Because these rock guys are all the same, and they're *all* used to the world getting down on their fucking knees and saying 'please'."

He lifts a stern brow.

"Don't do that, by the way."

My face burns as I quickly shake my head.

"Of course not."

"If you find him, don't mention being a fan. And don't pretend for a second that the two of you are friends. He's not your friend. He's your target. Just like you're his fucking prey."

I shiver as I nod quickly, my pulse quickening as I try to swallow the task that I'm about to set out and do.

"And like I said," Chuck shrugs. "If you're not up to this… there's the door. But if you *do* want—"

"I want it," I blurt, nodding stiffly.

He eyes me coolly.

"You find me Jackson Havoc, kid, and you can have *my* fucking job."

2

MELODY

"Wait, are you *serious*?!"

June, my friend and roommate, who also happens to be an *amazing* if not totally under-appreciated singer-songwriter, squeals into the phone.

"You *got it*?!"

I give a grin and a quick wave to Martin, the building's doorman, as he opens the door for me with his usual flourish. Then my attention swivels back to June.

"Oh, I got it."

"Fuck yeah, Mel!" She screams. "I mean *fuck* yeah!"

"Hey, thank your pal Becca for me."

June snorts.

"I don't think she was expecting that you'd *actually* get the job. I'm pretty sure she was doing my friend—*you*—a favor to get in my good graces. She's been hounding me for some lame puff piece about women and indie music for like a month now."

"Wouldn't that story be good for you?"

"I mean, if Becca wasn't a hack writer, sure."

I choke on a laugh.

"So, which of those pitches you prepared did the trick?"

"None of them, actually." I groan. "I did it, June."

She sighs, knowing exactly what I mean by "it".

"Well, hey, it worked. I mean, we both knew mentioning Judy was a layup into that gig, right?"

"Yeah, well…I kinda wanted to do it on my own merits," I groan as I step into the elevator.

"Look, take it from someone who's been fighting that 'on your own merit' fight for years. When opportunity comes knocking? Just freaking take it. You can prove your merit once you've got your foot in the door."

I smile wryly. "Fair. Thanks."

"Don't let it sour the day. You're going to be great at this. Of course, offer still stands to be my personal lyric writer. You can be Bernie, I'll be Elton."

I grin, rolling my eyes.

"Has the pay gone up?"

"From my generous offer of infinite sandwiches and zero dollars? No, not at all."

"Those sandwiches good towards my half of the rent?"

"Yeah, you know what? On second thought, definitely go with the journalism gig."

A laugh bubbles from my lips.

"So, do you have a story to do yet?"

"*Oh yeah*," I mutter. "But…" I frown as the elevator doors open to a familiar hallway. "I actually gotta let you go. I'm at Judy's."

"Oof. Good luck. Fill me in on the story later?"

"For sure."

"Later."

I hang up and slip the phone into my pocket. Then, with a heavy sigh, I raise my hand and knock on the door.

"*Hey* girlfriend."

A plume of acrid tobacco and weed smoke surrounds her like a smoldering halo as the door swings open. I resist the urge to gawk at the plunging—and I do mean fucking *plunging*—neckline of what could only generously be described as a top and not intimate lingerie.

"My God, Melody, what are you wearing?" She makes a face.

I look down at my very basic black slacks and white blouse business-casual outfit from the interview earlier.

"Are you working for the cops or something now?"

I sigh as I raise my eyes back to her.

"Hi, Judy."

"*Mom*. It's *mom*," she mutters, moving back to let me in.

BROKEN LINES

I step into the large, light-filled West Village apartment. As is her custom, my mom pats the frame that sits over "To Judy Blue. Xoxo," written in sharpie on the wall above the fairly famous signature of Will Cates.

The note on the wall is the "card" that came with the gift of this very apartment, back when I was eight and Will, the now deceased rhythm guitar player for Velvet Guillotine, and my mom were dating. He ended up running off with a Victoria's Secret model two years later. But the huge apartment was in my mom's name and paid for in full.

It's weird, knowing that those hit Velvet Guillotine songs you hear in almost every bar are the reason I grew up—from at least aged eight on—with a roof over my head. Not in a car, or in the back of random tour busses, or in hotel rooms, or crashing with "friends" of Judy's. Which is what I remember from those years before we moved here.

I shut the door behind me and follow my mom's swaying, shuffling steps down the hall. In the living room, I grit my teeth, keeping my eyes *away* from the wall above the couch.

Aka, one of the top reasons I never brought friends home from school. Aka, the source of relentless teasing growing up, and scorned looks from other parents.

Aka, the *gigantic*, framed print of my mother's Playboy Centerfold shot.

Judy sighs when she sees the way I'm fastidiously staring at the opposite wall.

"I don't know how I managed to raise such a prude."

"And I'm not sure where you found your definition of *raised*, but here we are."

She rolls her eyes. "Oh, don't start, Mel. It's exhausting."

I also have no interest in going down this road with her for the millionth time. Because it never fixes anything. It never changes a thing about the fact that I grew up in this weird shrine to her own narcissism, often *without* her even here for extended periods of time. It doesn't change that I learned to cook when I was nine, because Judy went to a concert and just "decided" to hop on the band's tour bus for the next five days.

In her mind, she was a "cool" mom. She was "avant guard" and "a free spirit".

In most legal definitions, what she was was an *absent*, derelict parent. And the whole "roof over my head" thing is just about the one aspect of being a mother she didn't fail me at.

The list of ways she *did* fail me is vast.

And dark.

And left me with invisible scars that'll never fully heal.

Do I want to scream in her face for abandoning me so she could go screw and party with famous people? Do I want to rip down that goddamn centerfold that somehow made *me* an object of scorn and misery through all my school years? Do I want to physically hurt her for the way she let a monster into our home, and into my bedroom when I was thirteen?

All. The. Fucking. Time.

But I know painfully well from the years I did spend yelling at her that it won't change a thing. It never hurts her to hear my pain.

It only inconveniences her.

Judy Blue: mother of the fucking century.

So instead of getting into it with her, I turn away. This time, in an effort *not* to lay eyes on the enormous nude photograph of Judy sitting spread-eagle on a pool table pouring champagne over her vagina, my gaze lands on the coffee table.

Which, currently, is decorated with a glass of something bubbly, an ashtray with a joint in it, and a mirror covered in lines of white powder.

Ahh yes, nostalgia. There's the home life I remember.

"Alright, let's hear it," she sighs.

I turn away from the cocaine to smile thinly at her.

"Hear what, exactly?"

"The fucking lecture. Just get it out. I'm sure you'll feel better."

"It's your life, Judy."

"*Mom.*"

I don't respond. She sighs.

"I'd offer you some, but…"

"Yeah, well, you know. Eleven in the afternoon is a *touch* early for me."

She rolls her eyes. "Oh, calm down, Melody. I had some company over last night. I just haven't cleaned up yet."

She sighs, slumping down on the couch and reaching for the spliff smoldering in the ashtray next to the narcotics.

"I raised you in the—"

"Yep, gonna stop you right there, Judy."

My mother glares at me as she puffs on the joint.

"I *raised you* in the spirit of rock 'n roll. And yet somehow, you turn out to be a little narc."

"Oh, I'm sorry, should we shoot up or something? I mean, gee, mom, it's almost noon! Chop chop!"

She waves me off, a bored look on her face.

"I gave smack up *years* ago, hon."

"How nice for you."

She sighs again.

"So, did you see my interview?"

I lean against the doorframe, forcing my gaze lower to her instead of up at the gynecological display on the wall above her.

"I did. I thought you were done giving those."

She snorts. "Yeah, well…"

She raises her hands, dusting one with the other as if she's "making it rain" dollar bills.

"*Right.*"

"Also, you do not say no to Rolling Stone, Mel."

"I wasn't aware you said no to *anyone*, actually."

Her lips purse tightly.

Am I being a bitch? Definitely. Does she deserve every damn drop of it?

Fuck yes.

"How'd my tits look?"

I frown. "What?"

"The interview. How'd the girls look?"

"I…have no idea, and don't even remotely care."

She lifts a shoulder absently, taking a sip of her champagne.

"I had them lifted a few months back."

"Congrats on the boob job?"

She sighs with exasperation. "I didn't have a *boob job*, Melody." Her brow furrows. "I mean, not since 2005. I had them *lifted*. What do you think?"

She cups her tits, jiggling them at me through her lacy top that looks like something someone even younger than me would wear to a club. Or a porn shoot.

"I think I've probably seen my fill of your boobs before."

"Christ, the morality police are here. Everyone cover up!" She snickers at no one before taking a long drag off the spliff.

I chew on my lip, trying to decide if I'm really going to even ask what I came here to ask. If it's worth wading into Judy's bullshit and getting sucked into her narcissistic tar pit.

"Oh, listen, honey, while you're here, I wanted to ask you something."

"You can't borrow any more money. I don't have any anyway."

Her "shocked and offended" look is so practiced I almost want to give her an Academy Award.

"*Wow*," she chokes. "Just…*wow*."

"Oh, *please*. What else could you possibly be dying to ask me about, Judy?"

"Uh, first of all, I don't want your money. I just got looped into something big and was thinking…" she shrugs. "I was just thinking that maybe my dear daughter might want in on it, too. *That's all.*"

"Is this code for buying drugs?"

She sighs heavily. *"No,* you freaking narc. But if you think you might be interested, it's an investment opportunity."

I snort.

"Really."

"Yes *really*, Melody. And quite a lucrative one. Have you been hearing about crypto coin?"

I groan as I start to turn "Okay, I'm out—"

"It's a once in a lifetime opportunity, Melody! And I'd just need to borrow like…twenty-thousand, *max—*"

"There it is!" I bark coldly. "Wow, Judy. You actually almost surprised me with that one!"

"Did you just come here to be a cunt or was there another reason?!" She snaps back.

I almost say no. I almost forget the whole thing, mentally write off the job at Ignition, and leave. But that's not a win for me.

It'd be another Judy win. It'd be one more thing I lose out on, because of her. One more opportunity I don't get, or miss out on taking, because my mother is too high to bring me to an audition. Or she's off banging a famous guy on a tour bus in Georgia and can't sign the permission slip. Or I'm too scarred and shattered and silenced to even *take* the leap because of what the monster she let in did to me those years ago.

My teeth grind and my lips thin lethally.

No. I will *not* let her take another opportunity from me.

I take a slow breath, trying to calm myself before my lips form the words.

"Is it true?"

Her brow knits. "Is what true?"

"What you said in that interview. About…" I look away. "About Jackson Havoc."

The living room goes quiet.

"Which part?"

I swallow as I turn back to her. "The part where you know where he is?"

She smiles.

God. Fucking. Damnit.

I groan as my shoulders—and the hope for a job at Ignition Magazine—slump.

When you live with a narcissistic liar, you get good at knowing their "tell", like in a poker game. And Judy's tell, without fail, is to smile like that whenever she's completely full of shit.

"Of course, you don't—"

"Well, c'mon, Mel!" She sighs. "Rolling Stone didn't want a boring interview! They wanted the good stuff!"

"They wanted *the truth*, Judy," I mutter. "Not your concocted fantasy."

She rolls her eyes, waving her hand haphazardly.

"They just wanted something juicy from yours truly. And they got what they paid for."

I groan, pinching the bridge of my nose.

"So, you don't actually know what happened to Jackson Havoc."

She shrugs. "I mean, I can guess."

But I don't need guesses. I need the truth.

"Any idea where he could be?"

"Why would I know that?"

"Because you screwed him? Or was that part made up too?"

She waves her hand again. "Oh, who can even remember these things, Melody."

Gross.

"But no, I don't know where he is."

This was a waste of my time. Why did I even come here? What the hell else besides more Judy bullshit was I possibly expecting to find?

With a groan, I turn to leave.

"I mean, I know where he's *not*."

I pause, glancing back

"What do you mean?"

Judy gets up and swaying a little before she slinks over to "the wall"

I cringe.

It's her "conquests" wall—a whole big wall of pull-out drawers slightly bigger than the ones you'd find in a library card catalog. And each one is stuffed with memorabilia and little "things" from the famous men she's slept with.

I groan inside, remembering a particularly traumatizing incident when I was in fifth grade. I'd managed to invite some girls over from school who hadn't yet been barred by their parents from hanging out with me—definitely only because said parents hadn't met Judy yet.

Mom was, shockingly, gone when Ashley and Jess came over. I told them there was cool rock and roll stuff in these shelves, and randomly picked one to pull out.

Except this one—marked as the drawer for Chris Hammerstein, the drummer from Dream Vice that mom was seeing for a month or so—slipped off its runner and crashed to the floor. And out spilled a pair of snapped drumsticks, three backstage passes from the Dream Vice "Vicious World" tour, a bag of old weed, and large plaster cast.

...of Chris Hammerstein's erect penis.

After that, Ashley and Jess quickly moved to the "don't hang out with Melody" list, and I learned to never *touch* these drawers again.

Judy pulls out one of the larger ones—the one marked "Will Cates". She rummages around, frowning, before suddenly her brows shoot up.

"Here it is."

She turns around, triumphantly holding a creased, faded postcard with a cartoony Statue of Liberty on it.

I frown.

"What is that?"

"Well, Will was going through this poetic Hemingway phase. It was after Guillotine broke up and after Jackson pulled that disappearing stunt. Will was hand typing things and writing people postcards. You remember, don't you?"

"I was like ten, Judy."

She rolls her eyes.

"Well, he was drunk one night—this was right before he got together with Chrissy, of course—and I guess he was feeling nostalgic. And he sent this off to Jackson."

Chrissy would be the aforementioned Victoria's Secret model Will ran off with, who ended up dying in the same motorcycle crash that took his life.

"Wait, he *knew* where Jackson was?"

Judy shakes her head.

"He thought he might. But…" her mouth twists as she passes me the postcard.

The front has a cartoonish picture of the Statue of Liberty with the words "The Empire State!". The back has mom's apartment address as the return, with the "to" address crossed out with red pen and a rubber-stamp over it that reads "Discontinued address. Return to sender".

Also, there's just two lines as the message.

Jackson - I hope the world is treating you kindly. Miss you so much, brother.

I stare at the card, running a thumb over the handwritten words.

Will didn't live with us all that long, but he was definitely mom's longest fling. And he was kind, and was good to Judy and I, which is more than I can say for most of the dickheads that came before or after him.

And yes, obviously, the question of Will being my father has come up before. Being that he lived with us for almost three years and took such an active role in taking care of me. Not to mention, buying us a freaking apartment to live in.

But for a woman who blathers to anyone and everyone about every single private matter she's been involved in, it's the one thing Judy's kept tight-lipped about. She'll never tell who my real father was. Or the hard truth is, it's likely she doesn't *know*.

Either way, I stopped asking a long time ago.

But I did use to imagine it might be Will. I was only twelve when he and Chrissy died. But I remember Judy being exceptionally sad. And for some reason, that made me sad, too. Even if I didn't fully grasp that a man who'd lived with us for those years—who'd cared for me and even taught me to play the guitar and how to sing—was dead.

In high school, I used to put pictures of myself up on my computer screen next to tabloid shots of Will and try and spot the genetic similarities. Sometimes, I thought I could see them. Other times, they weren't there anymore.

So, maybe my dad was Will. Or maybe my dad was some random roadie for Pearl Jam. Who the hell knows. And at this point, who even cares?

My eyes slip back to address—a Falstaff Island, in Maine—with the "Discontinued address. Return to sender" rubber stamp over it.

"I have no idea why I kept it. I found it under some junk mail in a drawer maybe a year after he and Chrissy got together."

Judy lifts a shoulder before she drains the last of her champagne. Her phone buzzes on the couch behind her, instantly yanking her attention. I watch her eyes gleam for a second as she dives for it.

My mouth thins.

I know this face.

"Listen, Mel, I have to run out for a quick thing. Feel free to stay?"

Drugs. She's running out for drugs. Nothing in the *world* snaps her attention faster than that.

"I have to go too."

"Oh, great!"

She smiles a fake, distracted smile at me as she practically levitates off the couch and brushes past me for the door.

"Just let yourself out, then?"

I don't have time to answer, much less fake a "good to see you, mom" at her back before she's out the door.

Same as it ever was.

I exhale slowly, shaking my head. I go to toss the postcard back in Will's drawer, when I stop.

This is stupid.

And it probably is. But seeing as Judy's interview was total bullshit, it's also the only lead I have in order to get the job I want.

And for once, she is *not* going to take an opportunity from me.

My phone camera clicks. I leave the postcard from one rock god to another on the coffee table, appropriately next to the cocaine and under the nude Playboy Centerfold.

Then I'm out with the only clue I have.

3

JACKSON

The first thought that hits me, as consciousness slaps its chubby dick in my face, is that someone is trying to murder me.

With a fork, to the head.

I wince, groaning as the pain lances into me, cutting into my fucking soul. Until I finally relent and open my eyes.

But of course, I'm alone. I'm always alone. And the would-be assailant isn't an intruder, or someone with an axe to grind.

The person trying to kill me is *me*.

In a sense. At least I only do a halfway decent job at it most times.

I groan as I lift my lids the rest of the way, grumbling and wincing as morning daylight stabs into my eyes. I roll before the sudden jerk of gravity stops me with a stomach-heaving yank. My pounding head swivels to the side, and I grunt.

Right. I'm on the couch. I never made it upstairs to bed last night.

My eyes squeeze shut, my parched lips rubbing together before I finally manage to swing my legs off the side of the couch. My bare feet touch hard wood, and I exhale slowly as I drop my head to the back of the sofa.

"Why the *fuck* is it so fucking light in here…" I mutter to no one.

I lift my head, turning with a wince to glare of the wall of windows on the far side of the massive, lodge-like living room.

Sleeping down here was a *shit* idea. At least in my bedroom upstairs, I've got real, actual blackout curtains. And an eye mask. And earplugs. And virtually anything else I could use to combat the intrusion of reality. Or, specially, mornings.

My least favorite fucking time of the day. Always have been.

But down here in the living room where I apparently decided to call it quits last night, I have none of those tools. And it's too goddamn bright in here.

I stab my angry gaze at the wall of windows again—this time, piecing together the string of sheets and towels strung up over the glass…with push pins, it would seem. A hazy recollection of an even earlier hour dawns in my head—a flashing memory of me angrily tacking up the sheets to block out the light.

Apparently, it only bought me a few more hours.

I blow air through my lips, dropping my head into my hands. My fingers shove through my dark blondish-brown hair, muscles rolling as I suck in another deep breath.

Better hangovers than you have tried, motherfucker.

I stand, grumbling as I stagger over to the makeshift curtains on the windows. I peel one aside, wincing as I glare out at the pristine northern Atlantic Ocean, past the cliff's edge.

Sometimes the view is nice. Okay, the view is always beautiful. But at times—specifically, morning times—looking at beautiful things just pisses me the fuck off.

I turn back to the huge living room. My eyes travel the dusty, cluttered floor, and then slide over the piano and the guitars leaning against it. Over the shredded and crumpled pieces of paper from the ripped-up notebooks scattered on the floor over the last month or so.

The empty bottles on the floor. And fireplace mantel. And windowsills. And…basically everywhere else where there's a flat surface.

I drop my forehead to the window and swallow as the vague memories of the night filter back in.

I stuck the fuck with it last night. The drinking, yes. But also trying—*trying* to fucking write. Something that wasn't complete shit, at least. For myself. For Iggy, on his birthday.

I glance to the left and right for a bottle that still has *something* in it. But I come up short. Instead, I close my eyes and think of my lost best friend. My writing partner. The man who was crazy enough to start a band with me.

Happy birthday, mate.

Drinking and snorting myself into an absolute stupor while trying to bleed genius out on a page felt like the best way to honor him last night. I turn again to let my gaze slide over the mess of ripped up lyrics and hacked out chords on the scraps of paper on the floor.

Not that it did anything. Not that I wrote anything.

That part of me ended when I came here, apparently. Ironically, to write, without the pressures of the world. Back when I was stupid enough to think if I got "mad", and *stayed* mad, the next logical thing that would follow would be "genius".

Mad, plus genius, equals mad genius.

At least, that was the hopeful reasoning. But, spoiler, when you stay mad, the only thing that comes is more mad. And a tension headache.

Maybe I had that genius once. Or I just got good at fooling myself and the rest of the world. Either way…

I glare at the pile of empties on the piano as the fading memories of last night sink into my psyche.

Fuck.

Either way, I'm out of fucking booze. That much I remember from before I crashed to the couch last night.

I groan and slump my face into my hands.

Shit. This is going to make my usual morning coffee exceedingly less fun.

I grumble and shove papers and old notebooks aside. The dark thing in my brain perks up a little when I finally uncover the silver mirror on the coffee table with the little white lines streaked across it.

Who the fuck needs coffee?

The coke hits my bloodstream fast, invigorating me and dragging me—at least slightly—out of the black hole I woke up in. I manage to stand again on wobbly legs, my pulse thudding faster as the drugs take hold.

Shirtless, jeans slipping off my hips, I cross the huge open living room. I pause for a second, catching my reflection briefly in the glass of a framed photograph of New York City up on the wall.

I've lost weight. I should probably eat more. Drink less. Snort less—or better, none at all. There's a lot of things I should probably do. But first, it's time to get even more high.

In the kitchen, I find the bag of weed where I remember tossing it last night. As a bonus, there's a joint I apparently rolled and didn't smoke next to it. I quickly rectify that with one of the stove-top burners, and pretty soon, I'm feeling even better. A couple of Percocets later, and I'm fucking *flying*.

But I also need booze. And probably groceries, I begrudgingly admit. But the mission is alcohol.

AKA, my medicine.

I pull on an old flannel shirt by the front door and slip on some boots without socks. It's cold outside, but I don't bother going back for a jacket or anything. I grunt angrily at the sunshine, jabbing a cigarette between my lips and lighting it with the last glowing bit of the joint. I yank a hat down low and pull on some sunglasses.

Fuck you, daylight.

My head floats as the Percocets take hold. Outside across the yard of the rambling old cliffside mansion that once belonged to an eighteen-hundreds shipping tycoon, sits the garden I set up a few years back. Next to it, the greenhouse, and the garage where I tinker with my bikes from time to time.

I almost pause and decide to spend the morning doing exactly that. But there's a mission to get to, first.

Operation: "procure whiskey before the beast in me destroys itself" takes priority.

So, I amble down the stone steps that delve down through the woods from the peak of the small island where the main house sits. Down below, near the rocky shore, there's a little boathouse. I hop off the dock that extends past the rocks into the small fourteen-footer moored to it. The engine churns to life as I kick away from the dock, drag on my cigarette, and point the prow across the bay towards Cape Harbor.

Coastal Maine is pretty as fuck, I'll give it that. Even if my head still wants to murder my body for consuming what it did last night. Most of it, though—the coast of Maine, that is—is full of fucking tourists.

Cape Harbor, mercifully, is *not*.

Population: seven hundred. Grocery stores: one. Liquor stores: two. Local shady wannabe drug dealer who can score me weed, mediocre cocaine, and most prescriptions I could think of: one.

Fucks to give about the enigmatic motherfucker who doesn't speak and barely even shows his face around town, who lives in the old Fleetwood estate across the bay on Falstaff Island? Aka, *me?*

Motherfucking *zero*.

And that's exactly how I like it.

The sea wind whips at my shaggy hair, stinging my cheeks above my scruff. I inhale deeply, swallowing the briny air and closing my eyes as I bounce over the slight chop.

Slowly, the general "feeling like ass" sensations from when I woke up fades. And by the time I'm close enough to read the "no wake" sign on the dock at Cape Harbor, I'm feeling fantastic.

This message brought to you by: drugs.

I slide the boat in against the dock and toss a line over the mooring post. I pull the hat down lower, buttoning my sleeves down all the way and up to my neck to hide the ink. Not that half this fucking town isn't lobstermen and other trade-types covered in ink of their own. But their tattoos haven't been on billboards selling fucking cologne or on concert posters and album covers.

I pull the slack in and cinch the boat tight before I turn and head up the gangway.

"Afternoon, Robbie."

I nod wordlessly at Albert; the old dock master whose job mostly consists of sitting under a beach umbrella with a line in the water while he crushes Bud Lights all day.

I'm seriously considering going out for his job when he retires.

"Pretty one out, ayuh?"

I nod, again, wordlessly.

"Ayuh, ayuh," he nods back, tossing his fishing line back off the side of the dock. "Well, you take care, Robbie."

I give him a thumbs up and another nod before I head past him up to the main road.

That's another thing I like about this place. Coastal northern New England isn't entirely different from Liverpool, in the United Kingdom, where I grew up. It's got the same gritty, seafaring, salt of the earth type people who know how to fish and know how to keep to themselves.

Which is perfect. The world should be more like this, as a whole.

To them, I'm just the weird fucker who lives alone in a rambling old shipping tycoon's mansion out on an island without a landline, cell service, or the internet. They can—and do—make up their own conclusions or stories as to how it is a guy who mostly dresses like a hobo managed to buy an island. The top theory I've heard whispered behind my back is "failed dot-com tech bro."

Sure. Let's go with that.

I come over once every three or four weeks to buy groceries, a lethal amount of alcohol, and sometimes, a felony amount of illicit and prescription drugs.

I pay cash. I usually keep my sunglasses on, and in ten years, I haven't said *shit* to anyone here. And it's exactly what I want.

Well, not *exactly*. But it's close enough to livable, which is more than I can say for whatever my life was before. Before I fucking disappeared. Before I vanished. Before I couldn't put up the good fight against my demons anymore.

I head to Shoreline Spirits first. I can skip groceries this trip. One, because—annoyingly—I was just fucking over here a week and a half ago. But also, until winter really sets in at least, I grow a lot of my own vegetable in the small plot or the greenhouse next to the garage. And I've got a massive freezer in the basement stocked to the gills with frozen meats and other stuff.

But also, even with the coke, weed, and Percs still buzzing through my system, I've been awake for almost two hours.

I *need* a fucking drink.

"Mornin', Rob."

George, behind the counter of the liquor store, nods absently at me. He only half turns from his Red Sox highlights on ESPN at the sound of the chimes over the door.

"Anything aside from the usual?"

I shake my head.

"Man of habit. This is why I like you, man."

I just nod.

Back when I talked—and I talked a fuckin' *lot*—I was polarizing. People either loved me, to an insane, deity-worship degree, mostly. Or they fucking hated me…also to a slightly deranged level. Especially the idiots who never even actually met or knew me, but who just decided that the internet needed to hear their vitriol against me.

It never really bothered me, because fuck those people—the worshipers and the haters, both.

But now that I *don't* talk? People just seem to…*exist* around me. I'm no longer polarizing. I just smile and nod, give a thumbs up here and there, and go on my merry fucking way. And even if it's pretty obvious to anyone who gives me three seconds of attention that I'm a barely functional drunk, I'm a *likable* barely functional drunk.

This town *likes* me. They don't love me. They don't worship me. They don't hate me and write weird fucking fan fiction on the internet about cutting my corpse into pieces.

They just like me, or else, they're indifferent to me.

I should have disappeared *years* before I did.

George squats behind the counter and lifts a big cardboard box with the amber glass necks of a dozen bottles poking up out of it. My weekly rations.

He rings me up, tells me to have a good one, and then goes back to his baseball as I heft the box and head outside. On a bench, I plop the box down, grab a bottle, and grin to myself as I twist the top off. I bring it to my lips, and I groan with the rush of endorphins as the booze flows over my tongue and down my throat.

Good morning, Vietnam.

I exhale slowly, relishing the familiar burn and heat of my vice of choice. Or vice of *top* choice—these days, at least. I shoulder the box, keeping the opened bottle in my hand as I stroll down the street to the post office, sipping as I walk.

It's just about the end of the month, which means I've probably got some kind of monthly financial statement and probably a message or fifty from Cliff, my manager slash lawyer.

Well, from him, but routed through three proxies, considering he's the only person on earth who know where the hell I am.

I'm across the street, about twenty feet from the post office, when *she* appears.

And I. Stop. Fucking. Cold.

It's not just that she's goddamn gorgeous. It's not just the wind whipping her pink hair across blue eyes, a button nose, and very, very fuckable lips.

It's not the beanie, skinny jeans, stiletto boots, leather jacket, and small leather backpack slung over her shoulder that fucking *scream* "New York City".

It's not the fact that in a town of seven hundred people, even if you barely make appearances and make it your mission not to know a single fucking one of them, you still get an idea of who's who. And she's the poster child for "from away".

It's not…

I scowl.

Fuck it, I lied. It's all those things. That's why I stop cold, bottle halfway to my lips as my gaze stabs into her—raking over her pouty lips and determined blue eyes. Over the pink-punk hair. Over the frankly phenomenal ass encased in those tight jeans.

New York Punk pauses outside the post office door and glances up at it. Then down to something on the phone in her hands, then back to the post office.

My eyes narrow.

What the fuck is this, and who the fuck is she?

I slip into the shadows next to Gerard's Hardware, eyeing her as she steps into the post office and up to Margie, behind the counter.

My jaw clenches.

This is fucking up my plans for the day, which included getting my mail as fast as possible, polishing off another fifth of this bottle on my way back to the dock, going home, and then getting obscenely drunk.

Instead, I'm skulking in an alley staring lecherously at the denim-clad ass of a girl probably half my age.

Needless to say, there are…*downsides* to living alone on an island. I grumble to myself, glaring death at Pink as I sip my whiskey.

Get the fuck out. Whatever you're here for, get it, and then get gone.

But she doesn't listen to my telepathic demands. Instead, she's got Margie laughing.

Laughing.

Margie doesn't fucking *smile.* I wasn't aware she was physically capable of mirth or joy of any kind. And here she is giggling.

Get gone. Get the fuck out of my town.

But once again, my wordless, telepathic demands are ignored. She doesn't leave. Instead, she fucking turns. And suddenly, I'm stiffening as Margie *waves* and stabs a finger…

Right at me.

Mother. *Fuck*.

Fuck. Fuck. Fuck.

I turn away, but not before those big blues of Pink Punk sizzle into me. Something roars deep inside, smashing against cage walls before I manage to pull away. I take an angry, greedy swig of whiskey as I storm down the side-lane next to the hardware store. I take a sharp right down the alley behind it and the drugstore next door. And I'm about to step back out onto the street and make a beeline directly to the dock—

When I crash into something.

Something small.

Something soft.

Something *pink*.

My feet lose their footing. I stagger back, feeling gravity yank my legs out from under me as I fall backwards.

The bottle slips from my hand, smashing to jagged shards on the pavement as I hit the ground. The box on my shoulder hits the sidewalk too with a cracking sound. Instantly, the base of it turns pulpy and wet as all eleven bottles empty through the fresh cracks along their bottoms.

"God. Fucking. *Damnit.*"

I hiss as I lurch to my feet, snarling as I loom over her and stab my gaze into hers. My mouth opens to rip her a new one, when I realize what just happened.

Shit.

I just spoke.

The girl—who now I'm not even sure *is* even half my age—freezes and stares up at me with this mix of uncertainty, fear, and second thoughts.

All of those are smart thoughts for her to have.

"Robert Johnson?"

I glare at her, saying nothing. She arches a brow, a slight smirk playing over her lips.

"Robert Johnson, the famous Mississippi Delta musician who's credited with inventing the blues?"

I shrug. My jaw clenches.

"You *just* talked."

Wordlessly, I brush past her, ignoring the stinging ache in my arm.

"Look, I know you're not— wait, hang on!"

The concern in her voice stops me. I turn to glance back at her, but when my arm throbs, my gaze goes there first.

Shit.

Blood soaks the arm of my flannel, dripping down my pinky to patter the ground with red drops.

"Hang on, *stop.*"

She slings the backpack off her shoulder and yanks the zipper open. My eyes drop to the collection of wadded up t-shirts, a notebook, a toothbrush, another pair of jeans, and a lace black thong…which she sees at about the same time, because she makes a little "eep" sound, pulls a t-shirt out, and yanks the zipper closed.

"Here, let me—"

I glare at her, yanking my arm back.

"Dude, I know you can talk, and you're bleeding badly. Can you just tell me where the hell the cut is?"

My eyes narrow, lips thinning.

"Oh my God, seriously?"

Before I can blink, she grabs the hem of my sleeve and shoves it up high

"Stop—"

Shit.

Her gaze lands on the tattoos on my wrist and forearm. The famous ones that sold sports bikes, and liquor, and fashion.

And records.

Lots and lots and fucking *lots* of records.

Her eyes drag up to mine, widening, her mouth falling open.

"Oh my God—"

"Stay the fuck away from me."

"Jackson—"

She gasps as I grab her by the neck of her jacket, shoving her back into the shadows against the wall of the hardware store.

"It's Robbie," I hiss. "My name is fucking *Robbie*."

"Just like you don't speak?"

My hand drops her jacket. My pulse thuds as my eyes flay her open, until she's shivering, her cheeks reddening.

"Go back to wherever the fuck you came from."

I turn and storm back to the docks, clutching the t-shirt to my throbbing forearm. It's not until I've blown past a napping Albert and cast off my mooring line—not until I'm gunning the engine and guiding the boat back across the bay, that I glance down at the shirt I've been bleeding into.

My brain glitches as my eyes narrow on the way too familiar logo, even after all these years.

It's a fucking Velvet Guillotine shirt.

Why do I get the feeling that the walls I've spent ten years building around myself, and this island, and this life, are about to come crashing down.

Walls that have stood for ten years, breached today by five-foot-four of pink *sass*

Fuck.

4

MELODY

Fear surges in my chest as I strain, muscles coiling as the waves crash over me once twice…

But the third time, the sloshing waves soak me to the bone as a panic threatens to drag me under.

Perhaps this was a terrible idea.

All of it. Not just convincing the old man on the dock to let me rent a boat, claiming "years" of practice. Those years of practice include paddle boating in Central Park and taking a canoe out, twice, at summer camp…when I was ten.

That was ten years ago now, and I'm about as proficient a boater as Rose clinging to a piece of driftwood as the Titanic, and Jack, sinks around her.

But taking this boat out is just—pardoning the Titanic pun— the tip of the iceberg. Maybe coming here at all was a terrible idea. Crossing choppy seas from a town I've never been to, to an island I've never heard of, to try and meet with the ghost of a fallen god who doesn't want to be found.

A fallen god who goes by the name of a blues legend and lives in what looks from here to be a haunted mansion on an inhospitable island covered in trees and jagged cliffs.

A fallen god who doesn't speak, but who looks like he spent the last ten years drinking himself into a ditch. But a fallen God who bleeds, nevertheless.

I saw the tattoos. I looked in his steely blue eyes. And there's zero question in my mind that "Robbie"—a hermit the whole town seem to regard affectionately as gruff but nice-enough drunk, is the very man or fallen, shattered god, I've been looking for.

Now, horrible idea or not, I'm on my way to do the impossible: lay eyes on and speak to Jackson Havoc for the first time in ten years.

I gasp as yet another wave slams over the edge of the tiny rowboat, soaking me through and making my teeth chatter. My hands grip the oars tighter, and I strain, wincing at the way the rough wood rips at my palms.

I shiver as the frozen fall air needles through my skin. But I keep going, glancing behind me and hoping to God I'm still aiming for the island and not to open sea. But it draws closer and closer, and the cliffs rear up like an angry dragon's teeth to swallow me whole.

And up on top, like a black keep from some sort of fantasy TV show, is castle Havoc itself.

It might be half an hour or possibly a lifetime later that I'm a half falling out of the boat as it hits the shore. My feet soak, splashing down into shallow waves as I stagger to the rocky beach like Robinson Crusoe.

Like a shipwreck survivor barely escaping a frenzy of sharks as I claw my way up to the beach. I reach behind me, grabbing the tether rope to the rowboat and pulling it up the beach after me. My muscles whine, and the palms of my hands shred even more against the salty-wet rope, making me cry out before I finally let it go.

I drop to my knees. I heave for air, shivering as I hug my soaked leather jacket around myself against the wind. I take a shaky breath and glance around before I groan.

In my desperate, near-drowning attempt to get to shore, I completely missed the *fucking dock*, jutting out into the water about twenty feet away, next to a boathouse.

Not that it would have saved me from getting wet. I was already soaked before I even got halfway to the island. And with my lack of sea-worthy-ness, I'd have probably fallen out of the boat and missed the dock entirely.

I groan, shivering as I look up through the trees. A rough-hewn, slightly overgrown stone walkway that looks like it turns into stairs leads up through the trees. My eyes trace those steps as they wind up to the peak of the island…up to the Dragon's Lair.

I take a deep breath and reach into my soaked bag. I had the foresight to put my wallet and cell phone in a Ziplock plastic bag. So even though everything I brought with me is completely drenched through, that seems to be working. Except when I pull the phone out of the plastic, my face falls.

It's working.

…But there's no cell service here.

Wonderful.

I groan, zipping the phone and my wallet back into the plastic and chucking them into my soaked bag. When I stand, I raise my gaze up the path into the trees.

Time to see this through to its conclusion.

I trudge off through the trees, gritting my teeth painfully at the way my soaked, salt and sand encrusted jeans bite into me at the seams. But I keep climbing. I keep walking until the pathway turns into stairs that seem to climb forever. My feet ache, made worse by my terrible choice in, now-soaked, heeled leather boots for this excursion.

I mean, I was expecting to walk up and ring a doorbell. Not cross the Atlantic Ocean and then climb a mountain, first.

Finally, the path plateaus into the flat peak of the island. And there before me, looming over the edge of a cliff, is the house itself.

I swallow as I step up onto the huge porch of the rambling old eighteen-hundreds mansion. Margie, the post office worker, mentioned that was this was formerly the Fleetwood Mansion—a pinnacle of excess built by a one-time shipping baron who has now faded into the annals of history.

Now, seemingly, it's the home of Jackson Havoc, a.k.a. Robert Johnson.

I stop in front of the enormous carved wooden door. There's no doorbell to be found, which makes me suddenly wonder if this island without cell service even has electricity. But there *is* a huge iron doorknocker, ornately molded into the shape of a lion roaring.

I raise a hand, grab it, and let it slam against the door twice. The thunderous sound booms through the door, vibrating in my body. I pause, stepping back and shifting anxiously as I wait for him to answer it.

Which of course, doesn't happen.

I bring my hand up again, gripping the huge iron knocker and hammering it twice more. When that doesn't work, I do it again. And again. And again, and again and again…until finally, I hear a roaring swear yell from inside the house.

Apparently, I didn't make that up. He *does* speak.

Footsteps thunder closer and closer, shaking me as if I'm back on the boat being tossed by the waves. I shuffle a step back, teeth chattering as the wind on top of the island summit slices through my wet clothes. I blush as I look down and quickly yank the leather jacket tight over my chest to hide the wet white t-shirt beneath.

The thundering footsteps get closer, making me shiver even more than the cold itself. But finally, they stop in front of the door. The doorknob wrenches and twists, and suddenly, the huge door swings open.

I shiver, shaking as I look up and instantly lose myself.

In steel blue eyes.

In a strong, clenched, grooved jaw covered with scruff.

In shaggy hair framing a face that one brought the world to its knees. A face that once sold millions and millions of albums.

A face that at one point was one of the most famous faces on the *planet*. And looking at him—the first time anyone knowingly has looked on him in ten years—it sort of feels like I just discovered El Dorado, the city of gold. Or Bigfoot. Or the Loch Ness Monster, or something.

We stand there staring at each other—me shivering, him with his arms outstretched and his hands on either side of the door frame.

Blocking me. Caging me out.

Making a point.

This is *his* castle. And I'm the intruder.

The second stick by in silence. I swallow, waiting for him to say something. But he doesn't.

Guess we're staying with the silence bullshit once again.

I take a slow, shaky breath, calming my nerves as best I can before I open my mouth.

"*Hi.*"

He says nothing. And the longer I look at him, the more I'm sure he's exactly who I think he is.

Of course, he is.

The same steel blue eyes. The same strong jaw. The same cool, barely contained animalistic viciousness behind his gaze.

"So...*hi*, my name is..."

I pause. I don't know why I pause. I don't know why the idea of telling him my name scares me. It's as if I'm on safari, and actually opening up to him and revealing myself would be like stepping over the boundary into the lion's den.

"I'm Melody," I blurt. "Hendrix."

It's not the first time I've used June's last name instead of my own. Because *my* last name comes with baggage. And history. Or worse, recognition.

When your mother has spent her life making your last name famously synonymous with "being a rock groupie" and "being a top-selling Playboy centerfold", the attention that last name brings—especially from men—is almost always less that well-intentioned.

Even as a teenager, I had to learn that the hard way. I head to learn for myself that the male cashier at the grocery store who recognized me based on my last name, and who was suddenly interested in getting my number, was *not* actually interested in me for me.

He—all of the "he's" who pulled similar moves—was actually interested in *Judy*. Or—worse, and ten times grosser—those kinds of guys were interested in trying to get *me* into bed as some sort of perverse "bang the daughter of your favorite rock groupie and playmate" fantasy.

Fucking *ick*.

Currently, though, I'm using Hendrix for the same reason I didn't want to name-drop Judy in my interview: because I *want* this story, but I don't want him giving it to me because Judy once dated his rhythm guitar player.

Jackson says nothing as the lie hangs in the air.

"My name is Melody Hendrix and I'm a…"

I pause.

Don't say reporter. Don't say reporter. Don't say—

"I'm a reporter."

Fury ignites behind his eyes. I cringe inside, wincing as he seems to loom even closer to me.

"I'm a reporter, and I work for Ignition Magazine."

His lips thin.

"Anyway, I'm here because I… I found you!"

I smile expectantly, hoping for some sort of recognition. Or a sentence. A single fucking word. But I get nothing. He just stares down at me like he's hoping his eyes will turn me to a pile of ash right here on his porch.

"And anyways I am a *huge* fan—"

A vicious grunting sound rumbles in his chest. I wince, remembering Cliff's warning.

Wow, you're off to a great start, idiot.

But I'm out of my element here. I'm in a place I don't know, with a man who, to be totally honest, scares the shit out of me as much as he ignites a fire in me.

But that's always been the allure of Jackson Havoc. It's what made him world-famous. The attraction to the darkness, like the seduction of a blade. That scary but warming look of his is the reason that millions of people flocked to him and his music…like moths to a flame they knew damn well would incinerate them.

But it was just *too fucking pretty* a light to stay away from.

Because the hard, cold truth is that Jackson—now as he was back then at the height of his fame—is *lethally* attractive. Illegally gorgeous.

I take a deep breath, centering myself and trying to conjure up some sort of ability to even speak words.

"I tracked you through a source of mine."

There's no way in *hell* I'm mentioning Judy. It's best to *never* mention Judy, to be honest…let alone the fact I'm related to her. Let alone the fact that she's my *mother*.

"Anyway," I blurt, still going, for some insane reason. Even though the frighteningly gorgeously man glaring down at me is still completely silent.

"Anyway, it brought me to the PO Box at the post office, where they told me it was no longer in service nor was there anyone named Jackson even living here—currently or ever. But when you showed up, the kind lady at the front desk mentioned *you* were the new owner of the PO box, and you might know…"

I'm rambling. *Horribly*.

I take a deep.

"So, yeah. I'm here because I think the world would love to hear your story. I think the world *deserves* to hear your story, and I think—"

"You talk a lot."

Even if he doesn't so much speak the worlds as he does rumble them, instantly, there it is, washing over me.

The famous Jackson Havoc voice.

Velvet and whiskey. Sex and fire. Woodsmoke and golden honey. It's that *infamously*, British-accent-soaked rumble that's somehow genetically programmed to make your heart thud and your knees weak.

It is *completely* unfair that this man found himself in show business, as a singer. Because when it came to Jackson, the audience never had a chance. They were fish in a barrel.

And Jackson was fishing with atomic bombs.

Somehow, though, I manage to not turn to a pile of ash, or a pillar of salt. I swallow thickly, looking up at him.

"I'm talking a perfectly normal amount."

His lips curl darkly. His eyes narrow. It's not a smile. It's the snarl before the pounce.

"I live purposely alone," he rasps. "On a fucking island…"

He slinks a step closer to me, arresting my breath and closing my throat. And it takes everything I have not to take a step back from him.

Scratch that. It takes everything I have not to turn and *run away* from this man.

His lips curl deviously.

"Believe me. In my world, you're talking *way* too fucking much."

I swallow thickly.

"Well, I'll try to be brief," I mumble. "As I said, I'm here hoping—"

"No."

My brow furrows.

"Excuse me?"

Jackson's eyes narrow coldly. And this time when his lips curl, it *is* a smile.

A sadistic, gleefully wicked, cruel smile.

"I said *no*. Now get the fuck off my island."

My heart sinks as I start to turn away.

"Actually, wait."

My brow shoots up, a hopeful smile spreading over my face as I turn back to him eagerly.

"Yes?"

Jackson's gaze bores in on me.

"You owe me."

I stare at him, shivering as my brows knit.

"Sorry, what do I owe—"

"Booze," he grunts. "You owe me twelve bottles of whiskey."

My brow furrows deeper.

"I'm sorry, I what?"

"You," he says slowly, smiling at me thinly. "Owe *me*. Twelve. Bottles. Of. Fucking. Whiskey."

He annunciates each word, as if I'm a child, or hard of hearing. My lips purse. But this time, I don't cower. I don't backstep or apologize.

This time, I glare right back at him.

Yeah, the power of the "demanding asshole rockstar god" sort of wanes when said demanding asshole rockstar god is now a voice-less hermit living on a island, drinking himself into a stupor.

"What, because you bumped into me?"

"Switch that. And yes. Fucking *exactly* because of that."

I scowl, pursing my lips as he stands there gripping the doorframe.

"Okay, *okay*," I sigh. "Fine, sure. I'll buy you new whiskey."

Jackson just stares at me, lifting a brow.

"Well?"

My brow furrows.

"I'm sorry did you mean right now?"

"I didn't mean tomorrow. I didn't mean a week from now. I didn't mean an hour from now."

I tremble as he a takes a step closer to me. And whatever I said before about the "power" of his royal rockstar assholeness waning or fading?

Yeah, lies.

Because when Jackson steps closer to me, it's like the very air ignites around me. It's like static crackles over my skin, prickling the hairs on back of my neck and teasing its way to places it very much shouldn't.

I swallow thickly, hoping to God the heat thudding in my core goes away. Because I am *not* a Jackson Havoc groupie. I love his music—I mean I *really* love his music. And the giddiness I feel being around him is because I'm standing in front of the very man who wrote and sang songs I absolutely adore, that were and continue to be part of the soundtrack of my life.

Not because I want to bang him.

…It's *not* that.

I shiver.

"*Fine.*"

He smiles thinly.

"Wonderful. You know where to find me."

He slowly turns as if to disappear back into the house.

"I just have a few conditions."

It takes everything I have not to flinch, or jump back, or *run* when he whirls back to me with a cold fury on his face.

"I'm sorry, are we bloody negotiating?" He snarls.

I shrug. "Perhaps."

Jackson rumbles a dark, cold, mirthless laughs.

"No, we are not."

"I'll tell you what. You answer a couple of questions, and I'll go get you as much whiskey as you—"

"Yeah, no, that's not even a little bit how this is going to happen," he rasps, making me flinch as he takes a step towards me again.

He towers over me, that dark energy that surrounds him dancing sadistically and seductively across my skin.

"What exactly did you expect in coming here, *Melody?*"

"I…I…" I stammer, hating that I do.

"You, what, thought you'd 'rescue me' from my isolation? Pitch me with an idea for a warm and fuzzy feel-good story about the former rock star 'finding his voice' again?"

He grins, making me shiver and take another step back as he advances on me.

"Or maybe, you just wanted a little *taste*, eh? That why you're here with the wet t-shirt contest look?"

He smiles coldly and viciously.

"We can drop the whole 'gutsy reporter' thing now if you want. Because if you're just a fan, as you just said, looking for a little memento?" He shrugs, smirking cruelly.

My brow furrows.

"I'm sorry, where are you even going with that?"

"It starts with you, getting on your knees," he grunts.

My face goes bright red.

"And ends with me emptying my balls down your pretty throat."

My skin *throbs*. My pulse jangles. I want to—and part of me *really* wants to—smack him. Or at the very least, to feel appalled, or completely disgusted, or furious.

Except I'm not.

I'm just…warm.

And tingly.

And pulsing, *everywhere*.

And that is so very completely unfair.

It's also completely unfair that I'm utterly at a loss for words. So instead, I just stand there like an idiot, gaping at him, my face red and my eyes wide.

Jackson smirks, folding his arms over his broad chest.

"You've got the mouth right; it just needs to be about a foot and a half lower—

"I'd rather *swim* back to town."

There it is: my voice. My armor. *Finally*.

Jackson lifts a brow.

"Both is certainly an option."

"So is biting your dick off."

His eyes gleam sadistically. His lips curl, but then slowly flatten into a thin line.

"We're done here," he grunts. His face dims as his eyes pierce into me. "Now get the fuck off my island."

He turns away, back to the darkness of his mansion.

"*Fine.*"

Jackson steps into the house and reaches for the door.

"Fine, I'll leave. If you answer *one* single question."

He pauses, his broad shoulders tensing before he turns to level his gaze at me.

"Once again, you're mistaking this for a negotiation. Let me reassure you one more fucking time: it is *not*—"

"Why did you leave?"

He doesn't say anything. He doesn't react. And yet, it's the absence of a reaction that gives him away. It's the way he keeps himself perfectly still, like he's holding something back.

"Just answer me that," I press, quietly. "Why, at the height of your fame, at the height of *everything*, did you run? You had everything—"

"Stop talking."

"Look, if you want me to leave, I will; fine. But I came all the way here. I *found* you. And I'm guessing in, what, ten years, no one else has—"

"You *need* to stop talking. Right now."

"But *I'm* here," I urge. "And I'll leave, I promise. I'll leave and I'll sign whatever NDA I'm sure you've already concocted in your head to send me. But before I do, I just want to know why you were so desperate to drop the keys to the kingdom and flee to—"

"And *I* want to know!" he thunders, shaking me, and making me falter back a step. "How it is you never fucking once asked yourself if I *wanted* to be found."

I rake my teeth over my lip.

"Look, no one will find you, even if you give this interview. I promise you that. The magazine will cover it a hundred different ways. *I'll* cover it. I won't even tell my editors where I found you at all! I just want to tell your story—"

"*My*. Fucking. Story," he rasps angrily. "Not the world's. Not Rolling fucking Stone's—"

"Ignition—"

"Not. Your. Fucking. Story."

He roars the words, and the color drains from my face as he storms into me, tapping his chest with a snarl on his lips.

"Mine! My life. My story. *My* fucking island," he spits. "That you can get the fuck off of, *right goddamn now.*"

"*Look*," I say evenly. "If I found you, someone else can, too. And all I'm saying is, they might not—"

"Do you know how far of a drop it is off that cliff behind this house?"

I pale, swallowing.

"I've been away from society, just like you said," he growls. "For *ten* fucking years."

I shiver as he takes another step towards me.

"Maybe I've forgotten my humanity. Maybe I've forgotten right versus wrong."

My heart thuds in my chest, racing in fear as he looms over me. I step back, but my foot slips on the top step of the porch stairs, and I start to fall back…

Until suddenly, his powerful hand shoots out, making me gasp as he grabs the collar of my leather jacket. I choke, hanging in a sort of limbo of a half-fall, with Jackson snarling into my face as he keeps me from toppling backwards.

"But do you know what I *haven't* forgotten?" He hisses as he leers close, drowning me in that swirling dark magic.

"How far of a fucking drop it is off that cliff."

My eyes go wide. I shiver as I feel the tug of gravity at my back.

"So, here's what I'm going to do, Melody Hendrix from Ignition fucking Magazine. I'm going to count to five. And by the time I hit three, if I can still see pink hair in my vision, I'm wrapping it in my fist, dragging you to the edge, and letting *you* figure out how far a drop it is to the waves."

I stare at him, my pulse deafening in my ears.

"Do I make myself crystal fucking clear?"

I swallow. My face feels ashen, my eyes bulging. But quickly, I nod.

"*Lovely*," Jackson snarls.

He lets go of my jacket. I catch myself on the railing before I fall back, but still manage to awkwardly trip down the last two steps.

"*One.*"

There are times where you should stand your ground. There are times where you need to plant your foot down, and let the bullies know you won't be pushed around.

Except in the roughly five minutes I've now spent in Jackson Havoc's vicinity, I've come to the conclusion that maybe ten years alone on an island pretending he can't talk has *actually* pushed him off the deep end.

There are times to stand your ground and say no to being pushed around.

This is *not* one of those times.

I don't even wait for "two" before I'm whirling and *bolting* for the path back down through the trees.

Away from the fallen god of rock 'n roll.

5

MELODY

What a fucking asshole.

The phrase "never meet your heroes" rattles through my head as I half run, half *flee* down the stone steps back down to the water.

I'll admit that I'm scared. I'd be lying if I said the huge, towering beast of a man who just roared in my face, threatening to *toss me off a cliff* didn't scare me.

But even with the fear, I'm angry. I'm angry at myself for running. I'm angry at myself for not sticking with what it takes for the story. It's not exactly like I planned on *dying* for a job at Ignition Magazine. But that said, do I actually believe Jackson would commit murder and throw someone off a cliff?

I shiver.

No one around here even knows his real name. No one even knows that you're here at all.

I rush down the rest of the stone steps, scatter-brained and weirdly playing out the opening of the true crime special on Netflix based on me, after they never find my body. I try and imagine the actors they'll get to play me, or Jackson.

Or the old man at the dock…aka "the last man to ever see Melody Blue alive." The man who will have regrets the rest of his life for renting a boat to an inexperienced boater, who took that boat into choppy water never to be seen again.

Oh sure. They'll interview the hermit living in the old mansion up on the cliff. The man who the whole town will vouch for as a nonverbal but gentle type. The one none of them sees is actually a fallen god, lording over all of them from his clifftop manor.

I groan, shaking the macabre thoughts of my own demise from my head. Then I rush down the last of the steps to the shore. I'm already mentally trying to prepare myself for the horrible boat ride back across the bay. Which is going to be ten times worse going this way, considering I didn't even get the story I came for, plus I'm *already* cold and wet before even step foot into the boat—

Oh, God.

I pause, my heart lurching up into my throat as my eyes scan the empty beach. I take another step onto the rocky shore, my eyes darting back-and-forth, peering at the rocks as if somehow the boat I rowed over here in will magically reappear.

Because currently, it's nowhere to be seen.

My chest constricts. My lungs squeeze. I bolt back and forth across the rocky, sandy little beach, which is only maybe twenty feet across.

My eyes aren't playing tricks on me.

There is no boat.

I stare at the waves crashing against the rocks. And I realize they're much higher up the shore than they were when I arrived.

I groan.

I pulled the boat in from the water. The water rose. The boat, that I didn't actually tie to anything, is now gone and probably washed out to sea.

My face pales, and my mind gleefully goes back to plotting its twisted true crime Netflix special. I imagine the chapter where the Coast Guard two states away finds the remnants of my boat washed up on shore.

But then, shaking my head free of those thoughts, I think about reality. Not the Netflix special. Not the dramatized version.

The *real* version. The very real reality that at the moment, I am soaked to the bone, cold, scared, and trapped on Jackson Havoc's private little island.

Alone with him.

I stare at the place where the boat should be. As if somehow, my hopes and wishes will make it reappear, ending this nightmare.

But that's not happening.

My head swivels to the dock, my lip catching in my teeth.

There *is* a boat. It's just not mine. And while stealing Jackson's boat should be as appealing as waiting to see if he really does throw me off a cliff...what's he gonna do? Swim after me?

I smile thinly as I bolt for the dock and down the wet planks to where the motorboat is tied up. But quickly, my hopes sink like rocks in the tide.

It's not tied up. It's *chained* up. And locked.

Fuck you, world.

I jiggle it and try yanking at the chain. But it's no use. For a second, I even entertain the idea of finding a tool of some kind in the boathouse to jimmy open the lock. But the door to *that* is locked fast, too.

This is a dead end.

Shivering, I shuffle back to the shore. I turn, swallowing a cold lump as I stare out at the water. Slowly, I shuffle backwards until my foot catches a rock. I fall back, landing on my ass on the cold damp, rocky sand. Numb, I open my bag, snatching out my wallet and cell phone still in the Ziplock bag. But it's the same thing as wishing for a boat that doesn't exist anymore.

There's still no cell service.

Still no boat.

Still nothing to do but either stay here and freeze or haul myself back up to the house of the grumpy, snarky asshole who just threw me out.

I shiver as I toss the phone back in my bag and stare out at the ocean. It's not dark yet, but it's going to be in a little bit. Sooner than I want.

I sit there another few minutes, wallowing in my own misery. But finally, reality pressing down on me, I stand. Then I turn to look up at the stairs that lead back to the house.

Shit.

6

JACKSON

I'M SHAKING by the time the door slams in her face.

Shaking trembling, and barely containing myself.

A roaring fire that I extinguished years and years ago ignites inside of my chest, engulfing me in flame. Until I squeeze my eyes shut and grind my jaw painfully tight to extinguish the heat.

I grasp the edges of the door frame in an iron grip, sucking in air through my teeth.

But I'm still staring at the tree line through the peephole in the door long after she disappears. Part of me that's been buried for longer than I've been missing wants to follow her into the woods, stop her, press her to a tree and bury myself inside of her as she squeals for more.

And yet...perhaps underneath that carnal desire, there's a *small*, tiny, broken hidden piece of me that just wants to save a stranger in need.

I roll my eyes.

Or not.

I turn, my jaw setting. There has *got* to be fucking booze somewhere in this goddamn house.

I start in the kitchen. Logically, the demon in me has already found whatever I've stashed away. Whatever I've hidden has long since been discovered and consumed. But that doesn't stop me from hunting.

I poke under the sink, in cupboards, behind cereal bowls, behind the toilets. I look in places no stable human should be hiding liquor *from themselves* without admitting they have a problem.

Fine. Fuck it. I have a problem.

And I don't give a single shit.

The quest for booze becomes a quest to forget the girl who just showed up on my doorstep. It leads me to parts of the house I've barely been in in years. The attic. The guest rooms for guests that have never appeared, or even been invited. Under the couch. Behind the dryer.

Finally, however, success strikes like Ben Franklin's kite getting hit by lightning.

But it comes with a price.

The bottle of scotch is twenty years old. It's not twenty years old because it's *good* scotch. It's twenty years old because it's shitty scotch I left here twenty fucking years ago. Back when I first picked up this house. Back when I left this bottle where I just found it today, in the bass drum of the drum kit in the half-set-up recording studio in the east wing of the mansion.

It's a gag gift I left for Iggy, for when we were all going to come here and record our next opus.

Before everything changed.

Before we ended up never coming here together as a group.

Before I was the last one here—an aging, fallen idol, living in a monument to what was.

Either way, reaching into the base drum and locking fingers around the glass bottle brings a mix of relief to finally have my poison. But also, the pain that comes with anything linking me to Iggy.

To Will. To Asher.

To anything and everything that was, before it all fell apart.

But at least I have the relief I need.

I stop by the living room on my way back to the kitchen. And the demon in me halts my steps when it spots the mirror on the coffee table.

Who am I to deny him?

Bending over the table, I inhaled the last remnants of my cocaine, making a mental note to text Scott the next time I'm on the mainland to arrange for more.

The coke buzzing in my system, I uncork the bottle, exhaling slowly as I bring it to my lips.

I was right; it's absolute dog shit whiskey. But beggars can't be choosy.

Or, fuck it. This beggar will *always* be choosy. But for the time being, I'm fine with what I have.

I jab a cigarette between my lips, angrily whipping a lighter out of my pocket and touching the flame to the tip. I suck greedily, letting the nicotine calm the raging beast inside my veins as I glare at nothing.

And yet, all I see is her.

Pink hair. Great ass. Sharp, no-bullshit blue eyes. And a mouth that infuriates me as much as it makes my dick hard.

I frown. Back on the mainland, when I was devouring her with my eyes from behind, I pegged her for half my age.

But now, I've had a closer eye-full of her. And now that I'm lecherously and vividly imagining the ways I'd wrap that pink hair in my fist and see how hot those lips would look stretching around my cock...I'm questioning how old she *actually* is.

My eyes narrow. Okay, she said she's a reporter. She works for a national magazine, for fuck's sake. Somehow, I don't get the impression that print media is so hard up these days that they're hiring high school kids.

But maybe I'm wrong.

I groan and exhale smoke, doing my best to drag my mind away from the X-rated thoughts of all the depraved, illegal-in-some-states ways I'd like to absolutely *sully* little-miss-pink-hair. Instead, I try and focus on another task.

Writing is out of the question, as having fuck-all to show from last night's frustrating attempts have proven.

Instead? Bikes it is.

I stalk to the front door, with every intention of spending the next hour or ten drowning in bad scotch, cigarette smoke, and engine grease. But when I get to the door itself, I stiffen.

I just caught a flicker of something through the peephole.

My mouth thins.

No fucking way.

I step closer to the door, and peer into the tiny hole in the center of it. I go still as my gaze focuses on the dripping wet girl standing on the pathway at the edge of the trees, looking dejected.

And *pissed*.

But even pissed and soaked to the bone, I growl to myself, my eyes slicing into her. She's looking at the door between us so dejectedly. So angrily. So... unrelentingly. She takes a deep breath, stretching her shoulders. And for the first time, I truly drink in exactly how...bedraggled she is.

Truth be told, it looks like she fucking *swam* here. Those jeans aren't just tight, they're soaking wet and clinging to every single—and I do mean *every* single—curve of her hips and her ass and her thighs.

She pulls at the jacket that she'd previously been holding shut, and when it opens, my breath sucks through clenched teeth. My pulse jangles. That fire I've spent ten years ignoring burns hotly in my veins.

The white shirt she's got on under that jacket is soaked through. Whether she's wearing a bra or not is irrelevant. Not when I can see the dusky pink, hard pebbles of her nipples poking through the cotton, even from here.

Enticing me. Goading me.

Shattering my resolve to keep this door shut.

I shake my head, wincing and frowning as I suck in another breath.

What I *want* to do is open this door, drag her inside, and have my goddamn way with her like a caveman. Or not even inside. Just put her on her knees right there on the front porch—as I suggested before—and see *exactly* how fuckable those lips really are.

My pulse hums hotly. Gripping the doorframe, I force myself to look away from the temptation on the other side of it.

I need to get my shit together. There's a chance I've been away from society a *touch* too long.

I take another breath, sliding my gaze back through the peep hole. Outside, she slips her bag off her shoulder and reaches inside, pulling out a Ziplock bag containing a phone and a wallet.

I smirk.

Okay, she didn't actually swim here. But by the looks of it, she came over in something closer to a bathtub or an inner tube than actual boat.

Curious, though. I wouldn't expect little miss New York City pink-punk-hair to be capable of boating.

I grin.

Well, and apparently, she's *not*. Not without getting herself soaked to the bone on the way over, at least. And it's not even that choppy of a day.

She takes a solid breath, pushing her wet pink hair out of her face. She mutters something to herself, her face tightening like she's psyching herself up for something.

Oh no fucking way.

And then, as I stare at her through the peephole, she marches across the yard, up the stairs, and right up in front of my door. She brings a hand up and grabs the door knocker again.

Apparently, this sassy little prick-tease doesn't take no for an answer.

I watch in cold amusement as she slams the knocker again and again relentlessly. I try to ignore it as she knocks again. But the longer the knocking goes on, the harder it is to ignore.

Not just because of the sound pounding through my fucking skull. Because all I can do is imagine the fist hitting it, and the arm attached to that fist. And the body attached that arm. And the face that sits atop that body.

And that *ass*.

What the fuck is wrong with me?

Finally somewhere between ten and three-hundred knocks later, I snap.

"What the fuck do you want!" I roar through the door.

There's no reply, but the knocking stops. I blink, wondering if maybe I scared her off again.

That is, until she gets one more goddamn knock in.

Fucking hell.

7

JACKSON

I BRING the bottle to my lips, drinking deeply, before I stab my gaze back through the peephole one last time. I settle my hard gaze on her, my eyes narrowing lethally.

Yes, she's attractive. Yes, in another world—in my old world, maybe—I'd already have her in the back of a tour bus, legs over my shoulders and my cock balls deep in that sweet little pussy. Maybe I'd have her sing my lyrics while I fucked her, just because I'm an egomaniacal prick like that. Or on her knees, tonging my balls until I came down her throat or across that pretty face.

But that was the old me. New me is... I want to say, "a changed man", but that's a lie.

The new me? He hasn't changed at all. He's just gotten darker. He's just allowed himself to step out of society. He's let himself reach the most devious, primal versions of himself.

Just because I abstain from the company women—or anyone, for that matter—does *not* mean I'm somehow a better person.

In fact, there's a chance it's done the opposite.

She brings her hand up one more fucking time. But I beat her to, yanking the door open, *hard*. Melody shivers, swallowing as I narrow my eyes at her.

Devouring the gorgeous little pink temptation standing on my doorstep.

Again.

I grind my teeth, feeling the lust in me surge as she looks up into my eyes.

I frown. For a second, I want to say she look familiar. Or maybe her name is familiar? But I shake my head, resisting the urge to roll my eyes at myself.

Every girl's name sounds familiar. Every female face looks familiar, when you've been me. When you took a garage band to international stardom at the age of twenty-one. When you toured the world seven times over.

I've lived a *lifetime* of hedonistic excesses. So, like I said: every single girl in the world has a way of looking "familiar" to me. But with her, that's not a possibility. She's all of… what, twenty-one? Nineteen?

That one hundred percent takes her out of the "maybe we've…*met* before" pile, given that the last time I was out "meeting" women was a decade ago.

I frown, shaking the ramblings from my head.

"Well?" I snarl.

I'm not trying to scare her…

Fuck it, no, that's a lie. I *am* trying to scare her.

Scaring her gets her the fuck away from me. I'm scaring her to make her go back to her a little boat, or dinghy, or pool noodle, or whatever the fuck she washed up on my shores with, and back to New York City. Where Cliff will promptly be in touch with her with the biggest, most fuck-you NDA she's ever laid eyes on.

And that'll be the end of it.

After that, I can go back to what I have here.

Silence. No faces around me. No prodding fucking questions around me. Just me, my guitars, my bike garage, my island, my drugs, and my fucking booze.

I just need her gone, first.

"Surely you didn't forget how to use a boat in the eight minutes you were standing on my doorstep before, did you?"

Her brows furrow as she looks up at me.

"Excuse me?"

And there's another thing. And maybe it speaks more to my own ego than it should that this is where I go with this. But fuck it. My ego made me a fucking *god* when I was younger. It made me rich beyond kings.

Kinda hard to shit on it after it did all that for me.

But the thing that goads me when she snaps at me like that—when she glares at me with this bored, disdainful, petulant little sneer—is, well, *that*.

The bored disdain. The petulant sneer.

The *immunity*.

No one is immune to me, *especially* not cute little—however-the-fuck-old she is—pink-haired, leather-jacket-wearing city girls like her. In fact, she's the fucking archetype of girls who, historically, have literally bent over backwards to do whatever depraved shit my dick and my dark heart has come up with.

To pretend I'm alive.

To pretend the past is a forgotten memory.

To pretend throwing myself into excess and pure hedonism erases the horrors that came before the fame.

But she breaks that mold. That *sneer* breaks the archetype, however fucking cute it is.

I grit my teeth.

"Well, no one brought you here. That's a fact."

"That's your assumption."

"No, it's a *fact*. I know that because no one in their right fucking mind from the mainland would bring you here without my express permission."

She lifts a brow.

"Got the local's that scared of you?"

I resist urge to smirk. She's got balls, this one.

"Which means you either stole, bought, or borrowed a boat to get here yourself. And judging by your appearance—"

"What the fuck is wrong with my appearance?" she snaps.

"Judging by the *state* of your appearance. Like the fact that you're fucking...*wet*."

I growl that last word thickly, letting it linger in the air between us. And I relish the way her neck blooms with redness.

"So, now it's your turn."

She stares at me with confusion.

"My turn for what, exactly?"

"To answer the fucking question," I growl through gritted teeth. "Did you or did you not forget how to boat in the eight minutes you were standing here before."

She looks away, her teeth chewing on her lip. Slowly, my eyes settle on her, and my mouth thins.

"Well?"

"My boat…"

She clears her throat roughly, twice, turning to stare out at nothingness, just to avoid my prying gaze.

"My boat…"

I laughed coldly.

"You lost the boat, didn't you."

She whirls back to me, her eyes narrowing.

"I didn't *lose* it."

"Is it in your pocket?"

She glares at me.

"Is it where you left it?"

"The tide came in and took it away, okay!?" She hisses, shaking her head and glaring at me, her lips twisting.

That look really, *really* needs to stop making my cock so hard.

"And exactly how is this my fucking problem?"

She frowns. "It's not your problem. I'm just relaying the information."

"And what precisely should I do with this information?"

She sighs heavily.

"Could I just use your phone?"

I smile. This should be good.

"No."

She rolls her eyes.

"Could I *pretty please*, oh legendary rock god of who-fucking-cares-island? Could I *please* use your phone?" She drawls sarcastically. "Then I'll be out of your hair as soon as I can get someone to come get me."

"Who."

Her eyes drag back to me narrowing.

"Someone?"

"Be specific."

Her look says she wants something heavy to fall on my head.

I'm amused by this.

"A water taxi?"

"Doesn't exist here."

"Then, I don't know…that guy from the dock."

"Albert. It's not gonna happen."

She sighs with exasperation."

"Is there a reason you're enjoying this?"

I sigh heavily, hanging my head.

"I'm sorry."

She looks at me quickly, her eyes narrowing suspiciously.

"What are you sorry for?" She says hesitantly.

"I'm sorry that you did all that sleuthing…"

I smile at her.

"I'm *so* sorry that you did all that work, and came all this way, just to find me. And I'm sorry that through all of that, *no one fucking told* you that I'm a complete. Fucking. *Prick*."

She swallows, glaring at me.

"That's not being glib, sweetheart," I growl. "That's not being funny, or cute. I'm just kind of a dick."

"Yeah, no shit."

"Wonderful. And now what did we learn today?"

"That…you're a huge dick?"

Those words from her lips instantly make my cock swell.

Even more.

I smile thinly.

"Never ever meet your heroes, sweetheart."

She smiles thinly.

"Your assumption that you are in any way shape or form *my hero* is…quite sad."

My lips thin as I glare at her. But we say nothing, and the silence hangs over us. Eventually though, she takes a slow breath.

"So…what exactly should I do?"

"How strong a swimmer are you?"

Her eyes snap back to mine, growing fearful.

"I'm not swimming that."

"That's probably the smartest idea you've had all week. Certainly, a better one that coming here to find—"

"Are you going to let me stay here, or not?"

I laugh coldly. But it's to cover the hunger on my face at the idea of her staying here.

In my house

In my bed.

Bouncing on my cock…

"I haven't decided yet."

"Well, guess what? I'm not really in the mood to play ego games with a narcissistic douchebag. So, either tell me if I can stay here, or—"

"Or what, you'll swim?"

"Or I'll steal *your* boat."

I exhale slowly.

"You're kind of annoying."

"And you're a shitty drunk," she throws back.

"I'm an *exceptional* drunk, thank you very much."

Melody rolls her eyes.

"You're an exceptional asshole who *happens* to be drunk a lot."

Her eyes drop to the bottle in my fist.

"Or, *all* the time, apparently."

My lips curl.

"Watch it."

"Is the truth uncomfortable?"

"Not as uncomfortable as sleeping outside is going to be for you when it drops to forty degrees tonight. My boat is locked, by the way."

She swallows, her face paling.

"Well, that shut you the fuck up."

She looks away, sucking on her bottom lip and hugging herself against the chill moving in.

I sigh heavily.

"*If* I let you stay…"

My eyes sweep over her.

Shamelessly.

"What will you do for me?"

I love—*love* the way her neck and cheeks turn pink.

"My gratitude for not making me sleep outside or swim across a freezing cold bay?"

"And?"

"And if you push for something more than that, trust me that I'll cut your dick off."

I bite back a grin.

Yep. New York girl, through and through.

I take another slow breath, my eyes never leaving her sharp, defiant glare.

"Fine," I finally growl. "Enter."

I step back, nodding my chin into the depths of the house. But Melody stays where she is, eyeing me coolly.

"Would you like the bell hop to get your bags, *miss*," I mutter tersely.

She chews on her lip, picking at her cuticles as her gaze stabs into the inside of the house. Then, that gaze slowly slides back to my eyes, where it hardens.

"I'm serious. You try anything and I swear to fucking God—"

"House rules," I grunt, cutting her off. "Stay out of my shit. Stay out of my way. Stay away from my food, don't touch my booze. And most importantly…"

I smile at her thinly.

"Most importantly, get the *fuck* over yourself. I'm not gonna touch you."

But I sure as fuck am gonna think about it, every goddamn second that she spends under my roof and under my gaze.

8

MELODY

Thank God.

Just as his Royal Assholeness relents, the clouds seem to open up above me, and the rain begins to pelt down.

Great timing.

Or maybe it's just that *all* of this is just plain awful timing.

When I step into Jackson's home, I honestly expect to walk into some kind of temple of rock 'n roll hedonism. I expect to see smashed furniture, broken glass…maybe bodily fluids sprayed across the wall.

Drugs, alcohol, and perhaps passed out or even dead groupies strewn across the floor.

Instead, the house I step into is actually…nice. I mean, it's a fucking mess. There's beer and whiskey bottles littering most surfaces, and old newspapers, and dirty clothes. And at least four or five guitars that I can see from just the doorway strewn across various couches, the staircase, a coffee table, and a piano—which is also covered with empty bottles and crumpled bits of paper.

But…it's actually an incredible home, and you can still see the former grandeur from its gilded-age roots.

I follow Jackson through the front entryway into massive, cavernous, ski-lodge sized living room. And when I step into that, my breath catches as my eyes go wide.

The far wall is all windows and glass doors—like Gatsby's ballroom or something equally Fitzgerald-ish—that look straight out over the ocean, past the cliffs beyond. And directly in front of them at the back of the house, an overgrown patio that looks as if it may have been an old Japanese-style tea garden.

With the black storm clouds gathering outside, and the rain beginning to fall, it's got this incredibly moody, atmospheric look that takes my breath away.

I pause, turning to stab my gaze through the slightly magical, dusty particles cascading in the light splaying out across the room. I take in the guitars, the piano, the trash, the bottles of booze everywhere…

My gaze slides back to the coffee table, and my lips thin. There's a mirror, with remnants of white powder all over it.

A scene straight out of my mother's apartment.

"You want a bump?" He grunts as he walks past me towards what looks like a spacious, light filled kitchen through another doorway.

"Uh, yeah, I'm fine, thanks."

Jackson pauses and turns to look at me over a shoulder, a small smirk on his face.

"Oh…" he lifts a brow. "*I see,*" he says drolly.

I frown.

"Excuse me?"

He just chuckles and shakes his head.

"Nothing. I'm just thinking that music reporters for Rolling Stone from other eras—"

"I don't work for Rolling Stone."

"*Ignition.* Fine, whatever." He shrugs. "I'm just saying twenty years ago, you'd be right in there, nose-first with your ass in the air saying please."

Silence hangs in the living room as I stare at him, shaking my head.

"*Wow.* So, this is like your thing, then?"

The smug look on his face clouds.

"Is what my thing."

"Talking like a crude teenager who just discovered bad words? Just being a massive dick and seeing how far that takes you with girls—"

"I see you've heard about my massive dick."

My face burns hotly.

"*No*, that is *not* what I meant—"

"So, that's just how you imagine it in your head?"

I stammer, my pulse thudding.

"*No*! That is not how I imagine your dick!"

Shit.

"So, you *are* imagining my dick."

"Oh my God, can you stop?"

His lips curl as one brow raises.

"That's a no on the coke?"

"*Yes*," I mutter tersely. "That's a no. *Thanks*."

He rolls his eyes as he turns away into the kitchen.

"Let me guess. Daddy is a cop? A suit? No…that's not it. Daddy is—"

"My dad *left*, actually," I blurt.

Immediately after, I regret volunteering that information to a needling asshole like Jackson. As if he needs more ammunition to use on me, and here I am offering up my soul to the devil on a silver platter.

And, predictably, his lips curl deviously.

"So, that's a yes on daddy issues, then?"

I glare at him as I bring one hand up to flip him off.

"*Outstanding*," he growls hungrily.

I hate that it makes my pulse beat quicker.

Jackson slips back into the kitchen. I turn, scanning for a place to sit. The couch with a guitar leaned against it is covered with blankets, pillows, and…looks slept in.

Recently.

The thought of sitting where this devil has been sleeping is… body-heating.

In a way it very much shouldn't be.

Instead, I stand there, shifting in my still-wet boots, feeling the damp denim cling to my legs as I turn to look out the windows at rolling black clouds rapidly swallowing the sun. I might be in the devil's island laid. But, *damn* is it pretty, in a dark way.

I give a quick glance into the kitchen to see his back to me. My bag slips off my shoulder, and before he can spot me and accuse me of trying to spy on him or something, I pull my phone out and snap a few pictures of the view. Then a wider shot of the windows themselves. Then an even wider one, showing the full "genius mess" of the space.

Then I slip my phone back into my bag and do my best not to think about the fact that I'll be spending the night here, under this roof, with *this* man.

"You hungry?"

His voice commands from the kitchen. I turn away from the windows at the sound of it and raise a curious brow.

"Yeah, actually," I exhale, feeling my stomach rumble as I head towards him. "Thank you."

Jackson barks a cold laugh.

"I wasn't taking your order, sweetheart."

I step in the kitchen to see him pulling things out of the fridge. When he glances back and sees me standing there, he nods his chin at what looks like a pantry.

"There's peanut butter and jelly...maybe some bread in there. Go nuts."

He turns back to where he's buttering and oiling a cast-iron pan. And next to that, my eyes land on a huge, juicy looking, seasoned steak. My stomach gurgles. But I sort of get the impression steak is *not* on the menu tonight.

Not on *my* menu, at least.

Instead, I step into the pantry and find a jar of unopened raspberry jelly, a half-eaten jar of peanut butter, and some bread that looks…basically not moldy. Back at the kitchen island, I quickly slap the sandwich together, ignoring the delightful smells of cooked garlic and steak simmering in the cast-iron pan on the stove.

I've almost finished wolfing down my sandwich—not even realizing how completely starving I've been all day—when Jackson finishes. He turns around and sits on a stool at the kitchen island, setting down a plate piled with a delectable looking steak and some grilled potatoes. And of course, his bottle of whiskey.

I stare, my mouth still full of stale peanut butter and crusty bread as I watch him slice into the juicy steak. Jackson pauses with the bite halfway to his lips and raises his steely blue eyes to stab me. His gaze narrows.

"Don't."

I blink, quickly dropping my eyes back to my plate.

"Don't what?"

"Don't look at me with those fucking puppy eyes," he growls. "You're not a guest. I didn't *invite* you here. And this isn't me putting you out. You are…"

He raises his eyes to the ceiling as if searching for the right word.

"You're a refugee here," he finally drawls out with a smirk. "A shipwreck survivor, by the look of it."

I smile thinly.

"Thank you so much for your *generous* hospitality."

"Keep up the niceties," he shrugs, tucking back into his dinner. "It won't buy you a steak, but you might just get yourself another PB&J."

Dick.

One bite later, I'm done with my sandwich. But Jackson seems to take his time relishing each and every bite of his steak and potatoes. With chasing each morsel with a half-swig of whiskey that I can smell across the table.

Though I said I'd pass on the narcotics—and I always do—it's not like I'm straight edge or some sort of prude. Of course, I drink. I mean, not as much as Jackson drinks. But I'm pretty sure no one on the planet drinks like him.

No one that's still *alive*, at least.

I clear my throat and steeple my hands on the table as I watch him.

"So, how long have you been—"

"Nope."

He doesn't look at me as he chews his food. But his head shakes side-to-side.

"What do you mean, nope?"

"I mean fucking nope," he grunts. "This isn't an interview. This is my dinner, and I plan on eating it in silence."

I nod, snapping my mouth shut. But after another few seconds, he abruptly stops and put his fork down. He grunts, raising his eyes to mine.

"Is there a reason you're watching me eat?"

I blush, looking away.

"You…wanted silence."

"Silence, yes," he mutters. "Not to be studied. It's unnerving to be watched while you eat."

"*Okay, okay*. Sorry. I won't watch you."

He grunts as he takes a swig of his whiskey.

"How about you make yourself useful, girl who couldn't get a job at Rolling Stone."

I glare at him.

"Who says I couldn't—"

"You mean aside from the fact that you're working for *not* the biggest music magazine, but one of their way-less-popular competitors? Yeah, lucky guess."

My lips purse.

"May I continue?"

I roll my eyes. "*Why not.*"

"As I was saying, why don't you make yourself useful—"

"If this is your way of asking for sexual favors again, this is going to get ugly for you real fast, asshole."

"That was my way of segueing into the suggestion that you clean up the kitchen or do the dishes or something. But the way you seem so eager to always bring it back to the realm of sex has me getting *very* cozy with the idea of fucking that mouth instead."

I couldn't contain the way my face heats like a furnace or stop my jaw from dropping at his utter audacity even if I tried.

Which, I apparently can't do around him, at all. Contain myself, that is. Myself, or the way my pulse races. Or the way even being in the same room as this man poisons my very thoughts to inky black filth.

I have no answer to the sexual part—as in I literally don't know how to respond to it without embarrassing myself or flubbing over my words. So, I skip that and delve into the first part.

"You want me to clean your kitchen?"

"It was one of two suggestions. Don't forget you have options."

I swallow thickly as my skin tingles with a forbidden, scandalized heat. Completely stepping over the invitation to blow him, of course, I want to lash out at Jackson for the absurdity of wanting me to be his maid.

And yet, as much as it boils my blood to even admit it to myself, he's not *wrong*. I'm not a guest here. Actually, being that I showed up unannounced, I'm not even a journalistic interviewer right now. More like paparazzi just showing up at some famous person's house. And I need to actually recognize that.

Yes, Jackson is a royal dickhead—King Asshole. But, to his credit, I *did* show up announced to demand an interview with a man who clearly doesn't even want to be found. And I'm here for the night because I screwed up. *I'm* the one that lost the boat.

So yes, while he's an annoying prick, I am putting him out a little bit. The least I can do is clean up or something, right?

I clear my throat smiling as I turn away from the heap of dirty dishes in the sink, back to him.

"Okay. I'll do it."

He lifts one single, hungry brow, and my core throbs.

"*The dishes*, asshole," I mutter.

Jackson smirks, saying nothing. At least, nothing audible.

The predatory glint in his eyes says enough.

He finishes off the last of his steak and stands, bringing his plate to the sink and adding it to the pile with a flourish—for me, I'm sure.

He turns to lean against the counter as his gaze settles on me. My eyes slip over the way his t-shirt clings around bulging biceps covered in tattoo ink; his arms folded over his broad chest. I shiver quietly.

Sweet Jesus, it's impossible to even be in the same room as this man without feeling his effects. And once again, all I can think of is how fucking *unfair* it is that a dark power like Jackson was unleashed on the masses across TV and airwaves.

The public never stood a *chance* with him.

My gaze slips over his arms again, before I frown. I pause, looking at his injury from the shattered whiskey bottle. My brow furrows at the bloody-looking gauze, hastily taped—with *masking tape*—to his arm.

"You should probably get that looked at."

Jackson glances down at his arm and shrugs.

"It's fine."

"It...really isn't. That looks disgusting."

He grunts. "I'm fine."

"Can I dress that for you?"

"I'd rather you *un*dress something else."

I swallow the heat from my face.

"I meant can I change your bandage before you get some gross infection, and you lose a fucking arm or something."

He eyes me coolly, arching a brow.

"First aid kit is in that cupboard."

He nods his chin to a rack of drawers next to the pantry doors. I bring my plate to the sink, balancing it precariously on the pile, before I go and retrieve the kit from the cupboard. I approach him warily, hovering just out of reach of him for a second longer than normal. Before, finally, I cross that last divide between us to sit next to him.

Jackson takes a sip of whiskey—from a glass at least, now—as he drops his tattooed, muscular, veined arm across of the marble countertop of the kitchen island.

"I'm at your mercy, doc. Do your worst."

But the charm is lost on me, because I know how very wrong that statement is. Because boat-less, phone-less, and trapped here alone with the demon king of rock 'n roll who seems to exhale pure lust and desire?

He's not at my mercy at all.

I am *very much* at his.

9

MELODY

The rain begins to thud hard against the kitchen windows as I peel the gross bandage off his arm.

I wince at the messy looking scab underneath. But the cut isn't deep or even that big it's just…messy. It's not like he needs stitches or anything, but it does need to be cleaned and bandaged correctly.

Like, without masking tape, for instance.

I reach for the rubbing alcohol.

"This may hurt."

Jackson says nothing when I bring the soaked gauze to his cut. He also doesn't move or flinch as I clean the crusty scab. When the cut doesn't look like special effects makeup from a trench-warfare movie anymore, I dress it with antibiotic ointment and then wrap his forearm in a clean bandage.

It's not until I step back to admire my work that I realize I've been touching him, for the last five-to-ten minutes.

I shiver heatedly.

I was so focused on what I was doing that I haven't realized that my fingers and arms have been brushing *his* arm the entire time. And now that I'm aware of it, suddenly the heat is transferred to my own skin, where it catches like a brushfire.

I stand quickly, closing the first aid kit.

"Okay, all good," I blurt hastily.

Jackson eyes the bandage and raises his eyes to me, even if I'm fastidiously avoiding his gaze.

"Okay," he sighs. "Fine."

I frown.

"Fine…what?"

"Fine you can stay."

I glare at him as the light outside turns black, and the rain begins to hammer down harder.

"I thought I already was staying?"

"Well now it's official. You're welcome."

He stands, ignoring my glaring stare as he disappears back into the living room. I follow behind him, shifting uncomfortably as my still-damp clothes and boots rub awkwardly.

I pause, glancing around the room. For a place with no cell service that looks like it was built almost two-hundred years ago, I almost expected this house to not even to have electricity. But he clearly does…I mean there are lights on, and there's a big refrigerator in the kitchen. So, he must have some sort of generator, or wires laid under the ocean or something.

Which also might mean he's got a washer and dryer.

I clear my throat at his back.

"Could I…possibly use your dryer? I'm still pretty wet."

Jackson pauses. Slowly, he glances back at me with what can only be described as a heated look.

"And?"

I frown.

"And…I was hoping I…"

My words fumble and falter as he turns fully towards me. But when he starts to slink towards me, like an apex predator causally approaching the prey that's already been immobilized, my face explodes with heat.

I want to be incensed and outraged at the way he keeps so causally invading my personal space or turning me to smoldering ash with those eyes. Or scandalizing me with his crude, wildly inappropriate comments.

I want to hit him, or hurl insults at him. Or call him a pig. But instead, my head—treacherously—invents all sorts of other…*physical* things it wants to do with this god of a man standing in front of me covered in tattoos and swirling with forbidden lust and dark magic.

Did I hit my fucking head today or something?

Jackson moves slowly towards me. I tremble, feeling a pulsing heat simmer beneath the surface, fighting hard to break itself free.

"And what should we do about that?"

"About..." My breath catches as my eyes slip up to his. "About what?"

"About you being...*wet*," he growls quietly.

I have to physically stifle the gasp by slamming my lip shut. And Jackson definitely sees it. He smirks, pleased with the way he's ruffled me—*again*—as he looms over me.

"I..."

I stammer, trying to collect my wits before I finally find them. And when I do, my lips purse and I force myself to take a step back from him.

There *needs* to be air between us, or I'm going to suffocate in that dark energy of his.

"I *meant*," I say tersely. "Can I use your fucking dryer. Pig."

"You never learned about vinegar and honey did you."

"What?"

"As it pertains to catching flies."

I roll my eyes.

"Pretty please?"

He grins.

"I could get *very* used to looking down into your eyes while you say that."

My face simmers as my lips purse tightly. As my body shivers. As my core clenches traitorously.

"Can I or can't I use your dryer to dry my clothes off."

Jackson grins a lopsided, roguish grin.

"Be my guest." He gestures down the hall. "Second door on the left, down the stairs to the basement. Washer and dryer are all yours."

I exhale slowly, feeling a sense of normalcy *finally* wash over the entire situation.

"Thank you."

He smirks.

"What?"

"Nothing. I'm just trying to imagine what exactly you'll be *wearing* while you wait to dry your…*wetness*."

I blush deeply.

Fuck. I didn't actually think about that. Everything in my bag —the couple extra t-shirts, hoodie, spare socks, jeans, underwear, etc., is all *also* still damp from my boating misadventure.

"I…" I stammer, chewing at my lip. "Do you…"

"Nope."

I stare at him.

"What?"

"Nope," he shrugs. "I don't have anything for you to wear."

I glare at him.

"You're serious."

"As a heart-attack. But you're more than welcome to go naked," he shrugs, turning to stroll from the room. "I promise, it's not gonna bother me one bit."

"*Good to know,*" I mutter at his back.

"And if you need someone to give you a hand taking those wet clothes off…"

I simmer.

"*Fuck you.*"

"Honey and vinegar, sweetheart," he grunts. "Honey and vinegar."

"Fitting you keep saying that what with being as obnoxious as the fly you seem to think I *want* to attract."

He smirks.

"Buzz buzz, baby."

I glare at him, feeling my face flush I spite of myself as he turns and strolls causally out of the room. I grumble to myself, turning before my eyes land on the blankets tossed across the couch.

The ones he clearly slept in.

My core knots.

But screw it. What else do I have? I grab one of them, along with my wet backpack, and stomp down the hall to the second door, which leads down to his basement…a perfectly normal, regular basement. Or at least a perfectly normal regular basement for a mansion built almost two hundred years ago, I guess.

Just like when I first set foot in the house upstairs, part of me expects to find some sort of sex dungeon or some other hedonistic rockstar wildness down here. Pleasure slaves chained to the wall. A drug farm. Something else to allude to the hedonistic infamy of the man who lives here.

Instead, I find a perfectly normal washer and dryer next to a shelf holding fabric softener and dryer sheets.

It's so normal it's almost off-putting.

I strip quickly, shivering when the cold air hits my wet, clammy skin. My mind wanders to the thought of security cameras, or some other less noble reason for him to have surveillance down here, and I quickly wrap the blanket around myself.

I'm tossing my clothes into the dryer when it hits me.

The scent of him, wrapping around me as tightly as the blanket. My chest constricts, my body shivering with a dark, throbbing heat as the masculine, woodsy, horribly and disturbingly *attractive* scent of the devil from upstairs invades my senses.

Like a virus.

Like a black magic potion.

Like something dirty and private I should look away from. But instead, can't stop voyeuristically staring at.

An electrically sensual feeling tingles over my skin, puckering my nipples and quickening my pulse. I blush fiercely, trying to push it to the side and explain it away. Maybe I *did* hit my head today. Or maybe the peanut butter I ate upstairs was past its prime.

Or maybe being around Jackson is intoxicating me, like being around mercury fumes, or asbestos.

I shiver, tightening the blanket around myself as I quickly set the dryer for thirty minutes and then step back.

But then, I'm faced with a choice. Do I…hang out in the dimly lit basement of a creepy old house I've never been in before? Naked except for a blanket that smells intoxicatingly like a viciously magnetic rock god wrapped around me? Or do I venture back upstairs, entering the lair of said viciously magnetic rock god? Again, naked, except for his blanket wrapped around me.

It's an impossible decision. But eventually, I end up splitting the difference.

I manage about nine minutes in the basement before the shadows get the best of me. Then, I'm scampering back up the stairs, clutching my phone, swaddling the blanket as many times around me as it'll go before I step into living room again.

But this time, it's empty.

No Jackson.

I'm halfway back down the long, elegant if not dusty hallway before I stop myself. What am I doing? *Looking* for him?

I pause, frowning at myself. The crude, drunken, obnoxiously attractive man of the house *not* being in the living room—especially when all I'm dressed in is a blanket and his scent—is a good thing.

That's a *great* thing, actually.

So why the hell am I seeking him out, when I should be setting up barricades? Or lighting a signal fire outside for a rescue from this place?

I roll my eyes at myself, and I'm about to turn back to the sanctuary of wherever Jackson *isn't*, when I hear it. I hear it, and I go absolutely still.

It's the sound of an acoustic guitar.

I frown as I glance around, trying to pinpoint the location. Lost in the sound of it, me feet carry me on their own accord down a hall, ignoring my brain screaming to let it go and get back to that whole "lighting a rescue fire" plan.

I meander through a stunning library, through some other sort of parlor or sitting room, and down another hallway. Until suddenly, I'm standing in front of a cracked-open door.

And from behind it floats the sound of pure, honeyed *gold*.

My pulse hums in my ears, my eyes widening as I approach the door. The notes of the acoustic guitar pour over me like liquid heat, and tease across my skin like a sensual lover's touch.

My breath catches as I realize I'm listening to him playing *live*, not a recording or something. And when that realization broadens to the possibility that I'm the first person on *earth* to hear him play a guitar in about ten years, my very soul seems to surge and swell.

It's not just that Jackson Havoc was lethally attractive, like weaponized sin. It's not *just* that he was a very talented songwriter, and an extremely gifted musician.

It's that the *way* he sang and played just…moved people. It's the same way his searing looks in the kitchen and living room turned me into a puddle, even if I wanted to hate him.

My mind recalls a magazine article from ages ago that once described Jackson as having the stage presence of Freddie Mercury, the allure of Mick Jagger, and the sex appeal of Prince, or Elvis. And they couldn't have said it better.

In an interview with Playboy, John Mayer once crudely referred to his then-ex, Jessica Simpson, as "sexual napalm".

But, that's Jackson: Pure. Undiluted. Sexual napalm. And when he plays a guitar, it's like the bomber doors opening up, ready to engulf the world in his fire.

My mouth goes dry as I move closer to the crack in the door, peering inside as my jaw drops.

It's a recording studio. Or it *was* one. Or is on the way to becoming one. A lot of it seems to be covered in white sheets, like it's either under construction or being dismantled. But either way, standing there in the middle of the space, in-between a big grand piano and what looks like a drum-set covered in a sheet, stands Jackson.

His back is to me, his head bowed. His broad, muscular shoulders roll as his biceps curl with the finger pattern he's walking up and down the neck of the acoustic in his hands. And the sound that comes out of it is just…

Fucking *hell*.

It's gorgeous. And rawly sensual. And full of heat, and pain, and darkness. It's not a tune I recognize, either. But whatever it is, even without any words, it's turning to me to molten lava as I stand there with my face pressed to the crack in the door.

A door that all of a sudden creaks an inch open.

Loudly.

Jackson stiffens, whirling so savagely I gasp and falter back from the door. I hear him grunt something vicious, and I'm halfway to turning and *fleeing* back down the hall, when the door opens with a yank behind me.

A powerful hand grabs my arm, making me jolt and blurt out a weird "eep" sound as he yanks me around to face him. I shiver, my eyes wide as I look up into his dark, smoldering, steely-blue gaze.

"Now what the *fuck* do we have here."

10

JACKSON

TOUCHING HER IS A MISTAKE.

And yet, I keep. Fucking. Doing it. Because here I am again, with my hands on her soft, throbbing skin.

Again.

And just like the times before, the sensation is like the first hit of a new drug. Exciting. Illicit. Dangerously addictive.

And I just want fucking *more*.

But at the same time, this is one addiction I need to stop cold before it takes root. I erased myself from the world ten years ago to disappear to this island and…I don't know. Lose myself in madness. And maybe genius. To find how deep the hole in my soul actually goes.

To hope to whatever god or muse or inspiration that might still dwell down there that I've actually got something left in the tank.

But I didn't come here to dance around little fucking temptations like Melody.

Easier said than done.

I groan as I look down at her—those big blue eyes looking up at me, that soft, gorgeous face framed with pink hair. Those *entirely* way-too-fuckable full, pouty lips that make my dick throb.

…and why the *fuck* is she standing here wrapped in a goddamn blanket?

The surging crash of carnal versus creative explodes in my head. What I *want* to do is put her on her knees with those soft lips wide and ready for me. I want her on all fours, that tight little ass up in the air as I bury every thick inch of my cock deep into every greedy little hole she has, until I've given her ten years of pent-up sexual release.

But her even being here is fucking with me. I've been….well, not *happy*. But fine. I've been "fine" in my dark little hole on my island for the last ten years. I've been fine as a nonverbal nobody of a ghost. Fine without the headlines, the fame, the bullshit.

I've been fine with nothing and no one around me reminding me of what I was.

What I am.

Her being here isn't just a disruption to my plans of slowly drinking myself to death, alone. It's a constant reminder that I've failed in *actually* disappearing. It's a reminder that while I might have left the world behind, the world hasn't left *me* behind.

She needs to leave. She needs to get the fuck away from me.

""I—I'm sorry, I didn't mean to inter—"

"Yes, you did," I rasp darkly, my face lined with anger and my eyes narrowing at her.

"Just like you interrupted me in town earlier. Just like you took it upon yourself to haphazardly launch an invasion of my island to interrupt me again."

"I didn't—"

"Just like you interrupted me *again*, when you let your own fucking boat float away."

She moves to pull her arm back. But I grip it tighter, relishing the way she shivers and gasps as I suddenly yank her closer. Melody's eyes bulge, and she *just* barely manages to grab the blanket with her other hand, stopping it from falling off her entirely.

But the movement has her tripping even closer to me, almost falling right against my chest. My pulse roars as the heat of her nearness taunts the beast inside of me.

"You've been interrupting me and my life *all fucking day*," I growl thickly, forcing myself to put a stop to this. To end this slow descent into yet another addiction I'll never, ever climb out of.

This ends. Now.

"Which is why first thing tomorrow, you're *out* of my fucking house. You're *off* my fucking island and out of my fucking life."

I ignore the look on her face as I drop my grip on her arm.

I was enjoying the teasing, provoking flirting that was clearly ruffling her feathers before. But we're past that.

I have to be past that.

"After that," I snap. "You don't come back here. No interview. No fucking questions. And yes, you can fully expect the most fuck you NDA you've ever even dreamed of to be delivered to your front door before you even get back to New York."

She swallows thickly, wilting under the fury of my gaze.

"I…I'm sorry—"

"No, you're not."

My eyes narrow coldly as I shake my head.

"You're not. Your kind is never sorry."

"My *kind?*"

"Parasites," I grunt. "Paparazzi, journalists, the media at large…you're all fucking parasites."

I know I'm being a dick. Luckily, I'm a pro at it.

Melody looks down, her brow furrowing.

"I….I really am sorry. I didn't mean to crash into your life, I just…" She swallows, dragging her gaze back up to my glaring one "I really am a huge fan, and I just—"

"I'm *sure* you are. What are you, seventeen?"

She snorts, sneering coldly at me.

"Better hope not, considering the number of ways you've crudely propositioned me today."

A shadow crosses my face.

Shit.

My jaw tightens, brow arching.

"Well?"

Melody looks away.

"I'm twenty, actually. And I've been listening to Velvet Guillotine my entire life."

Well, that's a brutal reminder of my age.

"I don't give a flying fuck if you are actually a Guillotine fan. It's not gonna do fuck-all to get you an interview with me. In fact, all you've accomplished just now is making me feel old."

Her lips curl coldly.

"You *are* old. Sorry," she says flatly.

"Sure does looks windy outside." My eyes narrow. "And cold. And wet, and not in a fun way."

The threat isn't lost on her. Her mouth thins, lips pursing as I smile coldly, lording my asshole-ness over her.

"Thought so."

I clear my throat.

"Name one."

"Name one what?"

"Name one single Velvet Guillotine song, super fan. You do that, and you can stay. I'll even let you sleep inside."

She sneers at me. Goddamnit, why is it so fucking tempting when she's combative with me.

"You've already *said* that I can—"

"One. Song."

I lean back, crossing my arms over my chest.

Melody rolls her eyes.

"From which album?"

A smirk curls on her lips.

"Any album. Dealer's choice. I'm just looking for one single fucking song from this great super fan—"

"*Bleed For You* or *The Hunted* from the Requiem for a Queen album. Though, *Deliver*, from End of the World is a great track. I also really loved the alternate take of *Lydia*, off the extended version of Blood on Main Street. *Never Found You Again* is beautiful, but I do like the live at Madison Square Garden version where you played with Dylan Mercer on keyboards the best."

She pauses when she sees the reluctantly impressed but still scowling look on my face. She seems to allow herself a slow, smug smile.

"Well, you did your homework for your surprise interview."

"It wasn't homework."

"Sure it was."

"The fuck is that supposed to mean?"

I smile cruelly, nodding at the phone clutched in her hand.

"As in you prepped for your assault on my solitude. To impress me, or whatever you thought that would accomplish."

"You *delusional* asshole—"

"It means I'm guessing every playlist on that phone of yours is a plastic, shit-tastic soundtrack to a mall."

She snorts.

"You have no idea what I like to listen—"

"Shitty boy bands? Tragically bad modern covers of great songs? Watered-down bland hip hop? Maybe some especially plastic K-pop?"

She rolls her eyes, swipes her phone open and then shoves it into my hands.

"Choke on it, asshole."

She looks smug as I take the phone, which is open to her Spotify app. I feign a bored look as I scroll through her playlists. But I'm quickly repressing the urge to raise a brow.

Shit.

She's got good taste. Like, really good taste. Classic Motown. Kick-ass 60's and 70's rock. A whole playlist of ultra-rare punk shit. Nick Drake. Jeff Buckley.

Fuck.

Annoyed that I haven't stumbled across the smoking gun I was expecting to find, I thumb off her Spotify app. And immediately proceed to start snooping through the rest of her phone.

"Well?" She snaps sarcastically. "Did I make your cut, douchebag?"

I just grunt, lifting a shoulder. She still thinks I'm passing judgment on her musical tastes. I've moved on to scrolling her photo albums for something scandalous.

Which I soon find.

It's not nudes or anything. But the selfies of Melody in a changing room taking shots of herself trying on bikinis is…

Interesting.

Alluring.

Very enticing.

And in complete opposition to my plan a minute ago of cutting her out and casting her away so I don't fall into a new addiction.

I grit my teeth as I slowly swipe through the shots, drinking in the creaminess of her skin. The awkward and yet enticing smiles she's trying to flash for herself. The way the bikinis hug her tits and that ass.

"What?" She finally blurts, a little trepidation in her tone since I still haven't said a thing.

I just smile as my eyes land on the last shot from the changing room photoshoot—this one of her in lacy pink lingerie instead of a bikini. Which is even better.

Or possibly worse.

"Hello? Your highness?" She snaps thinly.

My eyes slowly raise over the phone to see her glaring at me.

"Well? Ready to apologize yet?"

"For?"

"Assuming you know shit about me or my taste in music?"

I shrug.

"Sure. I don't care. I stopped looking at your playlists two minutes ago."

Her brow furrows.

"Then what the fuck are you looking at?"

I grin.

"You."

Her jaw drops as I flip the phone around and show her what I've been devouring with my eyes. Melody's face explodes with heat, her hand whipping up faster than I ever would have imagined, trying to snatch her phone back out of my hands.

Which I quickly yank up high, so that she can't.

"Give me that!" She screams, her face bright red.

"This is a great look on you."

"Give me my fucking phone back, you fucking creep!"

My smug grin fades to a scowl as my eyes narrow at her.

"Don't think for a second I didn't see the pictures you took of my basement, or my living room, or my patio," I smile thinly at her. "You fucking creep," I mimic the urgency and high tones of her voice from seconds ago.

"This is not an interview," I hiss thinly. "This is *not* a fucking photoshoot. This is not *anything*, except an invasion of my goddamn privacy."

I shove the phone back into her hands. She takes it, shaking a little.

"Okay, okay. I'm sorry. It wasn't for the article, I was just…it's a nice view."

"You got a thing for laundry detergent?"

"No, it's just…I don't even know why I took that picture."

"Then you'll have no trouble deleting it." My eyes narrow. "Now."

Melody wets her lips, swallowing as her eyes meet mine. She nods, dropping her gaze back to her phone and tapping the screen.

"There, okay? I deleted all pictures of your house."

"Great. This way."

She gasps as I grab her arm again, yanking her after me back down the hallway, through the library, and then down the next hallway back into the main living room. I let her arm go, hating the way my hand itches to touch her skin again.

Then I jab a finger at the couch.

"You sleep here. You go nowhere fucking else. And I *will* be checking your phone in the morning to make sure you weren't skulking around taking fucking pictures."

"You don't have to do that," she murmurs, looking contrite. "I know, and I'm sorry. I won't be taking any more pictures."

"I know. If you do, I'm taking the phone."

I smile thinly.

"*Including* the ones of you in a bikini and lingerie."

Her face turns crimson.

"*Right here,*" I grunt again, pointing at the couch. "You don't go into any other room in this house until morning. Is that clear?"

The contrite looks fades as that simmering defiance bubbles to the surface again.

"And if I have to pee?" She snaps.

I turn to wave a dismissive hand at the doors out to the patio

"The great outdoors welcomes you," I say dryly.

I need to get away from her. Because I'm quickly slipping back into dickish flirting, when I should be scaring her. When I should be ignoring her entirely until she can just *get gone* from my fucking life.

I whirl, storming into the kitchen and grabbing the almost empty bottle of shitty scotch from earlier. I pour a heavy splash into a glass and turn as I bring it to my lips.

Melody is sitting on the couch, wrapped in the blanket. And for the very first time, it occurs to me why it is she's got that thing wrapped around her.

Because her clothes are in the dryer.

Because she's fucking *naked* underneath that thin throw blanket.

I groan as once again, my set-in-stone plans to ignore her and cast her away from my world begin to crumble under the weight of my lust for her.

The glass touches my lips again, and I sip angrily and deeply, draining it. I grab the bottle this time as I storm back into the living room.

"No fucking pictures," I grunt like a caveman, trying to avoid even looking at her as I storm for the hallway that leads to the stairs.

"Thank you."

I flinch, pausing as her soft words hit my back.

"For what," I growl quietly.

Don't turn around. Don't you fucking turn around.

I do it anyway, taking a long, burning sip of the scotch as my eyes swivel to land on her. Rain rumbles down, and thunder booms outside. She flinches as lighting shatters the dark outside.

"For letting me stay. For not…you know…making me swim or something."

I don't say a thing.

I don't trust myself to.

"Tomorrow," I finally manage to grunt out. "Tomorrow, you're getting the hell off my island, if I have to ferry you over myself."

Because I need you fucking gone.

She nods.

"I know. I get it. And thank—"

"Don't fucking thank me."

My eyes narrow.

"Just get gone."

11

JACKSON

Seventeen Years Ago, London:

"You know who I bet fucked a lot?"

I glance up from the guitar in my hands to where Iggy is sprawled out shirtless on the couch, drumming against the back of it. A haze of smoke from…several different substances hangs like fog in the lavish hotel suite. And the very faintest glow of morning is beginning to creep in around the edges of the shaded windows.

"Oi, Iggs, we talkin' about your mum again?"

I grin at Will's voice from behind me, followed by the familiar flick of his zippo. Iggy glances past me, grinning himself as he raises a middle finger.

I blink, trying to focus as I glance around at the scene of absolute carnage around me. The picked-clean bones of our last-night's decadence of the after-show party lie tumbled around the room. Topless and naked groupies drape like discarded clothes across couches and the floor, and I can hear someone—God only knows who, or *by* who—getting absolutely *railed* in one of the bedrooms down the hall.

Behind me, Will sits slumped in a chair smoking a cigarette and drinking heavily from a bottle of scotch. The blonde passed out at his feet with her head against his knee suddenly stirs, fumbling and reaching a hand up. Will passes her the smoke, which she drags on—comically, as the big Velvet Guillotine flag that she probably bought at the show last night falls off her shoulders, baring her tits.

"Gene Simmons," Asher mutters from the corner of the suite, where he seems to be fastidiously dividing coke into the most even lines ever achieved by a drug user, all with two utterly *blasted* looking girls in miniskirts and tube tops perched on his knees.

As if anyone in this room needs more of *anything* in our systems right now.

"You asked who fucked a lot. Gene Simmons," he shrugs.

Iggy raises a brow.

"Fair guess but disqualified for obvious reasons."

"Obvious reasons like being in *Kiss*," I snicker..

"*FUCK KISS!*" All four of us crow at once before devolving into drunken, drug-slurred laugher.

I don't even know where the Kiss-hate originated from. I mean, aside from the fact that they're a mediocre band with like one good song who basically got famous for wearing Halloween makeup.

Needless to say, we all *hate* lame gimmicky bands.

"Simmons is a good one, but, nah." Iggy shakes his head, dropping his drumsticks and reaching for the bottle of whiskey on the floor next to the couch he's draped across. He takes a heavy gulp.

"Dean Martin."

"*Fuck*, good one," Will mutters.

"Right? Like, you know it. But you don't *really* know it until you do. And then it's just like…that guy *fucked. A lot.*"

I chuckle, slipping a cigarette between my lips as my fingers tease the neck of the guitar in my hand. The brunette I dragged up here after the show, who's been slumped high as fuck next to me on the couch for the better part of the last four hours, turns to me. She spreads her legs, making sure with all the subtly of a freight train that I'm fully aware of what garments she *did not* dress in tonight.

I'm twenty-five, rich as fuck, the lead singer and guitar player for the biggest band on the planet, and I've just been named both *People Magazine's* "Sexiest Man on Earth" and *Guitar World's* "Most Fuckable Rockstar".

I should be up to my *eyeballs* in pussy right now. And I may be yet. But not now. Not when I've got the faintest hint of a melody line humming somewhere in my head as my fingers run over the strings.

When I get a spark, I don't stop for *shit*. Not for food, not for booze, not for drugs. Not even for pussy.

I ignore the brunette—Shana? Shania? Sharina? I don't fucking remember because I doubt I heard it at all. But apparently, she's done waiting.

Her hand slides to my thigh, boldly sliding up towards my dick as she slips to her knees in front of me.

"I'm busy."

"You can play while I do it." She rakes her teeth over her overly done bottom lip. "Actually, that'd be hot."

"And I already said fucking *no*," I grunt.

"No means no, darlin'," Iggy snickers from his couch. "Jackie's waiting until his wedding night anyway."

The four us snort laughter when the girl's brows arch in pure confusion.

"Another time, babe," I shrug, pushing her hands away from my thigh. "But I'm working. Go play with Iggy."

My friend gives me a sharp look as the girl turns to him hungrily. Asher snickers from the corner.

"Oi, that's forbidden fruit, luv. Alice will have your ass on a goddamn spike for that. And best knock that shit off, Jack," he snickers at me. "Or Alice'll cut *his* balls off, with *your* balls."

"Don't threaten me with a good time," Iggy grins before he glances at the brunette. "Go play with Will, sweetheart."

The girl turns to frown at the scene behind me, where the formerly comatose blonde is now gyrating in our friend's lap as he shrugs with mock helplessness.

"But he—"

"I *sincerely* doubt he minds dividing his attention," I grunt.

Will looks out of his mind drunk. But he grins a sloppy grin at me as the brunette strolls over to also climb into his lap.

None of this is real. I mean, it *is*. But even three or four years into our "success", it feels like a dream. Or at times, a nightmare. But certainly, surreal or even fake either way.

Like a deep trance I'm going to wake from at any point. Like I'll open my eyes one day and it'll turn out I'm still back in Liverpool. Still washing dishes at restaurants and working part time for the construction company—all while forgoing sleep so I can write and practice at night.

"You know who wouldn't mind?" Iggy slurs as he drops his head back to the couch.

"Dean Martin?"

"Bloody *stud*."

"You pricks talking about me?"

I roll my eyes even before I turn to see him. And when I do see Kurt Harrison, strolling out of the hallway from the direction of the bedrooms in just a pair of boxers, my brow furrows. I don't *hate* Kurt, he's just kind of a douchebag.

But it's his bloody music that makes me want to hang myself.

Though branded "rock 'n roll", Kurt's basically a one-man fucking boyband with a guitar and a leather jacket for "cool" points. His shitty "rock influenced pop songs" fucking suck, and it's well known that his success comes at least half from the fact that his uncle is an executive with Columbia Records.

Kurt was an ignorable, utterly forgettable name that usually made me turn the station on the radio. Until some genius at our label decided he should open for us on the first half of this tour. Now, it's like perpetually having that party guest who drinks all your booze, does all your drugs, and doesn't know when to fucking *leave*.

"No one was fucking talking about you, you dumb wanker," Asher mutters. "Now put some pants on."

Kurt turns to grin at him. And in one movement, he crosses to the table Asher and his "friends" are sitting at, leans over it, and snorts up one of the thick lines Ash has been perfecting over the last fifteen minutes.

I arch a brow, glancing at Iggy, and then at Asher. But, Ash is cool. Or at least, cool enough to not blow his top that easily.

"What's the matter, Ash?" Kurt grins as he rubs his nose. "Seein' guys in their underwear make you think of your home life back with your dad? Bet you've seen a lot of that, what with him being a poof and all."

Asher's father, the relatively famous jazz bassist Leonard Sins, *is* in fact, gay.

Also, literally no one cares, especially Asher.

"Shit, mate, I've been meaning to pass this your way," Asher sighs. "Dad wanted me to tell you 'great effort and enthusiasm', but he said to maybe use less teeth next time, yeah?"

The four of us snicker as Kurt bristles, glaring at Asher. But before anything can happen, a small shape materializes out of the dim hallway behind Kurt. My head swivels, and my eyes narrow at the disheveled looking girl tugging at the strap of her dress.

The room goes quiet.

She looks scared. And the bruises on her neck and wrists look new. But most of all, she looks *young*.

Too young.

Too fucking young to be walking bruised and bow-legged out of Kurt Harrison's hotel room at five o'clock in the fucking morning.

"What the *fuck* is this?"

Iggy's eyes blaze with fury as he lurches from the couch. He glances at me, then back to Kurt as he jabs a finger at the girl.

"What is this?" He snarls.

Kurt rolls his eyes. He turns, and the girl whimpers—not in a good way—when he slaps her ass.

"Time to go, babe."

She smiles weakly at the rest of us as she pulls something out of her bag.

It's a ticket, to the show earlier tonight.

"Could…I mean, would you all sign—"

"No fucking autographs," Kurt mutters. "Get the fuck out."

Her face falls as she nods numbly. She turns and quickly makes her way to the hotel suite door. The room is still silent when it shuts behind her. But Kurt seems to ignore it as he grabs a pack of cigarettes off the table next to him and sticks one between his lips.

He frowns as he lights it, glancing at us.

"What?"

"*What?*" Iggy says thinly. His eyes narrow as he jabs a finger at the door the girl just left through.

"What the *fuck* was that?"

"That was *fun*," Kurt rolls his eyes. "You should quit being so pussy whipped by one fucking woman and try it sometime before your balls fall off."

"How old is she?"

Kurt stiffens, turning to glare at me next.

"Huh?"

I stand slowly, my jaw gritting as I put the guitar down.

"How fucking *old* is she?"

Kurt's brow furrows as he glances around the room.

"What is this, Sunday confessional? Cause you lot are the oddest bunch of nuns I've ever fucking seen."

"Answer the question," Will mutters. "How old was that—"

"Old enough to come to a fucking rock show!" Kurt spits. "Old enough to slink her way backstage and invite herself up to the afterparty. And old enough to take my cock in every fuckin' hole! *That's* how old she is!"

My jaw clenches as I move towards him, my hand curling into a fist.

"Your place on this tour isn't carved in stone, motherfucker," I snap coldly. "And I swear to God, if you jeopardize any of—"

Kurt barks a cold laugh, cutting me off.

"*Yeah*, it's gonna be me fucking pretty girls that throws off the tour," he spits before whirling to jab a thumb at Iggy.

"Not this junkie with his fuckin' gear."

I tense, turning to stab my gaze into my friend. Iggy's eyes dart side to side, his jaw tightening.

"Oh, for fuck's sake, if the rest of you are fuckin' blind…"

Kurt storms over to a table across the main suite, with Iggy's drumstick bag lying on it.

"Oi! Don't fucking touch—"

But Kurt ignores my friend as he dumps the bag out across the table, scattering drumsticks, a snare tuner, a pack of cigarettes…

And a bag of yellowish grey powder.

And a grimy spoon and a lighter.

And a syringe.

Kurt turns, spreading his arms as he glares at Iggy.

"Keep your fuckin' nose out of my bedroom and back up in your glass tower, you fuckin' junkie."

He eyes us all before he storms back to the bedroom. He comes back a minute later, dressed, giving us all one more glare before he storms out the door.

Slowly, in the ensuing silence, I turn back to Iggy.

"Jack—"

He jolts when I surge into him, grabbing him by the arm and mostly shoving him out of sight of the other guys and the groupies, into the hotel suite kitchen.

"What the *fuck*, man!?" I snap as I slam him into the fridge. "We talked about this!"

Iggy's jaw clenches, but he shakes his head.

"C'mon, Jack, it's fine."

"The fuck it is."

"Mate, it's just a pinch," he holds up a thumb and forefinger. "Just now and then." His face falls. "C'mon, Jackson. You don't know how it is when Alice can't come on the tour."

"So, you fucking *call her*," I hiss. "You've got more money than God, Iggs. You get on a plane, and you go visit her. You don't do *that* shit!"

It's sort of our one unwritten rule as a band. Well, aside from not screwing anyone else's girl: no fucking heroin. We might drink, smoke, snort, and pill-pop ourselves fucking stupid on a near nightly basis. But intravenous shit is a hard no.

And Iggy knows that.

"Goddamnit, Iggy—"

"Jack, I know." He sighs. "I know. But it's honestly not what you think."

I glare at him.

"It's *not*, I promise. It's literally just a pinch, every now and then. It's just to take the edge off, mate. I'm in control, trust me."

"*Iggy*—"

"Jackson."

He smiles that lopsided, disarming smile of his I've known since we were ten. I sigh and smile warily back.

"I'm in control. I swear to you."

I glare at him. "Better fuckin' be."

He grins again and puts a hand on my shoulder.

"More importantly," he winks. "What was that riff you were playing back in there? Because that sounded fucking *good*."

I eye my best friend one more time, and he chuckles.

"I'm on top of it, mate. Don't worry. I'm not going anywhere."

12

JACKSON

Present, Falstaff Island, Maine:

I wake up hard.

By which, I don't mean it's difficult to wake up—though, it usually is. I mean I wake up *hard*. As in, my cock is thickly at attention and obscenely tenting the sheets on my bed.

But then again, I also went to sleep fucking hard, too. In fact, I've been hard since she was foolish enough to hand me her phone. Since I went through her photos.

But no. It actually started before that.

I've been twisted up and throbbing with a dark desire since she showed up dripping wet on my front porch. Or maybe since she crashed into me back in town. And it's been an uphill battle ever since.

I don't even know what the fuck it is about her, either. She's stunning, of course. She's gorgeous and cute and sexy. But it's not ostentatious. It's not like some photoshopped Victoria's Secret model showed up on my front stoop on all fours with a plug in her ass and "daddy's cum slut" written in lipstick on her tits.

I groan as my mind immediately puts *Melody* into that same visual. Which doesn't do shit to help the massive tent in my sheets.

But the real-life Melody isn't wearing a ton of make-up or dressed provocatively—unless you count parading around my house in a blanket and I'm guessing nothing else. And unlike most of the women I've known in my time on this planet, mostly in the limelight, there's nothing shamelessly eager or wanton about her.

Which *always* bored me.

The models, the actresses, the groupies…any of those women who pleaded and debased themselves just to get a look at me backstage. The ones who wanted to get into my orbit by *any* means necessary.

Parasites, the lot of them.

Melody, however, seems to be immune to my usual magnetism.

Sure, I've been out of that limelight for ten years. I've spent the last decade alone, not talking, descending more and more into my own demons and biases. Until I'm basically the hermit the town across the bay thinks I am.

But still. She's not just immune to my…*charms*, I suppose you could call them.

She's repulsed by them.

But maybe that's a good thing.

I frown. No, scratch that. That's *absolutely* a good thing.

I shake my head as I sit up in the bed. Being that I slept in my own room last night instead of the living room, it's pitch black, as I've got the blackout shades down. I flick on the bedside light, wincing at the brightness as I glance at an empty bottle on the nightstand next to me.

Right. The shit scotch. Which I drank all of.

My gaze slips to the ripped-out pages of notebooks strewn across the bed and the floor. Right…right, there was that. I left Melody downstairs at, what, nine? Ten? Except I didn't go to sleep until well after two-thirty in the morning.

Instead, I stayed up drinking and trying to tap into whatever creativity I've got left, to write *something*. To find some last drips of whatever I used to have.

Laughable.

This whole goddamn house is littered with torn up pages and filled notebooks and the backs of magazines scrawled with lyrics and chord progressions I've shoved into dark corners.

It's all shit these days. Or maybe it's not and I just stopped giving a fuck about any of it. Or maybe I can't even tell what's shit and what's not anymore.

I grunt as I slide out of bed and yank on some sweatpants. I dig through my clothes for a t-shirt that doesn't smell terrible. But…maybe it's time to do some laundry.

It's definitely time do some laundry.

Shirtless, sweats hanging off my hips and the hangover nipping at my ass, I hit the button to raise the blackout shades on the windows.

I frown in confusion.

It's still dark outside.

For a second, I wonder if I've actually only slept an hour or two, and for some reason, I've woken up before dawn or something. But then I glance at the clock on the far wall and scowl.

First of all, why the *fuck* am I up at seven o'clock in the goddamn morning, because I haven't woken up before eleven-forty-five in *years*. But second of all, being that I am, why the *shit* is it still pitch-black outside?

But that second question answers itself when thunder erupts outside, followed by a crack of lightning. Actually, that might very well answer the first question, too.

I groan and sit on the edge of the bed, rubbing the bridge of my nose. I'm tempted to swig some cold medicine, stuff some earplugs in, and go back to sleep. But…goddamnit, I'm up. And now my body is up too, and demanding caffeine and alcohol. In the reverse of that order.

Grumbling, I yank the door to my bedroom open and plod out into the hallway, then down the stairs to see what the hell I can dig up in the way of coffee and booze. And then I step into the living room and stop cold.

Because the whole place looks…*amazing*. By which I mean, "clean".

I can actually see the surface of the coffee table. I can see the hardwood floors and the area carpets. What I can't see is a single ashtray, or mirror dusted with cocaine, or empty bottle anywhere in the entire goddamn room.

The sheets are off the windows, and the real, actual curtains are drawn back. The books on the shelves are arranged. The half-dead plants in the corner look…well, still half dead. But the soil at their base looks wet like someone actually watered them for once.

The framed pictures on the wall are straight. The couch cushions are arranged. The blanket she slept in is folded neatly and draped over the back of it. Even her stuff that she dried last night is folded in a neat little stack on a chair, next to her backpack and her boots.

I step back, arching a brow as my gaze slowly travels across the room.

This doesn't look like my hovel of a living room. It looks like a photo shoot from Architectural Digest. It looks like Elle Decor was in here Elle Decoring my shit up.

I want to hate it.

I *really* really want to hate it that she—Melody, obviously—cleaned up my goddamn living room. I want to hate that she mettled in my shit and got rid of…who even knows what hidden genius balled up in the pieces of paper across the floor that are no longer there.

But…shit does it looks nice in here.

I frown as I slowly walk the length of the room into the kitchen, where my jaw promptly hits the floor.

The transformation in the living room was incredible. The transformation in the kitchen is nothing short of a miracle. Mostly because what was here before was a fucking biohazard.

But now? The dishes are done and put away. The stove doesn't look like a nuclear waste dump. The fridge is…no longer growing new versions of penicillin.

But more importunely…

Where the hell is Melody?

I glance around, raising a brow as I scan the empty living room. And then, dimly, softly in the background, I hear it.

Music.

My ears tune, and my jaw and gaze harden in the direction of the recording studio I never finished. The one that was never used to record shit. The one I'm the only one who ended up playing in.

When our first record hit the stratosphere, we of course all did the stupid shit you'd expect a bunch of kids who'd never had money before would do with sudden fame and fortune.

We went fucking *nuts*.

Cars, drugs, girls, clothes, apartments all over the world, lavish trips to Vegas…all of that. And of course, *gear*. The rarest custom guitars. The most expensive equipment we could get our hands on. All of that shit. But I, being, well, *me*, took it a step further. As always.

I didn't just buy a bunch of gear. I bought a whole mansion on its own goddamn island, with visions of us all making it our getaway home. Complete with a recording studio, where we'd record our follow-up masterpiece.

None of that ever happened.

I mean I obviously bought the house. But once you're big, you lose control. Even if you fight like hell to hang on to it.

When you're making the record company that much money? When you're that high and drunk off your own ego, bullshit, and, of course, *drugs*, control is taken from you. The ship is steered by more experienced, sober individuals. Which is at times probably a good thing.

Except it meant we never all came here. Not ever. I managed to get Iggy out here; *once*. But that was it.

I blink as the music—an acoustic guitar, floats through my head again.

As of last night, I'm the only person to have ever played in that studio I set up here. As of this morning, it would seem that streak has ended.

Dark clouds roll across my face.

I told her to stay in one place and not to fuck with my shit. She ignored that, but I'm willing to overlook it—mostly—because she cleaned the absolute shit out of my living room and kitchen.

But this is a bridge too far.

She's in my studio—my inner sanctuary, where *no one* has ever been. And she's fucking around with my guitars.

You don't *touch* my guitars. Not even Iggy would have done that without asking. Soul Scream once had to cancel the last four shows on one of their US tours. Because at a hotel party in Chicago, their lead singer, Leighton James, decided it would be hilarious to stagger drunk into my suite, grab one of my guitars, and start hacking out *We Are the Champions*.

Publicly, Leighton James broke his arm after getting drunk and falling off a balcony into a pool—or, *mostly* into a pool.

In reality, he had some help going over that railing.

My eyes narrow, and my teeth flash as I stalk through the house towards my studio. No, I'm not going throw Melody off a balcony. But I am about to unleash some unholy-fucking-hell on her for—

I stop short, two feet from the half-open door to the studio.

I stop. The world stops. Time stops. Fucking everything else about reality just grinds to a halt. Because in that instant, all I know is the sound of her voice floating through the air.

Holy. Fucking. Shit.

It's like nothing I've ever heard before. But even more insane, it's like nothing I've ever *felt* before, and all I do, all day, every day, all my life, is feel the world through music.

But hearing Melody sing is like seeing a new color. It's like experiencing an emotion you've only seen described with words that never did it justice.

It's clear and yet smokey. A soft and breathy alto tone that somehow also exudes power and strength.

And it brings me to my metaphorical knees.

I'm aware of nothing else as I slowly move towards the door. As I get closer, I start to pick out the actual words, and hear the guitar she's strumming—gorgeously and expertly, for that matter—and somehow my jaw drops even further through the floor.

She's singing Warren Zevon's *Keep Me In Your Heart*.

I blink. For one, this happens to be one of my favorite songs of the last thirty years. But for two, what pink-haired, New York City hipster twenty-year-old even knows who the fuck Warren Zevon *is*?

I approach the door like an utterly hypnotized freak. My eyes are hard and prying, my jaw dropped as I peer through the opening of the door.

I was wrong—about time and the world and all that shit stopping before. I mean, it *did* stop before when I heard her voice. But it well and truly fucking *ceases to move* when my gaze stabs through the doorway.

On Melody, standing in the recording studio, with my old acoustic slung over her shoulders.

Wearing a bra-less t-shirt, and little pink panties.

And nothing else.

That's when the entire rest of the world around me truly ceases to exist at all.

My jaw clenches, and I couldn't even hope to stop the low, deep, animalistic growl rumbling from my chest even if I wanted to.

The music stops. With a sharp, choking gasp, Melody whirls to me, her eyes bulging wide as mouth falls open in a silent scream.

She scrambles to pull the guitar strap from around her shoulders, quickly but carefully placing it back on the little stand to the side. Still silent, she whips her gaze back to me. Her arms cross over herself awkwardly, as if trying to use her small hands to block my hungry gaze from devouring the obvious pebbles of her hard nipples.

The way her panties cling to her pussy.

A dark, pink color floods up her neck and her cheeks as she backs against the control board behind her. Her eyes dart here and there as if looking for a way to escape. A place to run and hide.

There's not.

Not for me.

Not right now.

Our eyes lock. And before I know what I'm doing—before I can tell myself to fucking stop it, or to run in the opposite direction or to go drown myself drugs, drink and whatever other escape I can lay my hands on—I'm crossing the room, fast.

And I don't stop until I'm right in front of her, arms on either side of her, caging her in.

Capturing her.

Ready to devour her fucking whole.

13

MELODY

I JOLT AWAKE to the sound of thunder.

The gasp tightens to a knot in my throat, choking me as reality rips me from the dream I've just been drowning in.

Drowning, or more like…writhing.

Moaning.

Whimpering for more.

And yet as good a dream as all of that *should* make it sound, this was not a good dream.

It wasn't.

I feel my face tingle with heat as I try and ram that mantra down my own throat. Because I have to get it through my brain that the sex dream I just had—*about Jackson*—was in fact, a nightmare.

My brain, unfortunately, seems to refuse to accept that reprogramming. Spitefully. Instead, it decides to replay the events of my...*vivid* dream involving the king asshole who lives here.

Every. Single. Toe-curling. Detail.

In my dream—no, *nightmare*, I reminded myself—Jackson was playing guitar alone on a stage. I can't remember or maybe I never even knew within the dream itself if there was an audience or not at that point, because the concert venue was dark except for a single dim light shining down on him.

Shirtless, jeans slung low on his hips like the leather pants in the infamously scandalous *Exorcise My Love* video. A song that is *actually* one of my top favorite Velvet Guillotine songs. I'd just never in a million fucking years tell Jackson to his face that one of my favorite songs of his is the one where he's basically fucking the camera dressed like Brad Pitt in *Fight Club*.

I mean, I'm not insane.

But the dream. In it, I found myself walking across the stage towards him, from behind. I was dressed like...well, like a Velvet Guillotine groupie of some kind. But like this weirdly erotic or stripper-esque mix of an Alice in Wonderland costume mixed with rock 'n roll hedonism. I don't know. There were fishnets.

I got within a foot of him, awestruck at the sounds of pure sexual energy humming from his electric guitar. Before suddenly, he turned, looked right at me, licked his lips, and said "you're dessert."

The next thing I knew, I was—shamelessly—on my hands and knees, ass up in the air, shivering as Jackson pushed my skirt up. Gasping as he ripped my fishnet stockings with his bare hands.

Moaning as his tongue dragged like hot silk over my pussy, making my thighs shake as I screamed into the crook of my arm. I could feel him move up behind me, a big powerful hand gripping my ass as he started run the swollen head of his huge cock up my slit.

And then the house lights came on, and I was suddenly surrounded by a *sea* of strangers, all cheering like this was the perfect finale to the show.

That's when the thunder woke me.

I rub my eyes, feeling the sheen of sweat across my body. The house is warm, and the blankets I heaped over myself last night, expecting to be cold, have only added to that overbearing warmth.

For a second, I consider trying to burrow back to sleep. But I'm up, and now my dumb brain is awake replaying that horrible dream.

I shiver, thighs squeezing together as I exhale slowly, waking even more.

My nose wrinkles as my eyes scan the dusty, cluttered, whiskey-bottle-littered room I've spent the night in. It's a gorgeous, stunning old home. Or at least it is somewhere underneath the layer of dust, grime, dirty clothes, and crumpled bits of paper littered across, well, basically everything.

How does he live like this?

My eyes land on the coffee table in front of the couch. My brow furrows as I stare at the mirror dusted with white powder. Like a little slice of home.

I ignore the narcotics in front of me and sink into the couch at my back, wrapping the blanket tighter around myself.

Home…

It isn't lost on me that I haven't mentioned my last name or who my mom is to Jackson. Partly because I don't want him to think I got the job interviewing him because of who my mother is. Even if, perhaps I did.

But the biggest reason is that I'm not sure if that last name and who I'm related to will open doors or get me thrown ass first back out of his.

I glance around the room one more time, turning to look at the time again before finally exhaling.

He can't live like this. This is gross.

I stand and go to tug on my jeans before my nose wrinkles. Most of my stuff is dry from the dryer last night. But denim is denim. And both pairs of my jeans are still slightly damp.

For a moment I shiver, realizing I'm standing in Jackson's living room in a t-shirt, no bra, and panties. I swallow as my eyes dart to the doorway to the front entryway with the huge, elegantly curved staircase that leads up who knows where.

But then again, there was one moment last night when I woke up somewhere around two in the morning and heard him pacing the floor somewhere in the house above me.

That was *two o'clock in the morning*. And it is currently…I glance at the clock and groan. It's five in the morning. And we're talking about a former rock god here.

There is no way in fucking hell Jackson is awake right now. I mean logically, there's no way he'll be awake anytime *today* with the amount of alcohol he's clearly been putting away. But definitely not at five in the morning.

I shuffle into the kitchen, wrinkling my nose again as my eyes slide over the disgusting state of it. I head to the pantry where I remember spotting something yesterday when I went to grab my peanut butter and jelly makings. And, sure enough, when I open the door, there's the apron hanging there.

I slip it on and then turn to take in the state of the kitchen with a heavy sigh. I'm not about to dive head-first into cleaning Jackson's house because he "suggested" it last night, as payment for his "grand generosity" of "allowing" me to sleep indoors.

Gee, thanks.

No, I'm doing this because this is my weird Zen thing.

When I can't sleep, or if I'm stressing, or can't get my mind to stop chasing itself in circles, I clean my apartment. When I did eventually see a therapist—or two, or three—about my childhood, *years* after, when I was eighteen, I never really brought up the cleaning quirk. But I'm sure they'd have quickly traced it back to the days and nights I'd spend alone as a kid, while Judy was lost for a week at Warped Tour, or Coachella, or whatever random band's tour bus she'd managed to slink herself onto.

And when I was scared, maybe a little bored, and alone, I'd start tidying things. Maybe the order gave me comfort in a home life rife with *dis*order.

First things first, I get the coffee machine going. The storm is still rumbling around outside, and the sudden bursts of thunder keep jarring me. So, I end up sticking headphones in my ears and turning on some saved-offline music on my phone.

The warm, familiar sound of Warren Zevon purrs into my ears as I roll up my metaphorical sleeves, and dig in.

An hour later, it's starting to look like a residence a human actually lives in. I collect all the empty bottles. I wash the cocaine dust residue off the mirror in the sink, which gives me flashbacks to the times growing up when I had friends coming over to the apartment and I had to hide my mother's drugs.

Bottles, mirror, and then the trash littering the entire room. But the tricky part there is some that of it is *actual* trash. But there's also other scraps here and there that only *appear* to be trash until you unfurl them. And the first time it happens, I realize what I'm holding in my hands isn't trash.

It's lyrics.

I go still, my eyes sweeping over the handwritten words and rambles sprawling across the crumpled-up page.

It's… sporadic. It's rambling, and not too coherent. But these are lyrics written by Jackson freaking Havoc. And recently, at that.

It's not lost on me that I could smuggle some of these scraps of lyrics home with me and probably sell them for a *lot* online.

But I'm not going to do that. Instead, I put it to the side and dig into more of the trash. But the more pieces of crumpled paper I unravel, the more lyrics I find.

I put them all in a stack.

A little while later, I finally make it into the disaster zone called the kitchen. And it's truly a fucking disaster. But just the same, I get to work.

And yes, I do question why the fuck I'm stomping around in my underwear at six-thirty in the morning, cleaning Captain Dickhead's house for him. There's a certain Machiavellian streak in me that wonders, or hopes, horribly, that this might... I guess *ingratiate* me with him.

That maybe, just maybe, the likelihood of an interview that lands me this job at Ignition is there if he comes downstairs and finds his place clean and not littered with trash.

But mostly, I know it's because I'm awake, and because yes, I'm a bit of a neat freak.

After another little while, I step back to admire my work. I grin smugly, pulling the earbuds out as I survey the now-sparkling, biohazard-free kitchen.

I glance at the time. It's now only seven in the morning. But I've hit my wall with cleaning, and the place looks fantastic anyway. Back out in the living room, I sit on the couch with the huge stack of lyrics I uncovered. Slowly, I read them, feeling a strange warmth settle though me.

They're rough. They're disorganized and random. But... there's a poetry to them that moves something in me.

Yes, Velvet Guillotine was always known as this collective of hard-partying, headline-grabbing, shenanigans-seeking young terrors. But if they'd *just* been that, they'd have fizzled out early.

There are a thousand bands out there who partied or still party just as hard as Velvet ever did. But what truly made them notorious, if not legendary, was that that wild, reckless spirit didn't just materialize in tabloid headlines.

It was right there in the dark genius of their music.

Of *Jackson's* music.

I pause, sucking on my lip as the memory of seeing Jackson play yesterday comes seeping back into my thoughts.

Maybe that's why I had that dream.

I shiver. But then, I pause, glancing at the time.

It's only seven-ten. And again, his royal prickishness was still awake, and probably drinking himself into a stupor, at past two in the morning.

There's no way he's up anytime soon.

Heart racing as if I'm breaking and entering, or trying to find hidden presents before Christmas, I rush down the hallway I went down yesterday. I go through the library, and the parlor, until I'm back at the door to the recording studio.

I push the door open, feeling my very soul surge a little bit as I step into air charged with the promise of creativity. My feet carry me through the uncertainty of being in here, until I'm standing in front of the little stand holding the very same acoustic guitar Jackson was playing yesterday.

I don't think. I just reach for it, like it's been left out for me, and slip the strap over my shoulder.

It was Will Cates who bought me my first guitar one random Wednesday when I was nine. Then he sat me down that very day in my mom's apartment and showed me how to play the opening to The Velvet Guillotine song *Lydia*.

Not *Jingle Bells*. Not *Hot Crossed Buns*, or any of the other extremely entry-level "first time playing guitar" type songs.

Nope. Straight into rock 'n roll.

Will taught me to sing, too. I mean, I was already singing all over the apartment. But he showed me how to use my breath, and how to hit notes the right way. How to train my ears to know where the melody is going.

My eyes close, and excitement flushes through me as my fingers touch metal strings. I used to love this *so much* it hurt. I mean I still love it, it's just…

My smile falters.

It's just that it was taken from me. By a monster. When I was thirteen.

After that night, I…

I exhale slowly.

After that night, the joy I found in playing and singing became a private-only thing for me. The guitar playing, yes, I could maybe still do in front of people.

But not singing. Never singing; not after him.

My eyes close as my fingers walk slowly over the strings, feeling the power in them as if they're still vibrating from their master who played them just yesterday.

And then, unbidden, and without trying to even coax it out, my mouth opens.

And the words pour out of me.

I go with Warren Zevon, because I was just listening to him, and *Keep Me In Your Heart* is one of my all-time favorite songs. And standing there, in what I know is a forbidden room, holding a forbidden object, I engage in what is—at least for me, since that night—the forbidden act of singing out loud.

And I'm lost in it. Lost in the love and joy for life itself that I feel when I sing, or when music just flows through me.

I get so lost in it, in fact, that it's not until I hear the thick growl behind me that I realize I'm not actually alone at all.

I have an audience.

And when I gasp and whirl to stare at him in shock and horror, my heart climbs into my throat. My pulse hammers like an invader in my ears, and my vision blurs as I lock eyes with Jackson.

And here I am standing here in a t-shirt, no bra, and panties, like something out of a porn shoot.

But the man standing six feet away from is absolutely *dripping* with sexual energy and raw lust. And as much as I want to look away—to drag my eyes kicking and screaming away from him—I can't.

Because no one can. Because Jackson is sexual freaking napalm.

The man is, what, forty? Forty-two? Beyond that, he seems to eat like a pig and drink like an Irish dock worker. And yet *absurdly*, the man has the body of a cage fighter. The body of a fucking god.

Grooved, lethally hardened lean muscles covered in tattoos. I mean he's illegally hot. Or what *should* be illegal is the way I'm staring at him hungrily.

But this isn't fair. This deck is stacked. I mean for fuck's sake; he's standing there caging me in with his hands on the door frame with no shirt on. With sweatpants slung so low on his grooved hips that I can feel a heat pulse between my thighs.

So low that I can't stop my eyes from traveling down the etched v-cut of his hips, or down the dark trail of hair that leads lower and lower and lower…

God help me.

And then suddenly, explosively and determinedly, he's crossing the room towards me.

I gasp, shivering as he surges towards me, his eyes never leaving mine until he stops inches away. His gorgeous, viciously handsome eyes stab into me. I move back, only to find the control panel of the recording studio right at my ass. I move as if to slip to the side, but my breath sucks in as his hands slam to the counter on either side of me, boxing me in.

I stiffen. And I wait for the inevitable.

I wait for the freak-out, or the collapse. I wait for the numbness, or for my mind to go to that cold, windowless place it goes whenever a man gets close to me like this.

But none of that happens. It should, but it doesn't. I don't freeze or go numb. In fact, I'm warm and throbbing everywhere.

I tremble, my pulse humming in my ears as the world literally spins around me. It's like the heat of him and the force of him like some sort of magnetic magical dark energy sinks into my very skin, arresting my every though and choking the breath in my throat.

I don't get mushy and weird about celebrities. I mean for god's sake my mother has dated half the famous men of the rock 'n' roll scene of the last twenty years. For God's sake, Jackson's own rhythm guitar player *lived* with us, virtually as a stepdad to me, for years.

But it's not his celebrity status that has me choked up. It's not the fact that he's famous or that I grew up listening to his records, or the knowledge than any woman in the world in this position would be losing her fucking mind to be trapped in cage by none other than Jackson Havoc.

It's just...*him*. It's this dark sorcery. This lethal magic that surrounds him. I'm fully aware that it's the same dark energy that made him so magnetic on stage and sold so many records and so many concert venue seats.

But right now, all it's selling is my soul.

To him.

And I'm about to sign whatever dotted line this devil wants me to sign.

14

MELODY

Jackson's eyes flare with a steely blue fire. He leans down closer and closer, my breath choking until I'm positive he's just going to fucking kiss me.

But he doesn't, and the thin, smug smirk on his lips tells me he knows goddamn well that's what I was thinking. Instead, his mouth brushes past my cheek to my ear, and I tremble from head to toe as the sheer heat of him radiates through my body.

"*My, my, my,*" he purrs thickly.

The tone is so low and gravely, but I swear it's like he's touching me with his voice.

"I came down looking for coffee and maybe breakfast. But I think this is even better…"

My breath chokes, my pulse thudding in my head. My mouth fighting to form words. Literally *any* words.

"I—"

"*Fuck* toast and coffee," he rasps, like silk and leather into my ear. "I'll have that sweet little pussy for breakfast."

My heart climbs into my throat, absolutely choking the shit out of me as my face turns crimson. My pulse ignites like liquid fire underneath my skin, and my jaw falters open.

I fight to say anything back...anything at all. Even if I have no idea what my answer should be. Because half of me wants to scream at him and maybe slap him as hard as I can. But the other half of me wants to sink against his chest, raise my chin, kiss him as hard as I can, and then let him do *whatever he wants* to me.

And I have never, ever *once* felt like that around a man. Not ever, and not even a little bit.

For a time, I thought I was asexual. Or even sexually confused, and that trying to force myself to go on dates with guys felt off because I was playing for the wrong team.

But that's not it. I have desires. I get turned on, and I have fantasies—about men.

I just can't enact them *with* men. I can't be intimate, or even bring myself to last through a single kiss without losing my shit and having a freak out. All because of the motherfucker who destroyed me when I was barely a teenager.

Except, something's different. The closer Jackson leans, and the more his sinful words and heated breath teases over my skin...

The more excited I get.

The more caged in by him I become, the more I feel pure liquid desire pooling in my core.

Not coldness. Not stiffness. Not my body and my mind shutting everything out until the date who just tried to kiss me awkwardly pulls away to ask if I'm having a stroke or if I'm about to throw up.

There's none of that right now. For the very first time in my life, a man is pulling closer to me, and wanting me…

And I'm wanting him back.

Horribly.

I shiver, biting back the whimper that desperately tries to tumble from my lips. Maybe it's the sheer power of him. Or that goddamn dark energy surrounding him. There's a part of me that still wants to slap him and call him a pig.

But there's no revulsion. No chilling effect. I might want to tell him to fuck off, but I know damn well if and when I did that, my words would be laced with desire and lust.

And he'd see right fucking through them.

Instead, I stand there gasping, my breath coming in choked whimpers as his mouth brushes my ear. My eyes roll back, and tendrils of fire sizzle through my entire body.

Jackson's hand suddenly slides over my hip. And for one second, I get one flash of naked fear. One single glimpse of the cold, arresting, paralyzing terror that's happened every single time a boy—and it's only ever been a boy, never a man, like him—has tried to touch me, even innocently, since that night those years ago.

Since the night the real devil—not the charming one in front me, but the real, actual devil who my mother let in—came into my room.

But this time, somethings different from any other time since that night. Jackson's hand—a strong, firm powerful man's hand—doesn't touch me lightly. His grip tightens. His fingers dig into my flesh, and one of them traces slowly and deliberately over the thin strip of naked skin between the hem of my shirt and the lace of my panties.

And for the very first time ever since that night, another person's hand on me doesn't turn me to cold stone. This time, there's only fire, and it warms and cracks the ice around that part of my soul until the cold edge of fear rips away.

And something hot, fierce, and forbidden rushes through my core.

Something that aches for more.

"Pretty sure I had dreams about you last night," he rasps darkly into my ear.

His finger strokes my skin, lazily tracing back until he hits the small of my back. I shiver, feeling his palm rest against my skin as one finger lazily dips under the lace to stroke the very top of the cleft of my ass.

I can't breathe. I can't think. All I can do is stand here and slowly melt into a fucking *puddle*. Unable to talk but wanting to tell him to take everything—wanting to tell him to do whatever he wants to me.

Because in this one insane moment, all I want is everything with his man.

"Now comes the important choice," Jackson growls deeply, that honeyed, whiskey-soaked, entirely-too-sexy accented voice of his teasing every fantasy in my head.

His hand strokes across my hip, slowly moving to the front as my whole world turns to fire.

"What…"

I can't talk. Why am I even trying to talk?

His hand slowly moves up my side, sliding up under my t-shirt and making my skin prickle in heat. He traces up each bump of my ribs, higher and higher until the edge of his thumb brushes the very side of my breast.

I moan, my eyes rolling back, my throat tightening as his breath washes over my ear, teasing me. His hand twists, and when he cups my breast fully, I absolutely melt.

His touch brushes across my nipple before he takes the throbbing little bud between a thumb and finger and pinches.

I whimper…*eagerly* and desperately.

Jackson growls into my ear, and his body surges against mine hard—pressing me to the counter behind me. I whimper when I feel something hard, something thick, something…*huge* throbbing against my lower stomach through his sweatpants.

Oh my fucking God.

His fingers twist and tease my nipple. His teeth rake over my earlobe, turning me to liquid fire.

And then suddenly, horribly, it hits me.

She hits me.

Judy.

And suddenly, all I'm hearing is the replay of that goddamn interview from a few days ago. For some horrifying reason in this moment, all I'm hearing is my fucking mother's voice cackling as she tells Connor Newsome about her sexual exploits of the past.

About her vague, maybe bullshit, but sweet Jesus, maybe *not* bullshit insinuation about the very man pining me the counter behind me, about to swallow me whole.

And suddenly, the record scratches.

The bile rises in my in my throat, and my core turns to ice. And then comes what I assumed would come a minute ago: the naked fear. The shut-down. The sickening feeling in my stomach that comes with being touched.

I explode. With a gasp, I suddenly shove Jackson away with a snarl on my lips.

"Don't you fucking touch me," I blurt, choking, gasping, sucking in air as the swirling room tries to bring me to my knees.

Jackson's brow furrows. But his hands drop from me, shattering the rest of the moment as he steps away.

His eyes narrow.

"*Please*," he mutters quietly.

I shake my head violently, hugging myself as my lips curl.

"No," I snap. "No, I'm not fucking *begging* for any—"

"No," he hisses sharply, anger lacing his one. "No, I mean *please* as in give me a fucking break."

I blink. *What?*

Jackson laughs coldly as be backs away from me.

"Like this wasn't your plan all morning?" He snorts. "Or last night, for that matter?"

My jaw drops as I stare at him.

"I beg your fucking pardon??"

"I said *give me a fucking break*, sweetheart," he snaps. "You just *happened* to be cleaning up my house…"

"If your house wasn't a fucking biohazard!" I yell back. "Maybe it wouldn't need to be cleaned for basic fucking health reasons! And I couldn't sleep after someone was banging around upstairs at two in the morning!"

"Couldn't put fucking pants on either, I suppose."

My mouth forms an O shape.

"Oh my *God*, you narcissistic pig—"

"What was the plan?" He snaps. "Prance around in some little lace panties for me? Put on a fucking sexy maid outfit? Bend over for me? Spill something on my fucking crotch?"

My face goes red as he sneers at me.

"I've met some real star fuckers in my day, sweetheart. But whoring yourself out for an interview—"

My hand connects with his famous face.

Hard.

Me slapping the absolute shit out of Jackson reverberates through the sound-perfected room, until everything goes silent.

My face falls in horror as we go still as statues.

But he doesn't whirl on me. He doesn't explode, or hit me back, or roar or yell or scream. He just slowly turns back to me, and his eyes go livid as they stab into me quietly.

"Jackson—"

"Get. Out."

The words are pure ice, chilling me to my core.

"Jackson…" I swallow. "I am *so* sorry. I…I didn't mean—"

"GET THE FUCK OUT!" He thunders, ripping a choked gasp of fear from my throat.

But then suddenly, the absurdity of the situation hits me. He's mad because…yes, I slapped him. But it's more than that. I mean it's not like I *stabbed* him.

And then it hits me.

He's mad because…what, because I wouldn't put out for him? Because he had the gall to assume any woman around him who even looks at him wants to fuck him, or act out whatever porn fantasy he's woken up with?

The heat from earlier chills to cold fury. And suddenly, I'm not scared anymore. I'm just fucking pissed off and a little disgusted.

My lips curl as I stare up at him.

"You *frail* little man baby," I sneer. "Your *poor* fucking ego—"

"My ego is fine," he rumbles darkly. "It's your ass that's going to be bruised when you land on it, after I throw you out the fucking door in ten seconds."

I stare at him, shaking my head.

"*Pathetic.*"

"Nine."

"So. Fucking. *Pathetic*."

"Eight."

I swallow, the "last stand" in me melting away.

"*Seven*."

Suddenly, I'm scrambling past Jackson, out the door, and then bolting down the hall. I can hear him marching after me as I bolt into the living room. I can feel his eyes on me, my back to him and my face bright red as I start to shove my things into my backpack. I'm sure he's staring at my ass as I yank on the still damp jeans and boots.

I don't look back at him. I just ignore him completely, my face absolutely fuming with heat and embarrassment as I bolt for the door and throw my bag over my shoulder.

I was *not* trying to fucking seduce him. Jesus fucking Christ. That's not why I was dressed like…well, embarrassingly like that. But he doesn't want to hear that. He won't hear that.

At the door, I stop, whirling leveling my eyes at him. He's just standing there in the archway from the entryway to the living room, leaned against the doorframe, arms folded over his bare chest with those sweatpants still slung infuriatingly low on his gorgeous hips.

"*For the record*," I snap at him. "I wouldn't sleep with you if you were the last man on fucking earth."

"Whatever helps you sleep at night sweet—"

"Have a nice life, douchebag."

I whirl, and I storm out the door.

15

MELODY

For the second time, the words "what a fucking asshole" flash like neon in my head as I flee Jackson's clifftop manor.

I mean *what a fucking prick*.

At the tree line where the path leads down to the dock, I whirl to glance angrily back at the house.

It isn't that Jackson has shut himself away from the world. It's more like fate or karma has imprisoned him here. Because the world does not deserve to have Jackson Havoc let loose upon it, like Satan himself rampaging across the lands.

Fuck you, asshole.

Mercifully, the storm seems to have let up. The sky still looks like the apocalypse. But the rain has stopped, and the winds have died down. I might still have no idea how in the world I'm going to get off this island. But at least I've got that.

I stomp angrily down the stone steps—angry at myself, angry at him. Angry because I let go of my defenses for one second and look where that got me.

Humiliated. Mocked. Scorned.

My lips curl into a sneer as I continue down the steps towards the shore, without a single goddamn idea what I'll do when I get there. Swim maybe? A signal fire? Or maybe I can line the beach with rocks until a low-flying plane picks me up like a shipwreck survivor.

Because I will *not* be the subject of a Netflix true crime special. Certainly not one that shines any fucking light on the king asshole who rules this island. Women already swoon at fictional versions of Jeffrey Dahmer.

Jackson would probably have an armada of boats full of panty-less women surrounding his island if that special ever aired.

I'm trying to mentally calculate exactly how far of a swim it's going to be back to the mainland when I surge out of the woods onto the rocky beach, and my jaw drops.

Because miracle of fucking miracles…

My boat is back.

I don't even know how. I don't care. And I'll thank whatever deity needs thanking later. *After* I get the fuck off this godforsaken island away from the devil himself.

I rush over to where the boat is half beached a little way around the rocky bend of shore, caught on an old log trapped between two boulders. I run my hands over it as if it's some kind of mirage and I need to make sure my mind accepts this is real.

Yep, it's real.

Without a second thought, with another look back, without another single fuck given towards Jackson, I toss my bag in, shove the boat into the surf, and clamber in, splashing water up my jeans all over again.

But fuck it. I can get dry jeans. I'll find them along with my sanity, self-respect, and wits when I land back in the real world again.

I grip the oars tight and put my back into the wind. Then, I'm rowing as fast and as hard and as desperately as I can.

Away from him.

I'M COMPLETELY SOAKED by the time I hit the mainland, because—of course—I made it halfway back before the rain started to pelt down again. That and surprising no one…I'm still a terrible row-boater.

When I do climb out of the boat, my plans instantly change.

Forget jeans. Forget my wits. Forget my self-respect, apparently, as well. Because the first place I land after assuring the guy on the dock that I'm fine after disappearing for almost twenty-four hours, is the only bar in town.

In my head, when I go barging in through the door of the Clam Shack, I'm the outlaw from a western movie slamming through the saloon doors. The fantasy of my soured, mean face sending the locals fleeing for cover makes my lips curl deviously.

But once again, reality is a sad imitation of my imagination.

Instead, the only reaction I get when I stumble dripping wet into the bar is for the grizzled looking bartender with a gray beard to glance up from the sports section of a newspaper.

The bravado, fury, and wind go out of my sails as I clear my throat.

"… Are you open?"

The guy lifts a shoulder, nodding. He turns his gaze back to his sports section, completely ignoring me.

I clear my throat again.

"Uh, great. Thanks."

I swallow, trying to collect my wits as I walk over and find a seat at the bar. Gray Beard looks up, raising an eyebrow instead of actually asking what I want.

"Hi yeah I'll have…I'll have vodka."

The brow stays arched.

"With ice. Thanks."

The bearded bartender keeps eyeing me as a squirming in my seat.

"I… I think I left my ID at…my house?"

I smile at him. Gray Beard just shrugs his shoulder again and turns away, reaching for a glass.

Apparently, legal drinking age matters about as much here as sending a search party for missing young female tourists after they rent boats and disappear for an *entire* day.

Which is to say, it apparently doesn't matter for shit.

Gray Beard slides a glass that looks like it has entirely too much vodka in front of me. But at this point I'm actually thankful for the over-pour. He holds up five fingers without saying a word.

"Do you take cards?"

The thin line of his mouth pretty much answers the question.

"Right, right. Okay. Is there a—"

He nods a chin past me to one of those rip-off ATM machines on the wall that charges you ten bucks to take your own money out.

"Great…thanks," I smile. "Should I pay now, or—"

He just nods.

"Got it."

A minute later, I come back with cash in my hand and take my seat at the bar. Gray Beard makes me change as I sip on the medicinal tasting cocktail in my glass.

What. A. Fucking. Asshole.

Jackson, that is. The devil king of fuck-off island.

I glower. An NDA? He wants to send me an NDA? Fucking *gladly*. I'd rather no one in the entire world knows how I spent the last twenty hours of my life.

Especially the last one of those hours.

Nearly kissing—and doing much more with—Jackson Havoc.

Ugh.

I sip the drink, feeling it soak directly into my bloodstream on my empty stomach. A glance down the bar shows me Gray Beard is back to his sports section. But, whatever.

I clear my throat. He doesn't look up.

"Does Ja.." I frown. "Does Robbie come in here much?"

The man sighs and raises a bored eye to me.

"Johnson. I mean Robbie Johnson."

He shrugs and then shakes his head once before diving back to his newspaper.

I cringe as it suddenly hits me.

Oh my God, I totally misread this. The guy behind the bar isn't being an asshole, he's just *nonverbal*.

I exhale, glad it's not just this guy being a prick, like a town-wide epidemic of assholeness. Jackson being patient zero, of course.

"I'm so sorry!" I say cheerily, dragging his gaze back up. "I've had a weird day," I sigh, shaking my head. "I didn't realize you were…"

He arches a brow, looking amused.

"You know," I smile. "Like Robbie."

"Mute?"

I blink as the word croaks from his lips.

"Excuse me?"

Mother *fuck*. Nope, he does talk. He was just being dick.

Great little town you've got here…

"I said, mute," he rumbles in a scratchy voice. "Like Robbie."

I wince, twisting my face.

"Yeah...I don't think that' a very PC way of saying that?"

"A what?"

"Politically correct? I don't think you're supposed to say that."

"Mute?"

"Yeah."

"Since when?"

"I think a while."

He shrugs. "Okay."

"I think the preferred term is nonverbal."

He smiles thinly. "Well, I'll just have to remember that the next time The Lower East Side decides to come knocking, now, won't I?"

I just smile and look down into my drink.

"And for the record, Ms. PC," he grunts. "Robbie doesn't give a shit if I call him mute. Cause he's *mute*."

Yeah, that's because "Robbie" is a fucking liar and a scumbag.

We sit in silence after that—Gray Beard deep in his sports section, me in my drink and my thoughts. Hoping to God the vodka chases away, well, all of it.

The memory of his lips dragging millimeters from my skin. The lingering heat from his body—so toned and chiseled and...*hard*, against mine.

The filthy, whispered promises growled into my ear.

I shiver, shaking my head before I glance back at the bartender.

"Where's the best place to get a cab around here?"

He glances up in amusement.

"Where you headed?"

As far away from here as possible.

"The airport in Bangor."

He chuckles.

"That's a two-hour drive."

"Okay. So…taxis?"

He chuckles again as his head shakes.

"No taxis in Cape Harbor."

"Does Uber—"

"Nope."

My brow furrows. I mean I took a taxi *here*, when I got off the plane the other day. How the hell do you get the fuck out of this town?

"Matt Michaud could drive you. He brings folks into Bangor from time to time."

My face brightens. "Oh yeah? That'd be great!"

He nods slowly "Ayuh. Probably run you a hundred bucks."

It could cost a million bucks and I'd still be in that car.

"Okay, great, where can I find—"

"He'll be free tomorrow."

My face falls.

"Tomorrow?"

"Yep."

"Is there anyone who'd go to Bangor today?"

Gray Beard just sighs heavily.

"*Right*. Got it."

My brow furrows. Shit, I need a place to stay.

"There's not a hotel or anything in town—"

"There's Laurie's place. The Northeast Motel, two streets north."

I glance outside through the dingy window at the rain pouring down.

"I don't suppose..."

"Taxi situation hasn't changed in the last three minutes."

Fuck this town.

AFTER POUNDING the rest of my drink and then bolting through a deluge of rain, I'm running the corporate card Chuck gave me to use on the trip—the same one that bought my plane ticket and the taxi to Cape Harbor—at the dingy Northeast Motel.

Laurie, the owner, seems to be of about the same pleasant, outgoing disposition as the bartender back at the Calm Shack. But she does take cards, mercifully.

Utterly soaked, my hair clinging to my face, I shuffle into the motel room and slump against the door. I drop my bag and eye the bed, but my nose wrinkles.

It's just one night. One night here and then you can get back home.

I exhale slowly as I shove my hair out of my face.

The phone on the bedside table instantly jangles, making me jolt. I frown as I kick my soaked boots off and shuffle over to answer it.

"Hello?"

"How's my story?"

I blink. It's Chuck.

"Mr. Garver…" I frown, shaking my head. "How did you—"

"I've been trying to call you for the last twenty-four fucking hours, Melody," he grunts.

I glance at my soaked bag, which I haven't even touched since I staggered back to shore.

"When the corporate card just pinged at a motel, I called the front desk and had them direct me to your room."

I exhale.

"Right, and I'm so sorry. I should have checked first about using it for—"

"Forget it. How's my story going?"

I make a face, thinking of my single-minded plan to get the first car out of town tomorrow, and the first plane back to New York.

"It's…"

The dismal trail off has Chuck sighing heavily.

"*Fuck.*"

"I'm sorry, Mr. Garver, it's just proving to be a more…" I frown. "*Difficult* story than I expected."

He grunts.

"Listen, Melody, you seem like a good kid, so I'm gonna level with you. I'm getting the inside scoop on a hot story involving Black Horizons getting back together and recording a new album."

"Oh, *wow*, that's awesome—"

"I'm gonna run it instead of your Havoc piece unless you get me something real, like yesterday."

My mouth twists.

"Oh. Yeah, okay, I—"

"Just so I'm being clear, Melody," he grunts. "Without this piece, you don't work here."

My heart sinks.

"Sorry kid. That's the industry."

I nod glumly.

"So, unless you've got *anything*—"

"I found him," I blurt.

Chuck chokes on something.

"The *fuck* did you say?!"

"I…I found him."

"You *found* Jackson fucking Havoc?!"

My lip catches in my teeth. Why does telling Chuck feel like I'm doing something wrong? Like I'm spilling a secret I'm not supposed to?

"Where?"

"I…" I clear my throat. "I'd rather not say."

I'm not an idiot, and Chuck is an obvious shark. I'm also acutely aware that I haven't actually signed anything about working at Ignition, I just have Chuck's verbal "you're hired".

The second I tell him where I found Jackson, there's nothing to stop him from hanging up and getting someone else up here to finish it off.

He chuckles.

"A bitter, seasoned journalist already. I like it. You got proof?"

"I do, yeah."

"What kind of proof?"

I suck on my teeth before lightening hits me.

"Pictures. A couple of them."

I grab my bag and dump it out across the bed. I deleted the pictures I took from my camera roll, but not from the trash folder.

"*Pictures?* You're fucking shitting me!" Chuck wheezes gleefully. "Of Havoc himself?"

"Of his house. But I can get some of him, too."

My escape plans vanish in the face of actually owning this. Of actually securing this story. Of final seizing something for my own without Judy wrecking it.

"Fucking *outstanding*. You got cell service in…where the fuck are you again?"

"Maine."

"Whatever. Send me what you've got so far."

I grin as I paw through my wet clothes until I snatch up the plastic Ziplock bag…which currently holds my wallet.

And nothing else.

My heart sinks as I start to frantically shove my stuff around the bed, shaking out t-shirts and my spare jeans to see if it the phone is there. I groan to myself as my face falls. Fuck *me*, did I lose it in the boat or something?

"Melody?"

Think. Think. Think…

When it finally clicks, my heart drops into my stomach.

I didn't lose it over the side of the rowboat. Only, diving into the freezing cold North Atlantic might be a preferable place to go back and fetch it than where I just remembered it is.

Jackson's house. I freaking left it at *Jackson's* house, in the kitchen when I took my earbuds out after finishing cleaning.

SHIT.

"I—crap, you know what?" I sigh into the motel room phone. "No service."

Chuck swears. "WiFi? You can email them to my—"

"No WiFi, I'm afraid."

He sighs heavily.

"Christ, kid, where the fuck are you, the arctic circle?"

"I heard there's a cafe with a hotspot that opens tomorrow," I lie, mentally scrambling to come up with a plan to somehow get *back* to King Asshole Island and get my fucking phone back.

He grunts.

"*Fine*. That'll have to work. But while you wait, I want more pics, too. Get me something of the guy himself, Melody."

"You bet, Mr. Garver."

He exhales slowly.

"God *damn*, you really found him?" He chuckles. "This is gonna be fucking huge, kid. HUGE. Get me the rest of this damn story."

"Definitely."

"He knows you're the press?"

I nod. "Yeah, he knows."

"And he's consented to a story?"

I wince.

"Uh…yep," I lie again.

But whatever. Shoot first, figure out how to get Jackson to legally agree to let me write and publish a story about him later.

Chuck snorts.

"Don't bullshit a bullshitter, Melody," he snickers. "If you don't have it yet, just work on it. These star-types…they just need to get leaned on sometimes. They need their fuckin' egos stroked. So…lean on him."

I furrow my brow, not saying anything. Chuck sighs.

"What."

"It just seems…I dunno, Chuck. I mean the story is interesting, or I think it could be. But he ran off from the world for a reason."

"A reason we're going to print and make a cover story about. A reason that you're going to write a great story on, and it's going to define your career."

My lips twist. Even with how much of a prick Jackson is, it just feels…scummy to go into this "leaning" on him to force him into allowing me to do this story.

"Melody," Chuck grunts. "Let me fill you in on a little secret. Guys like Havoc? They can pretend they're running from the fame and the press and whatever they want to bullshit themselves about all they want. But these people…they live for this shit. It's a drug to them. Believe me, he wants this story to break, too."

I nod slowly, my thoughts sliding back to the island.

And him.

And his hands sliding over my body, turning me to fire.

I shiver as my thighs squeeze together.

"If you want everyone to like you, Melody, believe me…journalism is the wrong business for you. If you want that, go be a rock star or some shit. You get me?"

I nod. "I got it, Chuck."

"Good. Now go get me that story, Melody. Yesterday. Get it whatever it takes."

16

JACKSON

I PACE my living room like a caged bear, back-and-forth, my jaw grinding painfully.

What the *fuck* was that.

And what fuck was I thinking? This isn't backstage at Madison Square Garden. This isn't the after party at some fancy hotel. And she's not a fucking groupie bending over begging me to stick it wherever I fucking want.

She's the *press*. And I let her the fuck in here.

A reporter—one who is now on her way off this island ready to tell the world a: where I am. And b: probably that I'm some lecherous tit-grabbing monster.

Fuck.

I storm out the front door and bolt down the path towards the shore. But when I get there, half expecting to see Melody trying to use a rock to bash her the lock off my boat or trying to build a fucking raft out of God knows what, that's not what I see at all.

I see *nothing* on the rocky beach when I get there. No Melody. No sign of her trying to break the lock chaining my boat to the dock. I frown, but when I look out over the bay, my eyes narrow.

It takes me a half a second, but then I realized the small figure sloppily rowing away across the bay back towards town is *Melody*.

Melody in a boat. Not my boat.

Her boat.

My lips curl as my eyes narrow even thinner.

I think I just got played. That whole story last night about her boat washing away and not being able to get back to shore? Bullshit, apparently. Because there she, is in her boat, on her merry fucking way.

Which means she was only here to be the enemy I've always known she was. She was only here last night to spy on me.

My mind flicks back to the photos I scanned on her phone. Sure, my thoughts linger for a second or ten on the ones of her in a bikini or in that pink lingerie. But then I replay the shots she took of my living room. Of the backyard, and the laundry in the basement.

And those are the pictures I *saw*, before I was distracted by the racy ones.

I grind my teeth furiously as I stab my gaze across the water at the figure rowing away.

Who the fuck knows what else she took pictures of? Who knows what secret app she had recording our conversations, or photographing the rest of my house like a little sneaking spy while I was still asleep this morning?

I've got half a mind to jump in my own boat and roar after her. But the fire fizzles as the hankering need for coffee and substances roars up inside. That, and I look down and realize I'm not even wearing shoes. Or a shirt for that matter.

My eyes raise to the sky, which also looks like it's about to drop a monsoon down again across the water.

I grunt.

Yeah, fuck this.

I stomp back up the stone steps back to my house. Inside, I slam around in the kitchen, angrily grabbing a mug from the shelf of now-clean ones and pouring myself some coffee. I glower, sinking back against the counter in my thoughts.

And those thoughts are squarely on one thing.

Melody.

But the anger from before is…well, not *gone*. But, clouded. It's…diluted, by *other* thoughts surrounding Melody.

Specifically, the feel of her skin beneath my fingertips. The way her nipple hardened so eagerly against my hand. The sound of her breath catching and her moan whimpering through her lips. The way her hips pushed against me.

The way I wanted her. The way I still want her, truth be told.

But fuck that. She's the fucking enemy. She's the spy that slips over the trench wall at night to cause untold chaos and mayhem while everyone sleeps. Like me.

Another thought hits me, and I scowl as I stomp back into my living room. I storm over to the stack of papers she's shuffled together into a stack on the coffee table and grab them up in a fist.

I shuffle through them angrily. My thin gaze slides over lines and lyrics I've scrawled and then cast away over the last few months. I paw through them for another minute before I stop, frowning at myself.

What, like I'm gonna fucking *know* if she took something?

Before hurricane Melody swept through here, there was probably three-hundred pieces of paper ripped and balled up, strewn across this room alone. And most of that shit I came up with so deep into a bottle, I have no memory what the fuck I even wrote down anyway.

Do I seriously think I'm gonna notice something missing?

I sigh heavily. Fuck it. If something shows up on eBay, I'll have Cliff rip her a new asshole. And if she just took it to brag to her friends or to tape up in her bedroom or on her bathroom mirror like some sort of weird memento from our meet?

Screw it. Let her have it. Fuck if I care.

I glower as my thoughts melt from black to red with lust.

There's a...*different* sort of memento I would've rather she take with her. One more in the vein of marks across her skin. One more in the vein of my cum dripping out of pussy into her panties the whole boat ride back to town.

I shake my head, brow furrowing.

I trudge back into the kitchen and snatch up the mug of coffee again, grunting as the hot liquid rolls over my tongue. I lean against the counter, when suddenly something catches my eye to the side. I glance over, and my lips curl.

She might be a shitty sailor. But it would seem Melody is it even fucking worse spy. Because right here, still laying on the kitchen counter, is her phone.

Instantly, flashes of those bikini pictures flood my mind. My jaw clenches and my pulse throbs heavily. And yes, my dick thickens eagerly against my sweats I reach for the phone.

I stop and roll my eyes.

You thirsty motherfucker.

What am I, twelve? I glare at the phone. The fucking thing is locked anyway, and it's not like I have any idea with the passcode is.

I sigh and drop it back on the counter. Problem solved in any case. If she *did* spy, and prowl through my house sneaking pictures and information while I slept? It's all still here.

Mission failed, you little spy.

But, while the phone may be locked, I can still see her music app open on the lock screen. I smile curiously.

She was listening to Warren Zevon. Just like she was *playing* him when I surprised her in the recording studio.

I frown. But, again, who the fuck listens to Warren Zevon aside from guys my age, or guys way older than me, for that matter?

Pixie-pink, sassy little New York City hipsters do *not* listen to Warren fucking Zevon. Except for Melody, apparently.

My thoughts simmer, until one from yesterday bubbles back to the surface. Why the fuck is it about her that seems…familiar.

It's not *her*, per se. But that name, maybe?

I roll my eyes as I slump onto the couch and slug back some coffee.

It's Melody. Not something insanely exotic. And if it sounds familiar? Well, like I thought to myself before: *every* woman's name rings a little familiar when you've lived my life.

My brow furrows as I glare into the coffee. I'm not proud of my past, and I've never been the sort of deranged drunk frat boy type who brags about his "conquests".

But just the same, my past exists. And I can't change that.

When you're a god amongst mortals—when you walk out on stage and truly feel like a deity come down from the heavens to be worshiped by the masses—you leave your humanity behind. You leave it back there with humility and humbleness.

Because when you're that high, and when you're that much of a god, there's no place for things like humbleness, humility, or humanity.

People think rock stars dive headfirst into excess and hedonism because it's there for the taking. They don't realize that the *reason* that happens is because there's no other place to go after you've breathed air that high up.

You think Mick or Keith, or Lennon or McCartney, at their height, were going to, or *able to* spend their time fucking grocery shopping? Do you think they could go on strolls through the park, or grab a pint at a local pub?

Fuck no.

No, because the life of excess becomes a drug you need to survive. Because the next drug, or the next fuck, or the next illicit thrill becomes everything you think about. It becomes a driving force that compels you and bends you to its will.

I spent more than a decade of my life chasing that high and falling deeper and deeper into that pit before I got out. I didn't *even* get out. I just found a quiet, dark corner of that pit and fucking stayed there so I wouldn't sink any lower.

And I was fine in that hole…up until roughly *yesterday*.

Up until pink temptation crashed into me. And slid under my skin. And destroyed my defenses and my resolve. Until for the first time in ten years, all I wanted to do was bury myself in her in every fucking way possible.

And the longer I sit here growling into my coffee, the more that desire continues to flicker hotly to the surface.

Even if she is a little fucking reporter spy.

My shoulders roll, my fingers gripping the coffee mug tighter.

In any case, judging by the way she lit up out of here without her phone, it would seem this matter is done. What's she going to do, go write a story about me without pictures, notes, proof, or for that matter, my fucking permission? No publication in the world would print that.

She's got nothing except, what, her *claim* that I live here? I've got a town full of people across the bay who've known me for *ten fucking years* as a nonverbal, friendly enough drunk hermit named Robbie.

Good fucking luck with that, Melody.

I drain the last of my coffee as other demons begin to claw their way to the front of my psyche.

I need to meet my guy and re-up my...*prescriptions*, so to speak. And maybe get some groceries and toiletries while I'm over there. But what I definitely need to do is check in with Cliff and have him prepare the nuclear-level NDA that's going to land on Melody's front door.

She doesn't have shit in the way of evidence. But I need to be sure I squash the rumors, too.

THREE VERY WET HOURS LATER, my pockets and a backpack thoroughly stuffed with federally criminalized narcotics, prescription pills, some toiletries, a couple groceries, and more alcohol than a human should possibly consume in a week, I head back to the docks.

It's still raining, but it seems to have momentarily lightened up enough that getting home will just suck instead of being impossible.

Albert, who was missing in action when I first pulled up—probably because it was raining like *hell*—is back at his post, under the overhang outside the door to the dock offices. He looks up and smiles as I walk past, nodding his chin at me. I nod back as I head towards my boat.

"Always nice to have family visiting, isn't it?"

I pause, my brow furrowing as I glanced back at him.

I'm...casually conversational with most people in this town. Of course, "conversational" is a matter of perspective. It's more that they feel comfortable talking to me, and I feel comfortable pretending I can't talk at all.

The long sleeves go a long way with covering the tattoos. The scruffy chin covers the jawline some people might recognize from album covers or billboards. The baseball hats, or the fishing cap, or any number of beanies I wear, coupled frequently with sunglasses, do the rest.

And not talking? That's because, and I don't really give a fuck if this comes off as conceited, but I do have a fairly famous voice.

Like, *very* famous.

And even if the fine people of Cape Harbor aren't big rock 'n' roll fans, I've always gotten the impression that a Liverpool accent—a.k.a. "the Beatles voice"—would stick out like on the coast of Maine like, well, a fucking Beatles voice.

However, at the moment, I sorely wish I wasn't "nonverbal". Because I would love to know what the fuck Albert is really talking about, and I'd love to ask him with more than my eyebrows.

Said eyebrows raise questioningly at him in any case. But Albert just smiles and nods.

"You just missed her. I mean by maybe ten minutes. Damn, Robbie, I didn't realize she was your niece yesterday when she rented the boat!"

What. The. Fuck.

"I'd have driven her over myself if I knew she was coming, buddy," Albert smiles at me. "You know, while she's here, you might want to get her some boating lessons. Seems like she's more of a city type, but if she's going to keep going back-and-forth between town and your place, might be that she needs some lessons." He glances up at the sky. "Especially in this soup. When you head back over, just make sure she knows it might be best to stay put for the rest of the night."

My pulse thuds. My eyes narrow. And I slowly turn to stab my gaze across the water to my island.

"When you head back over just make sure she knows..."

I grind my teeth.

That implies—no, that boldly *states*—that Melody is in fact *back* on my fucking island.

I was ready to let this go with the atomic non-disclosure agreement that was going show up on her doorstep this evening.

But now?

Now, this is fucking war.

17

MELODY

Shit.

It takes me longer—much longer—then it should to find my phone once I'm inside.

Initially, I couldn't believe my luck when I rode up to the shore to see his own boat missing from the dock. And here I was ready to either storm my way in with a rock and demand my property back, or wait until dark and literally break in to steal my phone back.

Except I didn't have to do that, because Jackson was gone.

But the longer I stay in this house, the higher the chances are of him coming back—and of finding me here.

And I'm not sure that's a scenario I want to see play out.

Eventually though, I find the phone. It's still in the kitchen where I was pretty sure it was, but now it's across the counter next to refrigerator instead of where I left it.

My face blooms with heat.

Sneaky fuck probably tried to get back into my pictures to look at those...*embarrassing* ones of me in a fucking changing room trying on bathing suits.

Creep.

Except when I think of Jackson trying to spy on me dressed, or rather, *undressed*, like that, I don't actually get creep vibes. I get...warm.

In places I shouldn't. And it won't stop spreading.

I shiver, trying to shake it off and swallow it down. I snatch up the phone and pocket it before turning to head back through into the living room.

I make a beeline to where I dropped my bag by the front door. Except I'm not even halfway there when said front door slams open.

My heart jumps into my throat, and I skip back a step, gasping as the huge, roughened silhouette of Jackson himself fills the doorway. I suck in a breath, and my eyes bulge as I stumble a step back.

Jackson prowls inside, his eyes leveling on me viciously, lethally, as he steps in and slam the door shut behind him. He leans back against it, one hand coming up to stroke his strong jaw as his eyes turn me to ash.

I swallow, defiantly lifting my chin, refusing to show fear. Which gets increasingly harder as the second tick by, and his dark gaze narrows dangerously.

"Breaking and entering? That, I didn't see coming."

I swallow my trepidation, glaring right back.

"I didn't break shit. The door was unlocked."

I lift the phone from my pocket and wave it in the air.

"And this is my possession."

"On my property."

I roll my eyes.

"What are you going to do next, hit me with 'finders keepers losers weepers'?"

Jackson smirks, his eyes smoldering as he glares at me. I bristle, swallowing as I slide the phone back in my pocket.

"Well, you got what you broke in for. Unless I should check the house for my valuables."

"Says the guy who doesn't even lock his door."

"Because I live on a fucking *island*."

We both flinch at the sound of thunder rumbling outside. My skin prickles as jagged, torn lightening splits across the dark sky through the windows.

It would seem that temporary break in the storm is ending, and fast.

"Well?" I glare at him. "Am I free to go or are you calling the cops?"

I smile sweetly.

"Oh, but that's right, you're not gonna call the cops."

He lifts a brow.

"What precisely makes you think that?"

"The fact that you have cocaine spilling out of your pocket?"

His gaze immediately drops as his hand whips to his side. There's nothing there, of course. I mean, I *did* see a glimpse of Ziplock baggie coming out of the edge of his pocket. The rest I put together.

Apparently, I hit a nerve.

Jackson exhales and raises his eyes back to mine. A look of slight amusement mixed with aggravation and annoyance crosses his face.

"*Clever*," he grunts.

"So, I guess that's a no on calling the cops on me then?"

He sucks on his teeth for a second, crossing his arms over his chest.

"Hmm."

I blink, jolting as he suddenly moves right towards me. I flinch and step back, but he stops right in front of me.

Smiling.

My brow furrows.

"What?"

"I just…" he sighs. "I was a dick, before."

My brain glitches as it tries to process what he just said.

Wait, what?

"Uh…okay?"

He shrugs. "Look, I don't talk to people much, and…I don't know. Maybe I'm a little lonely out here. My manners have gone a little unused in the last ten years, and it wasn't cool to accuse you of being a spy or whatever."

I stare at him, blinking in disbelief.

"You're…you're serious."

He nods slowly, a warm, kind smile spreading over his lips.

"I am. And honestly, I'm humbled that you liked the house so much that you wanted to take pictures of it. I mean it's a beautiful home, and I have to say, it feels good to see someone else appreciating it."

My brows arch. I'm looking, and I'm looking *hard* for the hidden knife here. For the hint of malice behind his eyes, or the forked tongue hidden behind his teeth.

But there's nothing there. And suddenly, I realize I might just be the first person in a decade, if not ever, to get the real, honest version of Jackson.

A smiles spreads across my face.

"I mean, it's a gorgeous home."

He grins. "Thanks. I know the view is a little darker outside now, but feel free to take as many pictures as you want."

"You're sure?"

"Completely."

I grin. "Okay, if you're sure."

I slowly pull my phone out, waiting for him to try and snatch it or something. But he just casually looks away towards the windows.

"It's stunning when the storms roll in from the ocean like this. I should really get a good camera or something out here."

I unlock my phone with a few taps and bring it up to start capturing the swirling black clouds outside.

And then he's on me in a second.

I gasp as his hand shoots out faster than I'd ever imagine, grabbing my wrist tight. And before I can even process what he's doing, his other hand yanks my phone—my *unlocked* phone—out of my hand.

"You fucking *asshole*!"

Jackson glares at me with a sneer, that charming little—well, *act*, I guess it was—dropping like rock from his face. His lips curl as his eyes flicker with steely blue fire.

The devil reveals himself, after all.

His gaze swivels to my phone in his hand. I lunge for him, but he easily keeps me at bay with one arm as he breezily scrolls through my fucking phone.

"You can't do that!"

"I'm literally doing it right now."

"Fuck you! That's my personal property, and my personal information on—"

"And if it turns out it *is* just *your* personal information, then we're fine," he smiles thinly. "But if there's more pictures or anything else pertaining to me or my house on this, I'm keeping it, and you're fending for yourself outside."

I hiss at him, lurching for the phone again. But he's...big. And even if he's more lean-muscled than some kind of gym-addicted muscle man, he's still strong as hell.

My teeth grind as I watch, helplessly trying to squirm past his arm against me as he casually pokes around my phone. I mean it's not like I have anything horribly scandalous on there.

I tense, brow furrowing.

I mean I don't *think* I do. Aside from those stupid changing room pictures—

"Innocent schoolgirl gets seduced and dominated by rough hung professor."

My fucking *soul* shudders in horror. My entire being shrivels, turning to ice before shattering into pieces on the floor at my feet as Jackson speaks the words.

"Oh, *please*," he chuckles darkly as I go still against his arm, my face white.

"Please, tell me you have *no idea* how this website *possibly* got opened in your incognito mode browser tabs."

I try and swallow, but I can't. Instead, I wish for an asteroid to come crashing through the ceiling and end my torment and suffering. But no luck.

Yes, I know damn well what the video is. I mean, I don't let men touch me, but…I'm only fucking human, and I have needs and urges.

It's just that, ideally, those needs and urges stay *completely fucking hidden away*, never to be flayed open in front of me.

And certainly not by *this man*.

I finally manage to swallow the lump in my throat. I still can't actually look him in the eye, but I at least raise my gaze to his mid-chest.

"Give me. My phone."

He chuckles.

"Didn't even fight it. Respect. But hey, pro tip? You're supposed to *close* your incognito tabs once you're done flicking the bean."

I cringe, hollowing in on myself as my gaze drops back to the floor.

Jackson sighs.

"Alright, I think we're done here. You can have your spank material back."

"Fuck you."

"Yeah? Even if I'm not your professor?"

He snickers as he lowers the phone into my vision, now mercifully back to lock screen. I snatch it hastily and shove it into my pocket before I yank my arm away from his grip.

Whirling, I numbly grab my bag up and march for the door.

"Well, *bye*."

"Have a nice life," he mutters at my back.

I yank the door open. But when the thunder cracks like a bomb, I half scream, half fall, half scrabble back into the house at the sheer violence that illuminates the sky.

My face pales as I creep back to the door, staring up at the Mordor-looking darkness now swirling in the sky and turning the entire world black.

Shit.

I stand there frozen the doorway, watching as the rain begins to pelt down hard outside. My stomach and my heart and drop at the prospect of of even making it down the stone steps to the shore, much less much less boating all the way back across the bay to the mainland.

Behind me, I hear a low rumbling chuckle. I scowl darkly as I whirl to glare at him.

"I'm sorry, what exactly is so funny?"

"The fact that given a perfectly sunny day in a goddamn inner tube, you're a shit sailor."

He smiles thinly.

"And today? Well, today is *not* a perfect day."

I turned back to the blackness outside which is now pelting rain down so hard it's thundering off the roof. I swallow, chewing on my lip as I try to imagine how the fuck I'm exactly going to get back to safety.

"I suppose…"

Jackson drawls behind me, making me tense at the velvety tone of his voice.

"That despite your trespassing, and breaking and entering, and generally fucking up my shit…not to mention your filthy pornography addiction…"

My lips purse in embarrassment and fury as I glare daggers at him.

"I suppose I could overlook all of that and open my home with generous arms to the bedraggled masses."

He grins smugly at me, but his eyes still have that dangerous, lethal edge to them.

"I am not *bedraggled*, thank you very much."

"No? Give it about one second outside, and I guarantee you're gonna look bedraggled as fuck."

He settles onto the couch, lacing his hands behind his head and kicking his feet up onto the coffee table.

"You lose that leather jacket and head out there in just that white shirt, and I might just open a beer and watch this bedragglemeant."

"*Pig*," I hiss.

"Prude."

We eye each other the room, the tension crackling as much as the storm outside.

"Well?" he growls, still smirking at me. "Are you staying or are you going. Either way, shut the door after you make up your mind."

I glare at him before turning once more to look out at the black carnage outside. I swallow, torn between the maelstrom outside and the devil sitting on the couch behind me.

And then suddenly, as if it was even remotely possible, the entire situation manages to get worse. Because outside, the rain begins to turn into *snow*.

Heavily.

There's no way in hell I'd live trying to boat in this. There just isn't. Slowly, I turn back to him and take a deep breath.

"Staying," I said quietly, wondering what the fuck I've just signed myself up for.

"I'm staying."

18

MELODY

The lights flicker as the storm outside howls against the house. I sit awkwardly in one of the chairs across from the sofa, feeling very "in the way" as Jackson hauls piles of chopped firewood in from somewhere outside and dumps them by the fireplace.

He shakes the snow and sleet off of his hoodie and then pulls it off. My eyes, traitors that they are, immediately lock onto the grooved abs and v-cuts of his hips as the hoodie pulls his t-shirt up, like horny teenagers.

"The lodging is free. The show costs extra."

My face heats as I whip my gaze up to see Jackson smirking at me.

"Fuck you, I wasn't looking at you."

"Uh-huh."

He turns, squatting down as he starts to stack old newspapers, little twigs, and then logs in the massive stone fireplace set into the wall. The lights flicker again, and I gasp audibly.

"Power come from cables that come over across the bay on the sea floor," he grunts, answering my unsaid question without turning as he brings a lighter to the newspaper.

The fire catches, and I watch him with probably way too much interest as he leans in close to blow on the flames. When they catch the twigs, and the fire crackles bigger, he sits back.

Thunder booms outside, and I flinch, gasping again as the lights flick on and off.

"There's also a generator if—" he sighs, turning to raise a brow at me. "You know what? Maybe stop worrying about it. But you know how you *could* be useful?"

My lips purse, trying to hide the flush on my face as I glare at him.

"If this involves taking my clothes off or *blowing you*, I'd be prepared for teeth if I were you."

Jackson snorts, rolling his eyes.

"You've got a *very* high opinion of yourself."

"No, but I've got twenty years of highly detailed, published opinion on *you* for reference. Which I don't think I even need with the way you've behaved for the all of one day I've known you personally."

"That's adorable."

"*What.*"

Jackson turns to toss another log on the fire.

"That you think you in any way shape or form *know* me."

I bark a laugh.

"Let's see if I have this in line. You're a narcissistic prick and an egotistical maniac with a massive substance abuse problem. You see yourself as 'above' the 'normal' people of the world, and your poor ego actually gets bruised when the people around you don't fall to their knees in worship. How am I doing so far?"

He rolls his eyes, sitting on the floor and leaning back against the side of the fireplace.

"Like you've read way too many puff pieces about me in shitty music magazines like Ignition."

"And yet, the prophecy comes true the second I step through your front door."

He sighs. "Well, were you done with your professional analysis of me?"

"Not even close."

"My my, then. Let's have it."

"You're a pig and probably a sex addict."

"Says the porn-watching prude."

"That doesn't even make sense."

"It's called juxtaposition."

"No, it's called *reaching*, because I'm hitting more truth than you want."

His mouth thins.

"Let's see," I go on. "You think you're God's gift to women and have this absurd and toxic mindset that just because you're famous and you have a dick, the entire female population of the world owes you pleasure. Which is why you think it's okay to corner young women in your house and *grope* them—"

"Does groping usually come with a side of desperate moans, whimpers, and greedy hips pushing a *very* warm pussy against my thigh?"

My jaw *drops*, my face heating to roughly the temperature of the sun as I stare at him.

"That…! That is *not* fucking—"

"It's definitely true. I was there, remember?"

"You know what?" I snap.

"Please, don't keep me hanging."

I sneer at him.

"I honestly can't wait to go home and write the truth about you, so that everyone knows what a douchebag you actually are."

"Hmm, yeah," he rubs his chin. "Sounds like quite the revenge-fetish fantasy. Just one teeny problem, sweetheart."

He grins.

"You can write your little fan fiction with as much angst and vitriol as you want. You can even leave out the part where you were ten seconds away from *begging* me to relive that heat between your thighs."

"You motherfu—"

"*But*" he growls. "No publication on earth, even shitty, desperate ones like Ignition, would print your little story without proof," he starts ticking his fingers. "My express permission, or at the very least, a verifiable admission from me. Without any of those, though, all you've got is one very strange erotic fan fiction involving yours truly."

I glare at him, simmering in the chair.

"Now, as I was saying, why don't you make yourself useful and go grab us a drink from the kitchen?"

"I'd rather—"

"Yeah, I'm sure that list is vast and *very* angsty and interesting. But save it for the fan fiction, sweetheart."

He stands, ignoring my lethal glare as he moves past me, to the kitchen where he dropped his backpack—presumably full of drugs and alcohol—earlier. I hear him moving around, and the sound of a bottle being cracked open.

And then, as sudden as the lightning still flashing outside and making the lights flicker in here, it hits me.

Without proof, my express permission, or at the very least, a verifiable admission.

It's that last part that clicks with me, the part about "verifiable admission."

Say a famous person is giving an impromptu press conference, like on the steps outside a courthouse or something. They're not handing out signed consents for every reporter there. They're giving *implied* consent to print their words, so long as it's verifiable that the video, or voice recording, or the notes, are of *them*.

I happen to be holding a recording device—my phone—in my hands. And both Maine, where we are, and New York, where Ignition is, are single party consent states when it comes to being recorded.

My eyes gleam.

Yeah, maybe this is pretty low. It's definitely morally gray, at best, to do what I'm about to do. But…I make peace with that, being that Jackson is, well, *Jackson*.

Quickly, I open my phone and navigate to the voice recording app. It doesn't matter that there's no internet out here. It'll record and save it locally on my phone, and I can email it to my work laptop later when I get back to New York.

Genius.

I tap the record button and quickly put the phone face-down on the armrest, just as I hear footsteps coming back from the kitchen.

"Cheers."

I blink in surprise when a glass—a *large* glass—of whiskey is thrust into my face. My eyes drag up to see Jackson standing over me, sipping his own drink as he eyes me.

"Oh, I…"

He sighs. "Please tell me you're not sober, or don't drink or something. You're approaching a superhuman level of being a square prude."

I smile thinly as I snatch the glass from his hand.

"I *drink*, thank you very much. Just not as much as you, jerk."

"Let's hope not."

He taps his glass to mine before going back to the sofa, where he lies back and kicks his feet up again.

I swallow.

"So, why did you come out here?"

He levels a withering, cold glare at me, and I roll my eyes.

"What, I can't be curious? Do you have any idea how many people out there are asking themselves this exact question? Jackson, I'm just curious."

"As a fan," he says dryly.

"Yes, as a fan."

"Who works for a music publication as a reporter."

"I'm just asking as a fan."

A fan who happens to be secretly recording your answer...

Jackson looks away, taking a slow sip of his drink.

"Fame is fucking boring."

I nod, eyes locked on him, waiting for more. But, as the seconds tick by, my brow furrows.

"And?"

"There's no and. That's just it. Fame is boring. I got bored, so I left."

"Yeah but—"

"Oh my *God* are you a pain in the ass," he grunts, sighing heavily.

I let it sit a minute before I open my mouth again.

"Why here? I mean why does a rich rock icon who's already got the Beverly Hills mansion, the loft in New York, the townhouse in London, and all of that, buy an old mansion on an island off the coast of Maine?"

Jackson's gaze flicks to mine.

"I like islands. It's the Brit in me."

I smirk. He grins, draining his drink before standing and walking past me again towards the kitchen. When he returns, he's got the whole bottle, along with a fresh pour in his glass.

"Top you up?"

I glance at my own glass, which I've barely put a dent into.

"I…think I'm good."

"Catch up, enemy."

I frown. "Excuse me?"

"The enemy. The press. Tell me you've seen *Almost Famous*."

I grin as I get what he's saying. "Right, the enemy. That's me."

He makes a "drink-drink" motion with his hand. I flush as I bring the glass to my lips and take another sip.

"Ever heard of the Big Pink?"

"*What?*"

"The Big Pink. You asked why this place."

My brow furrows.

"Is this a crude joke?"

He smiles darkly.

"*Dirty girl.*"

I hate…*hate* how much my body responds to him uttering those two words. I hate that my core clenches. That my thighs squeeze together. That my pulse jumps with lust.

I quickly shake that crap away.

"While I do appreciate how your mind went there," Jackson adds, "It's not a pussy reference. It's an album from The Band."

I know this music trivia about "The Band" who were once Bob Dylan's backing band. Of course, I do. But from him? *Yeah*, my mind went somewhere…filthier when he said, "big pink".

"They—"

"They bought a big pink house in Woodstock, New York, to record an album," I interrupt. "I'm familiar with it."

"So, you thinking about pussy was just a distraction?"

I flush.

"I was *not* thinking about pussy."

"You should try it sometime."

My face burns.

"Sorry to ruin your male fantasy, but I'm comfortably straight."

He grins.

"I meant that you should *think* about pussy—such as your own—more often."

I simmer as I look away, sipping my whiskey.

"You know what? This *is* fun," Jackson grunts. "My turn."

"Oh, I don't think—"

"Why, because you're the one conducting this interview on me?"

He smiles at me thinly, his eyes narrowing.

"But you're just casually asking questions, right? As a *fan*, right?"

I swallow.

"You're right, this isn't an interview."

"So, we're just two people having drinks together then, it would seem."

I shrug. "Sure."

"Then it would seem that's it's fairly my turn to pry into *your* personal life."

He sits back, sipping slowly.

"Tell me, Melody…would you say being a pain in the ass and your generally prickly personality is your own little perpetual fuck-you to your father for abandoning you?"

My eyes narrow coldly as my lips thin. Jackson smiles.

"Now, was that prying?"

"*Yes*."

"Good. Well?"

I glare at him. "You don't want to go there with me."

He laughs coldly.

"Sweetheart, I have a doctorate in shitty parents. And if you're expecting me to answer anything else, you're going to need to pony up first. Question for question. That's how this'll work."

Bastard.

But I shrug as I smile casually. "Fine, whatever. What's your question?"

"How old were you when your old man dipped out."

"Zero. I wasn't born yet. He and my mom…" I clear my throat. "I don't think they exactly knew each other well."

"What do you wager, bar bathroom? Back seat of a Nissan?"

"Gross?"

"Everyone's thought about it."

"I cannot begin to tell you how wrong you are."

He shrugs, knocking back more of his whiskey.

"Did you ever meet him later? I mean when you were older."

"I thought this was question for question?"

"You *really* like rules, don't you?"

I roll my eyes at his smug grin.

"Well?"

"No; never."

I sigh as I look away, shaking my head.

"I mean he wrote me these letters for a while, where he'd call me Prudence—"

My mouth slams shut as my body jolts in horror. Why the *fuck* did I just willingly volunteer any of that information to Jackson? I mean here we are playing verbal chess, and I'm giving him moves.

"Like *Dear Prudence*?"

"Forget it."

"You're the one that brought it—"

"Well let's pretend I didn't," I snap. "My turn?"

He shrugs. "Have at it."

"Do you think you have a problem?"

His brows lift.

"I do. But it seemed cruel to leave her outside during all of this weather."

"Har-har-har," I mutter dryly. "You know what I meant. Do you think you have a drinking problem?"

"Do *you* think I have a drinking problem?"

"Honestly?"

"As if you'd waste an opportunity to be as brutal with me as possible?"

I bite back a grin.

"I think yes, you do have a problem. Definitely with alcohol. Probably with other things too."

He whistles quietly as he starts to *very* slowly clap his hands.

"My, my, Melody. I can't believe you cracked this cold case wide open. You know, you might actually be the very first person on earth who's come to that conclusion."

I glare at him.

"You don't have to hide behind sarcasm."

"Yes, but it's so much damn fun."

"As fun as avoiding the real question I'm trying to ask?"

"As a fan?" He mutters.

"Yeah, as a fan. But you're still working your ass off to dance as far away from my first question. I mean if you don't want to talk about it, just say so. But don't give me that 'fame is boring' bullshit. You were *beyond* famous for like ten years before you disappeared. You could have dipped out at any time with more money and fame than you knew what to do—"

"*Fine.*"

His gaze whips to stab into mine, narrowing coldly in a way that rips a shiver down my spine.

"You want me to stop *dancing* around one of the most brutal, dark periods of my entire life, Melody?" He snaps.

My face falls.

"Jackson, I—"

"I *left* because my best fucking friend in the world killed himself, and it was such a stupid, worthless fucking waste. I *left*," he snaps, his voice getting darker as the volume rises. "Because instead of leaving me the fuck alone, the entire goddamn world, and mostly parasites like yourself, spent a *year* asking me about it, over and fucking over again. And if I'd stayed around that for another second, I was going to either blow my fucking brains out Cobain style, or…"

His eyes close as his mouth this. I sit there stunned, staring at him with my pulse thudding as he breathes slowly in and out.

"I left because after Iggy died, this shit was *not* fun anymore."

I don't say anything. Because there's nothing *to* say. He sips his drink, I sip mine, and we sit there in the crackling light of the fire as the storm thunders outside.

Eventually, after he's drained another glass or two, he mutters something under his breath and stands.

"Jackson, I'm sorry. I didn't mean—"

"Leave it."

He stalks past me to a far corner of the living room. I half expect to hear the sound of a fresh bottle cracking open.

Instead, I hear…*notes*.

I stiffen, eyes widening as I listen to Jackson walk back over. When he moves past me, my pulse quickens with excitement as my eyes drop to the acoustic guitar in his hands.

Holy shit, he's going to play again.

Maybe it makes me a dork, or a pathetic fangirl. But, whatever. As much of an asshole—albeit a gorgeous asshole—that Jackson is, and as much as we've been warring and nipping at each other's heals like dogs since I arrived…

I really am a *huge* Velvet Guillotine fan. I mean that band, and this man's voice, have been the soundtrack to most of my life. And now, hate him or not, I'm about to watch and listen to the king dickhead himself *play*.

I bite back my own giddy, eager grin as he sits on the couch.

"Do you—"

"Stop talking."

I swallow, nodding as I sit back in the chair, my eyes glued to him in the firelight.

"And try to keep your drool in your mouth."

My brow narrows.

"You *arrogant* fucking—"

But then he cuts me off. Not with words, or a look, or even crude gesture. What shuts me up and leaves me spellbound is that Jackson starts to *play*. And it's...everything.

His eyes close, hunched over the acoustic on the edge of the couch. Firelight and shadows dance over his face, his muscled forearms, and his veined fingers as they slowly dance over the strings.

I'm confused by what I'm hearing for one single second. But then it hits me with a stunned realization that he's playing a slow, stripped, acoustic version of *Wreck Me Gently*, Guillotine's first radio hit.

That original version is loud, and thrashing, and drips pure rock 'n roll excess. But the reason that song became the hit it was, and why the band who played it went on to the stratosphere instead of being catchy one-hit-wonders is because there is *so much* under that gleaming, screaming, rock veneer.

Underneath, the lyrics are *gorgeous*, and haunting, and painfully real. And I've always thought that's what people always really dug into when that song first dropped. It was the words—Jackson's words—about the fear of the chase, and then the even greater fear of what you do once you catch what you've been chasing.

In a weird, eerily prophetic way, that first song set the tone for Velvet Guillotine's entire career arc.

And suddenly, Jackson starts to sing, and the whole world stops moving.

Yeah, ten years away from screaming in arena tours, and ten years of drinking and skulking away have changed his voice.

But fuck me if it isn't *better*. It's literally even *better* than it was before. It's older and roughened. It's even more soaked in honey, smoke, and whiskey. The weary timbre of it sends chills down my spine and—shamefully—brings a heat to every single hidden place in my body.

And then, like they always do, the song ends. His eyes are still closed, the firelight still flickering over him like magic. The last notes of the acoustic hang long and slow in the still air of the room, until they fade too.

It's not until he opens his eyes and turns to me that I realize how very much under a spell I am. How much I'm staring in amazement at him. How my eyes are glassed over, and my mouth is hanging open.

"Watch that drool, sweetheart."

My burns, snapping me out of the reverie. I quickly collect myself, blushing hotly as I take a strong drink from my glass.

"When it crushes down like that…the world, regrets, whatever," he mutters quietly. He shrugs. "That's the only way I can get out from under it."

"That was…" My head shakes. "That was incredible."

He lifts a shoulder, nodding quietly.

"And I know the feeling," I shrug. "I…when I learned to play guitar, it was helpful when I'd get lost in some of the bullshit around my life. My dad leaving, my mom being…" I frown. "Well, my mom in general. All her boyfriends…"

Jackson lifts a brow. And suddenly, he's standing, walking over to me, and holding out the guitar with one hand.

My eyes bulge.

"Uh, what?"

"Play."

Heat flicks like flames up my neck as my brow wrinkles.

"Oh…no. No, I'm fine."

"Let me hear you play."

"No."

Something cold starts to dig it's claws into me. Something monstrous.

Something slipping into my room when I was thirteen, and my mom was out on a bus somewhere.

"Melody—"

"I don't play in front of people."

Something with a sickening chuckle, and evil eyes. Something who told me to "sing pretty for me".

Something that left me broken, empty, and unable to even cry afterwards, with the words "rock 'n roll, baby," snickering on his lips.

"I don't play in front of people either, but I just did."

"Well, good for you," I snap coldly.

He rolls his eyes, pushing the guitar towards me.

"C'mon! Drink some liquid courage and fucking play, you baby."

My jaw tightens. My vision starts to blur and go dark on the edges.

"Jackson—"

"And don't tell me you don't sing, either. I heard what I heard the other day."

"Jackson, please—"

"*Melody*," he sighs, shoving the guitar at me.

"*Please...don't...*"

I jolt as the guitar gets pushed into my lap. My body goes cold, my vision narrowing to pinpricks as my throat starts to close.

"*C'mon*, Melody. Play something."

"I—"

"Sing pretty for me."

My vision goes out. My throat closes completely, and I'm vaguely aware of the glass slipping from my hands to shatter on the floor.

"Melody?"

The room spins, cold claws ripping and tearing at me, dragging me down into the blackness as I lurch forward out of the chair.

"Melody!"

The darkness swallows me whole.

19

MELODY

My breath chokes, gasping as I bolt upright.

"*Easy*, hang on."

Hands touch me and grab me. Hands try to push me back down.

I scream.

"Melody!"

I blink through the panic and the terror, and my vision starts to clear. My eyes blink again, and I realize, and remember, where I am. And when I frown up at the shape hover near me, it materializes into Jackson.

I swallow, feeling my pulse begin to slow. Jackson looks at me with concern, his brow furrowed deeply, his jaw set tight. Behind him, the fireplace crackles, but…I frown as I glance around us.

"Why is it dark?"

And it is. Aside from the fireplace, the house is pitch black. No lights on in the kitchen like they were before. No lights down the hall, as they were before. The only light comes from the flames licking hungrily at the logs in front of me.

"The power went out just as you…"

He frowns, leaning closer to me, his eyes narrowing.

"What was that?"

"Nothing."

I swallow as I sit up again, hugging my knees to my chest. I take a breath, looking away from him as I chew on my lip.

"Melody—"

"It was nothing, okay?"

The marked silence from him has me glance out of the corner of my eye to see him looking at me with cold suspicion.

"Are you epileptic?"

"What? No."

"Diabetic?"

"*No*," I sigh. "No, I just…" I shrug. "I guess I need some food?"

I'm not going there with him. Or anyone. I'm not prying that nailed down, padlocked, cemented door deep in the recesses of my mind open. Not ever.

The therapists I saw years after what happened explained that in some ways, it would be easier to talk about it then, at eighteen, rather than when it initially happened. But in other ways, they said, it was harder.

Trauma calcifies. It heals in unpredictable ways, leaving scar tissue mosaics you might not be able to explain. So, by the time I did open-up to trained professionals, a lot of what had happened was just…locked away already.

Buried. Covered in a mile of mud.

Jackson eyes me.

"So that's a no on playing guitar, then?"

I laugh, loudly. Which is weird because it should make me flinch, or angry, or ball in on myself again. But it's *just* the right level of dark humor given the situation to bring a smile to my face.

"Think I'll pass for now."

"As long as you don't pass *out* on me again."

"I'm guessing it wouldn't be the first time you have passed out girls in your company?"

He frowns.

"You've got a low opinion of me, don't you."

"Sorry. Just a joke."

I swallow, moving as if to stand up.

"Hang on, cowgirl."

Jackson moves to stop me, but I scowl and slap his hand away.

"I'm fine."

I stand, and instantly, my head swims and my legs give out. But instead of falling onto my ass, or my face, I fall forward…

Right into Jackson's arms.

Heat blooms across my skin as my palms go flat to his broad, muscled chest. His big arms wrap around me, his hands at the small and mid of my back as he pulls me against him.

I don't fight it.

I don't go catatonic, or freak out, or turn cold.

Instead, my pulse thunders in my ears. My body shivers a little as electricity tingles across my skin, raising every hair and tuning every nerve. I can feel my face throb with heat as I raise my eyes to his.

Still lethally cool and steely. Still illegally gorgeous. Still alarmingly *un*-alarming to me.

Because he very much should be.

Because every time since what happened to me that a guy has touched me, or been this close to me, I feel fear. Because the idea of standing chest-to-chest, wrapped in the arms of a man with firelight crackling over us has forever been a completely unrealistic fantasy to me.

And I've tried. I've really, really tried. I've gone out with the tamest, most house-cat guys in the world. Guys who were sweet, and completely not pushy, and understanding that my preference was to go slow.

They all blew up anyway.

And now, here I am with the opposite of that. Not in a public park, or a cafe, but in an isolated home, locked in an embrace I'm not entirely sure I *could* break out of if he didn't allow it to happen.

With a man who is the opposite of tame and sweet. A man notorious for getting what he wants from women.

A professional hunter, and he's got me locked in his arms, holding me like I'm already his next meal.

But I'm still not scared. I'm still not freaking out, or losing consciousness, or screaming at him. And the worst, most cringing, most mortifying part of all of this, is that I don't *want* to scream at him or push him away.

I want him closer. I *want* his hands on me, because it's just hit me that for the first time since the night of the monster, another person's touch is making me *calm*, not terrorized.

My face burns hotly.

Actually, the worst, *most* mortifying and horrible part is that he isn't just make me feel calm and safe.

He's making me feel desire. And lust. And a need for more.

Jackson's hands stay firm on my back. They're not wandering, or pushing for something else, or any of that. But it's like the sheer presence of them on me, with my heart thudding against my chest and his, has me sinking into this sinful, heated place.

His touch has me pulsing and burning with fire, and power, and agency.

And I don't want that feeling to go away.

"C'mon," he growls as he starts to pull back. "Let's at least get you sitting—"

"*Wait.*"

I close my eyes as my hands tighten to fists in his shirt, stopping him. I breathe in and out, my pulse fluttering and my head swimming as my teeth rake over my bottom lip. And I'm positive I'm about to make a complete fool of myself. But those hands on me feel too good. His presence is too disarming, and calming, and empowering all at the same time.

And besides, pretty soon, this storm will pass. I'll go back home, and that'll be it.

When the hell else will I have a chance for my first kiss, at twenty years old, to be with the hottest, most infamous rock star on the planet?

I take one more deep breath, clinging to his shirt. Before slowly, I raise my head and halfway open my eyes.

"Jackson—"

His mouth slams to mine. His lips crush against me in a thunderous, explosive rush, nearly bringing me to my knees. Which might actually happen if it wasn't for his arms holding me against him.

The crash stuns me. It makes sparks and alarm sounds explode in my head. But he doesn't let up. He doesn't pull away or ask me if this is okay.

And maybe it isn't.

But right now, locked in his embrace, and lost in his ferocious kiss, frankly, I don't give a fuck.

20

JACKSON

For ten years, I lived a life of excess. I was reckless, and selfish, and I left a trail of carnage and destruction in my wake. I lost friends, hurt people, torched bridges, and generally went through my day-to-day existence like an uncaring, unfeeling agent of chaos.

I was an asshole, is what I was.

But I was blinded by the fame, and the money, and the women, yes. I was addicted to the way the whole world fawned over me, falling over themselves to make sure I felt like a god.

We were all like that—Iggy, Will, Asher. Just four star-blinded, greedy little assholes, crashing through the world like a gold-plated, diamond studded, whiskey-soaked, cocaine-fueled wrecking ball.

No regrets. No attachments. Trust no one except each other. Maybe all that was toxic as fuck, but it brought us to the top of the world. It turned us to *gods*, and we had a hell of a ride doing it.

That is, until the bottom dropped out.

Until one of the four legs broke. And after that, the whole fucking stage fell down. When Iggy went, that was the end.

And so, I faded away. I walked away from all of it that night when I was supposed to walk out on a stage for the bazillion fucking voyeuristic strangers drooling over the prospect of watching me bleed emotion. The night I was supposed to pretend *any* of them knew Iggy at all, or knew me, or my pain, for that matter.

That was it. That was lights out.

But I countered my life of excess and spotlight too hard. I didn't course-correct, I veered off the fucking map into no-man's land. And instead of fixing myself, or seeking forgiveness, or understanding, or fucking nirvana, or whatever, I've spent the last ten years sulking, ticking the days off, and drinking myself into a black hole.

Until this very. Fucking. Moment. Until the very second my lips crush to hers. And suddenly?

Suddenly, I'm seeing in motherfucking *color* again.

I groan as I sear my mouth to hers, hungrily sucking her bottom lip into my mouth. She whimpers, clinging to me even harder than she was a second ago, which was what shattered the last of my resolve.

"*Jackson*," she moans breathlessly into my lips as she presses herself into me, grinding her body against mine.

The fire in me roars, my hand at the small of her back yanking her tight as my other one slips up to grab her jaw possessively. She whimpers as I hold her firmly, not even giving her the option to back away from me or to break this kiss.

Because one kiss, and she's fucking *mine*.

Melody shudders when my tongue teases her lips, demanding entrance. She gives it, shivering and holding me tighter as she tastes my tongue—exploring it as I explore her mouth. Her body trembles, like this is all new to her.

Fuck.

I tense, and for a moment, I almost drop this entirely and back the hell away.

It was always my one rule: no virgins. No girls with fantasies of their first time being with "legendary rock 'n roll sex god Jackson Havoc." Who the fuck knows why, but for some reason, that was always like my one tether back to reality from the tinsel bullshit world of no regrets or consequences.

I wasn't going to ever be anyone's first. Not because some ridiculous Disneyworld idea of a first time "being special" or any nonsense like that. But because to me, fucking or being fucked for the first time is pretty much forever linked with misery. With shame.

With a darkness that's stayed with me ever since.

That and girls who actively *want* to lose their virginity to a sweaty, shirtless motherfucker drunk out of his mind and high off his ass in the back of tour bus are fucking psychotic. Or, confused.

Either one is a recipe for disaster in that world.

I pause, and I swear to Christ I'm about to pull back and skip this whole thing. That is…

Until Melody's tongue delves into my mouth. Boldly. Teasingly. Igniting me and crumbling whatever plastic hazard signs I was about to put up.

She kisses me back, and the brakes go out.

My hand tightens on her jaw, eliciting a moan deep in her chest as she kisses me harder. The hand at the small of her back slips under her shirt, and she shivers as her fingers tighten against my chest. I grip the hem of her shirt, lifting as my other hand drops to help.

And she goes right for mine. She grabs the hem of my shirt, feverishly shoving it up my abs and my chest as she kisses me with a fucking vengeance that sets me on *fire*.

Holy shit. The timid little prude mask just fell off. And I fuckin' like it.

We pull away from devouring each other's mouths just long enough for me yank my shirt off, and then rip hers the rest of the way too. My eyes drop to her tits, spilling out of her lacy bra, and I growl. I mean I literally *growl*, like a starved beast.

Which, after ten years here, might be exactly what I am.

But it's not just thirst. It's not that I'm jacked up and rearing to go. It's *her*.

I've had…offers, in the years I've been away. I mean, not offers like I got as *me*. But "Robbie", while not an internationally recognized sex symbol, and, you know, *nonverbal*, has caught the eye of a woman or three in and around Cape Harbor.

Robbie wanted none of that. Because that hunger for flesh in me died the day I walked away.

So, when I look at Melody, and all I want is to tear her fucking clothes the rest of the way off and devour her fucking whole, it's not because I've been without.

It's because I want *her*.

Her bra falls away as my mouth crushes back to her. I groan, relishing the way her hard puckered nipples dig into my chest, and the way her skin feels so fucking soft against mine. At the way she clings to me so eagerly, like she wants this as much as I do.

Kinky is sexy.

Consent is sexy.

But feverish, wanton, uncontrollable lust? Now that's the ultimate aphrodisiac. And when I feel that emanating off of her very skin when she slams her mouth to mine and claws at my back, I get rock fucking hard.

Melody whimpers when my hands drop to that tight ass and yank her up into me. She gasps, her legs wrapping around my waist as I turn and move to the couch. I drop us both down into it, one hand still grabbing her ass, the other tangling in her pink hair.

My mouth devours her lips and her tongue. Her moans. Her eagerness. She arches her back, moaning my name over and over as my lips slip to her jaw and then the soft skin of her neck. I dive further down, leaving hickeys down the curve of her tits before I wrap my mouth around a hard, light pink nipple, and suck.

"Oh *fuck*…" She chokes, jolting from the couch and gasping as her fingers shove into my hair.

I smirk to myself. This is me at like five miles per hour, and she's about to come in her panties for me. But I'm not taking this to top speed just yet.

Top speed with me is...*hard*. And rough. And...intense. And while so much of me wants to drag us both down into that hedonistic depravity, I also don't want to freak her the fuck out.

Not yet, at least.

Instead, my mouth savors one nipple and then the other, nipping them with my teeth and sucking hard to soothe the ache. Melody writhes and squirms for me like she's in heat, and all it does is make me want to rip those jeans off and bury my cock balls deep in her right this second.

But I'm not with my appetizers yet.

She shudders, her stomach caving under my lips as my mouth sucks and licks down to her navel. I move lower, making her whimper as my fingers pop the button of her jeans. I unzip them, slide my fingers into the sides, and hook them *and* her panties in my fingertips.

I look up at her through the valley of her tits, our eyes locked as I slowly drag her pants off of her. More and more of the creases of her hips tease into view. More skin. More moans. A little scar on her upper thigh.

Her eyes go wide as I slide to the floor, dragging her jeans and panties with me before flinging them away. I move up, my hands skimming her thighs and pushing them wide apart as her face goes crimson and her eyes bulge.

"*Jackson...*"

My eyes drop to her pussy, drinking her full nakedness in for the very first time.

And fuck. Me. Sideways.

She's perfect. She's sexy as *fuck*, with those light pink nipples, the caving stomach, the curved hips and the swollen, pink, *dripping fucking wet* little pussy barely a foot away from my mouth.

I've told myself I need to restrain myself. I've told myself to keep it vanilla, since I don't know her, and this isn't a cocaine-fueled afterparty at the W Hotel. But the second I lay eyes on *all* of her, in all her stunning, sexy, dick-swelling temptation?

Yeah, fuck that.

She gasps as I move up over her, pinning her to the couch as my lips brush her earlobe.

"*I want,*" I rasp against her neck, making her shiver. "You to grab your legs behind your knees and pull them back."

My teeth nip at her earlobe, making her choke on a whimper.

"And I want you to be good girl for me and spread those pretty holes of yours as wide as you can, so I can fucking *devour you.*"

I don't wait for an answer. I just crush my lips to hers, kissing her punishingly before slipping down to the floor again. I look up at her with dark lust on my face. But she holds that look, biting her lip, her face throbbing with need as she nods. Her hands slide under the backs of her knees, and I groan as she does *exactly* as I asked.

Good girl.

My hands skim up her thighs as I lean close. But whatever grandiose plans I had of teasing her and drawing out the pleasure until she was begging me for my tongue shatters.

Let's be real: I've been away from women for *ten fucking years*. And I now have—bar none—the prettiest, sweetest little pussy I've ever laid eyes on four inches in front of my mouth.

Yeah, sure, "drag it out."

Lies.

My tongue plunges into her, and I'm in *heaven*. So is Melody, judging from the way she throws her head back and moans like she's literally already orgasming.

Her legs quiver as I drag my tongue up her silky, honeyed lips until it swirls over her clit. She bucks, gasping wildly as her body shakes and squirms under my mouth. I slide my tongue back down, pushing into her like I'm fucking her with it, before I move back to her clit.

My lips hover over the little bud, sucking as my tongue takes that clit over its lap to spank the fuck out of it. I'm relentless, tonguing and sucking and swirling around her clit until she's thrashing on the couch. Her hands drop, her legs falling over my shoulders.

I rectify that with light slap on her ass, making her yelp and then moan.

"*Uh-uh*, sweetheart," I rasp into her inner thigh. "Be a good girl and keep those legs up for me."

Her eyes explode with lust, and she nods eagerly as she grabs her legs back up. I double down, humming into her clit as I push two fingers into her greedy pussy. *Christ* is she tight—

so fucking tight it's like she's trying to crush my fingers with her cunt. But I slide them deeper, curling them up against her g-spot as my tongue swirls over her clit.

Her whole. Fucking. Body leaves the couch. I mean the girl literally levitates, screaming "Jackson!" as her orgasm detonates like a goddamn bomb. But I don't let up. I keep her buzzing right there in the stratosphere with my tongue and my fingers, just drowning myself in her sweet pussy as she comes over and over for me.

But I want more. I want *everything* with this girl.

She's still shaking and shuddering when I slide my tongue back down her slit, tonguing at where my fingers are still fucking her.

And then I go lower.

I *did* tell her to spread both of her pretty holes for me.

"*Jackson…*" her voice shakes a little, going up a half octave as my tongue dances low. "What…*oh fuuuuuck…*"

My tongue slides over her ass, swirling over the little ring as her eyes roll back.

"*Holy fucking SHIT…*"

I groan into her, tonguing her ass in slow circles as my fingers stroke in and out of her pussy and my thumb rubs her clit. Her thighs quiver and clench. Her stomach tightens, and I watch her mouth fall open in a silent scream as her eyes bulge from her face.

"*J-J-Jackson—!*"

"I want you to come like a *dirty* little slut for me," I rasp against her. "Fucking come for me, Melody. Come like a good girl with my tongue in your ass and my fingers making that pussy drip all over the place. Come, baby. Fucking *come* for me, right the fuck now."

My tongue stabs into her, my thumb rolls over her clit, and my fingers curl right against her g-spot.

She never stood a chance.

With a honeyed, erotic, broken scream that shakes the fucking house and turns my cock to *steel*, she explodes for me. She comes over and over, her grip on her legs giving way, and her body thrashing and writhing on the couch until I finally let her breathe.

For now.

Because what she might not know yet is that now, I've gotten a taste. And I'm reasonably sure alcohol and drugs are about to slide into second and third place on my list of addictions.

Because her pussy just claimed first.

And we're nowhere *near* to being done.

21

JACKSON

"*Holy fucking shit*, what the *hell* was that?"

She's smiling, practically a puddle of smiles and flushed skin as she melts against the sofa. I grin as I nip at her thigh, making her gasp with this cock-thickening little moan wrapped around it.

As if my dick could be any harder right now.

I let my lips tease over her skin, nibbling up and down that thigh until I brush higher to the crease right next to her swollen, flushed pussy. And it might honestly be the prettiest sight I've ever seen in my life.

My jeans drop as I shove them and my boxers down and kick them away. My hungry, rock-hard cock slaps against my abs as I let my tongue drag up her pussy. Melody moans, her hips rising on their own accord.

"*Greedy girl*. Did this little pussy want more of my tongue?"

Her breath catches, and she drops her gaze to stare at me with wide eyes as I lazily tease her cunt with my tongue.

"Or maybe, you want to explode for me again like a bad girl with my tongue in your ass."

Her face darkens to a deep red, her chest rising and falling heavily. Her mouth forms an O shape as my tongue drags up and down her dripping wet lips.

"Or maybe…"

She shivers, gasping as I slide up between her legs, moving over her until my lips are an inch from hers. I lower my mouth, and before she can protest, I kiss her deeply, letting her taste her own pussy on my lips.

The eager little tease kisses me right back, hungrily.

"Or maybe," I rasp again against her mouth. "Maybe I need to *fuck* this tight little pussy like it deserves to get fucked, and feel you milk the cum from my balls while you come all the fuck over my thick cock."

I shift my hips, letting my swollen dick brush hotly against her thighs.

And instantly, something happens. Melody stiffens. That heat and drug-like ecstasy in her eyes *vanishes*. Instead, she goes cold, the color draining from her face as the light just winks out of her eyes completely.

My brow furrows as I peer down into her face, watching in real time as she just shrivels away from the whimpering, sexually submissive but eager little orgasm machine I just had writhing under me.

"Mel—"

And suddenly, I see it. I see it like looking into a fucking mirror—a jagged, broken one that cuts me even if I can't look away. I look into her eyes and see something only people like me—*like us*—can really understand.

"Hang on…"

She flinches as my hand comes up to cup her cheek. Fury—not at her, but because I know what this—erupts in me, blackening my heart as I pull back from her. Her breath is coming in ragged hitches, and I understand this pain.

I know this trigger.

Because I've heard it click a million fucking times since the night my childhood was taken from me.

I yank my boxers on, tugging my shirt back on too before I grab a blanket. I wrap her in it, both to cover her and take away that sense of nakedness she's feeling. But also, to put a barrier between us.

Because I know she needs that.

She's still shaking as I tug it tight around her and then sit beside her on the couch. Every ounce of me wants to hold her and bury her in my arms as if to shield her physically from the demons and monsters rampaging through her head right now.

But I won't do that. Instead, I just reach out and take her hand, squeezing tightly. She flinches, but it snaps her out of. With a blink and another shiver, her eyes rip from whatever hole they were just in, turning to stare at me as her face falls.

"I—Jackson, I…I'm so—"

"Don't you dare fucking apologize," I rasp quietly. I squeeze her hand again. This time, she squeezes gently back.

"I—I didn't mean to—"

"This isn't happening, sweetheart," I say quietly, shaking my head. "We're not—"

"No, I want—"

"*No.*" I shake my head as my eyes lock with hers. "I see you, and I know what's going through your head. You don't have to prove shit."

Her brow furrows, a flicker of anger sizzling behind her eyes.

"Excuse me?"

"You don't have to do anything to prove to anyone, even yourself, that you're fine, or over it," I mutter. "Trust me."

She swallows, her face paling.

"I don't know what you're talking about."

"Yes, you do."

She looks away, yanking her hand back.

"It's none of your business."

"No, it fucking isn't."

She swallows, brushing the back of her hand across her eyes.

"I..."

"I know what you're feeling, for what it's worth."

She whirls on me, her face angry and broken, tears welling in her eyes as she hugs the blanket tight around herself.

"You can't *possibly* know—"

"No?"

"No, Jackson!" She snaps. "Fucking a million random groupies does not equate to surviving sexual assault!"

She blurts it like a dare. Like she's goading me into saying something, or being an asshole about it, or looking disgusted.

That bait won't work on me. None of that shit is going to happen.

"And you think losing yourself in a decade of meaningless, anonymous sex is a symptom of a *healthy* sexual development?" I throw back at her.

She closes her eyes, turning to look away at the fire.

I exhale slowly. Iggy's the only one who ever knew about my past. Not even Will or Asher. Just me, Iggy…and *her*.

The fucking cunt that preyed on me like a monster.

And yet, for some reason I literally cannot wrap my head around—because it's not even like I'm wasted or coked up in that way where you just can't stop shit from spilling out of your mouth. But whatever it is, for some reason, I *want* to tell her.

Maybe it's because I can see how broken she is. Or because I see myself in her. Because I was just like this, once. Only I dealt with it in wildly self-destructive ways.

"She was my stepmother."

My words break the hanging silence, and Melody stiffens.

"I was twelve."

I want a drink. Motherfuck, I want *all* the drinks, to numb this even as it spills from my mouth. But I stay where I am, staring straight ahead into the fire as my past sinks it's teeth in my jugular.

"She drank a lot, and my dad was usually gone—work, getting fucked up, fucking around with other women. Anything he could do to *not* be at home. The first time it happened…"

My jaw grinds.

"It just happened. And when it was over, she just stayed there in my room—in my bed—smoking cigarettes until my dad came home."

Melody half turns, her face crumpling as a tear slides down her cheek.

"I was used to him hitting me around. But that night, he beat the living shit out of me, until I lost consciousness. He hit her, too, and called her a whore and all that shit. But he decided it was my fault. I'd gone after what was his, to stick it to him, or whatever."

Her hand touches mine. My fingers twist, lacing with hers; tightening.

"I thought that was the end of it. But it only made things worse. After that, he started disappearing more and more. And every time he was gone, she'd be there—drunk, slurring, telling me to be quiet. Telling me to be a big man for her…"

My eyes close. My jaw grinds painfully as I swallow back the nightmares from my youth.

It's different with boys. When it happens to them—to us— we're not really seen as victims. We're given high-fives. Slaps on the back. A cold beer. A grin and a "atta boy".

So only Iggy ever knew. Because he came from as fucked up a place as I did, with an uncle who liked to put cigarettes out on Iggy's arm, or hit him with buckle end of a belt for basically anything.

Iggy knew that keeping that shit inside wasn't because we were scared, or because we felt some fucked up need to protect the ones who hurt us.

It was self-preservation. Keeping it locked deep was how you kept waking up every day and kept breathing.

Obviously, half a lifetime of excess and self-destruction later, I understand how fucked up that is. And how poisoning it was to keep those things inside. But it was what it was.

"Eventually, he caught her with me again. And again. And every time, she'd cry and sob and tell him what a pervert I was, and how I wouldn't leave her alone or couldn't keep my hands off of her. And every time, I was sure it was going to be the time he finally just kept going until I was dead."

I shake my head bitterly.

If there's a hell, they're both there. And I fucking hope it burns.

"Then one time, he walked in with a gun."

Melody's face pales, and her hand tightens in mine.

"He sat there in my room, pointed it at me, and told me to keep going. And that if I stopped, he'd fucking shoot me."

I close my eyes.

"The next day, he was gone. He just went to work or wherever, and never came home. She didn't work, so she took it out on me—called me a bastard and a home wrecker, and all this shit. So, I left, too. Went to stay at Iggy's house, which was its own nightmare, but it was better than that."

I draw in a slow breath, turning to look at Melody. I take her other hand, bring them to my lips as I kiss her knuckles.

"*I know* the fury and the pain of those broken pieces inside, Melody," I growl thinly.

Tears slide down her cheeks. Slowly, she starts to move closer to me.

"You have *nothing* to prove—"

"*I want to be touched*," she chokes in a hushed whisper. Her face caves, her eyes squeezing shut. "I *need* to be touched. By you."

I pull her softly into my arms, wrapping them around her as she pulls curls into my lap.

"I was thirteen."

"You don't need to tell me this."

"I know."

Her breath exhales against my chest.

"He was dating my mom, and when she was gone one night, he came to my room…"

She shudders against me.

"He's…" she shivers. "He's why I don't sing in front of people anymore. And I used to *love* to sing," she says softly. "I mean I really loved it. I still do, I just…can't. Because he…he…"

Fury explodes deep in my chest as my hands tighten on her. I grit my teeth, eyes narrowing into the fire.

"He…" her voice shakes. "When he was touching me, he told me to 'sing pretty' for him."

Fucking Christ.

That's what did it. That's what pushed her into that hole, before. Because I fucking said the *same thing* her fucking monster said to her.

"I'm so sorry…"

"No, it's…" she shakes her head, dragging in a shaky breath. "I hate him for what he did to my body. But it's like I hate him even more for what he took away from me."

The rage threatening to explode out of every pore in my body actually shakes me. The pure, murderous rage I feel for the motherfucker who silenced her and took something as personal as the expression of music—singing—from her, is staggering.

"*Who*," I rasp thickly, shaking in my rage. "Who the *fuck* is he."

She tenses, and when she looks up at me, her eyes are narrowed coldly.

"What," she sneers. "Mad I'm not the delicate little untouched flower you thought I'd—"

"I'm fucking *mad* because I want to *destroy him*," I snarl lethally.

Melody pales. But she moves deeper into my arms.

"I—I can't tell you."

"Can't or won't."

"Jackson—"

"Just tell me who this fuck is, Melody," I hiss.

She shakes her head.

"He was…he still *is* kind of famous. My mom signed a bunch of NDAs and other things. I think there was some money involved. I don't really know."

"Tell me who this monster is, and I swear to fucking Christ—"

"Jackson *please*."

The urgency in her voice stops me and clears the red mist from eyes momentarily. And when I drag myself from that rage and look down into her eyes, I remember what's important here.

Her. Not my own, possibly selfishly tinged need for vengeance. *Her*.

"Just…let me keep this one locked up, okay?"

I reach up, pushing a lock of pink arm her face as I nod.

"Okay."

She sinks against me, and my arms tighten around her.

"Thank you."

"For?"

"Seeing me," she says softly. "And not seeing the shame or the—"

"I see you."

I lean down, my lips kissing the top of her head.

"And all I see is perfection."

I hold her like that as the fire crackles and the storm blows outside, until her breathing gets regular, and her body sinks into sleep against me.

It occurs to me that this is literally the first time in my life I've ever held a woman until she falls asleep.

Imagine that.

22

MELODY

I open my eyes to…whiteness.

And I'm alone.

My brow furrows as I stir, shifting under what feels like a mountain of blankets heaped over me. Slowly, I open my eyes, but then half-close them as the bright whiteness blinds me.

I shift, sitting up as I open my eyes again. This time, I take in my surroundings, and I blink as I stare out the windows.

Snow. That's the blinding white light that just woke me up. Outside, the storm from last night has turned to a blizzard of some kind, with flurries whirling and blowing hard against the house.

I shiver, realizing it's somewhat cold in the house, even though the fireplace is still crackling with what looks like fresh logs. And of course, the million blankets heaped over me.

I tense when I realize I'm naked beneath them. But then, slowly, heat floods into me as it all comes back to me.

Kissing him. Falling into a dark, sultry hole with him that I never wanted to come back out of. His mouth on me, his hands on me…

I shiver. And then, his truths.

And mine.

For a second, embarrassment and shame that I actually let my dark past out—to *him* of all people—has me groaning as I sink into the blankets. There's only three people who actually know about what happened to me those years ago. Judy, I count, feeling the sting of betrayal and anger, but choosing to breath it out. My roommate June, because we got *embarrassingly* drunk one night and spilled dark secrets to each other. She just doesn't know the *who*.

And *him*, of course. The monster.

He can't hurt you.

Not anymore.

I exhale, hugging myself and choosing to not dwell there in that nightmare from my past. Yes, he's still out there. He's not dead or horribly maimed, or in prison. No one, to my knowledge, has tortured him or cut his dick off.

He's still famous. I still turn to ice if I walk into a record store and see his fucking face on a greatest hits album, or when Ticketmaster decides to send me a robo-email gleefully reminding me that he's playing in New York.

My lips purse. My teeth grit as I shake my head.

Let it go.

I slowly run through breathing exercises that usually help me distance myself from trauma. And as I do, my thoughts wander to last night, and heat simmers through me. My skin remembers Jackson's hands on me. My lips remember the taste of him...

I blush fiercely. And of me.

At twenty years old, with *zero* dating or consensual sexual history to speak of? With my inability to even let a guy touch or kiss me?

I have a fucking *doctorate* in making myself come. I mean, no joke. I'm *very* good at knowing what I like, and what does it for me.

Hey, a girl has needs, even if she won't let someone else attend to those needs.

But, in all my years of...self-exploration, I've never once come *close* to the places where Jackson took me last night. Which was somewhere past outer space. All I know is, his tongue, and his fingers, and his filthy words ripped me from my reality and took me someplace fantastical last night.

And I'm not sure if I ever want to return to reality again.

I flush, simmering under the blankets as I bite my lip. But then, my brow furrows as I look around the empty, slightly chilly living room.

Where *is* he, actually?

I glance at the clock on the far wall. It's barely eight in the morning. Which seems like an unlikely time of day for someone like Jackson to be awake. I frown, trying to put together the puzzle. But when it clicks, a little of that euphoria and giddiness that came with thinking about last night dims.

He's not up and awake at this hour. He's just…not here. As in, not still sleeping on the couch with me, after I embarrassingly fell asleep on his chest.

The heat on my face cools.

I fell asleep, and he probably immediately went back to his own bed, after extracting himself from clingy-mc-clingy. Aka, me.

I groan as my heart sinks. Great. He probably thinks I fell in love with him or something last night.

I mean, I had an amazing time. And even if I initially want to cringe that I told him what I told him…it actually feels good to have done it. It feels like a little of the background noise I usually carry with me is quieter. Like the weight I usually feel is lightened.

But *please*. I don't regret any of last night. He might have redefined what I consider the definition of an orgasm last night. And I'm relatively sure I'm not going to find that kind of ecstasy *anywhere* else, which is a sobering thought. But it's not like I've fallen head over heels for the man.

Jackson—however incredible he felt last night, and as amazing as it felt to open up with him—is still Jackson.

He's still the drunken Mad King Asshole of Ego Island.

I shiver. Yes, last night was fun. But at least I didn't lose my mind completely and give him my freaking virginity or something. I mean you'd have to be psychotic to want your first time to be with drunken, drug-abusing egomaniacal rock star.

I swallow, making sure that sticks good and deep before I take a breath.

I glance around, spotting my underwear and the rest of my clothes with a blush before reaching over and yanking them under the blankets. I slip them on, gasping a little as I'm yanked further from warm, cozy sleep into wakefulness.

Icy cold panties will do that.

When I'm dressed, I finally stand, wrapping one of the blankets around me as I pad into the kitchen to make some coffee.

My brow furrows. The coffee is already made.

I pour a mug in mild confusion, inhaling the steam as I bring it to my lips. Okay, maybe he's got it on a timer or something? But then I turn, still frowning as I glance back at the fireplace. Okay, the logs crackling in it are clearly fresh, not smoldering embers from last night. So…what the hell is going on?

And then, I hear it.

Thwack. Thwack. Thwack.

Frowning curiously, coffee mug clutched in my hands, I walk over to one of the kitchen windows and peer outside.

My face instantly flushes.

The thwacking sound is Jackson, swinging an axe high and then down to chop a log into firewood. And even though the snow and wind is whipping and swirling around him, he's in just jeans, boots, a Henley with the sleeves pushed up, and a beanie.

And *fuck me*, does something about that whole situation make my legs weak. And makes my core tighten and throb with heat. I don't know what kind of messed up, monkey-brain caveman shit this is, but watching him—muscles rippling, jaw set tight against the swirling snow as he manhandles that axe—takes me from zero to hundred in *seconds*.

My thighs squeeze together, my eyes gleaming with desire as I just stand there in the window, sipping my coffee and watching him like a complete creep. Like a horny teenage boy spying on the girl's locker room or something.

He keeps chopping another ten minutes or so before he starts tossing the pile of firewood around him into a wheelbarrow. He rolls his shoulders, dropping the axe in as well before he turns and shoves it though the snow back towards the front of the house.

I'm still in the kitchen when I hear the front door open and then shut with a loud bang. I can hear him muttering and grunting about the cold as he kicks his boots off. Then, my eyes follow him from my lurking spot in the kitchen as he stomps into the living room with an armful of wood to dump next to the fireplace.

Suddenly, he turns, and I blush as his eyes lock with mine. A devilish smirk curls the corners of his perfect lips.

"Morning," he grunts.

"Good morning."

My eyes devour him. And the lust I feel surging inside of me honestly scares me a little.

"The place should start warming up soon. I have a generator out by the garage that was supposed to kick on last night and didn't. But I just reset the pilot on that, so, it's running…"

He frowns and walks over to a vent by the floor, crouching to wave his hand over it. He grunts.

"There it is."

I just swallow, feeling heat of my own pool between my legs. Feeling my chest constrict as my nipples harden.

Jackson sighs, tossing another log on the fire before he settles on the sofa and drops his head back.

But I already know what I'm doing.

I step out of sight of the living room. Quickly, I shed my clothes, shivering, even though I can also feel the heat kicking on. Naked, and trembling with desire, I wrap myself in the blanket again and step out into the living room.

And I walk *right* to him.

"There's coffee—"

He arches a brow as he glances up and sees the look on my face. His eyes don't pull away from me at all as I prowl right up in front of him, look him right in the eye…

And drop the blanket.

Jackson's jaw clenches, his eyes narrowing to dangerous, hungry slits as he nakedly drinks in my body.

"What are you doing, Melody."

"This."

I sink onto his lap, trembling with anticipation. Shaking with need. I lean in to kiss him, but I jolt when he stops me fast, gripping my arms as he frowns.

"What the fuck are you—"

"Returning the favor from last night," I husk, desire roaring in me as I push forward to kiss him again.

Infuriatingly, he fucking stops me. Again.

"What the *hell*—"

"You don't *owe me* shit," he growls. "And you don't have fuck-all to prove. To me, to yourself, to any—"

I break free of his grip, and this time, my mouth slams into his; hard. Jackson growls deep in his chest, and whatever walls he had up a second ago crumble as his hands grab me possessively.

I whimper as I feel his grip tighten on my waist, squeezing as his hips rise to grind into me. I moan, feeling how fucking hard he is already, even through his jeans. My head spins as my lips open, our tongues sliding together in a sultry dance as my nipples drag against his chest.

"This isn't because I owe you," I murmur heatedly against his mouth. "This is because *I want you*."

I kiss him again, or rather, he grabs my hair and bruises his mouth to mine so hard I see stars. I shudder against him, rolling my hips against the hot, thick bulge in his jeans before I can't hold back anymore.

I want this. And I want it with him.

I pull away from his mouth, whimpering as his teeth rake over my bottom lip. My mouth drops to his neck, kissing and nibbling at his skin as I shove his Henley shirt up his gorgeous body. Jackson growls, muscles flexing as his hands slide into my hair. I shiver, dropping lower and lower to kiss his chest, and then his abs as I sink to my knees on the floor.

His eyes lock with mine as I glance up at him.

"Melody—"

"Are you going to let me suck your cock or not?"

I whimper when his hand in my hair tightens, yanking me into him as he leans down to kiss me violently again. As he does, I shiver as I hear him yanking his belt and jeans open. I feel him shoving them down, and I throb with needy lust as I feel his cock slap against my tits.

Holy fuck I'm really going to do this.

And I goddamn really am.

He pulls away to yank his t-shirt off, and my eyes finally drop to—

Holy. Fucking. FUCK.

I just stare—shamelessly, because I can't possibly look away—with my mouth hanging open and my eyes bulging from my head.

Jackson's cock is fucking *enormous*.

I mean, I've erect dicks before—"porn-watching prude" that I am. But sweet fucking Jesus…this is another category entirely.

He's long, and *thick* as fuck, with a swollen head that somehow turns my stomach to knots and makes my tongue wet my lips.

I've wondered about how I'd feel seeing a man like this again —like for real, and not in an internet porn video. If I'd be repulsed. Or scared. Or angry. But all I feel when I stare at Jackson's absolutely gorgeous—and I do mean *beautiful*—cock, is desire.

My hand shakes as I reach for him. My fingers wrap around what feels like hot silk over pure steel, and when he grunts, I shiver as lust pools between my legs. My hand strokes gently up and down, and before I can second-guess myself or ask too many what-ifs, I just go for it.

I lean down, open my mouth, and wrap my lips around his swollen head.

I don't know who moans louder—him, or I. But it happens at the same time. I whimper, humming around his cock as I slowly push my lips lower on him. He tastes salty and sweet at the same time, and I shiver as my tongue laps at his head.

My eyes raise to his, and my heart thuds as his lust-hooded gaze locks with mine. I moan as I suck him deeper again, before sliding my lips from him with a wet sound.

"How—"

I stop myself.

Don't you dare ask him how it feels, dork.

Instead, stroking him lightly, I bite my lip as I look up into his eyes.

"Show me how you like it."

The way his jaw ticks like he's barely controlling himself turns me to fucking fire. And the way his eyes flash almost dangerously as my body aching for him.

But slowly, he just shakes his head.

"No."

"No what?"

"Don't ask me that," he rasps quietly. "Just…don't."

"Why?"

I move up, still shaking with heat, still stroking his huge cock as I bring my mouth closer to his.

"Why shouldn't I ask you—"

"Because the answer might scare you."

Pure need explodes in my center at his words. If he was trying to frighten me with what he just said, he failed. Because it did the opposite.

It made me want him even more.

And maybe that's a sign of something truly fucked up inside of me. Or loose wire, or…something. But it's there, and I can't ignore it.

"Try me."

His eyes flash cold blue fire.

"I'm fucking warning you," he growls thinly.

"No, you're treating me like a delicate little flower."

"You don't want to play the way I play, sweetheart."

I shiver.

"Try me."

"Melody…"

I lean in, feeling untouchable and on fire as I nip at his bottom lip with my teeth, dragging them over it as I pull back.

"Fucking try me."

Something clicks in his gaze. A darkness explodes behind his eyes.

"You want to play with me, little girl?" He rasps in a tone that sets me on fire.

I whimper, nodding as my thighs soak with desire. I gasp as his hand slides into my hair, grabbing it in a fist that sends electricity rippling through me. His muscle clench as he uses his grip to push me lower.

I moan, dropping back down until I'm eye-level with his swollen, throbbing cock.

"Open your mouth."

The words tease over me like hot silk, electrifying me and making my core quiver. I whimper as I do what he says.

"Now wrap those pretty lips around my cock, and I want you to *suck* like a good girl."

His hand tightens in my hair as I lean down, look up into his eyes, and slide my lips over his thick head. Jackson groans, his jaw tense as his muscles strain. I moan, taking more of him into my mouth before sliding back up.

I do this a few more times before I slide off and look up at him again.

"Show me."

I can see the war playing out in his eyes—wanting to not hurt me or push me too far past my comfort zone. But also, the roaring desire to take complete control of me and use me exactly how he wants.

"Do it."

I shiver, throbbing with a desire and a raw need I've never come close to feeling before.

"Fucking do it exactly how you wa—"

I choke as he grabs my hair and shoves his cock deep into my throat. My eyes bulge, tearing at the corners as my hands grab his hips, my nails sinking into his skin. Jackson starts to back off, but I dig my nails in tighter, shaking my head as my eyes look up at him through the wetness.

Our gazes lock, me on my knees with his thick cock stretching my jaw. Him brimming with dark, sultry energy—his muscles clenching and bunched, his eyes aflame as they lock with mine. And there right in front of me, I watch the control leave him. I watch a shadow slide over him that has my thighs quivering.

"I said *suck*."

Oh, fuck yes.

He pushes his hips forward, grabbing my hair in his fist as he rams deeper. He draws out as I choke, letting his glistening cock slip from my mouth. Spit drips in sticky strands between his crown and my lip as my watering, lust-filled eyes look up at him with pure need.

With a growl, he pushes himself back between my lips and sinks deep again. I moan, grabbing his hips as he thrusts in and out, pushing his crown over my tongue, past my lips, and past my threshold again and again. I gag, but I don't stop. My airwaves block again and again as he fucks my mouth and pushes his cock to the back of my throat.

But I *don't. Fucking. Stop*.

Not because I'm afraid. Not because he has control over me or that I'm at his mercy.

Because I've *given* the control.

Because I fucking want this.

This is loss of control and agency on *my* terms, and the more he fucks my mouth, and groans, and reaches down to pinch my nipples as I choke on his fat cock, the more I'm sure I might *literally* come without even touching myself.

"Such a pretty little slut, choking on that big dick," he growls luridly, making my eyes roll back as I tremble.

"Fuck, you look so pretty with my cock filling your mouth."

I whimper, pushing myself further, swallowing him as deep as I can as spit runs down my chin.

"I bet that pretty little pussy is on fire, isn't it?"

I moan as I hum around his cock.

"Isn't it."

A whimper tears from my throat as I nod, looking up at him with desperate, teary eyes.

"I want you to play with that greedy cunt for me, sweetheart. I want to watch you rub that little pussy until you come while you swallow my dick."

My hand flies between my legs, my eyes bulging at how obscenely wet I am. I moan wildly around him as he thrusts into my mouth, my fingers desperately rubbing my clit hard as my legs begin to shake. Jackson's muscles clench, his jaw grinding as pure fire sparks from his eyes into mine.

"Come for me, sweetheart," he snarls, his face a dark mask of lust and depravity that turns me to molten fire. "Fucking come for me while I pump my cum down this greedy little throat."

I explode. My fingers press hard against my clit, my thighs clamp shut, and I *moan* as he buries his cock deep into the back of my throat.

"Swallow my fucking cum, babygirl. Swallow it like a good fucking girl."

I feel his cock swell somehow even bigger. His abs ripple, his groan hisses through clenched teeth, and suddenly, I can feel it. I can taste it as his cum sprays across my tongue and down my throat—pump after pump as I keep rubbing my clit and coming again right there with him.

My head swims, and my body is shaking everywhere as he slowly tugs my hair, pulling me off his slick cock. For a second, reality hits me as I feel how swollen my lips are— how I can feel spit and cum dripping down my chin. Shame begins to cloud my thoughts, before suddenly, he's pulling me up into him. And before I know what's happening, he's crushing his lips to mine.

"Mm, wait, Jackson—"

But he doesn't stop. He just keeps kissing me and shattering my own hang-ups of what a mess I must be.

I pull back again, our eyes locking.

"I—I mean, I should brush my teeth, or—"

"Do you really think I give a fuck?"

This time, when his mouth slams to mine, I don't stop it. I kiss him right back, opening my mouth as our tongues dance and explore. Until suddenly, with a growl, he's pulling away, flipping us over, and shoving me down into the couch.

He drops between my thighs, shoving them lewdly open before he ducks between them. His eyes lock with mine as his mouth sinks against my pussy, his tongue dragging over my slit.

"Oh fuck...Jackson!"

I'm a mess. I'm flopped like a rag doll on the couch, my legs spread wide and shamelessly, my hair a mess, my lips swollen from him fucking my mouth, and spit and cum dripping down my chin onto my tits as he *devours* my pussy.

It's pure hedonism.

It's pure depravity.

And for one single second, I wonder if this is what slowly losing control feels like. I wonder for one second if I'm letting go, or if I'm being dragged into something I'll regret.

But then, his lips suction around my clit. His tongue swirls over it as his palm slaps my ass. My back arches, my head throws back as my mouth falls open in a scream of pure release.

Of pure exhale.

And when I come, the doubt and the worries shatter like glass.

If I'm being dragged into something, it's more than willingly. And if I'm losing control and falling into his sin? Heaven, or hell—or, let's just say "Jackson"—take me.

Hedonism, thy name is Havoc.

Ready and willing, thy name is *me*.

23

MELODY

"I'm going to go out on a limb and assume that even with your…prickly personality, there are people who might be wondering if you're okay?"

Curled on the couch, I lift my head from the guitar I've been lightly playing around with.

It's not lost on me that he didn't say anything when I picked it up. As he said nothing when I started to quietly play a few chord progressions. He just…let me, without comment, or so much as a lifted brow.

Flat out, I don't sing in front of people. Nobody. But I'll still play a guitar if I'm feeling comfortable. Like with June, even if she's miles better than me.

Apparently, giving in to my most base, depraved, dark fantasies and desires with the god of hedonism himself has a comforting effect on me.

That said, when I lift my head at his snarky comment to see him smirking at me, I lift a middle finger.

Jackson chuckles.

"Or maybe not?"

My brow furrows as the reality within his joke sinks in.

"There are some people who'll be worried about where I am, actually."

Like June, definitely. Or maybe, you know, my new boss, who I last talked to…what, one day ago? A week? I've somehow lost all sense of time here on Havoc Island.

I frown.

"There's definitely no cell service out here?"

He shakes his head.

"But…I might have a solution. Come with me."

I stand, setting the guitar down to follow him. "Comfortable" Melody is fashionably dressed in a button-down flannel shirt of Jackson's which goes to mid-thigh, and panties.

Apparently, "comfortable Melody" has a laissez-faire attitude surrounding pants. Or modesty.

But when I catch up to Jackson at the front door, I pause.

"Wait, are we…"

"The solution is outside in my wood shop in the garage."

I make a face. He rolls his eyes.

"Though *chivalry* is notably lacking a picture of my face next to it in the dictionary, I'd go, but…" he clears his throat. "You sort of need to come too."

"Why?"

"Because Robbie can't talk."

THE SOLUTION to the snowstorm outside ends up being Jackson wrapping me in a blanket and charging through the snowdrifts until we crash through the door of his garage. He sets me down and slams it shut behind us. I shiver as I wrap the blanket tighter around myself, my eyes roaming the garage.

It's a wood shop on one side, full of tools, a workbench, and sawdust everywhere. The other side seems to be motorcycle garage, with two vintage looking bikes in varied states of disassembly.

Jackson walks over to a box on a shelf next to his workbench and unclips what looks like a radio microphone attached by a curly cord.

"You know what this is?"

"A budget recording studio?"

He grins.

"It's a HAM radio, sort of like what truckers use on the highways. I know for a fact Albert's got one in the dock master's office. If you want, I can operate, and you talk. You can have him make a call for you or fire off an email, if you want to tell anyone where you are. Friends, boss…" his brow arches. "Boyfriend."

I roll my eyes, blushing.

"Seriously?"

He shrugs. "Was I that obvious?"

"Subtle as a root canal."

He smirks as he turns a dial, bringing a crackling sound over the speaker.

"It's one way at a time. So, you'll talk, and end whatever you have to say with 'over', at which point I'll release the button so Albert can respond. Good?"

I nod. "Good."

He turns, but then stops to glance back at me.

"You really told him I was your *uncle*?"

"My *weird*, grumpy uncle."

"Yeah, that tracks."

I giggle as he turns, hits a switch, and then holds down the button on the microphone as he holds it close to me.

"Ask for Albert, mention who you are and where you're calling from."

I clear my throat.

"Um…Albert? Albert in Cape Harbor? This is Melody over on Falstaff Island?"

I raise a brow at Jackson.

"Over," he mouths.

"Uh, over."

He lets go of the button, and static fills the garage. But a few seconds later, it crackles.

"Melody! Albert here. You guys okay over there in the storm? Over."

Jackson thumbs down the button.

"Yeah! We're fine. Uncle Robbie is extra cranky about the cold. Over."

Jackson flips me off as he depresses the button. Albert chuckles.

"Oh, you tell that grump to simmer down. Tell him if the going gets that tough, I'll come on over myself with some drinks for him. Over."

Jackson rolls his eye. I giggle.

"Hey, Albert, I was hoping you could do me a huge favor. My phone isn't getting service out here, and you know that Robbie doesn't do internet or landlines. Would it at all be possible for you to call someone for me and let them know I'm fine, just snowed in, and will probably be able to contact them myself by tomorrow? Over."

"Absolutely, kid. No trouble on my end at all. Who am I calling? Over."

I exhale with relief.

"Actually, it's two people, if that's okay? Over."

"No trouble at all. Over."

"Thank you SO much. I really appreciate it. The first is June Hendrix." I rattle off her cell number to him. "Could you just let her know I'm fine, just snowed in up here? Over."

I swallow, hoping to God that June is savvy enough to just go with it and not be weird when some strange man with a Maine accent calls to let her know I'm bunked in with "Uncle Robbie".

"Got it. And the second? Over."

"His name is Chuck Garver, my boss. You'll probably get his secretary." I run off that number before clearing my throat and wrinkling my nose. "Also, and I'm so sorry if this makes this weird, but…he thinks I'm on a work assignment, not visiting family. Over?"

Albert laughs heartily.

"Ayuh, I know that story. Don't worry about a thing, Melody. I'll just let 'im know you're snowed in and not to worry. That work? Over."

"*Perfect.* Thank you so, so much, Albert. I really appreciate it! Over."

"Not a worry, not a worry. Tell your Uncle Grumps we'll see 'im after this snow lets up. You two take care over there, ayuh? Over."

"Will do. Thanks again, Albert. Over."

"*And out,*" Jackson mouths quietly.

"And out!"

A LITTLE WHILE LATER, I'm back on the sofa, noodling around on the guitar. But I pause, frowning as I look up and realize Jackson's been gone from the immediate vicinity for…a while, actually. I set the guitar down, standing as look around.

"Jackson?"

When I hear nothing in response, I walk over to the front door, peering through the peep hole for signs of footprints in the snow outside. The snow itself has stopped falling, and my eyes search the ground for signs of Jackson maybe slipping out to his garage while I was playing.

But no dice.

Strange.

He's not in the basement, and I'm about to furtively go explore upstairs—which, I actually haven't seen at all yet—when I hear it.

Music.

My face heats as I pad barefoot through the house in the direction of the studio. And sure enough, when I get to the half-open door, there he is just inside.

He's at the desk to the side of the control counter, hunched over an electric guitar. I watch quietly, spellbound as he fingers out a soft, sultry, bluesy line through a warm-toned amp beside him. But then he stops, frowning as he reaches for a pen and scrawls something in a notebook open in front of him.

He grins to himself, nodding with a sigh before he leans back in the chair and starts to play again. And I'm *spellbound*.

The notes pour off his fingertips like a lover's touch. And the words that fall from his lips—garbled, and haphazardly thrown together they may be—reach into my chest and touch something buried deep.

It's just one stanza—one verse or a refrain of some kind. But it's so fucking haunting, and so sultry and beautiful that I'm practically falling over myself to get closer to it—as if proximity will let it sink deeper into my skin like a tattoo.

That is, until I actually *do* get closer, and accidentally push the door open a crack.

Jackson jumps, the spell broken as he whirls on me.

My face pales as I wince.

"I'm *so* sorry—"

"Don't be," he shrugs. "Just garbage anyway, as usual."

I stare at him. "You're joking."

"I'm not. It's all garbage these days."

He starts to slip the guitar strap over his head.

"Wait!" I blurt. "Don't stop!"

My face heats as he arches a brow.

"I mean, don't stop because of me. Keep playing."

His eyes slowly trace over me, and when they halt midway down, and smolder, I frown quizzically. But when I glance down at myself, I blush when it clicks.

I've been standing in the doorway with my arm raised, elbow on the doorframe above my head as I leaned against it. And I'm still just wearing his button-down flannel. Which in this position, is now pulled up.

Flashing my panties.

I flush heatedly as I drop my arm. But Jackson's hungry look doesn't fade.

"I'd rather play something else," he growls thickly.

I shiver, biting my lip as desire pools in my core.

"What if I said yes…"

He growls as he starts to stand.

"But *only*," I add quickly, grinning at him. "If you play me something first."

I grunt rumbles in his throat.

"Sneaky."

I shrug.

"Except I don't take requests."

I shrug, clicking my tongue against my teeth.

"Well, then that's a bummer for you, because those are the rules."

"You've seen my track record with rules, yes?"

I blush, biting my lip as my thighs clench.

"If you want to play…you have to *play*."

He grunts, eying me with a scowl. But then, he cracks his neck as he sits back into the chair and reaches for the guitar.

"*Fine*," he grumbles. "What's the fucking request."

I restrain myself from jumping up and down.

"*Lydia*."

He groans, and I even know why.

There was an article years and years ago that blew up in a huge way, that called *Lydia* "Velvet Guillotine's *Wonderwall*", as in the infamous Oasis rock ballad. I mean, they *are* both similar in terms of that softer, more ballad-esque feel, and are both about broken love and the attraction to the tragic.

But it become almost like a meme. Every interviewer after that would seem to slip in some asinine question to the band about their relationship to the Gallagher brothers of Oasis, or if they'd ever collaborate or something. It wasn't even dumb questions insinuating that *Lydia* was inspired by *Wonderwall*—the songs musically sound nothing alike at all. But, as documented in other interviews, it apparently drove the members of Guillotine, and Jackson especially, crazy.

I know all this, and I'm *still* making it my request. Because—sorry, not sorry—it's an *amazing* song, and one of my favorites.

I smile as wide and as cutely as I can.

"Pleeeease?"

He sighs, hiding a grin as he shakes his head.

"Fuck it, fine. But after this, I'm ripping those fucking panties off, and you're planting that pussy right on my fucking tongue. Got it?"

I shiver at the demanding tone and the wicked promise.

"Got it," I murmur, swallowing.

He rolls his shoulders, drops his hands to the strings, and starts to play. And I'm smiling ear to ear through the whole thing. Every verse, every soaring chorus. Every way his voice breaks so perfectly, and the way the guitar lines blend like aural paint. The way one single song—one three-minute piece of music—can make your soul leap out of your body.

When it's over, and the last lines melt into the air around us, I've got my eyes half closed, my heart still racing.

"That was…beautiful," I whisper.

Jackson nods, putting the guitar to the side as he stands. His eyes cut into me dangerously, hungrily, making me shiver. But as my eyes slip to the side, I frown as they land on the control board for the studio, which is half covered in scraps of paper, scribbled notes, and jotted down chords.

My brow knits.

"What is all this?"

He grunts.

"Nothing, trust me. Just shit I've been writing and working on."

My jaw drops as I whirl to him.

"Are you really working on new songs?"

His eyes roll.

"I'm working on pure piss and garbage. Trust me, there's nothing there. It's shit."

"Can I read it?"

"Melody, I'm not trying to be modest. It's fucking garbage."

I turn to reach for one of the scraps of paper.

"Can I be the judge of that?"

"Only if you drop those panties while you do."

My face heats violently, my core quivering as desire pools between my legs.

"I…think that's a fair arrangement."

"Oh, do you…"

I whimper as he turns me towards the control board and bends me over it.

"Read away, sweetheart."

I shiver, reaching for a new page and letting my eyes drift over it. Which, admittedly, becomes a lot harder when I feel him drop to his knees behind me and pull my panties down to my knees. But I keep reading his words…even when I feel his strong hands spread me lewdly open from behind and feel his breath on my thighs.

His tongue drags over my pussy, and I moan, almost bunching the page in my hand into my fist. But, even as the waves of bliss wash over me, I force myself to read the words in front of me.

I want both—his physical lust for me, and the mad genius scribbled on the page in my hand.

And so, I take both.

I cry out as he tongues my clit, or when his palm spanks my ass. But I keep reading the lyrics—page after page of them, until I'm floating in this heady mix of his tongue and his creativity.

But, even as my toes curl, and as I drift closer and closer to exploding on his tongue, I stare at the words I'm reading.

They're…good. I mean they're really, *really* fucking good.

"I know you're trying to hold out on me, sweetheart," he growls into my thigh. I yelp when he spanks my ass and then slides a finger deep into me, stroking it against my g-spot.

"You can try all you want, but I *will* have you coming for me. I *will* taste this sweet little cunt when you explode all over my fucking tongue like a good girl."

His mouth attacks my clit again, devouring me as he strokes his finger against the spot just inside. My eyes roll back as I slump across the control panel with my legs shaking. The pressure builds, and when he sucks my clit between his lips and sucks hard, I can't hold out anymore.

With a jolt and a cry of pure bliss from my lips, I'm coming hard against his mouth. But even as I slide off the edge into the abyss, my eyes are locked on his words.

24

JACKSON

Melody's message to Albert about "calling people herself" by the next day doesn't come to pass. By nightfall, the snow starts to pick up again, whitewashing the bay and turning the whole island and town beyond it into a hazy fog of ice and snow. The next morning, it's the same thing, and it goes all day into the second night as well.

And into the third morning.

Yeah, I'm not boating anywhere in that shit.

Not, for that matter, that I have *any* motivation to facilitate her leaving this island. Or anywhere that isn't close enough that I can drag her into my arms and devour her whenever I please.

Which is exactly what I've been doing for the last three days.

And when I do, sometimes, I worry that I'm pushing her too far. It's become fairly clear to me that Melody is…not exactly experienced. And I don't mean that in as a negative or a critique in the slightest fucking bit.

The way that girl turns me on and makes me fucking explode is…transcendent. It's genuinely mind-blowing and hits me in a way that puts just about any other rush I've ever chased to shame—be it drugs, sex, success, fame, whatever.

But, still, it's clear what happened to her put the brakes on… exploring herself. Sexually, that is. And I've worried that my own tastes and appetites are beyond what she's ready for.

I play rough. I play hard. But I am *not* going to hurt her.

And yet, when I do try and tap the brakes, or hold back, it's like she can tell. And she goads me into letting off those brakes. She antagonizes me, like she knows needling me will make me lose control and be rougher, and more dominant with her.

I'm beginning to think little miss Pink Hair has *way* more of a submissive streak than she even knew about.

I frown, shaking my head at myself as I finish chopping vegetables for dinner. Ten years away from the world, and I get hooked like a fucking junkie on the first girl who steps foot on my island. But, again, it's not thirst. It's not like she's a "warm body" or any bullshit like that.

It's that she's *her*.

Sharp, thorny, difficult. Defiant and challenging as fuck. And yet, she's also delicate. And soft. And breakable. And it might be the mix of all of that—however polar opposites some of those qualities may be—that draw me in and won't let go.

It's like I have this constant need to war with her. To butt heads. But also, to protect her. To shield her from anything and everything. I want to swat that ass into submission while she chokes on my cock. But then, I also want to wrap her in soft blankets and stroke her hair until she sleeps.

What in the *fuck* happened to me out here?

I roll my eyes as I butcher the steak from my freezer, slicing it thin for the Vietnamese-style stir-fry I'm making for dinner. I use the knife to push the slices off the cutting board into the bag of marinade, and then deposit that into the fridge while I clean up a little.

When I've washed my hands, I go off to seek Melody out. But even though she's been here all of three days, I know exactly where I'll find her.

The studio.

She's drawn to it like, well, like I'd be if I were her. Like I *am* drawn to it and all recording studios. It's been interesting to me watch her slowly come out of her shell when it comes to music. When she first set foot here, I had her pegged as the enemy; the worst kind of reporter: a *music* reporter.

There's a quote I read somewhere once that said, "writing about music is like dancing about architecture," and it amuses me to this day.

Music journalists always got under my skin in an especially needling way. A regular reporter just asks dumb, obnoxious, prying questions about what you do. And it's annoying, and I usually fucked with them as much as I could. But, at the end of the day, you could just answer the questions, they'd smile and nod, and that was it.

But *music* reporters? No. They're a special breed of holier-than-thou. They think because they write about music all day—other people's music, I'd like to underscore—that they understand it. Or "get it". They think they're boss-tier level "fans".

But they're not fans. They're poison. With them, you can't just answer the asinine questions, have a drink and be on your way. No, they feel the need to pry deeper. To make you dance around the bullshit answer you gave, even if you both know damn fucking well it's the answer they were looking for anyway.

They're professional buzzkills is what they are. And *that's* what I pegged Melody for when I first laid eyes on her.

But she's not that. In fact, she may be the most non-toxic music reporter I've ever met. That, or, in my opinion, she's in the wrong fucking industry. She's on the wrong side of the battle, so to speak.

She's not a reporter. I mean not under the surface, that is.

Deep down, she's like me.

She's an artist. She's a creative. And part of me wonders just how much of her desire to write *about* music is because it's as close to *writing music* or *playing* music that she can get after what that motherfucker did to her.

My jaw clenches as I stalk into the living room, even just thinking about it.

One day…one day, come hell or high water, I *will* find out who hurt her.

And I'll fucking drown him in his own blood.

For the time being, though, I shake the fantasies of murder and castration from my head. But just as the fog of it is lifting, I wince as I trip over something next to the couch I didn't even see.

I glance down to see Melody's backpack, the contents half-spilled across the floor.

Shit.

When I stoop to push her things back into though, I frown as my hands stop on her notebook. I tell myself not to open it, but…fuck it. She's already pried into my own shit enough times anyway. And besides, it's probably just her notes for Ignition Magazine or something.

But when I open it, I realize how wrong I was. It's not journalistic notes. It's not dirty little secrets about yours truly.

It's *lyrics*.

My brows knit as my eyes drag down one page, and then another. And another.

Fuck me. Not just lyrics. *Good* lyrics. I mean the girl is twenty. And all due respect to twenty year old wannabe songwriters and poets, but that shit is usually about as "deep" as the black and white photos of telephone lines or train tracks that come out of a high school photography class.

But not these. This shit is *good*. Really, really good.

I smile curiously, reading another page before I snap the book shut and head for the studio.

She gasps when I step in behind her, pulling away from the guitar she's been dancing her fingers over to look at me.

Melody's dressed in what has become, A; her go-to outfit around the house. Which also happens to be, B; my new all-time favorite outfit on any woman ever: one of my button-up plaid flannels, which goes down to mid-thigh, and…

Well, ideally *nothing* underneath. But even if it's just panties, it's basically a look that keeps me at least three-quarters hard just about every single waking minute of the day.

"I need you for something."

She blushes deeply. Which just makes me grin wickedly.

"*Dirty girl*," I growl quietly, which just makes her turn a deeper shade of crimson.

"I mean with this."

I place her notebook on the counter and glance at her. Melody stares at it, her mouth pursing before she whips her gaze to me, looking miffed.

"Uh-uh," I growl, shaking my head. "Let's put those stones down, Ms. Glass House. Who poked around in who's personal writing shit first?"

She glares at me, but I can see her lips trying to stop the grin.

"Okay, fair," she mumbles. "So, you looked at my writing?"

I nod. She swallows as she turns away.

"Huh."

"Yeah, huh."

She clears her throat.

"So…what do you need me for?"

"I need your help, with this."

I grab the stack of crumpled bits of lyrics and chords from the shelf where I stacked them yesterday and spread them out across the counter in front of us both.

Melody looks confused.

"What I need," I rumble as I grab a chair and sit down next to her. "Is for you to help me finish something."

Her eyes snap to mine so fast, I wince for her.

"I'm sorry, what?"

"You heard me."

She swallows, her eyes piercing into me, as if trying to see how I'm fucking with her.

"I'm not."

She frowns. "Not what?"

"Fucking with you."

A flush creeps up her neck.

"I'm not. Melody, your shit is *good*. Like, really good."

"Stop."

"I've already told you I'm not fucking with you. Take the compliment. I don't exactly dole them out willy-nilly, and I'm betting you can guess how true that is."

She stares at me, chewing on her lip in that way that drives me fucking wild. Though I haven't told her that, for fear she'll stop doing it.

I take a slow breath as I nod at the pile of shit in front of us.

"I *need* to finish something, Mel," I growl quietly. "I have ten fucking years of one-liners, sketches, ideas, and a whole lotta bullshit. But I need—I *need*—just one fucking thing. Just one goddamn song."

She nods slowly, eying me.

"Why?"

It's the same question I've asked myself a million times over the last decade. Why bother? Why not just take the ludicrous amount of money that Cliff is investing for me and go buy a vineyard in the French countryside? Or a chalet in the Alps. Another damn island, but in Vietnam or something.

Why not accept that I had ten years of *massive* success—the kind where they'll be playing my songs for the next hundred years—and just let that be it?

Because I can't. Because if I do, I'll never know.

I turn to look at her. "To prove to myself it wasn't a dream. To prove to myself I still have it, or *ever* had it. To prove to myself I still have *something* in the tank."

My eyes drop as I draw in a breath.

"I did most of the writing for Velvet. But it was Iggy who always took us home. He's the one that always brought me over that finish line, or who took my madness and shaped it into something glorious. I mean I know he's on the writing credits to a lot of the songs, but I don't think a lot of people know that."

"I didn't," she says quietly.

I smile sadly. "Yeah, he was always an asshole about not wanting his name on things."

You're the writer, mate. I just hit things.

I grin as I hear his voice in my head. Then I glance at Melody again.

"I came here ten years ago to write. And a decade later, I've got…." I wave at the collection of random words and lines and chords in front of us. "This. I need you to help me put the pieces together."

She blinks, staring at the lyrics.

"I…Jackson, I'm not a lyricist—"

"Bullshit. Yeah, you are."

She rolls her eyes.

"Not a legendary, world famous one."

"Yeah, and neither was I at twenty."

"Jackson, come on—"

"I'm *not* fucking with you. And I'm not drunk…"

I frown.

"Okay, I've had a couple drinks."

She grins, rolling her eyes.

"But I'm serious, sweetheart. I want you to help me with this. I need you to help me."

Her lips twist as she looks down.

"Say yes."

She grins to herself.

"Say *yesssss*…"

She giggles.

When I reach over and brush the hair from her face, she turns to me. And when I cup her face and lean in to taste her lips, her cheeks flush.

"Say yes."

I sear my lips to hers, devouring her until I feel her breath catch and her lips break a millimeter apart from mine.

"Yes."

25

JACKSON

We eat first. Because no genius ever has come on an empty stomach. And of course, there are drinks. Because genius also never comes sober.

I mean, at least personally speaking.

It's late by the time we both head back to the studio. But, as with empty stomachs and stone-cold sobriety, no great musical genius has ever been written before a late hour. That's just fucking scientific fact.

Probably. Maybe.

With the lights low, we sit at the counter, each of us with a guitar, a pen, and a notebook. For the first hour, we're just sorting through ideas, trying to match lines with certain vibes—basically trying to separate everything into the right piles. That done, Melody picks one at random, and we get to work.

I show her a couple of chord progressions I've been monkeying around with. And I hum a few melody lines, too.

"What about…this one."

She pulls one of the scraps of paper towards us.

"This line as the start of a chorus. I love the internal rhyming and the sea metaphor."

I grin. So do I, on both counts.

I strum a few chord lines, shifting the tempo and cadence until it just clicks with the line she's picked.

"That's it," she blurts, just as it clicks with me at the same time. "That's the tempo. That's the feel, just how you just did it."

I nod, repeating what I just did as I try singing the line.

Fuck me, that's catchy.

"*Damn*," she breathes.

"Catchy, isn't it?"

"That's a hook right here."

I look up, and she grins at me.

"What's next?" she says eagerly.

"Next, we just need to write the rest of the fucking song."

"Oh, that's it?"

"I know, right? I don't get why more people aren't writing hit, internationally successful songs."

She giggles as she starts to strum the guitar, playing our progression over and over until she suddenly stops and grabs a pen. Before I can say anything, she's grabbing the crumpled piece of paper that has my first few lines scrawled on it and adding two more, in her own handwriting, underneath.

I stare at them as she jerks back.

"Shit, sorry, I should have done that on another piece, or asked—"

"Hang on."

I pull the page towards me, staring at the lines. My two, followed by hers.

"Forget what I just wrote. Cross it out. It's dumb—"

"Will you fucking *stop*?"

She winces, shying away.

"I'm sorry, I shouldn't have just—"

"What I mean is," I growl, turning to her. "Will you stop fucking *doubting* yourself?"

She swallows, blinking at me.

"Where this just came from?" I tap her lines on the paper with a finger. "I need more of it."

She blushes. "Jackson—"

"Play it again."

Heat blossoms up her neck. But her fingers find their placing on the neck of the guitar, and she slowly begins to play through the chord progression as I quietly sing the lines we just wrong.

Together.

We play through that same bit about five more times in a row before we both stop and look at each other.

"*Whoa*," she breathes.

"Yeah."

I nod, grabbing the pen and adding something that just came to me. And as we keep doing that—playing, stopping, adding, building—suddenly, an hour blurs by. And then two, and then three, until we're lost in this hazy world where time and reality don't really make sense. Where creative seems to hum off the both of us in a way I haven't felt in *years*. In over a decade.

I haven't felt the muse or whatever just flow out of me like this since Iggy.

But the words and the lines keep pouring out. The hours tick by until it's God knows what time in the morning. But there's not stopping, and it's like neither of us *want* to stop.

We're strumming through the second verse that leads into the swell of the chorus, trying to nail down the chord changes exactly, when I hear it. For a second, I think I'm imagining it. Or that it's some weird acoustic effect of the room and how we're sitting—overtones hovering in the air or something.

But it grows louder, and more purposeful. And when I glance up, I almost stop playing entirely.

Her eyes are closed tight, her face crumpled with emotion as we play into the first line of the chorus.

As we play, and she *hums*.

It's not singing. She's not saying the lyrics or even opening her mouth. And yet, the sounds the vibrate like silken strands from her throat are fucking *magic*.

I have to force myself to keep playing, else my stopping will jar her from whatever place the music has taken her—the place where she's actually almost singing, in front of me. The chorus swells, as does her humming, until it peaks...

I immediately strum right into the last bits of the second verse again. She falters for a quarter second, but the reverie doesn't break. Her eyes stay closed tight, like she's locked and lost in that place. And suddenly, as we slide right back into the chorus, I watch magic happen.

Her mouth falls open as her face wrenches with the emotions of the words. And when the first notes break clear and sweet from her throat, I watch a tear trickle from her tightly shut eyes.

And she fucking *sings*.

> *"There's a song in my ear, there's a hope that you're near,*
>
> *When I'm lost on the rocks and I'm sinking*
>
> *When the boats goin' down, all I'm thinkin',*
>
> *Is the melody you sang to me to sleep...*
>
> *Is the one pulling me down to the deep."*

The room goes absolutely silent. I meant to keep playing, but...I lose the ability when Melody opens that mouth and sings pure fucking emotion and magic.

Holy. *Fuck*.

A second of absolute silence hangs over us, before suddenly, her eyes fly open. Her face pales like she's just realized what she's done. And instantly, that emotion turns to ash on her face as she crumples in on herself.

"Oh my God—"

"Melody—"

She all but drops the guitar to the floor as she bolts from the chair. But, no.

This stops *now*.

I know she's in pain. I know that fucking monster from her past hurt her in ways no one—even me—will be able to process or understand to the fullest extent. I know opening her mouth and letting the emotions inside of her come out in the form of sound and voiced colors terrifies her. I know it shoves her right back into that dark fucking hole inside of herself.

But I'm not *letting* her go back there. Not anymore. Not when I've seen the freedom on her face when she actually gets to spread her wings.

"Stop."

She gasps as I jump from my chair, surging in front of her to block her flight from the room. She's shaking, her eyes wild as she tries to dodge past me. But I grab her wrists tight, yanking her into me. I grab her face, forcing her tear-streaked, terrified eyes to look at me.

"Jackson, please…I—"

"*Stop.*"

I shake my head slowly, stabbing my gaze right into the heart of her.

"*Sing.*"

She starts to cry.

"*Jackson—*"

"I know you're fucking scared, sweetheart," I rasp. "But I *know* what I just saw and heard. So, I need you to—"

"*I can't!*" She sobs, choking as she starts to shatter in front of me. But I don't let go. I don't let her look away from my eyes as I lock us together.

"*Yes*, you can."

"*I—!*"

"What he did to you *does not fucking define you.*"

The room hums with the ferocity of my voice and the sharp intake of her breath. She blinks, staring up at me with this mix of anger, fear, heartache, and determination.

"*Own it*," I growl thickly.

I reach for my guitar with one hand, stepping back from her as I sling the strap over my shoulders. Reaching behind, I flick the lights off until just the moon through the big picture window is the only thing letting us see.

She's shaking, her breath hitching in her throat as I step to her again and slowly turn her so that she's facing away from me, out to the ocean.

"*Own* your voice, Melody," I murmur into her ear. "Because it's fucking *yours*."

Her shoulder shake as she starts to quietly cry.

"*Own* it."

My fingers find the chord patterns on the neck of the guitar. I lean down to put my lips right by her ear.

"Don't sing for me. Don't fucking sing to prove anything. Sing for you, sweetheart," I whisper. "Sing for *you*."

My fingers strum out the chords of the verse, finding the tempo as I watch her back. Her shoulders stiffen, and then shake. And then rise and fall with her deep breath as she brings a hand up to wipe the tears from her eyes.

And then slowly, I hear it.

She hums the third line of the verse, and then the start of the fourth before suddenly, words tumble out. My jaw tightens, my eyes locked on her as the emotion builds. As the tension swells, and as the music crescendos into the chorus. And just as I hit that first chord…

An angel opens her mouth, and fucking sings down heaven.

> *"There's a song in my ear, there's a hope that you're near,*
>
> *When I'm lost on the rocks and I'm sinking*
>
> *When the boats goin' down, all I'm thinkin',*
>
> *Is the melody you sang to me to sleep…*
>
> *Is the one pulling me down to the deep."*

She makes it through the chorus twice before she breaks. She turns to me, tears pouring down her face.

But she's smiling.

Sobbing, smiling.

Free.

The guitar slings off my back onto a stand as I slam into her, my hand cupping her face as my lips sear to hers.

26

MELODY

It's the sensation of weight falling from my shoulders. Of air filing my lungs for the first time in longer than I can remember.

Of freedom.

And yet even through the tears of pure joy streaking down my face, and the feeling of walls crashing down around me, kissing him ignites something even more powerful inside of me. His hands on me unlock something I buried deep, alongside my voice when it was silenced.

Raw, unbridled *desire*.

Because it's not just my voice that's ripping free of a cage. It's a *need* that surges so suddenly and so explosively inside of me that it's almost hard to breathe. It consumes me like fire until I'm attacking his mouth with ferocity that almost scares me.

But with him, I'm unafraid. With him, touch becomes pleasure, not a weapon. Intimacy becomes something I crave instead of fear.

I've had his hands on me. I've drowned in the sin of his mouth.

Now, I want it all. I *want* what I've denied myself. I want to know what it feels like for him to be inside of me—for him to have all of me. And there's no stopping this now.

I moan as we crash backwards, his hands sliding over me and grabbing me tightly and possessively. Igniting me. Turning me to liquid fire as he all but rips the buttons off my flannel shirt.

I gasp as it falls open, my fingers shoving his t-shirt up his grooved body before he rips it off his head and tosses it away. We slam together again, and I shiver, relishing the hot sensation of his muscled body against my bare skin—my nipples dragging electrically against him as his hands slide down and into the waist of my panties.

I can feel the throbbing hard bulge of his cock pulsing against my core as we slam back against the piano in the corner of the studio. The lid over the keys is closed, and I moan into his lips as his big hands grab my ass and lift me onto the edge of it.

My legs spread, my core tightening as he slips between them. His fingers trace down the seam of my thigh, and I moan deeply when he slips them under the edge of my panties to run up my slit.

"*Jackson…oh fuck!*"

My jaw goes slack as two of his thick fingers sink into me, stretching me deliciously as he curls them deep to stroke against my g-spot. I yank at his belt, ripping it and his jeans open before shoving them down over his hip. His swollen cock springs free, slapping heavily and hotly against my thigh as I whimper and roll my tongue with his.

My hand drops to his cock, and I shudder at the feeling of him pulsing against my palm. My core quivers at the way his body tightens, and the masculine, deep growl that rumbles in his chest as my small fingers curl around him.

Stroking him.

Pulling him closer.

When I feel the swollen head of his cock tease against my lips, my breath catches. My body jolts, tensing with the need for him as I center him against my slickness. His hands tighten on me, his cock pulsing as he starts to sink between my lips.

"Just…go slow, first?"

Jackson freezes. Instantly, I wince. And when he pulls back, my eyes fly to his.

"Hold on—"

"*Fuck me…*" I whimper, my fingers curling around his cock, trying to pull him into me.

But he grunts, pushing my hand away and letting the electrifying heat of his cock slip from between my lips.

"Melody—"

"*Do it*! I want you—"

"*Stop.*"

I freeze, my breath choking in my throat as my face heats.

"You…*fuck.*"

"Wait, Jackson—"

My face falls as he starts to pull back from me.

"We're not doing this."

"*What? Why?!*"

"Because you—"

"Because I'm a virgin," I snap bitterly.

Hie eyes spark as his jaw tightens.

"*Yes.*"

"And why does that matter if I want you to—"

"It matters," he hisses quietly, his eyes piercing into mine. "Because I'm not going to be someone's ticket stub."

I swallow, my lips thinning.

"I'm not going to be your collector's item—"

"I don't want you because you're famous, Jackson," I whisper hotly. "I don't want you because you've sold a bunch of records, or so I can brag to my friends."

My eyes close, and I shiver when I feel his hand brush a lock of hair from my face.

"All I know, is when I'm with you—when *you* kiss me, or when you touch me—for the first time in my life, I don't want to throw up. I don't want to die, or crawl inside myself until it's over."

My hand drops between us again, my fingers curling around his throbbing hard cock. He groans, and I tremble as I feel his hands grip my thighs tighter.

"I want…Jackson, I *need* you to touch me."

My eyes open, and I shiver as I lose myself in his fierce gaze

"I need you touch me so I can fucking breathe."

He groans, pulling closer to me, his resistance crumbling in front of my eyes. He brings a hand up, cupping my jaw delicately, but with a power held back behind it I can practically feel.

"You might not like the air you get from me when you do," he growls thickly against my lips.

"Let me be the judge of that."

His thumb traces up my thigh, making my breath catch as the movement opens my legs wider.

"I don't play nice, sweetheart."

"I'm not looking for nice."

"I play *rough*."

Sinful, dangerous heat pools in my core.

"I'm not made of glass."

"If you need to stop—"

"And if you need to keep making up excuses for why you can't just fuck me—*oh GOD…*"

I cry out, gasping as he grabs my hip and drives his thick, swollen cock into me. The size of him takes my breath away, and the sensation of his sheer size stretching me open curls my toes as my pulse skips. I look down, and I'm stunned when I realize he's barely inside of me.

"Fuck" I whimper. "Fuck, Jackson—"

"Here's how this is going to work," he rasps into my ear, jolting me as I shudder and throb on the edge of the piano, stretched around his cock.

"For *once*, you're going to shut that mouth of yours."

There's a lethal edge to his tone that just…*fuck*.

It's not sweet nothings. It's not gentle affirmations or encouragement.

It's a decree.

It's a promise—not that I'm about to have sex for the first time. But I'm about to get *fucked* for the first time.

The illicit, dark edge to his voice should scare me, especially since I've never done this before. But it doesn't. The warning in his words should make me second guess all of this.

Not ache for it. Not be on the cusp of literally begging him to fuck me any way he wants.

And maybe that makes me a little fucked up. Maybe there are wires crossed inside of me from what happened those years before, where the sinister sharpness in his voice should make me fear.

But instead, it makes me *wet*.

"*Jackson—*"

Fuck.

I shudder, whimpering as he slams his mouth to mine, kissing me so hard it hurts. And yet, the hurt sends electricity sizzling out to every inch of my skin. It turns me to liquid fire as I feel his head surge inside of me.

"You're going to shut this fucking mouth," he rasps darkly against my lips. "You're going to spread those pretty legs, and you're going to take my cock as deep as I fucking want, like a good little slut."

I swear to God, I almost come just from his words. It's like his voice itself is teasing over my most sensitive, weakest nerve points. Like he's inside my head, ripping the doors off my most primal, darkest thoughts and fantasies to feast on them.

"You're going to take my cock as deep as I want, and as hard as I want. Aren't you, my good girl?"

I can't speak words. All I can do is whimper pathetically, nodding with wide, lust-filled eyes.

"I'll take that as a yes."

He drives in deeper, and I squeal in pure pleasure as feel myself stretching around him.

"In fact, the only thing I need to hear from your mouth, sweetheart," he groans thickly. "Is either *harder*, *faster*, or to tell me when you're going to come. Is that clear?"

I'm shaking and shuddering everywhere as I nod my head eagerly, my eyes wide. His lips brush down my jaw to my ears as he grinds into me, wrenching a whimper from my lips as his tease again my ear.

"That's my good girl."

Sweet Jesus.

He slides out, that thick, swollen head of his dragging over every nerve ending inside of me as I coil and shudder in pleasure. He runs the head up and down my slit again, pushing it over my clit before he centers and drives back in.

Hard, and to the hilt with one breath-arresting, toe-curling thrust.

Holy. *Fuck*.

His hand tangles in my hair, gripping it in a fist at the back of my head as his lips feast on mine—bruising and biting and sucking until I'm shaking all over from the intensity of the most vicious kiss in the history of kisses.

My body explodes with heat when he drives his thick cock deep into me. My thighs quiver, my legs locking around his muscled hips as my nails dig into his side.

"*Harder*," I choke, my eyes rolling back.

Jackson groans, and I cry out as he pounds into me. My nails dig into his skin, urging him on as I lose myself in the unbridled, forbidden heat.

"I thought I said *harder*," I whimper, goading him on as I start to sink into the pure ecstasy of everything I'm feeling.

Jackson growls a dark chuckle. His hand grips my hair and my hip tighter, and I cry out when his teeth bite the soft skin of my neck. He thrusts in savagely, his muscles coiling and bulging as he pounds deeper.

As he starts to utterly claim me.

As I start to completely lose myself in him.

"*Faster…*"

My hips rock to meet his thrusts, and my legs wrap tight around his muscled hips. I cling to him, urging him on with my head falling back and my mouth falling open. His lips and teeth drag across my neck, and his fingers leave their mark on my skin. My nipples rake across his hard chest as his thick cock drives into me over and over again.

"Jackson—"

"I know, sweetheart," he rasps thickly against my ear. "I can feel your greedy little pussy squeezing my cock so tight."

His hand slips from my hair and slides to my neck. And when his strong, powerful fingers wrap around my throat, suddenly, I know I'm about to lose all control.

"Now be a good girl for me, and fucking *come* on that fat fucking dick."

It's like the entire world erupts under my feet. It's like the sun explodes, blinding me and engulfing me in liquid fire. My entire body wrenches and spasms, the orgasm ripping through every single inch of me as my eyes roll back.

His mouth crushes to mine, suffocating me but also giving me air—swallowing my screams of pleasure as he groans savagely and sinks deep inside of me. His cock surges and pumps, spilling his cum deep inside as he holds me tight against him.

As his lips sear to mine.

As I lose any and all control and completely lose myself in him.

27

MELODY

My head drops back as I cry out, my face crumpling as my nails dig into his chest. His hips thrust hard, burying his swollen cock deep inside of me as I crash screaming over the edge of ecstasy.

Jackson groans, his big hands circling my waist and gripping my ass hard enough to leave bruises as he follows me into oblivion. My back arches, my throat closing with the pressure of my release as I ride him through my orgasm until I'm about to collapse.

And then, I do. Collapse, that is. It's like someone cuts the strings, and I fall like a rag doll onto his chest. I shudder, trembling and sucking in ragged breaths of air as his arms circle me and hold me tight. My head swims as I sink into him, my cheek against his skin.

Holy. *Fuck*.

Everything hurts. Everything is sore, and achy, and tender. Which is probably because I've spent almost the entirety of the last three days in bed with Jackson while we screwed each other to within an inch of our lives.

Well, mine, at least. I shudder, my skin sheened with sweat and marred with bruises in the shape of his fingers. I wince as I slide off him and tumble to his side.

Fuck am I sore. I've been sore for the last two days. And yet, we've kept this fuck-marathon going at an inhuman level for a frankly ridiculous number of rounds in a row—breaking only for the occasional shower, food, and beverages.

It's as if my pussy is unable to decide anymore if it's actual sexual need that has me ignoring the pure physical fatigue and spreading my legs around him for a fortieth time, or if it's just some sort of masochist competitive drive.

Or maybe I've just become a full-blown addict for his dick.

Actually, I'm reasonably sure that's literally what's happened here. Because I crave him like a fiend every single second of every single day. I crave the possessive way he pins me down and *fucks* me—not just making love or having sex. When Jackson's eyes turn that steely blue shade of fire, and his jaw ticks with desire…

Fuck.

It's like I morph into this dick-crazed addict for him. Moreover, it's awakened parts of me I've honestly never explored, or even really understood about myself. For instance, apparently, for all my usual sass and—admittedly—prickly New Yorker attitude, I'm actually submissive; sexually, that is. Or, at least with Jackson I sure as hell am.

Desperately, eagerly so.

Submissive and possibly a bit of a masochist. Not just because I can't seem to stay off him even when my body is flagging behind and sore everywhere. But because I think I might actually get off *because* of that at times.

The way I crumple to shuddering, gasping pieces when he spanks me hard, or when he bites my nipples, with teeth, when he drives into me.

I'm not about to start playing with clothespins and whips or anything. But there's at least a degree of pain that I think I actually crave in our play.

I should probably look up my old therapist and tell her to go ahead and buy that vacation home.

I shift against Jackson, but this time, I wince in real pain as my legs slide together.

"*Ow*, fuck…"

His brow furrows in concern as he glances down into my face. I smile weakly.

"Just…sore."

He grins. "I think we need to take a break."

"Yeah, well, tell that to *him*."

I nod my chin at his still impossibly hard, very swollen, very —somehow, even in my painful state—*incredibly* enticing cock.

Jackson lifts a shoulder.

"Eh. I stopped trying to reason with him decades ago."

I roll my eyes.

"Yeah, well, I'm officially closed for—*Jackson!*"

I gasp as he rolls me onto my back, pushing my thighs apart as he slides between them. Part of me screams inside that if he tries to fuck me again, I'm literally going to cry, even if *so much* of me wants him to. But…I mean, the human body has limits. Or at least, *mine* does.

"Jackson, ple—*oh…*"

But it's not his cock that moves between my legs.

It's his mouth. And when his tongue drags with maddeningly slow and yet exquisitely gentle strokes up and down my slit, my head rolls back in bliss.

"Oh God…"

"Jackson or Jack will do," he growls into my pussy as he slowly turns me to a puddle on his bed.

I'm still sore, but the way he slowly and teasingly devours me somehow melts that ache away. The delicate and devilish way his tongue *slowly* swirls over my clit until my toes are cramping has me arching my back off the bed. My fingers clench the blankets in fists, my mouth hanging open in a silent scream.

"You know what I want, sweetheart," he growls into my folds. "So, stop holding out on me. Stop trying to hold back and give me that orgasm. Let me taste your sweetness when you fucking come all over my tongue like a good girl."

My core spasms violently, my body jerking and writhing as the scream caught in my throat erupts from my mouth. I cry out, shattering for him when my hips raise greedily against his mouth as I come.

I collapse back into the bed in a state of bewilderment and vibrating nerve endings.

"If you're *actually* trying to kill me…" I mumble, turning to stare at him with hazy, unfocused orgasm eyes as he flops across the bed next to me. "You're doing an incredible job."

"Always nice to hear from a fan."

I giggle, rolling my eyes as I sink into the sheets. My head twists a little, my gaze dragging towards the late morning sun streaming in through the windows. Instantly, my face lines a little at the reality we've both been steadfastly ignoring.

The storm was over two days ago.

And already, most of the snow from it is melting away, too. And with it, the entire basis for why I've been camped out on Havoc Island for almost a week now.

When it was still blizzarding outside, I could tell myself *that's* why I was here. Even if, yes, it came with the benefit of a mind-blowing fuckathon with a sex *god*. Or with the benefit of finding my voice and writing with Jackson.

The storm, and the fact that I quite literally *couldn't* leave, acted like a sort of safety net. But that nets been gone for two days now, even if we've been doing our best to ignore it or bury that reality with sex.

Lots, and *lots* of sex.

"Want a lift?"

My brow raises as I feel him slide up behind me, wrapping his arms around me as we both look out the window at reality.

"To…?"

"Melody."

I frown as I twist my head to look at him.

"Storm's over, sweetheart," he growls quietly.

"So?"

His mouth twists, a brow arching.

"You've got people who are going to start wondering if you've driven off a cliff or something."

"They know where I—"

"Melody."

"Are you trying to get rid of me?"

He rolls his eyes.

"Hey, I'm just looking out for *me*. You go missing, and they're going to start poking around the last place you were seen, which happens to be my backyard. I don't need that kind of heat."

I giggle at his dry sarcasm.

"Watch it, or I'll disappear and Gone Girl your ass."

"Huh?"

"Gone Girl?"

"Is that a reference I should know?"

"The movie based on the book?"

His brow furrows in a lack of recognition.

"Oh my God, you've been on this island for *way* too long."

Jackson just shrugs.

"If it's not Charles Bukowski or Bastian Pierce, I probably haven't read it."

"Oh my God, I *love* Bastian Pierce. *Fucked Sideways* is a favorite."

He grins. "I'm partial to *God $ave The Queen*."

"Ooo, also great."

We're stalling, and we both know it.

Jackson sighs.

"So, you want a ride or not?"

"It might be faster than swimming."

"Less wet, too."

I gasp as I feel his thick cock pulse against my ass and where my thighs meet.

"Unlike some things…"

I blush. But slowly, I raise one leg, and I shiver as I push back against him.

"Melody…"

Trembling, my hand snakes back, and I bite back a moan when my fingers wrap around his huge, throbbing, gorgeous cock. I shift, guiding his head lower with a gaps on my lips as I feel it spread me open from behind.

"You're sore—"

"Make it hurt."

An hour and a half later, after a very much needed shower and a chilly boat ride across the bay, I step off Jackson's boat onto the dock. For a second, when he steps up after me and ties off the boat, I want to turn and sink into his arms. I want to kiss him with everything I have as the winter sea wind whips around us.

I frown.

Except, I can't do that. Not here. Not when Albert and the whole town thinks he's Robbie, and I'm his niece.

I mean, *yikes*.

Instead, I blush as I playfully squeeze his hand, like a dorky schoolgirl with a crush. He responds with a subtle and hidden swat of his palm against my ass, and I giggle as I skip up the gangway to shore.

"Well, you two look like you survived that one okay, ayuh?"

I smile at Albert at the top of the dock.

"Definitely. Everything good over here?"

He shrugs. "Can't complain. Well, 'cept the cable when out across town while the Sox were giving the Yankees a beating."

Albert smirks at me.

"You're a New Yorker, aren't you?"

"Yeah, but the kind that doesn't give a crap about baseball."

He chuckles, nodding as he laughs.

"Oh, and thanks for making those calls, Albert."

He shrugs. "Not a problem. Your friend June seems like a peach."

I grin. "She is."

"That boss of yours is real prick though."

I wince.

"Sorry about that one."

"He's called me personally about a dozen times since."

Fuck.

I reach into my pocket and yank my phone out, which I've had turned off for days since I don't have service on the island anyway. When I turn it on, my stomach flip-flops as the missed calls and texts notifications start chiming like a mad orchestra.

Albert whistles.

"Well damn. Did you go viral, or whatever they call it?"

I glance at Jackson, in full "Robbie" mode with his hat pulled low, his jacket zipped all the way up, and the almost comical looking sunglasses.

"I'm…going to go check my messages. I'll meet you back here at the docks, Uncle Rob?"

He smirks, but he sticks up a thumb before nodding his chin in the direction of the Clam Shack bar.

"See you soon, Albert."

"Ayuh."

I head up into the town and end up ducking out of the wind behind the same hardware store where I first bumped into Jackson. Which, now, feels like months ago. I open my phone and feel my stomach drop

Fuck me, I have over a hundred missed called in the last few days. A bunch from June, one or two from Becca, a *ton* from Chuck, and—oddly—more calls from Judy that I usually get in a year.

My brow furrows as I flip to my texts. Jesus Christ, it's even worse. Hundreds of them which never delivered while I was on the island, but are now all popping up at once. I catch the few from Becca first, which immediately freak me out.

> *Hey girl! I heard you're snowed in, but you HAVE to get in touch with Chuck. He's flipping the fuck out about this shit with your mom, and he wants this story you're working on bad. Call me.*

I frown. What "shit with my mom"? I mean, aside from the usual litany of bullshit surrounding Judy.

The ones from Chuck I can't even look at, because there are *a ton* of them, and they all seem to be varied versions of "call me right fucking now" or "where the fuck is my fucking story?!" Or "DID YOU FIND HIM".

I start to read through June's texts when my voicemail notification pings. On top of the avalanche of voicemails from the last few days, I apparently have a fresh one from Chuck that I missed by like ten minutes.

My stomach knots, but I hit the play button anyway as I bring it to my ear.

"Okay, this is my last motherfucking call, kid! I don't give a fuck if you're snowed in, because right now all I know is, this shit with your mom is about to go fuckin' nuclear, and I NEED that goddamn Havoc story yesterday. YESTERDAY, MELODY! I swear to fucking Christ, if I don't hear back from you in the next two

hours, I'm canceling that goddamn card you've been milking at that bumfuck motel of yours, and your ass is gone. Two hours, kid. I mean it."

My face falls in horror. Holy *shit*. One, that crappy motel has apparently been billing the Ignition corporate card since the day I checked in, almost a week ago. Which is…shitty. But more importantly?

What shit with my mom?

I'm a millisecond away from thumbing June's number, when my phone buzzes with an incoming call that makes me grin as I answer.

"Mind reader, I was *just* about to call you—"

"Melody *where* have you been!?"

I wince at the fear and concern in June's voice.

"I'm *so* sorry. Albert did call you, right?"

"The guy with the Maine accent? I mean, yeah? But that was like five days ago!"

"I'm sorry, I'm sorry," I wince, making a face. "Where I was staying up here got dumped on with snow, and the service is nonexistent."

June exhales.

"It's okay, I was just really worried about you."

My nose wrinkles.

"I know, and I'm sorry to have just gone off the map like that."

"I mean what music-related story are you even doing up there in the hinterlands?"

"I…" I swallow. "I'd better tell you in person. It's…kind of a big deal."

It's the other piece of reality that I've been putting to the back of my mind over the last week. The part where I'm sitting on the most explosive music news story of the last decade.

And I'm not going to tell it.

I wondered about it for a few days there—if I'd tell it but downplay it. Or if I'd tell it and somehow hide where I'd found him. But in the end?

No.

Jackson was right. It's not the world's story at all. It's his. His life, his decisions, his pain. His story.

I know this is going to cost me the job at Ignition. But I've made peace with that. I think, at least.

"Well, when you get here, I can't wait to hear it."

I chew on my lip.

"Yeah…about that. I…might be hanging out up here for a little while longer."

I grin to myself, feeling my face heat. No, there's not some weird trepidation in my chest or the big question mark of "if that's okay with Jackson". Because I know we've crossed that line somewhere in the last week, buried in snow, music, and ecstasy.

I'm not a child, and I know this isn't a Disney story. I know us fucking each other's brains out for five days doesn't mean we're a "we" at all. I know it doesn't mean I'm moving in with him or anything ridiculous like that.

But I know it means I don't want to leave yet. And a bit broken and bunch inexperienced that I am, I *know* by the way he looks at me and by the way he holds me tightly that he's not ready for me to leave yet, either.

I grin a goofy smile to no-one as I blush.

"I dunno. I just…I like it up here, and—"

"Melody are you fucking serious?"

There's a weird tone to her voice that sets me on edge.

"What do you mean?"

"Oh my God, you haven't talked to Judy."

Fuck. Now what.

"No, I literally just got to a spot with service for the first time in days. What's—"

"You haven't been online at all?"

"Nothing."

My brow furrows as a chill creeps over me.

"Wait, what the hell is Judy—"

"Mel, she's got another book coming out. A big one. That interview she had with Rolling Stone lit a *fire* under the whole 'where is Jackson Havoc' story."

I shiver. "You're joking."

"I'm really not. She's saying it's a tell-all *entirely* about him, too."

My skin crawls. "*What?*"

"Yeah, she apparently had this whole thing with him?"

Part of me wants to vomit. And the reason I don't is because I *know* Judy's full of shit. Just like I know this is her chasing a glimpse of limelight. Judy *did not* hook up with Jackson. And the reason I know that is because I would have heard about it, on repeat, years ago.

I groan.

"It's all just fantasy Judy bullshit!"

"Well, people are freaking out about it, dude. She's even going on The Late Show this weekend to talk about it, and...Mel?"

There's a hesitancy in her voice.

"What?"

"She's been dropping hints that there's a whole bunch about *you* in the book, too."

My jaw sets.

No. *Hell* no.

I didn't have a say when I was kid. When Judy would give some stupid interview and paint this cutesy picture of her raising me as free spirit on the road, surrounded by love and music, I didn't have the voice, agency, or even option to give my side of things. To refute that cutesy picture and paint the real one that involved hunger, fear, creeps, missing my own birthdays, not having friends...being molested when I was thirteen by my mother's own boyfriend.

My teeth grind painfully as my eyes narrow to slits.

I didn't have a say back then. Now, I've got a *whole* hell of a lot to say. And if Judy thinks she's going to milk some more cash out of desperate Velvet Guillotine fans with a book made from complete bullshit, and use *my* childhood and suffering to sell it?

She's about to get my full wrath. Because that is *not* happening. Not anymore.

"Look, Mel—"

"I have to go," I blurt. "But I'll see you soon."

"When?"

I close my eyes, my heart sinking even as I say the word.

"Tonight."

28

JACKSON

Every song ends. Every refrain comes to a stop, and eventually, the house lights have to come up.

It's just that for the majority of my career, I always made sure to be backstage somewhere buried in as much escape and distraction as I could get my hands on when those house lights *did* come up. Because I always hated that part of a concert, even ones where I was in the audience.

I hate it because it means the fantasy escape that you just fell into is gone. The experience of sharing music with a band and a bunch of strangers just ended. That shared temporary religion—and to me, that shit *is* religion—is over when the lights come up. Which is why once the option was there for me, I made sure to never be around when they did. If only to pretend that the magic lived on.

Standing in my living room watching Melody glumly stuff her meager belongings back into her backpack feels like being blinded by the house lights.

My jaw sets.

I'm not a child, or some heartbroken, puppy-eyed teenager. This isn't a movie, and I of all people understand that two adults spending a whole lotta time fucking each other does not a relationship or commitment make.

It's just that I'm doing everything in my fucking power to ignore the little voice in my head screaming that this is different. Because I have to. Because I need that voice to shut the fuck up.

Because she really is walking out the door right now.

There's a very Bruce Springsteen or maybe Humphrey Bogart part of me that wants to walk up to her, tilt her face up with a suave finger to the chin, and tell her take care out there. To kiss her once and let her walk out aching for more.

To watch her leave knowing I've left her better than she was before. That somewhere out there, there'll be some guy her own age to make her smile. And even though he'll never make her smile like me, and he'll *damn well* never make her scream like me, she'll be mostly happy, and almost certainly better out there in the world without me in her life.

I scowl.

Yeah, fuck whatever movie I lifted that from.

Instead, my heart smolders with a black cloud as I watch her zip the backpack and sling it over her shoulder with a heavy sigh. She looks up, and our eyes lock.

And she starts to cry.

Shit.

I erase the distance between us in a second, grabbing her in my arms. My dumbass Bogart "here's lookin' at you, kid" fantasy shatters, and I hold her fiercely as she cries into my chest.

I know she has to go. Of course, she does. She's got a life back in the real world, and friends, and a job.

And I've got…well, I almost want to make a self-depreciating crack about "whiskey, drugs, and no one around to annoy me". But it suddenly hits me that my weird romcom-tinged fantasy about "leaving her better than she was before" is actually the opposite of what it really is.

I'm the "her" in this situation.

I'm the one *she's* leaving better off than I was before.

I just hate that the "better off" part comes with the "her leaving" part. I mean I really, really fucking hate that part.

"I…" she sniffs into my chest, her fingers digging into me. Slowly, she raises her tear-streaked face and her swollen eyes to me. Her lip catches in her teeth, and my heart clenches.

"I could come back…I mean, if it's okay, I could—"

"I think I'd like that a whole lot."

She grins, her face flushing.

"I mean, someone has to clean up your shit."

"For sure."

"And keep you from drinking yourself into a coma."

"There's that."

"And write hit new songs for you."

"Calm down."

She giggles, choking on a sob as she hugs me again.

"Come on," I growl quietly. "Or you'll miss that ride to the airport."

She nods, and her hand slips into mine as we walk out of the house and down to the dock. Across the bay, Albert's nobly volunteered to drive her to the airport in Bangor, where she's catching a flight back to New York.

The boat skims across the waves, the air stinging our cheeks the whole way over to Cape Harbor. When we get to the docks, mercifully, Albert's out of sight getting his truck ready.

I use the opportunity to grab her, yank her into me, tilt her face up, and absolutely bruise the fuck out of that mouth with mine.

"You know my door is always open."

"I know your door is always *unlocked*," she giggles as her chest hitches with a sob.

"So, just let yourself in when you come then, yeah?"

She nods vigorously, wiping tears from her eyes as they lock with mine.

"Count on it."

"Hey Mel!" Albert's voice shatters the moment. "You 'bout ready?"

Melody pulls away from, her hands locked with mine until those too slip away.

"I'll be back," she mouths quietly.

I just smile, nodding as she turns to walk up the gangway. I follow a second or two later, watching as she slips into Albert's beat up old Chevy. Taillights bathe me in red as it pulls away.

With her.

With my muse.

With a piece of my heart I didn't even know I still had, and damn well know I'm not thrilled about losing.

When they're out of sight, I glance at my boat. Then over to the Clam Shack. Maybe someday—soon, ideally—this is a demon I'll walk away from.

But it sure as fuck isn't going to be today.

I walk directly into the bar, with every intention of drinking until I can't think of her face anymore.

But something tells me, it's going to be a very, very long night.

29

MELODY

Everything hurts.

It's something I've groaned to myself a couple dozen times over the last few days. But those times, it was through a hazy smile, my entire body still tingling with orgasm. And usually still wrapped in Jackson's arms.

This time, it carries more weight. This time, I really, really mean it.

Everything hurts.

My body, yes. I'm still bruised and roughened in places no one really ever wants to be bruised or tender in. But at least that part of the hurt has the memory of ecstasy and bliss attached to it.

It's the hurt in my chest—in my heart—that truly almost brings me to my knees.

But right now, it's also the hurt that comes with walking away from opportunity. Even if, ultimately, I'm actually not even sure it's the "big break" I ever really wanted. Maybe it really was all about Judy, after all. Maybe trying to land this thing with Ignition really was just about proving something to myself.

Which, if that's the case, I failed at. Seeing as the whole reason I even got the assignment was because I blurted out Judy's fucking name.

But it doesn't matter. All I know is, this ride is over.

It's late. Chuck glares at me across the desk, his shoulders slumping as I nod.

"I'm sure."

He sighs heavily.

"Well…*fuck*, Mel."

"I'm really sorry, Chuck."

"I mean, a fuckin' week up there, and *nothing*? I though you said you found him!"

I smile and shake my head sadly.

"Most of that was just getting stuck up there with that storm. I really, *really* thought it was him, though. I mean I had a local source who swore it was, and this guy even kind of looked like Havoc. But…" I shake my head. "It wasn't him, Chuck."

He blows air through his lips, sinking back in his chair.

"Shit. And with your mom's new fuckin' book coming out, this would have been gold."

I don't say anything as my lips twist.

"You're sure?"

"It wasn't him. Look, Chuck, I can pay you back for the plane tickets and the motel—"

"Stop."

He shakes his head, and when he looks up at me again, he's actually smiling wryly. He's even looking at my face instead of my tits.

"You did good, Mel. I mean, it'd be better if you'd found him, but you put the effort in. I can appreciate that."

My brows lift.

"Yeah?"

"Yeah. Not a lot of people would have stuck that out."

"Thanks, Chuck, I really appreciate that."

He shrugs.

"So…" My brows knit. "Do I—"

"Work here? Oh, yeah, no."

My shoulders sink, but it's fine.

"Sorry, kid. The gig was dependent on you landing the Havoc story." He shrugs. "That's journalism. Sorry."

"No, that's fine, I get it."

I know I've got the music news of the decade in my hands. But I also know I'm not telling it. Because it's not mine to tell, and it's not the world's to use up and cut to pieces.

Instead, I smile, shake Chuck's hand, thanks him again for the opportunity, and then walk out the door.

"Mel!"

Outside Chuck's office in the general bullpen area of the Ignition offices, I startle as Becca, June's reporter acquaintance who got me the initial interview here, runs up to me.

"Hey…" she makes a face when she sees mine. "Oh, *shit*."

I shrug. "Oh, it's fine. I mean, I didn't get the story. And the job was only mine if I did."

She gives me a slightly overdone sympathetic look and hugs me as if we're good old friends. I'm reminded of June's thoughts from before my trip that the only reason Becca even got me that interview is because she wanted a story with June.

"Hey, publishing is hard, Mel."

"Totally."

"Well, I'm sure there'll be something else!"

I smile. "Well, we'll see, I guess. And thanks, Becca. I mean for getting me the interview. I really appreciate it."

She shrugs and waves me off. "No worries."

Her brow ticks though. She glances around and then leans conspiratorially close.

"It's true, then?"

I frown. "What?"

"That you were really up in Maine looking for Jackson *Havoc*?"

I stiffen, heat flooding my face before I can swallow it back.

"Oh…yeah, but," I laugh nervously and wave my hand. "A total dead end. I had a source that had me convinced. But I think it was either a scam or just mistaken identity. There's a guy who looks like Havoc, but it's definitely not him."

Becca's eyes lance into me, peering deep in a way that makes me shift uncomfortably.

"You're sure?"

"That it wasn't him?"

She nods.

"Uh, yeah? Pretty sure!"

She clicks her tongue to her teeth.

"Man, too bad. That'd be a killer story."

"Yeah, seriously."

"Plus, I mean…dude was hot when he was thirty. What is he, forty-two now?"

I swallow thickly, shifting.

"Something like that."

"I bet he's a fucking *DILF* now."

My face and neck swarm with heat as I laugh nervously.

"I mean, aside from the 'dad' part of 'DILF', yeah, totally."

Very, very totally the "I'd like to fuck" part.

Becca smiles. "Well, aside from everything, how was Maine? I *love* going up to Portland."

"Oh, beautiful. Stunning, actually. I'd never been before. We got a crazy snow storm, but—"

"We?"

I stiffen.

"I…just mean we like the town where I was camped out." I shake my head. "Like total blizzard."

"Ooo, I bet that was gorgeous. Did you take any pictures?"

Several. It's just that a ton of them involve Jackson.

"I…yeah, actually!"

I smile as I slide my phone out of my bag and tap on my photos. Quickly, ignoring my thudding pulse, I select a couple shots I took that just show snow through a window, or of Cape Harbor, or of the ocean. Pictures that obviously *do not* involve Jackson, or his house. I swallow as I create a new folder and copy the selected pics into it.

"Sorry," I blush, glancing over the phone at Becca. "Just editing one of them real quick. Here."

I click on the separate folder of just the pics I selected and place the phone on the desk we're standing next to.

Becca gasps.

"Oh *wow*, it's beautiful!"

"Yeah, I'm…" I swallow as my core tightens. "I'm definitely going back. I loved it."

"I bet!" She grins at me. "Oh! By the way, since June is your roommate and all…I've been trying to reach out to her about this story I've been dying to write."

I hold back the smile, remembering my friend's reluctance to have anything to do with Becca's story.

"Would you ask her if she got my emails? And voicemails? I think I texted a couple times, too."

And would you take a hint?

"I'll totally ask her. I'm sure she's just been busy. She plays out like four times a week."

"Cool, thanks Mel—"

"MELODY!"

I jolt, whirling as Chuck's office door yanks open and he sticks his head out of it. His eyes bulge and then narrow when he sees me.

"You're still here!"

I pale. "I'm so sorry, I was just—"

"Shut up, you're not in trouble. Get your ass in here, though."

I tremble, my feet tripping over themselves as I rush to his office and follow him inside.

"Shut the door."

I close it and turn to see him pacing the room.

"Your mom might've just given you a second shot."

"She what?"

"You know she's going to be on the Late Show tomorrow, yeah?'

My jaw sets.

"Yes, I do."

"And you know that tapes *tonight?*"

"I didn't know that, but…okay?"

Chuck grins. "I've got a source on the set crew. You know, to pick up info before shit goes live to anyone else. That sort of thing."

I nod uneasily.

"Mel, your mom is taping that show right now, and my guy says she's spilling a fuckin' *treasure trove* of stuff."

"How does that—"

"A lot of stuff about *you*, actually."

I stiffen, blinking rapidly as my pulse kicks up a notch.

"I don't get what you mean."

"This new tell-all book about her thing with Havoc."

"She didn't *have* a thing with him, though."

He shrugs. "Who the fuck cares? She's going to sell a million goddamn copies anyway."

Chuck stabs a finger at me.

"You want a gig here?"

I frown. "Um, I—"

"Of course, you do!" He barks. "And I'll tell you what. It's yours, kid. I mean it. The job is yours, if you can leak me whatever shit is in that book about you before it hits shelves next month."

My jaw drops.

"*Next month*?! I thought she'd just announced this crap?"

He rolls his eyes. "C'mon, you know how these things work. She's probably had a ghostwriter or two hacking away at it for months. Your mom isn't a dummy when it comes to self-promo, Mel. I'll give her that."

I grit my teeth as my fury simmers.

"Well?"

"Sorry, what?"

"Well, what's in that book about you?"

I stare at him, shaking.

"I…*nothing*!" I blurt angrily. "Chuck, it's all *bullshit*!"

"Well then go play the nice daughter to mommy and get her to tell you exactly what that bullshit is! I can read between the lines, Melody. You and your mom obviously aren't chummy. So, if she wants to fuck you with this book of lies?" He shrugs. "Fuck her back first and leak that shit to me before her book goes to print."

"Yeah, but it's *lies*—"

"I don't give a fuck!!" He roars, shaking me as he pounds his desk.

"You want a fucking job at my *fucking* magazine, kid?! You think I give a shit if you can write an article? No! I want you because of your mom. And specifically, your mom's juicy Penthouse letters celebrity music gossip!"

I swallow as he jabs a finger at me angrily.

"I can't believe *I* have to keep pitching *you* on a fucking job here, Mel! But here it is one more time. Get me the juicy details of Judy's book, as they pertain to you, and you can have a gig here at—hey! HEY! Get the fuck back here when I'm talking to you!"

But I don't.

Fuck Judy. And very much fuck the idea of working here.

I storm out, ignoring Chuck's threats that if I do, I'll never work in publishing again. Because…I just don't care right now.

Becca looks at me with a pale face and a weird nervous smile on her face.

"Um…yikes?"

I smile thinly as I walk past her.

"Thanks again for getting me the interview, Becca. I'll let June know to call you back."

"Okay! Thanks! Oh, Mel!" She runs after me and smiles as she hands me the phone I apparently left on the desk when Chuck barked at me to come into his office again.

"Don't forget your phone!"

30

MELODY

"*Christ*, Melody!"

Judy's hand flies to her chest, her eyes bulging as she backs flat against her dressing room door.

"You scared the absolute shit out of me!"

One of June's friends, a sound tech who also happens to work on the set for The Late Show, let me into the studios while they were wrapping taping for tomorrow's show. I've been waiting for Judy in her guest dressing room. And I glare at her as she tries to catch her breath.

"What did you put in there?"

She frowns. "Beg your pardon?"

"Your *book*, Judy. What the fuck is in there about me?"

She rolls her eyes, turning to march over to a mirrored vanity ringed with lights. She pulls a compact out of her bag, and I am every shade of completely not surprised when it's revealed to be full of cocaine, not foundation.

I glare at her through the mirror as she dips the edge of a credit card into the white powder and takes a bump up her left nostril.

"It's just…" she waves a hand, blinking quickly as she sniffs. "It's just a book, Melody."

"Am I in it?"

She shrugs noncommittally and takes another bump up the other nostril.

"JUDY."

"Will you fucking *relax*!?" She snaps. "My God. Do you need a Xanax or something?"

"What I need is for you, for *once*, to just stop lying and living in this fucking fantasy land, and to just *tell me the truth*!"

She turns, her eyes narrowing lethally.

"Fantasy land?"

"Judy, just—"

"IT. IS. *MOM*!" She roars with a fury that actually jolts me. She lurches to her feet, glaring nastily and jabbing a finger threateningly at me.

"It's fucking *mom* to you, you ungrateful brat! And that *fantasy land* brought you into this world! And gave you a roof over your head—"

"Will Cates put a roof over my head," I snap.

"Because of *me*!"

"*Don't*," I hiss dangerously, shaking my head. "Don't you go down that road."

"And which road is that Melody."

"The 'because of you' road." My mouth thins. "Don't."

"Oh, please. It's *all* because of me!"

"NO SHIT!"

The words erupt from my mouth like the black cloud of death before the volcano blows. Judy pales, backing away from me as I surge across the dressing room towards her, my teeth bared savagely.

"Yeah, Judy! It was *all* because of you! Even—"

"Don't you dare—"

"EVEN *HIM*."

She swallows, blinking rapidly as her face lines and pales.

"That's…that's not fair—"

I bark a cold, vicious laugh.

"*You* let him in. *You* knew he was a fucking creep, and you *knew* how he looked at me."

"You…you just—"

"And you *left me* alone with him!" I choke, shaking as the tears start to rip down my cheeks. "You're my *mom*," I sob as my legs start to shake. "And you fed me to a fucking monster—!"

"You were so jealous of what I had!"

The words hit like a slap, even if I've heard them before. But other times, they were implied.

This time, she just took the gloves off.

"You..." I blink, staring at her. "You can't seriously—"

"You were always such a jealous child," she hisses through tears. "So greedy. Always wanting more more more."

"*Fuck. You,*" I choke.

"You knew how I felt about him," she sneers. "And you tried to take him for yourself—"

I can't do this.

I won't do this.

"And then you go throwing around accusations because you bit off more than you were ready to chew—"

"Judy."

"And you tried to *ruin* his name! His whole career! And if it hadn't been for me—"

"JUDY!" I roar.

She stiffens, blinking at me.

"*What.*"

"Goodbye."

I turn and walk to the door.

"The hell do you mean, *goodbye*?" She snaps.

I stop, half turning to look at her over my shoulder. Years ago, even months ago...even two weeks ago, this might have broken me. I mean really, truly, finally broken me.

But I faced this darkness, in the arms of someone incredible, on an island in Maine, surrounded by music and warmth.

And I'm not afraid anymore.

"I mean this is the last time we're going to speak."

Our eyes lock, hers growing wide.

"*Ever.*"

I turn for the door.

"Melody."

I start to open it.

"Melody, *stop*! Melody!"

I'm about to walk right through it and out of her life forever when she drops the bomb.

"If you walk away, you'll never know."

I stop.

Fuck.

Slowly, I glare back at her.

"Know what."

She swallows, drawing herself up, her eyes narrowing as she smiles thinly at me.

"Who he is."

My pulse skips a beat. I blink.

I know exactly what she means. I just hate so much that it's working to stop me.

"Tell me."

She purses her lips. My eyes narrow.

"Tell me who my dad is. Or was."

Her lip curls.

"You already know, anyway."

I stare at her, the floor dropping out as the room grows cold.

"It was Will, wasn't it?"

She says nothing.

"Tell me."

She turns slowly, lifting her credit card and the compact full of drugs off the vanity and scooping up a little bump.

"Judy!"

She ignores me as she sniffs the powder up her nose.

"Is it Will?!"

Slowly, she turns back, sneering coldly at me.

"You'll have to read the book." She shrugs. "And sorry. No freebies."

31

MELODY

The crowd lurches to their feet around me, clapping wildly. And for the first time since I walked in here, it yanks me from the dark cloud I've been trapped in. I blink, startling to my own feet and following the crowd in applause.

Which makes me the shittiest friend ever, I know. But it's also frankly a miracle that I even made it from midtown to the East Village without getting hit by a taxi. Or without just falling to the sidewalk and shattering like glass.

Up on stage, the amazing June Hendrix—aka, my roommate and best friend—takes a graceful bow. Her wild and yet gorgeous wavy tangles of red hair flops over her face before she rights herself and grins at the crowd.

"Thanks so much for comin' out tonight, y'all. Love you guys."

The crowd, predictably, eats that up. They eat up everything June does, like the Tennessee in her that seems to disappear in the streets of New York but comes roaring out on stage. And they're not eating it up because any of it is a gimmick.

They eat her up because she's *incredible*. And it's an actual crime that she's not selling out world tours.

Or even this dumb bar, for that matter.

Her fans are fiercely loyal. But they're a small bunch. For now, at least. Or who knows. In a fair world, she'd be all over the airwaves and playing Radio City Music Hall tonight, not Smokey's Joint way out on Avenue C. But, then again, the world is very clearly not a fair place.

After the show, I wait by the far side of the bar for June to slowly make her way through the small crowd waiting for her. Even in my foul mood, I grin a little when I see her posing for selfies with her fans, and even signing a copy of her last album on vinyl.

For a second, it hits me how weird it is to see June working *so fucking hard* to "make it". And conversely, I just came back from a week with a man who has spent the last decade actively hiding from having "made it".

The grass is always greener, as they say.

Eventually, June makes her way to me, where I've got a whiskey—her favorite—waiting for her. I've been trying to hide my emotions by clenching them back with brute force. And also, with drinking more than I usually do. I mean, it's her show. And even if I wanted to be here to show support, I didn't want to be sitting there in the audience glowering like I was at a funeral.

"*Fuck*, what'd she do now?"

I frown as she plucks the glass from my hand and says it before I can tell her how great she was.

"What?"

"Don't *what* me. Mel, you looked like you were at a funeral the whole show."

My face scrunches up.

"Fuck, I'm sorry."

"Don't be."

She reaches over to squeeze my hand, her face wincing.

"What'd that—and I say this from the bottom of my heart —*cunt* do?"

She knows me well enough to know how toxic my relationship with my mother is. And she knows I just saw Judy, because she's the one that got her friend to let me into the studio.

"I…" I smile as a mechanism of holding back a tear. "New subject."

"Shit. That bad?"

"Pretty fucking bad," I say quietly, taking a large sip of whiskey.

"Is it the book she's been blathering on about to every gossip blog on earth? Or something worse."

"Oh, it's the book." I exhale heavily as I stare into my drink. "I'm in it, apparently."

Her eyes widen as her face falls grimly.

"Jesus, there's no bottom floor with Judy, is there?"

"Not yet."

She winces as she puts a hand on my arm.

"She's not…*fuck*, Mel—"

I shake my head. "No, not that. I mean, not that I know of, at least. She wouldn't, though. I mean she can't, not with the NDAs."

June's mouth thins venomously. She doesn't know *who* the monster is—no one but Judy and I know that. But she knows about that night.

"Dude, you really didn't have to come out tonight."

"Yeah," I smile wryly. "I did."

To support a friend, yeah. But also, I think I just needed to be doused in creative output. I needed *music*.

And whiskey. Lots of whiskey.

"Well, cheers."

"Bottoms up," I mutter, knocking my glass back.

June raises her brows.

"Oh, it's gonna be that kind of night, is it?" She frowns. "And wait, hi, hello. How the hell was your trip? And what's with this story that you, by-the-by, never actually told me about?"

I'm pretty sure the black cloud over my head tells her everything she needs to know.

"*Aaahh*, shit," she groans. "Well, what's your next assignment going to be?"

"It's going to be…not at Ignition, whatever it is."

Her jaw drops.

"Did Becca seriously not come through? She's been blowing my phone up about that dumb fucking story for a week!"

"No, it's not her." I sigh. "I didn't get the story. So, there's no job."

Her face falls, but I shake my head.

"No, come on, let's change directions." I smile at her. "Your show was awesome."

"You stared death at the back of the guy in front of you through the whole thing like he owed you money."

I wince. "Sorry."

"I already said, don't be. You've been to more of my shows than basically anyone."

"I wasn't *totally* zoning out. That new one is great, by the way."

Her eyes light up.

"Wait, can I show you something?"

"Um, always?"

She turns to the bartender.

"Joey, is upstairs free?"

He shrugs. "Sure. Just pull the door shut behind you when you go up."

"Thanks." She turns to me, nodding her head. "It's their storage room, but Joey's the best."

Joey blushes as he rolls his eyes.

"And you're going to show me…what?"

"I want to play you something I've been working on, if you've got a minute."

"For you, Brad, I've got five," I snark back, quoting our favorite line from one of our favorite movies.

"Well, Judy's shit can't be *that* bad if you're quoting *American Beauty*. Come on."

"One sec." I turn back to Joey and tap my empty glass. "We're gonna need two more of these, please."

UPSTAIRS in the storage room above Smokey's Joint, I sit on a case of Pabst Blue Ribbon cans. June camps out on top of a big box of paper drink coaster as her fingers splay over the guitar in her hands.

"I'm still trying to get the chorus right. Like, I've got this one melody, but I'm not in love with it?"

I nod. "Go ahead."

She starts to play, her fingers tinkling over the strings. Then her voice comes in.

I *love* June's voice. She could literally sing me the ingredients off cereal boxes, and I'd sit there and listen to every vitamin and grain. She's incredible.

She gets through the verses and then into the chorus. And…I get what she means. It's good, and the lyrics are basically there. It's just…

"It could be better, right?" She frowns as she stops playing.

I lift a shoulder as I sip my drink. Honestly, it's been hard to focus, because it's taking roughly ninety percent of my brain power while watching her play the guitar and sing to not think of *another* guitar-playing singer.

Namely, Jackson.

And very suddenly, I *hate* that I left that island at all.

"Mel?"

I shake my head.

"Sorry." My brow furrows. "It's…okay, what if you took that last line? Where you're repeating 'you're gonna lose me forever' twice in a row?"

"Yeah?"

"What if you do…" I chew on my lip, until suddenly, it just falls out of me.

"You're gonna lose me, forever. If you never get, better."

The storage room is silent. I blink, frowning as I turn to her.

"What?"

Her brow lifts.

"June, what?"

"Um…so we're just, like, singing now?"

I stiffen. And it's literally not until she says it that I realize what just happened. I didn't speak the lines. I *sang* them.

"Huh," I say quietly.

"Yeah *huh*."

June puts her guitar down, looking at me intensely.

"Also, hi, are you fucking shitting me with that voice?"

"Stop."

"I will not. And I *love* the way you lifted the melody line on 'ever' and 'better'. Like, I love that."

"Oh…good."

I drop my eyes to my drink, feeling my face flush. When June says nothing, I look up to find her looking at me intensely.

"Oh c'mon, what?"

"Aside from *you* singing in front of me? And being fucking amazing?"

"Let's move past that."

She smiles curiously.

"You know I know your tell by now, right?"

I swallow as heat creeps up my neck.

"Wh—"

"Yeah, you've gotta stop saying 'what', Mel. And your tell is that when you're…I don't want to call it *lying*, but when you're holding something back, you get this little stiff-necked, head-back thing going on where your chin kinda disappears?"

"Wow, flattering, thank you."

She grins as I roll my eyes and look away.

"I think it's time we talk about this trip to Maine."

"There's…nothing to talk about."

I pray the giant gulp of whiskey I slug down doesn't look as suspicious as I think it probably does.

"I went to a tiny ass town with no cell service in the middle of nowhere and got snowed into my motel for a week. It was honestly pretty uneventful."

"Yeah?"

"Yep."

"What'd you watch?"

I frown. "Huh?"

"I mean, if I'm trapped in a motel for a *week*, and I don't have a guitar? I'm going to watch whatever is on TV until my eyes bleed. So, what did you watch?"

"I….uh…" I shrug. "I don't know. Nothing."

"No TV?"

"No?"

"What'd you read, then?"

My brow furrows. "What is this?"

"This, my friend, is the Spanish fucking Inquisition. Because you're full of shit."

"Excuse me?"

"Mel, *please*. You're not seriously going to tell me with a straight face that you spent a week up there just sitting in a motel room staring at the wall."

"But that's…basically what I did?"

"*Dude*. Bull. Fucking. Shit. You one hundred percent got laid."

"I did not!"

"What was he? Sexy rough and tumble lobsterman? Lumberjack? Are there lumberjacks in Maine?"

"I mean…probably?"

"Don't make me pick the low hanging 'big wood' joke, Mel."

I snort a laugh as I shake my head.

"You're insane."

"And you, despite being sucker-punched by Judy and unceremoniously booted from your brand-new job, have this… glow on you."

"I'm tipsy. It's the whiskey."

"Spelled D-I-C-K."

"Do you need new triple-A batteries for your vibrator?"

She flips me off.

"Okay, *A*, his name is James Dean."

"You didn't seriously name your—"

"And *B*," she ticks a finger, cutting me off. "He takes double-A's." She smirks. "Also don't go into my bedside table anymore, creeper."

"I was looking for the headphones you borrowed."

She grins, eyeing me.

"Who."

"*No one.*"

"Fine," she sighs. "Well, can I at least make a suggestion?"

"Will you make this suggestion anyway, no matter how I answer that?"

"Obviously."

"Well, by all means, then."

"You've got a little money saved up, right?"

I make a face.

"*Some* being the operative word there."

"Give it to me in terms of your half of the rent."

"About three months?"

She shrugs. "Hey, better than me. So, here's what I think you should do."

"Lay it on me."

"You don't have a job."

I nod.

"Judy is going to be everywhere you look for a while, with this new book of hers, right?"

"Unfortunately," I mutter.

"And, mystery man he may be, there's a lobsterman or a lumberjack in Maine with a dick that seems to put a smile on your face, make you glowier then I've seen you maybe ever, and. Also, a dick that *literally* makes you sing."

My face heats as my eyes roll.

"*June*—"

"You've got nothing tying you down here. In fact, with Judy on a media rampage, there's actually a fantastic reason for you to be someplace that doesn't get cell or internet service. And if that place happens to come with some quality dicking?"

"You didn't seriously just say 'quality dicking', did you?"

"*Wild* that I'm single, isn't it?" She sighs. "Mel, there's just the one obvious question here."

She looks at me pointedly, raising a brow.

"Why on earth are you *here*, when you could be *there*?"

32

JACKSON

I EXHALE SLOWLY. My eyes narrow at the blank page in front of me, my fingers drumming the guitar on my lap impatiently. Waiting for lightning. Waiting for genius.

Mad, or otherwise.

But I might as well be waiting on a miracle, or Oasis to get back together, or for someone to find Jimmy fucking Hoffa.

Because that shit is not happening.

A day ago—one single day ago—I had it. "It": that magical, mythical spark, or energy that all creative types crave. The flow of greatness coursing through you. Ideas exploding like fireworks in your head.

Yesterday, for the first time in almost a decade, I had it. Today, it's gone. And I'm very much aware it's no coincidence that my creativity isn't the only thing missing today that was here yesterday.

The plain, biting truth of it is, my muse left, and with her went the creative juices. With her, also apparently, went my ability to look at a blank page and see what's supposed to be written on it. To strum though chords and *hear*—in my fucking soul—the melody line that's supposed to go over them.

That's how I used to see and hear things. Then I didn't, for about ten years. And then suddenly, it was back.

Now it's gone again. Because today, all I see is a blank piece of paper. And I don't hear *shit* in my ears except, well, utter shit.

My brow furrows as I shove the blank page away. I stab my eyes out the picture window in the studio, glaring out at the big, gray Atlantic stretching to the horizon.

Fuck.

It's closing in on evening again, and I still haven't really slept since watching those taillights fade into the dark yesterday.

After watching Melody leave, I dealt with the punch to the throat life had just served me like the rational, responsible adult I am: by getting blind drunk at the Clam Shack.

Mitch behind the bar was good enough to let me sleep it off in one of the booths after closing—which is hardly the first time I've done that. But this time, waking up two hours later in a dark, closed dive bar with a swimming head and cocaine residue on my nostrils felt…

Well, slightly less "rock 'n roll" and a little more "what the *fuck* kind of choices are you making in your life at forty-two?" Which was sobering enough to get me off my ass, out the side door, and back to the docks to boat back over here.

Since then, I've been sustaining myself on spiked coffee and Percocets, and sitting here trying to bleed genius across a page. The same page, in fact, that's still blank and now shoved halfway across the desk in front of me.

I scowl in the lights-off dimness of the studio, lit only by the twilight outside. I take a heavy sip of my whiskey and coffee and exhale slowly.

If this were a song, or a movie or some shit, the cliche would be that after she's gone, I see the error in my habits and kick my demons to the curb. That through her, I find my true self, and become the best version of myself.

Cue: an uplifting "look to the future" type song as the credits roll. Springsteen or John Mayer would be all over that shit.

But life isn't a song. And the lessons don't come just because they rhyme the right way or highlight that cool metaphor in the chorus. Out here in the real world, there's a chance I've let these demons of mine devour so much of my soul that there's no coming back.

I swear as I shake those thoughts from my head. I'm about to put the guitar down, get up, and go do some *serious* drinking. But instead, my brow furrows. I reach over and slide another piece of paper towards me—this one sketched over with lyrics, with chord notations jotted down above them.

I smile to myself.

It's the song Melody and I wrote, together.

My breath exhales as I position the guitar in my lap, my eyes scanning the lines as I start to strum the intro we came up with. And when I start to sing, I let myself imagine that she's still here with me. Fueling me; pushing me. Igniting whatever it is inside of me that used to burn so bright I couldn't stop the magic from pouring out of me.

"There's a song in my ear, there's a hope that you're near,

When I'm lost on the rocks and I'm sinking

When the boats goin' down, all I'm thinkin',

Is the melody you sang to me to sleep...

Is the one pulling me down to the deep."

When I finish, I go right back into it. I start from the top as the words and the music that came from both of us fill the space around me.

This time, when I'm done, I close my eyes and let the final notes just sit there in the semi-darkness, hovering around me like a memory.

"Do you have, like, a tip-jar, or something?"

My eyes snap open. For a moment, in the darkness of the studio with my pulse thudding in my ears, I wonder if maybe I really have lost myself. That I've truly drank myself into a psychosis of some kind, because I'm actually hearing shit that isn't there.

Shit like words from the lips of a pink-haired, pain in my ass girl who I watched leave in a haze of taillights last night.

I start to stand and put the guitar to the side. But suddenly, soft hands touch my shoulders and a warm breath teases my ear.

Real hands, really touching me. This isn't in my head.

"Play it again?" Melody whispers quietly. "Please?"

The guitar slides back to my lap as my fingers begin to strum. My heart thuds in my chest as the words flow from my lips, starting from the top and singing the whole thing one more time. Until once again, the last notes and the final lines hang like silk strands in the darkness around us.

They're still hovering there when I stand. They're still vibrating over both of when I set the guitar to the side, take a slow breath, and turn.

And there she is.

My muse.

Every pink strand of her.

"Melody—"

"Okay, you *did* say I could come back…"

I grin a lopsided smile.

"But I mean, if you're busy," she shrugs. "I can find some other washed-up rock star on some other island to hang out with."

Could you? I actually have plans with another neon-haired pain-in-my-ass. You understand, of course."

"Of course."

I grin.

So does she.

And we get one more second of putting on this sarcastic façade before it breaks. She gasps quietly as I close the distance between us in one giant step, my big hands grabbing her waist and pulling her into me.

She's barely been gone for twenty-four hours. But when I crush my lips to hers and taste the sweetness of her mouth, it's like I've been without her for years.

And maybe I have been, and that's what was missing the last decade of my life spent wandering through a haze on this island, searching and hunting for madness or genius.

It turns out, I was just waiting for her.

The missing chord.

The killer line.

The perfect Melody.

33

JACKSON

THE WAY she moans into me is like napalm to my soul. The way she writhes in my arms so eagerly and grinds her pussy against the thick bulge in my jeans turns me into a fucking demon for her.

But the biggest thing is that her being back in my arms triggers a sort of caveman response. A savage, evolutionary need to make her *mine*.

Ruthlessly. Recklessly.

Repeatedly.

She whimpers when I scoop her into my arms, her legs wrapping tight around my waist as my hands grip her firm, tight ass with a savage hunger. My lips don't even leave hers as I stride purposefully from the studio and down the hall.

I keep carrying her like that—my lips seared hungrily to hers and my fingers kneading the globes of her ass—the entire way upstairs to my bedroom. And I don't let go until I'm tossing her down across the bed and stalking onto it after her.

Over her.

Pinning her down as my mouth devours her lips. And her neck, and her collarbone, until she's arching her back and mewling like a fucking kitten for me.

Part of me wants to rip or even shred her clothes off. To *literally* tear her panties from that honeyed little cunt with my fucking teeth before taking her like a goddamn animal.

The other part of me wants to take my time—to peel her clothes off inch by inch. To slowly reveal every suckable, bitable millimeter of her skin.

To unwrap her like a fucking Christmas present.

My mouth moves to her neck, sucking and biting the delicate skin there until she jolts and cries out with pain and pleasure. But I still don't stop, not until the marks I leave in my trail of conquest across her body turn red and purple.

Brands, marking her as *mine*.

My hands peel her sweater up, pushing it over her head as I lower my mouth to her tits. She whimpers, still pulling her sweater off as my mouth finds a hard nipple through her shirt and her bra. I suck, wetting the thin cotton until the pink, hard outline of her nipple is visible through the soaked fabric.

I move to the other, making her flush and making her breath catch as I suck that other nipple hard.

But the aching thickness between my thighs is growing painful.

My control is fracturing.

I kiss her hungrily before the shirt gets rips away. Her bra follows, and then I'm feasting on her nipples as her back arches in pleasure.

"Jackson…"

I move lower, dragging my teeth over her stomach as it caves beneath my mouth. I grunt, yanking in frustration at the button of her jeans. It finally gives, but as I pull them down, my hooded eyes slide to her big wide ones.

"No more fucking pants," I growl. "Not on you, not in this house."

Heat tinges her cheeks as she bites down on her lip.

"Was that a request?"

"No, that was a fucking demand. No goddamn pants."

She shivers as I yank the jeans down and off her ankles.

"What if I get cold—*ahh!*"

She moans, shuddering when I shove her knees back and swat her ass with my firm palm.

"I am *confident* I can keep this ass warmed."

"By…spanking me?"

She whimpers when I do exactly that.

"If that's what it takes to warm you, then yes," I grunt. "But also, with lips."

My mouth presses to the red mark from my hand on her ass, kissing the burn.

"With teeth."

She jolts, gasping a I bite at her ass, offsetting the sharp sting by dragging a finger up the absolutely soaked gusset of her panties. I can feel how fucking wet she is—how fucking dripping and slippery her little pussy is behind the thin defense of lace.

"And...and with what else?" She breathes, her eyes wide with lust.

She shivers, moaning as I slip a finger between the soaked-through lace and her needy little pussy, pushing her legs back again as I drag her panties with one finger all the way to her ankles.

"Tongue."

Melody squeals I shove her legs back, dip my head, and plunge my tongue deep into her sweet little pussy. Her hands claw at the bedsheets, her body writhing with ecstasy as I devour her whole.

I let go of her thighs, draping her legs over my shoulders as I plunge my tongue into her. I drag it over her, teasing her from her asshole up to her clit and back again—making a fucking *mess* of her until she's shaking and all but ripping at my hair.

My tongue drives into her again, as if I'm fucking her with it. Her body undulates and shudders, her moans filling my ears like honey as I move up to suck her clit between my lips. I sink two fingers into her impossibly tight little cunt, stroking them in and out and curling them against her g-spot as I suck her clit mercilessly.

"Jackson...*Jackson!* I—I—"

My fingers curl deep. My tongue swirls over her clit as I suck it between my lips. And when I push one single finger against her ass and let it slip inside, her body shudders and jolts as arches from the bed.

Screaming my fucking name.

"JACKSON!"

Her greedy pussy floods my tongue with her cum as she explodes, clenching tight around my fingers as she cries out. My tongue keeps rolling over her clit as she rides wave after wave, until she's shaking and quivering on the bed.

I shed my clothes and slide up between her legs. And she's still shuddering and writhing in the aftershocks of her explosive orgasm when I sink my head into her heavenly pussy and bury every goddamn inch of my fat cock deep inside of her.

"*Fuck me*!" She chokes, her nails clawing down my back as her legs wrap tight around my waist.

She moans, her face a mask of sweet agony as I pound into her, filling the room with the lewd, wet sounds of my cock claiming her little cunt.

"Your pussy is already milking the cum from my balls, sweetheart," I groan into her ear before biting the lobe.

Melody whimpers, turning to crush her lips to mine hungrily as her hips rise to meet my thrusts.

"Is that why you couldn't last a day away?" I growl against her mouth.

She moans as I sink into her, grinding against her clit.

"The real world out there just not as sweet without my cock making a fucking mess of this eager little pussy?"

Her mouth falls open, her face caving in pleasure as she clings to me.

"Oh my *God*, your—"

She moans as I bury myself deep.

"My cock?" I hiss. "My cock is what, sweetheart? Making you want to scream my name? Making you want to come again for me, like a good girl?"

"No, your *ego*," she groans, gasping, her eyes rolling back as my balls slap her ass.

"Your *ego* is out of fucking control—"

"Let's not pretend my ego doesn't make a fucking *mess* of this pretty little pussy, sweetheart."

The fact that her only comeback to that is to dig her nails into me, crush her lips to mine, and squeeze the life out of my dick with her pussy like a velvety vice is the only answer I need. I devour her mouth as I fuck my cock into her over and over, my hands tangling in her hair.

Her cries of pleasure fill the room and melt over my skin. Her nipples drag electrically against my chest, her thighs squeezing the fuck out of my hips as her face crumples in pure ecstasy.

"Jackson!" She cries out. "I—*I'm*—"

"Fucking come for me, sweetheart."

She explodes like a bomb, shuddering and writhing and arching her hips into me as the orgasm engulfs her. And I'm right behind her. With a groan, I bury my cock to the hilt in her spasming, slippery, heavenly pussy as my balls draw tight. My mouth crushes to hers as my cum spills into her—

pump after pump coating the walls of her pussy with my release as I hold her possessively in my arms.

She's shaking. Her breath is hitching wildly as her body quivers and clenches around me.

But I'm *definitely* not done with her yet.

I'll never be done with this girl.

She pouts as I slide out of her. But when I grab her hips and start to flip her over, her eyes go wide.

"Oh shit, Jackson—"

She whimpers when I use my knee to spread her limp legs apart. A demon takes hold of me—a primal savageness that flickers to life as I watch my pearly white cum lewdly drip from her pink, swollen, freshly fucked pussy.

I center my still rock-hard cock, and she moans.

"You're—are you *still* hard?"

"And are you still somehow under the impression that the sight of you naked—or clothed, for that matter—*doesn't* make me want to fuck the living hell out of you until neither of us can walk?"

Her face flushes pink as she turns to look at me over her shoulder. She shivers, her lust-hooded eyes smoldering as they lock onto my throbbing hard, glistening cock.

"Now spread your legs and take every inch of my cock in this messy little pussy like a good little slut."

I drive right back in, making her mouth fall open in a silent scream as her eyes roll back in pleasure. I groan, grabbing her hips, keeping her flush to the mattress as I rut into her.

Hard. Deep. Mercilessly.

Wetly.

I can feel the sticky slickness of her cum and mine coating my cock. And the sensation of fucking my cum even deeper into her turns me into a beast. I become hell-bent on filling her with so much of my cum that she'll feel me filling her panties tomorrow. Or even the day after that.

My teeth grit, muscles clenching as I fuck into her—fueled by the way her pussy ripples and grips at me. By her choked moans as she lies sprawled like a fuck-doll on the bed beneath me. My fingers dig into her skin, leaving marks on her ass. My other hand slides up her back, making her shiver as I grab a fist-full of pink hair and tug.

I want to fuck her so hard that she remembers the feel of my hips against her ass for a week. I want her pussy to remember my cock forever—to imprint it on her fucking soul.

I want even the slightest heat of my touch, or a single whispered word from my lips to make her knees week and her panties *soaked*.

And yes, maybe she's right. Maybe my ego *is* out of fucking control.

Or maybe, it's just *her* that takes away my control. My brakes. My ability to think rationally, or even pretend to control the beast inside of me.

But, judging from the moans and choked whimpers from the girl writhing in pure ecstasy on my cock?

I very much doubt she has much of a problem with it—be it my ego, or loss of self-control.

Or just my overwhelming hunger for her.

Always.

My hand tightens in her hair, twisting her head so that her eyes swivel back to lock with mine. And we don't break that look. I don't blink, and neither does she as I pound into her.

That is, until she comes again. And when she does, her whole face scrunches in sweet agony. Her mouth falls open, her body convulsing and undulating under me. Her pussy clamps down like a vice around my cock as she screams my name.

Which completely pushes me over the edge again.

Yeah, maybe I do have an ego. And listening to her moan my name while she soaks my sheets and my balls with her cum strokes it just the right way to make me explode.

But maybe—*probably*—it's just her.

And that's what takes me over the edge: watching *her*. Listening to *her*. Feeling *her*.

I bite down hard on her shoulder as my cock surges inside, pumping and spilling my hot cum deep in her clenching pussy.

Both breathless and shaking, we roll to the side. I stay inside of her as I wrap my arms around her like a cloak, swallowing her against my body.

She's still trembling and trying to catch her breath as she turns to me, her eyes shining with a grin on her face.

"I—I don't know how long I'm *welcome* to stay, but I—"

"Forever."

She blinks in surprise.

Shit, so do I.

But the second I do say it out loud, it just sort of clicks. Like it's the obvious answer.

"Stay forever."

She leans up as I lean down, and our lips fuse hard as my hands tighten possessively on her.

Kissing her. Holding her. Being here in a moment with her that I never want to end.

34

MELODY

"Forever" comes in small increments. First, it's days. Then, as those days blur together in a heated swirl of music and pleasure, it becomes weeks. Then the weeks become a month.

A *month*.

We spend our days and nights alone with each other, splitting the hours between bed and the studio, then bed, then back to the studio in a haze of lyrics and orgasms. Of music and pleasure, until I begin to lose track of what's a line on a page and what's the real-life fantasy I'm living.

Or maybe, they're just blurring together at this point.

At times, it feels like a rush—like I'm on this perpetual rollercoaster. Like I'm always smiling, and always lost in the man I share every waking minute and breath with. Other times, it's almost terrifying to realize how wrapped up in him I am. Or how real this is all becoming.

Or how helplessly and utterly head over heels I am for him.

We share a bed. And our bodies, throughout most of almost every day. We share space, and time together. We share a creative spark, too. Because after a month's worth of hours and hours pouring over lyrics and guitar lines and melodies, that one song we had before has turned into eight.

Eight. Fucking. Songs.

That's a mind fuck in and of itself. No one in the world but us has heard them, but sometimes I have to stop and make sure I'm actually in reality when it hits me that I've cowritten *eight* freaking songs, with Jackson fucking Havoc.

But even under the bright glow of him, I still manage to find shadows. Maybe that's my flaw, or maybe it's the way I was raised with my mom being the disaster magnate she is. Whatever the case, even when he's got me laughing, and smiling, and *moaning* in sweet agony, I've still got one eye open.

Waiting for the other shoe to drop. Waiting for reality to take this happiness from me.

Or maybe I'm just waiting for my shit to sabotage it for myself.

I try to hold the line with reality. I tell myself that as incredible as it is here with him, and as much fun as I'm having, that Jackson is…well, *Jackson*.

A beautiful disaster. A fallen god. And most terrifying, given the way he's got me and my naked heart in the palm of his hand, a man possibly incapable of a normal relationship.

And of course, the second I even think something like that, I cringe at myself.

This isn't a "relationship". Even if I'm—recklessly and dangerously—crazy about him. Even if I've opened myself to him, emotionally and *definitely* physically in ways I've never even come close to before, with anyone.

We're just two people who…write well together. Two people who seem to spark a creativity in the other that isn't there by ourselves.

Two people who fuck like I imagine Greek *gods* fucked—savagely, recklessly, and seemingly tirelessly.

But—because I'm *me*, I guess—that's another thing about us where I can't help but purposefully seek out the shadows. And in the case our…physical relationship, the shadows I find are *green*.

And monstrous. And they cruelly pick at every single insecurity and jealous itch I've got bottled up in the minefield of my emotional baggage.

I don't own Jackson. And it's even more insane to suggest I had any sort of claim on him *ten or more years ago*.

But just the same, it—his past, that is—sits there sometimes in the back of my mind like a big green lurking dragon.

I hate thinking about a younger Jackson and the God only knows how many women that came before me.

I mean, I *really* hate thinking about it.

But what turns me from green with jealousy to seething with red rage isn't the fact a grown, forty-two year old, extremely attractive and famous man had a personal life before I met him.

It's that I can't stop fixating on it. That's what I really hate. That I allow it to get under my skin. That I can't just let go and let his touch, and his mouth, and his words, and his *godly* dick utterly and completely worship me into pure bliss.

I mean, I *can*, and I do get lost in him. But other times, that green flicker of jealousy is back there somewhere, lurking in the shadows. Ready to torment me.

The one upside is, I've officially put the "Judy thing" to bed. Yes, there was a minute there where the horrific and nauseating thought that she and Jackson could have had history seeped like poison into my head.

But then, I realized I had the proof that Judy really was completely full of shit in that regard. Not only would I have never stopped hearing about it years ago if she and Jackson had ever been "together". But also, I would have *seen* the proof right there in our living room.

Judy's "conquest wall"—the walls of drawers containing little mementos from all the famous musicians she's had things with. The little drawers with eye-poppingly famous names like Mark Cooper, Leighton James, Brian Cummings, Slade, Tom Roberts…even Will Cates.

But for all the famous names on that wall of drawers, there's one I *know* I've never once seen taped onto any of them: Jackson Havoc.

And for once, my mother being a serial liar and completely full of shit is a reason for me to sleep sounder at night.

She never had him. And I hesitate to say he's "all mine". But with the past back where it belongs, and the world walled off around us here on our island of escape?

For now, he really is all mine. And life really is perfect.

Until it's not.

Walls don't usually just come crashing down randomly. There are cracks that happen first. A bad foundation. Leaks that weaken the inside of them until all you're really seeing is the painted veneer over a crumbling center.

It always starts with small cracks.

At first, I don't even see them. Then I ignore them. Other times, I cover them with more creativity, or more "letting go" and losing myself in the pure ecstasy of his body and his bed.

Slowly but surely, though, some of those cracks just keep getting bigger. And more obvious. Until no amount of orgasm, or song lyrics, or laughing it off when I have to help him physically walk up the stairs at night because he's too fucked up will cover them anymore.

I grin as I stir the pot of noodles on the stove. Glancing over, I check the timer on my soft-boiled eggs, and then quickly give the tamari a whisk. Then I sit back, my eyes gleaming as I survey the preparation in front of me.

This is going to be awesome.

At first, Jackson just raised a quizzical brow when I mentioned I'd be making us scratch-made ramen.

"You mean like the shit that comes in those little packets for pennies?"

"No, I mean like really good, fancy ramen."

"Fancy ramen..."

"Yeah, it's...it's like a thing, now."

"But it's ramen."

"Yeah, but it's—"

"Like the little packets with the flavor powder?"

"Yeah, but those taste like shit."

"Exactly. So why are we eating it for dinner?"

I grin as the exchange replays in my head. I'm at least ninety percent sure he was mostly just yanking my chain. But Jackson really did miss the whole "fancy ramen at hip restaurants" thing from years ago, so, there's that.

Either way, I fucking *love* it. And even though I've only made it like twice for June and me, I wanted to try it with what we had on-hand at the house tonight.

As I stir, though, my face scrunches up I sniff the air. A smell that's definitely not from my cooking seeps into my nose, and when I turn, I frown.

Would I *like it* if Jackson didn't smoke? Yes. I think it's a fairly gross habit, and even when he brushes his teeth afterwards, you can still obviously smell it.

But he's also a grown man, and I'm not his freaking mom. If he wants to smoke, he can smoke. It's usually at most two a day anyway.

What gets under my skin, though, and what he *knows* gets under my skin, is when he smokes in the house.

Like he's currently doing.

My eyes narrow on him, sitting on the couch with his feet up on the coffee table next to an open bottle of whiskey. His plaid shirt is haphazardly unbuttoned in a distractingly sexy way, and his jeans are slung low in an even *more* distractingly sexy way.

But there's the cigarette in his lips, smoke curling towards the high ceiling as he absently picks out notes on the guitar in his hands.

Even if it's a terrible habit, visually, is the image of him sitting there looking all sexy-poet-rockstar with a cigarette in his lips outrageously hot?

Hell yeah.

But it's a picture I can smell. And, guest I may be, I *do* currently live here. And secondhand smoke is a thing.

"Hey, Jackson?"

He looks up, grinning a roguish smile at me.

"Yes ma'am?" He drawls in a way that lets me really hear the whiskey in his tone.

I bite my lip.

"Could you…" I lift a shoulder. "Do you mind…"

He frowns, but then suddenly his brows raise.

"Shit."

"Sorry, I'm not trying to be annoying. It's your house—"

"Nah, it's fine. Just cold out there."

He grins, shrugging as he plucks the cigarette from his lips and crushes it out in the ashtray on the coffee table.

"Thanks," I smile. "Dinner's almost ready."

"*Hell yeah,*" he groans, his eyes glassy as he grins at me.

I smile back, but there's a shadow behind mine. It's almost eight at night, and while Jackson having a drink—or several drinks—with or before dinner is pretty much the norm, today, he's been at it a little harder than usual.

Since eleven in the morning, actually.

Yes, we were trying to finish up this latest song we've been working on, which has proven to be tricky to get the feel of. But still.

Eleven in the morning on a Wednesday is a little aggressive. So were the two Percocets I saw him pop at two-thirty.

And then there's the coke.

I'm not a prude, and I'm not even anti-drugs, even with the household I grew up in. I mean I'll smoke pot two or three times a year, maybe. I even tried cocaine once, when I was maybe eighteen, before deciding it really wasn't for me.

I'm not *against* people having an escape. Believe me.

It's just that he escapes…*a lot*. And it scares me sometimes, the more often I see it. Just like it scares me that he obviously *sees* that it weirds me out at times and goes to lengths to hide it.

Like today, when he ducked out of the studio to "grab something". But ten seconds later, I could literally hear the unmistakable inhale of coke into nostrils out in the hall. And when he came back, he was all wide smiles, glassy eyes, and idea that came at a mile a minute.

I turn back to finish the noodles, when I hear that same sound again, behind me in the living room. My lips thin as I glance back at him.

Jackson clears his throat, lifting his head from the cover of a notebook on the coffee table. He sniffs, rubbing his nose as he leans back to exhale at the ceiling. I watch him grin to himself as he reaches for the bottle of whiskey, taking a big gulp.

He's better than this. I *know* he's so much better than this.

I turn back again, trying to push it away. Trying to cover the cracks. I drain the noodles, finish with the tamari and the soft poached eggs, and test the broth itself.

Perfect.

I assemble both deep bowls, spooning in the tamari and the broth, placing the eggs, and adding in the bok choy, the thin slices of beef, and the mushrooms. Then I grab them both and turn to set them on the kitchen island.

"Hungry?"

"Why, are you on the menu?"

I grin as heat creeps up my neck.

"We can discuss dessert after."

He chuckles, lurching to his feet. I almost go to him when I see him swaying, but he catches himself with a hand on the arm of the sofa. He glances at me and grins sheepishly.

"Man, lightweight over here, huh?"

"Come eat, dork," I smile back.

But the shadow is there behind it. I watch him stagger in very much not a straight line to the kitchen, whiskey bottle in hand, almost taking out a side table on his way in.

I'm about to sit and dig in. But instead, I gasp as he surges right into me, scooping me into his arms and pining me to the counter behind me. I shiver at the primal lust in his eyes, and the igniting way his hands touch me.

I almost say fuck it to dinner, and his current state, and jump him right here. But then, my stomach gurgles, loudly.

Jackson chuckles as he pulls back from my lips.

"Yeah, let's eat first," he slurs, eying me hungrily. "You're going to need your strength later."

I grin, biting my lip.

"Promise?"

He just nods, his eyes smoldering as he brings the bottle up. My brow furrows.

"Hey…maybe slow it down?"

"Seriously?"

I shrug. "I mean…yeah, kind of. You've really been at it today."

"I'm fine, sweetheart."

"No, I know you are—"

He falters back, almost knocking one of the kitchen stools over.

"Jack—"

"I've been drinking since before you were born, Melody," he grunts.

Which is exactly what's worrying to me.

"I'm fine."

I nod quietly.

"Okay, just…thought I'd mention it."

"You always do," he mutters to himself as he turns to sink onto his stool.

"The hell does that mean?"

His eyes roll as he looks up at me.

"Look, Mel, I know you mean well. But I don't need a fucking nanny."

"Oh, no?" I smile thinly at him. "So, the last four or five loads of laundry just sort of did themselves? The last two weeks of meals just cooked themselves? The last—"

"No one asked you to do any of that."

"No one was *going* to do any of that, either!" I snap back.

His face darkens. He reaches for the bottle, and when my eyes dart to it, he sighs heavily.

"*Care for a drink*, Mel?" He mutters sarcastically.

"No, I think you're managing just fine for the both of us."

"What the fuck crawled up your ass today?"

My eyes go livid.

"Go to hell, Jackson."

"No, I'm honestly curious. Because if *anything's* going up that ass, it's my cock."

I hate how much the crudeness of his words turns me on. I hate how I literally imagine that sinful scenario happening right here and right now, even if I'm mad at him—him pinning me against the counter and bending me over it.

Shoving my jeans and panties down or the latter just to the side.

The feel of his thick cock pushing against my most intimate, forbidden place before sinking into me, making me choke and moan as he fucks me like an animal.

But I strangle that fantasy, putting my walls back up as I glare at him.

"Believe me that is not happening anytime soon."

"You don't seem like the kind of girl who could take that anyway."

Every single insecurity and green-tinged jealousy of his life from before me comes roaring out of the shadows.

"Fuck you," I spit.

He grins.

"Oh, am I wrong?"

"Can we just eat our fucking ramen—*stop it.*"

He stands, making me shiver as he moves around to my side of the kitchen island. His hands slide over my hips as if to draw me against him.

But the timing is terrible. Because I'm still *rip-shit* mad and very much still stewing in my jealousy.

"Take your hands off me."

"C'mere—"

"Jackson, *enough.*"

"Melody—"

"Stop it!"

I shove him back. He hits the countertop, blinking as he glares at me with a flash of anger and glimmer of sobriety.

But just a glimmer.

"Fine, let's eat," he mutters.

He whirls and shoots an arm out behind him as if to grab his bottle of whiskey.

Instead, his knuckles hit my bowl of ramen. Which knocks across the table into *his* bowl of ramen. Both bowls hit the ground with the sound of breaking glass and slopping broth and noodles.

The kitchen goes silent as my pulse thuds heavily in my ears, my gaze locked onto the ruined dinner on the floor.

"*Fuck*, Mel—"

"*Don't.*"

My voice is lethal.

"Just…fucking don't."

"Mel, it was an accident—"

"Stop talking."

"Look, I'll pick it up—"

"STOP TALKING!"

I yank my eyes from the mess to his face. My lips curl when I see him swigging from his bottle.

"Yeah, have another drink, Jackson."

He lowers the whiskey, frowning as he looks down.

"Lemme fix this."

He stoops down as if to start picking the mess up with his bare hands.

"Stop it, you'll cut your—"

"I *got it*!"

He doesn't got it.

Jackson steps on a puddle of broth and noodles and instantly loses his footing. I gasp, but he's laughing as he falls onto his ass on the floor.

"Fuck, are you okay?"

"See? I told you ramen is shit."

My concern drops like a bad habit. My eyes narrow to slits as he sits there laughing on the floor, bringing the bottle to his lips.

Fuck this.

I turn and start to walk out of the kitchen.

"Where are you—"

"*Away*," I snap.

And then I hear it. First, him slumping against the island.

Then the sound of cocaine being sniffed.

I whirl on him, marching over in a blind rage and sneering down into his glassy-eyed face. But Jackson just grins up at me, raising a hand.

"Little help?"

"*No.*"

"What?

"I said *no*, Jackson."

I start to turn away when his hand slides up to cup my ass.

I shiver. And for a second, I almost break. I almost cave, and sink onto his lap to kiss him, or fuck away this stupid shadow hanging over us, and between us.

But I don't.

"I'm going to bed."

"Melody—"

"Go drink yourself into a stupor for all I care. And don't you fucking *dare* come up tonight," I spit venomously.

"Mel—"

"Or I'll leave."

He goes silent. When I turn to him, he's glaring at me, still on the floor, still bringing that fucking bottle to his lips.

"I'm sorry," he grunts quietly.

"Yeah, me too."

Then I turn and march away. And I manage to keep it together until the second I'm behind the door of his bedroom.

And then, I lose it completely.

35

MELODY

Last night was awful.

The morning is worse.

For one, I'm alone. And the bed doesn't look disturbed next to me, which means he heard what I said about not coming up last night.

Even if I secretly hoped he would.

I'm also exhausted from not falling asleep until God knows when. But I'm up, and there's no going back to sleep now. Not with my brain already churning on full steam, replaying and rehashing everything that happened last night.

My hands push my hair out of my face as I groan.

I hate this feeling.

I slip out of bed and use the bathroom. I brush my teeth, slip on some clothes, and then head downstairs. I stop short in the doorway to the living room.

Jackson is still asleep—or passed out, at least—on the couch. He's shirtless, looking way too hot for how angry I still am at him.

He also looks mad. I mean he literally looks angry at his dreams. I almost wake him, so we can just cut through the shitty part and get right to the part where we're kissing again. But I don't.

I *do* want to get to that part—the part that comes after the anger and the fight. But I need to collect my thoughts first.

I turn to look out the windows at the ocean.

What I need is *space*.

"Mornin', Melody."

"Good morning, Albert."

I smile at the dock master as I climb up the gangway from the lower docks. Albert steps out of the small office and zips his coat up.

"How's island life?"

"Oh…" I shrug. "Fine, thanks."

"You're getting better in that thing."

I grin as he nods past me to where I've docked Jackson's boat.

"Helps that this one has an engine and not oars."

He chuckles, glancing up at the gray late fall sky.

"We're gonna get some weather soon, I think."

"What, snow?"

"Ayuh. Maybe not tonight, but soon."

"Huh. Good to know."

I start to walk past him, when he turns.

"Hey, Melody, I haven't really seen much of Robbie the last few weeks. How is he?"

I stop, inhaling slowly as I glance back at him.

"He's a pain in my ass, Albert. A pain in my ass."

He chuckles as I step off the dock and head into town.

I MOSTLY CAME over to Cape Harbor for some air and some space. But, while I'm here, I might as well grab some supplies.

I load up on groceries I think we might need off the top of my head, along with some fabric softener, and chocolate.

For me.

Then, bags in hand, I head back towards the dock. A shadow crosses my face as I walk past the liquor store.

Nope. Not doing it. If he's out of booze back home, so fucking be it.

I continue, and I'm passing The Clam Shack when the door opens and Mitch—the gruff old bartender I once knew as "Gray Beard"—steps out.

"Supply run, huh?"

"Yep, needed a little glimpse of society too, I think."

He smirks, folding his arms over his chest. His gaze drops to my bags of groceries, and he frowns.

"Skipping the liquor store this run?"

My mouth thins.

"*Yep.*"

"Hmm."

I clear my throat. "Well, gotta get back. Good seeing you, Mitch—"

"Hey, Melody?"

I turn back to him, raising a brow as he sighs and shoves a hand through his gray hair.

"I'm just gonna say something."

My brow furrows. "Okay?"

"Robbie needs help."

My brows go up. It's maybe the last thing I would have expected him to say.

"What?"

"Help. With his drinking. You seem like a bright kid. I know you see it."

I look away, nodding quietly.

"Look, this isn't my place to say, but I'm saying it anyway. He does need help. But he can't just quit cold."

He eyes me coolly.

"My mom had a problem, too. Believe me, I've looked at liquor stores and walked past 'em the same way I just saw you do it. But you can't just cut someone off. I don't mean because it's not nice. I mean because if you drink as much as Robbie does, quitting cold turkey is real dangerous."

My mouth goes small as I nod quietly.

"I know this seems ass-backwards with me running a bar and all. But I know some people who could help him take those first steps. If he ever wants."

I smile wryly as I nod.

"Thanks, Mitch."

AGAINST MY BETTER JUDGEMENT, I do end up back at Shoreline Spirits getting Jackson another few bottles of whiskey.

Mitch isn't wrong. I do vaguely remember reading somewhere about how going from heavy habitual drinking to not drinking at all *can* have pretty disastrous effects on your heart and other vital organs.

But God do I hate myself for walking out of that store with more poison for Jackson.

I'm halfway to the docks again when my phone goes off. Finally. The service is pretty sucky over in town, too. And usually when I come over about once a week, I have to wander around to find a bar of service or two so that I can check in with June and let her know I'm not dead.

Sure enough, when I stop at a bench and glance at the phone, the first few messages are from my friend—all usual stuff like "are you ever coming home" "miss you a lot" and varied versions of "how's the lobstersman dick?"

Fucking fantastic, thank you very much.

I type out my usual replies: that I'm fine. That I miss her too. That I'm figuring out when I can come back to New York for a while. That lobsterman dick is awesome. After that, I start to put the phone away, when I realize I've got other texts.

From Judy.

> *Call me. It's important.*
>
> *Melody, I want to talk to you about something.*
>
> *It's about the book. Call me.*

Goddamnit.

I wish I could ignore her. I wish I could shrug off whatever bullshit she's trying to throw at me this time, and just go on with my life.

But I can't. Because I know if I ignore this, I'll spend the next few days slowly losing my shit wondering what she was talking about.

Judy picks up on the second ring.

"Where—weeks!"

I groan. Shit. Bad service strikes again.

"Judy?"

"Melody, can you hear me?"

"Yeah. It's bad—"

"—Hear me?"

I sigh.

"YES, I can hear you. It's bad service—"

"Melody—warn you—book."

My jaw ticks.

"What?"

"The book, Melody. I—leaking—chapter—tomorrow—encourage media interest."

I roll my eyes angrily, my lips thinning.

"Judy, I don't fucking care. Do whatever you want. We both know you will anyway."

"No, Mel—book talks about—your—don't want you being surprised at all."

I frown. "*What?* Judy, I can't hear—"

"Father."

I tense.

"What?"

"Book—leak—the truth—your father."

My stomach drops.

"*What* did you just say?" I whisper hoarsely.

By now, I've assumed that Judy's cunty and cryptic shit back in that dressing room about me having to "buy a copy" of her book to find out who my dad is was typical Judy bullshit.

So why am I suddenly second guessing myself on that?

"Judy, you're breaking up. What did you—"

"Don't—you—caught off guard."

"Okay? Judy?"

The reception fills with static.

"Judy?"

The line clicks off.

Shit.

I pause, frowning as I try and put the pieces together. But then I stop. Because this is what she does. She just sews these seeds of doubt and chaos, and then smiles as they grow tall.

Fuck you, Judy.

I've got enough to deal with and think about out here without her shit.

I BOAT BACK over under two clouds—one, an actual dark cloud up in the sky. The other is my mood—black, stormy, and cold.

Albert's right. I have gotten better at boats. I tie off the line to Jackson's dock, and then climb the stone steps up through the woods to the house carrying the bags of supplies from town. My hip pushes the front door open, and I sigh as I step inside, fully expecting to find Jackson still asleep on the couch.

I blink, freezing.

What I don't expect is for the living room to be *immaculate*. The kitchen, too. And the hallway, and…basically every room I step into.

Slowly, I make my way back to the kitchen, putting the groceries on the counter as my eyes sweep the clean sink.

"I want to do better."

I gasp quietly, turning and flushing as my eyes lock with his. Jackson's standing in the living room—his jaw clean-shaven, his shirt buttoned, and a pained but firm look on his face.

"Jackson—"

"I *need* to do better."

I swallow, walking slowly towards him

"I'm not trying to change who you—"

"Yeah, you are," he growls quietly. "But I love that you are. And I *do* need to change, Melody. Because this?" He glances around at nothing, and then down at himself.

"This is *not* working for me."

I swallow as I stop in front of him. My pulse races as I look up into his eyes.

"Jackson—"

"You make me want to be a better version of myself," he whispers, his hand coming up to cup my face. His other hand slides to the small of my back, and my breath catches as he gently pulls me into him.

"You *are* the best version—"

"No." He shakes his head. "No, I'm not. But I'm pretty sure I could be with you."

His mouth slowly descends, like he's waiting for me to tell him to fuck off.

Instead, I grab him, choking back a sob as I go up on my toes to kiss him deeply. Our lips lock, tongues dancing as he growls and lifts me into him.

My legs go around his waist, and his hands hold me tightly as he carries me upstairs.

36

MELODY

I WAKE UP TO...*BLISS*.

Confusion clouds my senses as I try to connect the dots. But as my consciousness drags me from sleep, I suddenly recognize what it is I'm feeling with a heated gasp.

It's a tongue, slowly circling my clit.

I moan softly, arching my back as my legs spread wider. I keep my eyes closed, but one hand slides down my stomach, and then into Jackson's hair.

"That feels so good..."

He just groans into me, tonguing me a little harder now that I'm awake. My free hand cups one of my breasts, fingers teasing and toying with the nipple as Jackson's tongue plunges into me. I moan louder, shifting as the sensations melt through me.

His tongue drags up and down my lips, delving lower to circle my ass and being a cry of forbidden pleasure to my lips. He moves higher, sucking my clit between his lips again and dragging his tongue over it.

"Baby…"

I sink into oblivion. My body coils and writhes, and my skin ignites as his fingertips tease over it. His tongue keeps swirling, his lips fastened tight around my clit. And as he sinks a finger into me and strokes it against my g-spot, everything shatters around me.

I cry out, my back arching from the bed as the orgasm slams into me. I'm shaking everywhere, gasping for air and clawing at the bedsheats as he slides up between my thighs. I'm so wet that his huge cock just sinks into me, stretching me open as he drives in deep.

I moan, but his lips sear to mine, swallowing my pleasure as he rolls his hips into me. His hands and fingers stroke and tease over my skin, his muscles clenching and rippling against me.

Jackson grabs my wrists, shoving them above my head and pinning them with one hand. The other slides sensually down my body, teasing every little pressure point, my nipples, my stomach, and my clit, all while he fucks his cock in and out of me.

He grips my ass, squeezing hard and digging his fingers into my skin as he fucks me harder and deeper. I keep moaning, and he keeps devouring those moans as he kisses me viciously.

We rock together faster, my arms straining but failing to break free of his grip. My back arches, pushing my tits into his chest as my nipples drag like electric points across his skin. I can feel my breath catching, my pulse faltering faster and out of control.

Jackson's hand slips between my legs, and his thumb begins to roll my clit as he thrusts into me. I start to tremble, my eyes rolling back as I feel his mouth drag across my jaw to rasp into my ear.

"I want that fucking cum."

I fucking *explode*. Instantly. My entire body jolts and electrifies, my core clenches so hard it almost hurts as the orgasms rips through me. He grunts heavily into my ear, biting down hard on it as he rams his cock as deep as he can get. A moan shatters from my lips as I feel him pulse and throb into me, filling me with his hot cum.

At some point, still shaking, I'm dimly aware of him gathering me into his arms and carrying me into a waiting shower.

Where we do all of that all over again.

"You don't have to do that."

But I'm grinning as he pulls me close and kisses my forehead.

"Yeah, I do. You want to stay here, or come with?"

"With, please," I murmur quietly, smiling like an idiot as I lean up to capture his mouth with mine.

Fifteen minutes later, we're skimming over the bay towards Cape Harbor. Where Jackson is hell-bent on buying the makings for more homemade ramen.

We moor at the far end of the dock, which, from experience and testing, we both now know is just out of sight of the dock offices. Which makes it a usual spot for a lingering last kiss before he becomes "Uncle Robbie".

And that's exactly what we do, until my lips are bruised with his. Then, a light snow just beginning to fall, we head up into the town with our disguises back on.

Jackson heads to the grocery store. I head to the hardware store, where, oddly, I seem to get the best cell service in town. Sure enough, as I step under the awning by the display window, my phone erupts with a series of texts and notifications.

Again? It's been less than a day since I was just over here.

I frown as I quickly thumb through the messages and notifications. There's a bunch from my mom, a bunch from June, and a *ton* from what seems to be easily fifty numbers I don't know.

My brow furrows. What?

A helicopter whirs overhead somewhere as I shake my head. And I'm about to tap June's number, when something catches my eye. I turn, my gaze dragging from my phone to the display flatscreen TV inside the hardware store.

The one with a video playing of a birds-eye-view of a town.

I blink as a tingling sensation creeps coldly down my spine.

Not just any town. *This town.*

I look up, tensing as I realize the helicopter I just heard above me is literally the same one broadcasting Cape Harbor across live television.

Shit, was there an accident or something?

I'm about to walk inside the hardware store and ask Lyle behind the counter what's going on, when the shot on the TV changes. A different aerial shot suddenly fills the screen.

One that makes me turn to stone as my heart drops.

Oh fuck.

It's Jackson's house, on the island, being filmed by a circling helicopter. My face goes white as I lurch into the hardware store. I don't even respond when Lyle says hello, and I numbly fumble over to the flatscreen and reach for the volume on the side of it.

"And you can see here from our second chopper the very house where, allegedly, Mr. Havoc has been living for the last ten years. The bombshell article in Ignition Magazine goes on to allege that Mr. Havoc has been presenting himself under the alias Robert Johnson—presumably a musician's nod to the late godfather of blues music."

Oh my God.

Oh my fucking God.

"Holy shit," Lyle suddenly walks up behind me as I stand there numbly staring at the TV. "Isn't that your uncle's place?"

"We're trying to get a news team actually ON the island. And again, if you're just tuning in, an explosive article in Ignition Magazine that just published online this morning alleges that this is the home of missing musician and rock icon Jackson Havoc."

"But that's Robbie's place?" Lyle murmurs.

Holy fuck.

The screen switches to the front cover of Ignition Magazine's new issue—with an older shot of Jackson himself splayed across it. The screen fades to more pictures from the article itself, and my stomach knots.

I know those pictures they're showing of the inside of his house, and the yard, and the views, and him himself, sitting with a guitar on his couch.

I know them, because I *took them*.

"Ignition has also released short audio clips from their apparently exclusive interview with Havoc, which are playable on the online version of their article that dropped this morning.

"Fame is boring. I got bored, so I left."

I want to throw up. The recoding is *Jackson*—Jackson spilling his guts to me, unaware that I'm being a horrible person and recording him doing it.

I have to find him.

Now.

"And of course, you pair this with the bombshell from her upcoming book that Judy Blue leaked to her Instagram followers this morning, and I think we're about to have one hell of a news day."

I turn, and I *run*.

I'm only vaguely aware of there being *way* more people in town than I've ever seen before. And more cars, and vans with big TV antennas branching off the top of them. But I dodge that, zigzagging back behind the hardware store and then sprinting behind the crowds towards the dock.

I have to get to Jackson before—

It's his eyes that get me first. It's the look of cold, hard betrayal in his steely blue eyes, thirty feet away from me on the dock, that almost bring me to my knees. But I keep running, even as he rips his gaze away and starts to walk down the gangway towards the boat.

"Jackson! Jackson *wait—*!"

"You need to stay the *fuck* away from me, Melody," he hisses, yanking his arm from my touch as he storms away from me.

"*Please—*!"

"You stabbed me in the fucking back!!" He roars, making me choke on the gasp in my throat as he whirls on me with fury.

"I—*no!* Jackson, I didn't!"

"That was *my* voice!" He barks viciously. "Those were pictures of *me* at my fucking *house*!"

"I didn't write that story!" Jackson, I've been here with—"

"You are *exactly* what I knew you were the second I fucking saw you."

My heart wrenches, the color falling from my face. I'm dimly aware of people rushing towards the docks behind us, but all I can do is stare him with horror sinking it's claws into me.

"*Please—*"

"The fucking enemy," he says coldly. "That's what you are, Melody. That's all you've ever really been,"

The tears begin to flood down my face as I shake my head.

"*Please*! Jackson!"

"Get the fuck away from—"

"Mr. Havoc! Ms. Blue!"

I gasp, shuddering as a hand grabs my arm and yanks me around. Lights blind me, making me flinch away as microphones and cameras are suddenly thrust into my face.

"Mr. Havoc! Does this mean you'll be returning to the music scene? Do you plan on touring again!?"

"Mr. Havoc! What made you finally break your silence—"

"Jackson!"

"Mr. Havoc!"

The tsunami of shouting faces and flashing cameras, and space-invading microphones is overwhelming. I blink, trying to catch a single breath as I feel them push me back against Jackson.

"Jackson! Has your daughter known you were here the whole time?"

I blink, and it's like everything freezes. It's like a record scratches, and the music turns off.

"My...*what?*" Jackson rasps darkly behind me.

"Judy Blue just went live on Instagram and leaked it from her upcoming book!"

"Leaked what—"

"Is that why you're here, Melody?"

I gasp, stuttering back a step as a wave of microphones are shoved into my face.

"Are you and your father reuniting?"

The floor drops out.

A low, whining sound begins to blare in my ear, growing louder and louder, drowning out the rest of the world as everything goes sickeningly still.

"Jackson! When did you find out about Melody?"

My body is icy still and numb as I slowly turn towards him.

"What the fuck are you fucking talking—"

"*Is it true?*"

The words rip like torn bits of paper from my cottony mouth. I look at him, and it's like a whole world is burning around me. Like the color and goodness is being scorched away to reveal the dark horror beneath.

"Is *what* fucking true—"

"Did you…."

My face turns white, and my entire heart turns to glass.

"Did you sleep with Judy Blue?"

Jackson blinks. His jaw tightens.

"Why are you asking me—"

"*Because my last name isn't Hendrix*," I choke.

Jackson goes still.

"*It's—*"

"Ms. Blue! Ms. Blue! What was it like, writing your first cover piece about—"

Jackson's face goes pale.

"*Because Judy Blue is my mother.*"

I want him to laugh. I want him to explode, or yell, or...*anything*.

Anything except look at me with pure horror etched across his face.

Oh my God.

OH, MY FUCKING GOD.

His face crumples.

"*Melody—*"

I turn, I shove my way through the crowd of reporters, and I fucking *run*.

I run recklessly, barely able to see as the tears stream down my face and the sick begins to heave in my stomach. I somehow make it down the side alley next to the liquor store before I double over, spewing vomit and tears onto the pavement as my entire world turns to dust around me.

"Mel!!"

Bleary-eyed. Horrified. Sick to my very soul, I turn my throbbing head to the side as familiar arms wrap around me.

June.

I don't know how she's here. But I don't care.

"What do you need!?" She yells, her face as stricken as mine as she helps me up.

"Mel! What do you—!"

"*I need to get out of here.*"

"I drove. C'mon."

I see nothing. I feel nothing. I *am* nothing as she drags me from the alley and into her waiting rental car. I collapse into the seat, lifeless, to the point where she has to put my seatbelt on for me. She climbs in next to me, and the car shifts into drive as a swarm of reporters rushes the car.

"Drive...please."

The tires squeal as we pull away.

As the world fades away.

As everything I am and everything I know turns to acid dripping through my fingers.

37

JACKSON

Four months later, New York City:

"Happy Tuesday, everyone. That was the latest track from the Brooklyn band Aesop. I am Delphine, and you're listening to 90.7 WFUV.

Well, if you're a Velvet Guillotine fan, it's been a wild last few months with the—I guess you could call it the rebirth of the man himself, Jackson Havoc. Four months ago, we saw the dramatic return to the spotlight of the Guillotine frontman following a bombshell article in Ignition Magazine revealing that Havoc was in fact alive, and living under an alias in coastal Maine

Even more explosive than the Ignition article though, was that Havoc's return to the spotlight also came on the tails of an incendiary leak out of the upcoming book from one-time groupie and Playboy Playmate Judy Blue—a book in which she apparently alleges that Havoc is in fact the father of her daughter, Melody Blue.

In his one media appearance since his return, Havoc has refuted this claim. But, stoking controversy, abruptly walked away from further questions when rumors of his alleged romantic relationship with the younger Ms. Blue were brought to light.

Scandal aside—and really, what would a return by rock 'n roll's baddest bad boy be without some controversy—it would seem that Havoc is back in the world of the living, and if rumors are to be believed, sober, as well. The Velvet frontman is also back in New York City, where he's allegedly been secretly recording a new solo record.

I don't know about you, but I am a huge Velvet Guillotine fan. I think I probably saw them eleven times back in the day. So, if the rumors are true about a Havoc solo album? I am HERE for it, you guys.

Of course, while Havoc has been uncharacteristically OUT of the spotlight, it would seem Judy Blue is pulling enough of it for the both of them. Her explosive new book, which allegedly details a relationship with Havoc and a ton of behind-the-scenes details into Velvet Guillotine, drops next month alongside the launch of her new reality television show, House of Rock.

Billing itself as Kardashian-esque reality show, House of Rock stars Judy Blue alongside her current romantic partner, rock musician Kurt Harrison, as well as her daughter, Melody. The show's premise is the three of them living in a Soho loft while navigating the launch of Ms. Blue's new fashion and home goods line, Mr. Harrison's new record, and the younger Ms. Blue coming to terms with being rock royalty.

House of Rock premiers next month, but WFUV will be on-site at the Beacon Theatre in three days for the Kurt Harrison album release concert. In the meantime, in keeping in theme, here's classic Velvet Guillotine with Wreck Me Gent—

My fingers slam the radio alarm clock off.

Yeah, no. I'm all set with that at the moment, thank you very much.

In the ensuing silence, I groan and finally drag myself from sleep. I exhale slowly, rubbing my eyes before I sit up in the bed and glance around the basically empty apartment.

But then, it's time for my routine.

Routine keeps me sane. Routine keeps me living. And yes, maybe at times it feels like living with the house lights perpetually on after a show. But it's *living*.

More or less, at least.

These days, my routine starts about now, at ten AM. No, I'm not sleeping past noon or until it gets dark outside anymore, because I'm not staying up until four o'clock in the morning poisoning myself. But I'm still never going to be a morning person, because really, *fuck* mornings.

So, ten o'clock it is. I wake up, roll out of bed, and meditate.

Yeah. *I'm* actually fucking meditating, like some sort of new-age hippie guru bullshit. But it's supposed to do something good for my blood pressure. Which, after twenty years of sustained abuse, is…"hesitantly open" to the idea of something healthy.

To that effect, after meditation, I work out. Like actually working out and lifting weights. And after *that*, I shower, get dressed, and sit at the breakfast table of my loft. I drink black coffee—and these days, it's *just* coffee, without anything fun in it. And I eat a *way*-too-healthy breakfast devoid of sugar, cocaine, weed, or prescription narcotics.

I'm not going to lie. It's a fuckin' drag.

After that, I try to write, with "try" being the operative word. I don't have to commit words to paper. I don't *have* to walk away from the breakfast table with my magnum opus, and I don't have to cut my veins open and bleed pure genius onto the page.

The important thing is to sit down, stare at the paper, and see what happens.

One moment at a time. One day at a time. God grant me the strength, blah blah blah.

Except, I don't know. I stopped asking God for things a long time ago. And when you've been branded as the Antichrist by no less than three major publications in the course of your lifetime, honestly, it just feels a little cheeky to ask Him for anything anyway.

Besides, I'm not in the program. There are no steps I'm following except the ones I lay out myself, and I'm making peace with that.

The steps—as in AA, or NA—*do* work for some people. I mean I've met people in the last few months who aren't altogether that different from me. They just didn't have the random dice roll in life of becoming rich and famous to go along with their demons.

For some of them, the steps work. The program works. AA works.

For me, not so much.

Maybe it's the "rule breaker" in me that was never an act. I'm just *actually* bad at following a path someone else lays out in front of me. I'm the stubborn asshole who has to cut his own way through the world. And so, I guess that's what I'm doing.

Because, as the fucking radio keeps blathering on about... Jackson Havoc is back, baby.

Whatever the fuck that means.

Except, what it *seems* to mean is the same three questions over and over: Will there be a new record? Will there be a new tour? Will he form Velvet Guillotine again? But to these questions and more, my only answers are simply "fuck" and "off."

For now, it's one day at a time. Routine keeps me sane. Routine keeps me moving. But most importantly, routine keeps me *sober*.

I'm still learning about sober me. He's a little less fun, granted. But so far, he seems okay. He's certainly easier to live with, I'll say that much.

So, this is me now: the "best version of myself" as I once told...

Instantly, whatever positivity I've drudged up from somewhere deep inside evaporates like smoke. My jaw clenches as my eyes slip across the table to my phone.

Don't play it. Don't fucking play it.

I play it; the voicemail, that is. AKA, the *one* communication I've received from Melody since the day it all went to shit. My eyes close as her voice—cold and lifeless—echoes from the phone speaker.

"Hi, it's me. They told me you had a cell phone now, and that this is the number. So, I'm just going to say this here and then never again."

Her breath draws in, and my jaw clenches like I'm bracing for the hit.

"I was just using you, Jackson. For the story. Sorry, but it is what it is. What happened with us was wrong and fucked up, and it's for the best if we leave what happened on the island and move on. I am, and I think you should, too. It's over. Don't try and contact me, or I'll spin a very different narrative about what happened. And I think we both know; they'll believe me over you. This also goes for my mom's book. Don't fight the release or I *will* bury you. Goodbye."

That's it. Full stop.

The masochist in me is tempted to play it again—as I do sometimes. But not today. Instead, I just let the brutal sting of it sink into my skin as I grit my teeth and stab my gaze through the table in front of me.

I want to dive headfirst into conspiracy theory land: that, obviously, Melody was forced to leave that message. That she's under duress or something. And maybe that was a theory I could rally behind...

That is, until I saw her. Not face-to-face, but when she and Judy were on *Good Morning Manhattan* together a few months back.

Smiling. Laughing. Fucking *hugging* each other as they reminisced about being "raised by rock 'n roll". And of course, touting Judy's upcoming book: "Havoc Love".

I mean, fucking *shoot me*.

Cliff, my manager slash attorney, wants me to fight the book on the very obvious grounds of it being *completely full of shit*. And easily refutable shit, at that.

For instance, I am *one-hundred percent* sure I'm not Melody's fucking father.

How, one might ask, could I—a man with a storied history of casual relationships and questionable choices be so sure of this fact? Well, for one, I never *once* even touched Judy. Because, frankly, she always skeeved me out. She never once came across as a fan or the kind of girl who just wanted to "be with the band".

She came off as *eager*. As someone with stars or dollar signs in her eyes and the claws to get her way to the top no matter what. And I never once had even a passing interest in her.

But how—aside from knowing without question that I never screwed Judy—do I know I have a zero percent chance of being Melodys father? I mean, to avoid a he-said-she-said situation?

Well, there's the tiny, little, minute detail that I had a *fucking vasectomy* when I was twenty.

I'm not her father. I'm not *anyone's* father. But still, despite Cliff harping about it for the last four months, I'm not going to be fighting the book, legally.

But is it because of Melody's bizarre threat to 'bury me' with…something?

Not in the slightest.

It's because the girl I fell completely in love with on Falstaff Island stuck a knife in my heart. And even *thinking* about her, or the book, or any of it, makes me want to go out to the nearest bar or liquor store and consume everything in fucking sight. Or go out and buy a Scarface amount of cocaine to shove up my nose until my heart stops.

So, yeah. That's where I'm at.

In the end, it turns out "the enemy" really was the enemy all along.

Fuck her.

So, for now, like I said, it's one day at a fucking time. I'm old enough to understand I'm not *actually* a deity. And I've lived with my demons and my addictions long enough to know how fragile the current state of my sobriety is.

Not to mention, how lethally important it is for me to keep it going.

And so, the routine it is. Wake up. Don't consume drugs or alcohol. Eat breakfast. Don't consume drugs or alcohol. Try and write. Don't consume drugs or alcohol.

This shit is fucking exhausting.

Usually, the morning routine is followed by heading into the studio by early afternoon. I try not to keep pace with the absolute shit-storm of rumors surrounding me and my "return to the world". But, that one about me recording they basically nailed.

Well, sort of.

Apparently, half the internet thinks I'm desperate for a comeback and relevancy at any price. And the other half thinks I'll be recreating old Velvet Guillotine records note-for-note for some asinine reason.

The truth is, it's neither of those things.

I don't give a shit about a comeback. I give a shit about finding my creativity again. And what comes out these days, for the first time in possibly my entire life, is just *me*.

No chemicals. Nothing bringing me down. Nothing bringing me up. Nothing coloring the way I look at the world.

It's just me.

And who knows…maybe "just me" sucks. Maybe no one wants "just me", and the whole appeal before was me plus the thousand other chemicals helping me become a version of me. But all I know is, at this point, I truly don't give a fuck.

Today, however, I'm breaking routine. I'm skipping the studio because I have someplace else I need to be, and I've been putting it off for way too long.

Downstairs in my building's private garage, I slip the helmet on and throw a leg over my bike. This is my new favorite way to drive through this city. Because—at the risk of sounding like a completely egomaniacal douchebag—you can't really walk down the street when you're *me*.

People know me. People stop. People want my fucking autograph. They want a selfie. Whatever it is they want, I can't get a fucking cup of coffee without dealing with that shit.

But on a bike with a helmet on and a tinted visor, I'm anonymous. I'm just one more nobody on a motorcycle dodging taxis and pedestrians. Getting flipped off. Getting cursed at like I'm just some schmuck.

And I love it.

The engine revs as I leave the garage and pull onto 7th avenue. And I make it about a block from my building before I get stuck behind a bus.

Instantly, whatever inner peace, or centered wisdom, or any other meditative bullshit I've managed to wrap around myself in the few hours that I've been awake shatters around me.

Because right there on the back of the bus in front of me is a giant ad for that *fucking* reality show—with Judy, fucking *Kurt*, and Melody's faces smiling right at me.

Mocking me. Ripping my chest open and letting me bleed out on the street.

But then, the moment passes. The bus pulls away and makes a turn, and I rev the bike beneath me as I roar off to where I need to go.

To somewhere, and some*one* I've been putting off seeing for way, way too long.

38

JACKSON

THE REDHEAD and I stare at each other for the longest fifteen seconds in the world when she opens the door to her Central Park West townhouse.

The seconds tick by. I can't tell if the years have driven us further apart than I've ever thought they would. Or, if standing here in front of Alice Watts for the first time in a decade, it's as if no time has passed at all.

She blinks. I blink. Slowly, her head shakes side to side, and I watched a single tear trickle from the corner of her eye.

"You fucking *asshole*."

And then suddenly, my best friend's widow is throwing her arms around me and hugging me like a long lost child. She hugs me tightly—so tightly that my breath chokes even as a smile creeps over my face while I hug her back.

"*You fucking asshole,*" she chokes against my chest.

"I'm sorry."

I hold her as she clings to me.

"I'm so fucking sorry, Alice."

Slowly, sniffing and smiling, she pulls back to look up at me with a grin on her face. She gestures with her head, pulling me into the townhouse.

"Well, come on in, you bastard."

I chuckle, following her inside the stunning home. But it's not ostentatious. The place isn't gilded in gold, like all the ads for House of Rock portray the set of that show.

Alice's home is a *home*, and I smile when I look around and see framed pictures of Iggy on the wall. There are framed pictures of me, for that matter, and framed posters of tours I barely remember from almost twenty years ago.

A recording of a someone fantastic playing the guitar drifts from a speaker from elsewhere in the house—something I can't quite place even though it's fucking great. A Stevie Ray Vaughn live track, maybe?

I'm not sure. But I tune it out as I focus back on Alice. I follow her down a hall into a modern, light filled kitchen.

"You want some tea, or…"

She turns to look at me, raising a brow as if questioning this whole sobriety rumor she's probably heard parroted somewhere.

"Tea is great."

She grins as she turns to put the kettle on.

"You look healthy."

"Yeah, apparently exclusively sustaining yourself on literal poison for almost thirty years is bad for the skin."

"Huh. Never heard that before."

"Yeah, I read it on a blog somewhere."

She grins.

"Sobriety suits you; you know."

"I'm trying it on for size."

"Well, one day at at—"

When I groan, she chuckles.

"Yeah, I figured you wouldn't be doing any sort of steps."

"You know me too well, Ally."

"What, the annoying big brother I never wanted?" she quips, making me grin at the line she used to toss out when she and Iggy and I were barely teenagers.

She makes the tea, which I take black, and we sit at the counter letting the steam curl around our faces.

Alice clears her throat.

"Have you talked to Ash?"

I shake my head.

Even if I wasn't coming back to "the world" under the shadow of what happened with Melody, and that fucking article, and the goddamn book, and Judy, and all of it?

Even then, being back from the dead is weird.

Some days, you just want to go back to your old routines. You want to go back to your old favorite bars and see if they've still got the same stuttering jukebox in the corner, and same cranky bartender slinging the same not-quite cold beers.

You want the same songs to be on the radio. The same talking points to be on the news. Some days, being "back" just feels like a reset—like you're starting over from an earlier saved point in time.

But that's just not how it works.

I've been a ghost for ten years, and the world has moved on and gone on turning. When I left, yeah, I sent quick, brief notes to Will and Ash—the two closest things I had to brothers—telling them I'd be disappearing for a while.

That it wouldn't be long.

That I'd be in touch at some point.

Obviously, things shook out much differently.

When I left, we all had demons we were fighting. All of us were still grieving Iggy in our own ways. Ash had just lost his father, Will was dealing with the shitstorm he'd kicked up by crossing Luca Carvelli, of all fucking people to cross.

I never meant to disappear forever. But a month turned into two, and then five, and then nine. And suddenly, a year had passed. Then another.

And then Will was dead.

Even a nowhere town like Cape Harbor heard about that. And when it hit my ears…I guess it was like the final nail for me. That was it, and out went any lies I'd been telling myself about ever coming back.

I should have reached out to Asher. But I never did. And the longer I went without sending the letter I'd re-written about a dozen times, the easier it got to pretend I was the only one left.

Alice smiles quietly. "You should."

"Do you guys talk?"

She shakes her head. "Not for a long time. We met up once for a drink maybe two years after Will's funeral, but that was it. He…" she shrugs. "He keeps to himself. Or so I hear."

I swallow, looking down into my tea and watching the few bits of leaves swirl in the bottom of the cup.

"Look, Alice—"

"Jackson, you don't have to explain shit," she shrugs with an easy smile. "Really. Look, did I miss you when you left? *Yeah*. I mean, yeah, Jack, we all missed you. Me, Will, Ash…"

She looks away, wiping her eye.

"We all missed you a lot, Jackson. Of course, we did."

She exhales, taking a shaky sip of her tea.

"Do you know what we did on the one-year anniversary of you leaving?"

"Went through my search history and made fun of the porn I watched?"

She stifles a laugh.

"No, you asshole. We had a fucking funeral."

My brows knit.

"Seriously?"

"I mean, *yeah*, Jackson. It'd been a year. A *year* without hearing from you. And let's be real…back then, you going a *month* without a safety net was cause for concern. But a year?"

She looks away, wiping another tear from the corner of her eye.

"I don't think any of us really thought you'd survive a year, Jackson."

"Well, I hope someone collected on that bet."

She smiles wryly as I exhale.

"Alice, I was supposed to take care of you—"

"You did, Jack."

She rolls her eyes and shifts her gaze around the twelve-foot ceiling in the luxurious Central Park townhouse

"Jackson, *come on*. I mean, I know what you did."

I clear my throat, playing dumb.

"I have no idea what you're talking about."

"*Please*, Jack. I loved Iggy to death. But the man knew nothing about paperwork or money or banks or contracts or anything like that."

"What, and I did?"

"Jackson, there are squirrels in the park across the street that know more about contracts and financial responsibility than Iggy ever did. I know you had to basically force him under duress to put his own fucking name on the writing credits to the songs you two wrote together."

I smile, shaking my head.

"Goddamn was he a stubborn prick about that."

"Wonder where he learned that?"

I grin. Alice eyes me over the rim of her tea.

"But I know what you did. Or rather, I know it wasn't Iggy who did it."

I lift a shoulder.

"No idea what you're talking—"

"You put Eleanor's name on the songwriting credits to every Velvet Guillotine song."

I try and hold it back, but the grin creeps over my face anyway.

"Jackson, I was already going to collect as is. I mean I *am* the executor of Iggy's estate."

"Yeah, well," I shrug. "I wanted to make sure Eleanor would, too. She's my goddaughter, after all. I figured if I was going to disappear for, well, forever, this would make up for all the birthdays where she wouldn't get cool shit from me."

Alice blinks back tears as she puts a hand on my arm.

"*Thank you*," she whispers hoarsely.

"Iggy would have wanted her name on them."

She smiles sadly, patting my arm. "I know."

"How is she, by the way?"

"Your goddaughter? Great. Big." She rolls her eyes. "You know she's twelve now."

"Fucking Christ, she's *twelve*?"

"Time flies when you drop off the face of the earth, huh?"

"No shit."

I glance around, frowning.

"When is she getting home?"

Alice smiles curiously.

"She's here, and she's almost done."

"Done with what?"

Her grin widens.

"Practicing."

"Practicing what—"

The guitar over the speaker in the other room stops. And suddenly it clicks as my eyes widen.

Holy fuck.

That wasn't a Stevie Ray Vaughn live recording. That was someone *actually* playing. I stare at Alice.

"Oh, fuck off—"

"Mom?" A voice calls out from somewhere in the house above us.

"I'm in the kitchen, hon! Come on down. I want you to meet someone."

Alice sits back on her stool, sipping her tea as we listen to footsteps crashing down the staircase. And then suddenly I hear sneakers on the kitchen floor. I turn, and my eyes blink as I stare at a carbon fucking copy of my best friend.

Well, almost.

A carbon copy without the receding hairline. And with her mother's auburn hair and blue eyes. But God *damn*, it's like a twelve-year-old Iggy staring at me with that same funny smile and a look of bewildered recognition on her face.

"You're…you're Jackson Havoc."

I grin.

"And you're a clone of your dad. Well, minus the ugly bits. You can thank your mom for that input."

Eleanor grins, but then her brow furrows.

"I thought you were dead."

"Eleanor!" Alice hisses.

But I just grin back at my goddaughter.

"I kind of thought I was too, for a while. But I'm figuring out how to be alive again."

She shifts on her feet.

"Was that you playing?"

She nods.

"You're pretty fucking goo—" I clear my throat as she giggles. "I mean, you're pretty good."

"It's okay, you can swear. I'm not a kid, and mom does all the time."

I chuckle as I glance back to see Alice burying her face in her hands.

"I have no doubt about that."

"I wanted to be a drummer, like dad, but…" Eleanor shrugs.

"Yeah, I get it." I wink at her. "Guitar is *way* more fun, isn't it?"

She beams at me. "Totally."

Alice slides off her stool, walking past me to pull Eleanor into a hug and kiss the top of her head.

"Hon, can I talk to Jackson alone for a second?"

"Sure, I actually need to finish up for my lessons tomorrow."

Her gaze shifts to me.

"I'm glad you're not dead."

"Me too."

She disappears up the stairs again. A few seconds later, my jaw drops as I hear her launch into the intro of a Joe Satriani song that someone three times her age should have trouble playing. I turn to shake my head at Alice.

"Holy *fuck*, she's incredible."

Her mom grins with pride. But then, her face falls a little.

"Have you seen her?"

"Who?"

She gives me a look.

"Melody, Jackson."

I take a long sip of my tea as I shake my head.

"No."

"Have you figured it out yet?"

"Christ, Alice, I'm not her fucking father. I mean, I've had some interesting times, but I never once touched Judy—"

"I know, Jackson—"

"I mean for fuck's sake, Ally, I had a vasectomy over twenty fucking years ago!"

"*Jackson,*" she sighs. "I know you're not her father."

She frowns curiously.

"Fuck, you didn't connect it yet, did you?"

"Riddles are a bit lost on me these days. She's not mine."

"Well, Jackson, of course she's not."

She stares at me in a way that begins to unnerve me.

"Alice, *what?*"

"Oh, my God, you don't…" She shakes her head. "You don't see it?"

"See *what?*"

She blinks, and I look at her with concern as her eyes start to water again.

"Alice—"

She turns away, dabbing at her eyes with a napkin.

"I loved him, you know. Iggy, I mean."

"Of course, I know that."

"I mean more than anything. And I knew he was flawed—"

"Alice, come on—"

"*Please*, Jack. Iggy was a flawed man, and we both know it, even though we both still loved him."

She turns back to me, her eyes red and puffy, tears rolling down her cheeks.

"Jackson, of course Melody isn't yours. Just like she's not Will's, either."

My brow furrows.

"I don't understand what you're—"

"She's Iggy's, Jackson."

The world goes numb as the bomb detonates right in front of my face.

"Jackson, Melody is *Iggy's* daughter."

39

THERE'S a moment of free fall. It's the sensation of the bottom dropping out, and all of me plummeting into the black hole of an abyss beneath my feet. For a second, it's almost like the feeling of being high, or that moment when drunk turns into blackout.

Except the fall just keeps happening.

There is no bottom. Instead, I stand there, swaying on my feet, gripping Alice's kitchen countertop as my eyes stab into her.

"*What the fuck...*" I whisper quietly.

Her face scrunches up.

"Jackson—"

"What. The. *Fuck.*"

I start to back away, shaking my head.

"*No.*"

"Jackson, please sit."

"No." My head shakes violently. "No, there's no fucking way—"

"Jackson!"

Her voice strikes out, hitting me like a slap and shaking me from the free-fall. I blink, and finally, I can actually feel my own skin, and my own pulse thudding in my ears.

Alice shakes her head as she exhales. "We're all flawed creatures, Jack. I loved Ig, but he wasn't a god or a saint or something."

I swallow thickly.

"*How?*"

She takes a slow breath as she sits at one of the stools against the counter.

"It was during your first US tour. I…I couldn't do it. I mean, *yeah*, you all had been playing around England for a while before that. And I followed when I could…you know, when I could get off work and when I could join the tour and be with Iggy and all of you. But the United States? With a chart-topping record?"

Her eyes glass over as she shakes her head.

"Jackson, all I saw on TV were the girls just throwing themselves at all of you, and I couldn't do it."

"Alice, Iggy never *once* stepped out—"

"I know, I know."

She looks away.

"But I cracked. I couldn't take the wondering and just the waiting for him to call me one day and tell me it was over. Or worse, if he never *did* call. If instead, I just turned on the news or opened a Rolling Stone and saw him with some girl, and I'd be shattered. It would've killed me, Jack."

My fingers shove through my hair as I watch her shrink in on herself.

"So, me being me, I did it first. I ended it, and we broke up."

My brow furrows deeply.

"You…" I frown, trying to replay those manic, drug-and-booze-and-adrenaline fueled days on the road from almost twenty years ago.

"He was my best friend…" I choke. "How the fuck would I not know that you two…"

And then suddenly—dimly and darkly—a flicker of something hits me. A vague memory of Iggy after a show in…

I stare at her.

"Chicago," I breathe.

Alice wipes a tear away.

"*Yeah*. It was when you were in Chicago."

I slowly shake my head as it floods out of the dark corners of my memory.

"Ig was a fucking mess that night."

I don't know how the fuck I remember that twenty years later, and after an infinite number of nights when any number of us were beyond fucked up. But that one stands out. Maybe because it was our first US tour, and I was still in that business mind-set of making sure the machine kept churning.

The media may have seen me as this drug-fueled wild man—which, obviously, was completely true. But they didn't see the war general behind the scenes.

Back then, I was *hyper* aware of how tenuous our place in the music world was. One hit does not a career make, after all. And back then on that first North American tour, I was a *bastard*—a single-minded machine making sure the wheels didn't fall off.

My face falls.

I remember being so *angry* at him that night in Chicago. I was pissed that he was just fucking it up. That he was too drunk. We hadn't even started the show yet, and he was absolutely blitzed. I remember yelling at him and then feeling terrible when he almost cried.

Somehow, I remember wondering what that was about.

Now I know.

"*Holy fuck*," I breathe.

"It was a week, Jackson. And I was a *wreck* back in Liverpool. I mean I didn't sleep or eat, and it was just worse. It was *worse* than the waiting for the phone call or waiting to see a picture of him with some girl on some music blog somewhere. So, I snapped, and I flew to LA to meet you guys."

"I remembered that" I say quietly with a small smile.

I remember Alice surprising Iggy at the hotel, and I remember watching my friend drop to his knees in tears as he just hugged her around the waist. And I remember feeling so...not *envious*. But just sad, knowing deep down that I would never have that.

Knowing that I wasn't wired that way, like Iggy and Alice were.

Except, maybe I was. Maybe it just took me twenty years to find it.

And then lose it.

"We knew the break had been a mistake."

Alice starts to cry.

"But, just the same, he was with someone else while we were apart. He told me that straight out and honestly when we got back together. He'd been drunk, and sad, and all of that. But..." she shakes her head. "There was another girl. And it almost broke me."

She looks away.

"But I accepted it, because I loved him. I accepted that he'd been lost, and away from home. I was his only lifeline, and I'd cut that off because I was scared of losing him. And in doing so, he found something with someone else, just one time. And that..."

She looks up at me with teary eyes.

"That was hard, Jack. But I accepted it. And I accepted it a month later when he told me that girl had contacted him, and that she was pregnant, and that it was his."

I blink, my pulse thudding heavily in my ears.

I've never heard a *whisper* of this. I knew the man for almost his entire life, and I never heard one fucking peep about any of this.

I want to be angry. I want to feel betrayed, because I want to think I'd have told Iggy about all of this in a fucking second if the roles were reversed.

My eyes close.

But that's bullshit. I mean maybe I would have, but I can't make that call now in the glow and safety of hindsight.

"She wanted him to be with her."

My eyes open as I stare at Alice.

"What?"

"The girl. She wanted Iggy to choose, but…."

She smiles sadly.

"He picked me, Jack," she whispers with a broken, sad smile on her face. "Iggy picked me. He told this girl that he'd do whatever it took for the baby—I mean financially, parentally, all of that. But that he couldn't be with her."

I swallow as Alice looks away.

"She lost it, and she said no. I mean, no to all of it—the money, the help, him being a part of the kid's life. She cut him out, Jackson, and it really it fucked him up for a while."

Her mouth twists.

"You know, that's when he first used. Heroin, I mean. That was the first time, after she told him he couldn't be a part of this kid's life. She was in love with him, I think. And he was in love with an unborn child whose life he'd just been told he couldn't be a part of."

I want a drink. I want a drink *so fucking badly* it physically hurts. The world spins as I storm across the kitchen to what looks like a liquor cabinet of some kind, and all but yank the door off the hinges.

…Only to come face-to-face with a collection of tacky coffee mugs.

"I'm five years sober, Jack," Alice whispers quietly behind me.

I suck in air, feeling the shakes ripple through my skin until I feel her hand on my back.

"Sit down," she murmurs quietly.

I let her guide me to a chair as the waves of need begin to ebb.

"I…I'm sorry. I didn't mean to just dump all of this on—"

"Keep going," I croak.

"Jackson—"

"Just fucking tell me, Alice."

She nods.

"Look, I knew that there was another woman. I just didn't want to know *who* that woman was. And I've spent years locking that part of my life into a compartment in my head. And I didn't know who that baby was, either…"

Her eyes lock with mine.

"Until that article about you in Ignition came out four months ago."

I stare at her, gripping the countertop.

"What do you mean?"

She blinks back a tear.

"I mean this."

She turns, opening a cabinet above the microwave and pulling something down. When she turns back, she shoves a stack of envelopes into my hands.

"I didn't know what these were. I mean, I—"

She looks away.

"I guess I did sort of know what they were. They were Iggy's therapy. They were his way of connecting with this piece of him that he wasn't allowed to see, and whose life he wasn't allowed to be a part of. So, he wrote these letters."

I stare at the unsealed, unaddressed envelopes in my hands.

"I always thought he wrote them and never sent them. But apparently, he did. Some of them, at least."

I stare at what's in my hands, feeling my heart thud as I open one. But I already know what it's going to say. And when I read those first words on the top of that first page, my heart breaks a little.

Dear Prudence,

I had ice cream today. To you, that probably seems like something you get to do all the time when you're a grown-up. But the funny thing is, it actually gets a lot harder to do stuff like get ice cream when you're big.

When you're a kid, all you want to do is grow up. But once you do, the crazy thing is, all you wanna do is be a kid again.

Anyway, I had my favorite—mint chocolate chip. The green kind, because the other kinds are rubbish. Trust me on that, I'm an expert. But I was wondering...what's your favorite flavor of ice cream? It's okay if it's the not-green kind of mint chocolate chip. If that's what you're into, you do you, kiddo. And don't let anyone, even me, tell you otherwise.

I hope things are good. And I hope you're well and happy.

Stay young, kiddo. Growing up is kind of a scam.

All my love,

Dad

My chest constricts. My pulse thuds heavily as I raise my eyes to stare at Alice as her eyes brim with tears.

"I...I don't know if he wanted her name to be Prudence..." She laughs quietly, brushing the moisture away from her eyes. "You know Ig; Beatles nut that he was. Or maybe it was just his way of..."

The sob wrenches from her throat. She starts to collapse against the counter, and I go to her, holding her as she cries into my chest.

"That girl, Jackson...that's Iggy."

Alice looks up at me.

"I don't mean in the sense of God, or heaven, or spirits, or reincarnation, or any of that. But that girl came from a man we both loved dearly, and I don't think it's a coincidence that she and you connected like that. She's Iggy's kid, Jack. There's a reason she dragged you out of whatever fucking hole you spent the last ten years—"

"She didn't—"

"Jackson? Shut up."

Alice smiles through her tears.

"Of course, she did. She got you out of that hole and off that island. You're not drinking. You're writing. You're *recording*, for fuck's sake. People don't come into our lives by accident, Jack, and you can't let them go when it happens. Believe me, you'll carry that regret your entire life if you do."

We stand there another minute—two people connected by their shared love and grief for a man gone way too soon.

"Your tea's getting cold," Alice finally mutters quietly.

I smile, leaning down to kiss the top of her head before I pull away.

"I don't want to know why you and Melody aren't together—"

"It's complicated—"

"I told you I don't want to know, Jack."

She purses her lips, jabbing a finger at me.

"But I do want to know what the hell you're going to do about it."

No genius ever came to anyone in the morning.

Luckily, it's late, and dark, by the time I get into the studio after hugging Alice and Eleanor goodbye.

I'm shaking a little. There's still the lingering stab of pain in my chest from learning everything I did tonight. And yeah, I want a drink, or a line, or a pill so fucking badly that my very skin burns.

But it's not drugs or alcohol that I'm going to numb myself with tonight.

It's the past.

Specifically, a part of the past I haven't once been able to even think about in eleven years.

For the last two months, I've been coming in here almost daily. And I've been rehashing, rewriting, and re-recording the same nine songs over and over. One is something I started writing when I landed back in New York. The other eight are from Maine.

They're all cowrites, with Melody.

Recording them and reworking them over and over is both torture and therapy. It's like flaying a cut open and then re-dressing it, only to rip it back open again.

And again, and again, and again.

Because these aren't just my songs anymore. They're *ours*—hers and mine. And every fucking word is wrapped around the memory of a smile or a kiss. Every chord or melody line is the soundtrack to a heated moment, or a stolen moan.

We wrote the soundtrack to *us*. I just don't know what the fuck to do with it, now.

But those nine songs aren't why I'm here tonight. Instead, in the low, dim light of just a strand of white string lights hung across the far wall of the studio, I reach for a notebook I haven't managed to bring myself to even *open* in eleven years.

We were in the middle of recording an album when Iggy died. But that one was different. It wasn't a bunch of songs we'd written months or even years before, and honed to perfection on the road, to live audiences.

For this one, Iggy was halfway through his fourth read-through of David Quantick's book "Revolution", about the Beatles and recording The White Album. And being the absolute Beatles nut that he was, Iggy wanted to try something different. No road-tested songs. For this one, the two of us were literally writing them *in* the studio and letting them evolve as they were captured on tape.

We got about halfway through before it all went dark.

I still haven't gotten myself to listen to any of those tracks—either the finished, polished ones that were album-ready, or the rough drafts of just Ig and I bashing out a chorus on a hot mic.

But there's one song in particular I've always known was going to cut deep if I ever even thought of it again. There's never been enough drugs or booze in the world to numb me enough to deal with that one.

But tonight, clean, sober, and without armor or walls, it's time.

Tonight, I'm ready to finish Iggy's last song; *Oh Eleanor*.

I smile tightly, nodding to no one as I reach for my guitar.

"Alright, you son of a bitch," I grin. "If you were looking for a chance to haunt me or some shit, now would be a splendid time. Because I could use your help on this."

I don't know if Iggy hears me. But I do know that for the first time in longer than I can remember, when the pen touches paper, and when my fingers find metal strings, something just *flows*.

And it doesn't stop.

It's almost dawn by the time I stagger bleary-eyed out of the studio. I inhale the scent of New York, blinking back emotion as I look up at the dim light of morning with a smile on my face.

The song is done.

Thanks, Ig.

I stretch, cracking my neck before I turn to head over to my bike. But suddenly, something blocks my path.

Not something. Someo*ne*.

I frown at the girl with the wild red hair and the guitar case slung over her shoulder who plants herself between me and my motorcycle. Her eyes glare up at me defiantly as her lips thin.

I groan. Whatever the fuck this is, I am *not* in the mood.

"*Move*," I grunt.

"Do you know how long I've been waiting out here for you?"

I blow air through my lips as I bring a hand up to pinch the bridge of my nose.

"Look, I'm flattered. But, not interested? Now, if you'll excuse me—"

"*Wow*."

She shakes her head, her lips curling as she raises a sharp brow.

"Has anyone told you lately to get the fuck over yourself?"

I frown. "Excuse me?"

"I wasn't waiting out here to because I have any remote interest in screwing a drunken has-been twice my age, thanks."

My eyes narrow.

"I'm sober, actually."

"Neat."

I glare at her and then nod at the guitar case on her back.

"That yours?"

"Yes?"

"You're a musician?"

"No, I make cakes in the shape of guitar cases." She rolls her eyes when I don't react at all to her sarcasm. "Yes, I'm a musician."

I smile thinly. "Tell you what. That demo I'm sure you've been dying to give me?"

"I don't—"

"Go ahead and shove it up your ass, then you can hum it to me as I drive away. Sound good?"

Her eyes narrow.

"Okay, *A*, fuck you—"

"We've already established that that is most certainly not happening. Now, get the fuck out of my way."

I step around her, moving to the bike.

"I'm here because of *Melody*, you pompous douchebag."

I freeze instantly. My muscles clench tightly, my teeth grinding as my eyes narrow to lethal slits. Turning, I inhale slowly as I glare at the girl with the guitar.

"Who the fuck are you?"

"I'm June Hendrix."

"*Speak*, June Hendrix."

"Okay, could you maybe lose the shitty attitude and just talk to me like a normal fucking person? You also can go ahead and *not* talk at all. That'd work fine for me."

I suck on my teeth before I open my mouth.

"What about Melody?"

"I'm worried about her."

My mouth thins as I turn towards my bike.

"Not my problem."

"Oh my God, are you still bent out of shape about that fucking article?"

My teeth flash as I whirl on her.

"*A bit*," I snap. "Yeah."

"Well, get over—"

"Am I still 'bent out of shape' that someone lied their way into my home and good graces? While using a fake last name..." I cock a brow at her. "*Your* last name, actually. And am I still a little *miffed* that this person wormed her way into my life just so she could sell me out to a shitty B-list music magazine?"

June bristles as I step closer to her.

"*A little*," I snap viciously.

The girl in front of me swallows, but she doesn't draw down.

"You don't seriously believe Melody had anything to do with publishing that piece, do you?"

"Well gee, June, maybe I was misled by the fact that *her fucking name* is on the article as a co-author. Or, hmm, the fact that it's full of confidential information that I distinctly remember telling her and her alone, without, I should add, agreeing to being recorded while doing so?"

"Maine is a single-party—"

"*Fuck. Off.*"

I turn to leave again, the high I was riding earlier from finishing Iggy's song dissolving like acid into something far more bitter. Something far more insidious.

The need for substances.

My body shakes, my skin burning as my demons try and claw their way back into control.

"Look, she may have recorded you—"

"*May have* nothing," I hiss, whirling on her again. "She did."

June shrugs.

"Fine. She fucked up. But she didn't write that story. She didn't have anything to do with it."

"I'm sure."

I need to get the fuck out of here. But this time, as I turn, the precocious redhead grabs my arm and yanks me back around.

"Stop walking away from me, asshole!"

I frown. There's real emotion and edge to her voice, and for the first time since she accosted me a minute ago, I can see through the attitude and the anger.

And I see that she's *scared*. Like really, actually scared. My brow furrows as I glare back at her.

"I know for a fact she didn't write that piece, dickhead," she chokes. "One, because the co-author, Becca Scaldi? She's a hack writer, and a snake. And she's also dim enough to have left her phone open around me."

Her eyes harden.

"Melody may have recorded you. But she didn't give it to anyone or write the story. Becca stole the recording and those pictures off Melody's phone and emailed them to herself."

I grunt. But June's not done.

"You don't find it strange that Melody writes the bombshell music article of the decade, and then literally ceases to exist at Ignition? Doesn't write a single other story for them, despite putting them on the map?"

I smile thinly.

"I suppose she was too busy building her and Judy's fucking Real World reality empire to have the time to blow up anyone else's lives."

"Oh my *God*, you're such a victim!"

"Fuck off—"

"Okay, yeah, the article was a dick move and the media showed up at your door. But, c'mon, seriously? It got you back in the world. It got you recording again, so they say. What were you doing that was so great before? Being a hobo on some island?"

"Yes," I snap. "That's exactly what I was doing. And I was *happy—"*

"Do you have *any clue* how fucking charmed a life you've lived?!" June blurts, shaking her head at me with this look of incredulousness that cuts into me.

"Dude, you won the game! Cry me a fucking river about fame being too hard, or the fans being too much, or that touring is tiresome? I mean are you for real?!"

My eyes narrow.

"You done?"

"No," she snaps. "Because even without the Becca thing, or without my friend disappearing into Judy-world, I *know* she didn't write that piece. Because Melody would have never in a million years have added the part about her dad's letters in a published piece. That's *way* too personal to her. She doesn't tell *anyone* about those."

"Well, hate to burst your bestie bubble," I shrug. "But she told me."

"Yeah, and that's what scares me."

I frown. June swallows.

"It scares me, because I know her. And I know how she was before she went to your stupid island, and I know how she was when she got back."

She looks away, shaking her head.

"You changed her, you know. Like it or not, you did something to pull her out of a place in her head she's been in for as long as I've known her."

She glances back at me, her sharp eyes slicing into me.

"And I get the feeling, she did the same for you."

I flinch as my brain glitches. Flashes of heat, and desire, and lyrics and music, and that feeling I once told myself I'd never have like Alice and Iggy burn into me like hot ashes. My jaw grits as the memories of Melody and I back on my island come swirling through my head.

"Why did you say you were worried about her?"

June's lips purse.

"Because she's one of my best friends, and I've barely seen her in *months*. And when I have, she looks and acts like a ghost. Besides that, she's living with her mom."

"And?"

June's eyes narrow.

"She'd willingly live with Judy like you'd willingly stop playing music."

I look away, my pulse thudding heavily in my veins.

"Melody is *not* okay, Jackson," she says quietly, her eyes wide with fear. "And I'm pretty sure you might be the only one that can help her."

My eyes close as my lungs fill slowly.

"That's none of my concern, anymore."

"Are you seriously—!"

"Melody made it pretty clear how she felt about me being anywhere near her life."

My jaw tightens painfully as I turn away.

"That's it!?"

"*Yeah*," I grunt, walking over to my bike. "That's it. I hate to break it to you, but real life isn't a cliched fucking song lyric."

June barks a cold laugh.

"Then what the fuck are you even doing back? Because if that's the Jackson Havoc we all get now?"

I glance back to see her lift a shoulder.

"Fuck that. Go back to your fucking island and go drink yourself into oblivion."

"Yeah?" I snap. "Well, maybe I will."

She sneers.

"Or maybe you stop hiding behind this devil-may-care bullshit, admit that the reason you're so mad at Melody at all is because you're in love with her, and then go *do something* about it."

My pulse ticks in my ears, a humming sound vibrating out through my chest as my eyes stab into the rising dawn. And faintly, like they're coming from a passing car, the lines seep like ink into my soul.

When I'm lost on the rocks and I'm sinking

When the boats goin' down, all I'm thinkin',

Is the melody you sang to me to sleep...

Is the one pulling me down to the deep."

Fuck.

40

MELODY

Some prisons don't involve bars. But that doesn't make the person trapped inside of them any less a prisoner.

Trust me on that.

I lay still in the bed, looking blankly up at the ceiling. Fatigue clouds my head with a dull throb, even though I've just woken up from a nap. But naps are a Band-Aid, not a fix for the fact that I don't really sleep much these days.

It's hard to sleep in prison. Even one with invisible bars.

I swallow, taking a slow breath as I try to convince myself to sit up. Or go back to bed. Or…anything. But everything is sort of numb these days.

Everything is a little cold, and empty.

Welcome to the House of Rock, aka, my prison.

It's fair to say Judy's never been a very good mother. In fact, she was pretty terrible at it. But "bad" was before she got a real taste of money and power.

Now, she's a nightmare.

She's not just Judy the shitty mom anymore. She's "a brand", and the way it's all come together is almost disturbingly elegant. Almost as disturbing as the way she's started styling herself as a sort of "rock 'n roll Kris Jenner"—even copying the short haircut and mannerisms. Which the producers of the show *love*, of course.

My eyes close as I sink into the bed.

First came the article—the one based off my horrible recording. But I didn't write it.

Becca did.

It took me a little while, but I eventually found the deleted messages on my phone, where she'd emailed herself my audio recordings, notes, and photos from the island while I was talking with Chuck in his office that day I got back from Maine.

But Becca didn't do it alone. She had help with some of the details of what became her "big story".

From Judy, of course.

After the article came the "leak", which was entirely Judy's doing in order to drum up salacious interest in her fucking "tell all" book—the grotesque and revolting allegation that Jackson is...*yeah*.

My nose wrinkles.

The idea that people read that and saw the pictures of the two of us alone makes me want to throw up. Even if, for the most part, "the world" seems to see it as the disgusting publicity stunt it is.

For one, as just about every blog and every post on Reddit on the subject points out, I look *nothing* like Jackson. Someone on the internet even did one of those "parent morph" things where they blended pictures of Judy and Jackson, and the result bares zero resemblance to me.

Also, there's a retired nurse named Linda Cressley who's been doing the rounds on talk shows, claiming that she once worked in a health clinic in London.

A clinic where, according to her, none other than Jackson Havoc once received a *vasectomy*.

At age twenty; the same age I am now.

Jackson is currently *forty-two*.

Yeah, do the math.

But proof or public opinion aside, it doesn't really matter. The whole point of Judy letting that horrible story out was to catapult her and "the brand" into the spotlight. It doesn't matter that it's an outright lie. What matters is, people are talking about the book. And her.

And really, that's all Judy's ever wanted from the world: recognition, of any kind, at any price.

I'm still lying in bed when the door to my room—my gaudy new room in the Soho loft which doubles as the set for the fucking show—opens. Tanya, Judy's way-too-eager new personal assistant, comes bustling in without a knock, frantically typing on her iPad.

"Um, hi, Tanya?"

"Mel, girl, we're on a schedule here. I need you down at dinner like five minutes ago, cool?"

My mouth thins.

"Tanya, I need you to start knocking."

She laughs. I'm not sure I get the joke.

"Five minutes ago, hon," she smiles a plastic, phony smile as she taps her watch. "We're on a real tight schedule tonight, with the event and all."

My mood blackens to night. A cold chill creeps up my spine.

"Tanya, I already talked to Judy, and I *really* don't want to go—"

"Well, that would be weird if you didn't!" She laughs. "Now, come on down!"

"My stomach is feeling gross."

She frowns, pulling out her phone.

"Want me to call Dr. Konrad?"

My face turns white.

"*No*," I blurt, shaking my head. "No. No Dr. Konrad."

The bars of my prison of the last four months may have been invisible. But the jailers aren't. And Judy's "doctor friend", Dr. Jeffery Konrad, is the captain of the guard.

Dr. Konrad is the one that "substantiated" Judy's claims in the book about my parentage. He's the one who put together a fake assault kit that "proves" Jackson sexually abused me— Judy's nuclear option against Jackson if he comes after her book.

The good doctor is also the one who's kept me docile, dulled, and lost these last four months of filming and TV appearances, through a heavy prescription of antipsychotics and anti-anxiety meds.

With the press tour and most of the filming for Judy's fucking show over, though, I've stopped taking those.

But I'm still numb. It still feels like the last four months were a hazy blur of feeling nothing. And it's still an unnerving enough thought, that the idea of even seeing Dr. Konrad again puts the fear of God in me.

"You're sure?"

"I'm fine," I blurt quickly.

Tanya grins.

"*Great.* Shall we?"

I nod in defeat as I stand and follow her out of the room and down to dinner. The whole lavish loft is decorated like a super trashy Hard Rock Cafe. Neon, chrome, glitz, and decadence ooze from every corner.

All of this is Judy, of course. And *all of it* will be readily available as part of her new House of Rock home-goods line.

Because of course it will.

The queen bitch herself glances up, sighing with a stern look when I step into the dining room.

"Melody, I *know* you saw the schedule for today."

She frowns.

"Do you need Dr. Konrad to get you something—"

"*No*," I hiss through clenched teeth, sitting heavily in the chair across from her. "I do not."

Judy frowns, her eyes piercing into me as she straightens her shoulders. Which has the effect of making her already gravity-defying tits—which she's recently had "lifted", again—jut out at me menacingly. She sighs as she lifts her gaze past me.

"Tanya, be a dear and give us a minute?"

"Absolutely, Ms. Blue," Tanya gushes in an eye-rolling way. "The car will be out front in forty-six minutes to take you all to the show, by the way."

"Perfect."

I hear Tanya's heels click-clacking away, followed by the sound of the dining room door shutting behind me.

Judy's smile falls.

"Melody, so help me God—"

"*What.*"

"What?!" She snaps. "I'm building you an empire, and all I get is snarky fucking—"

"You're building *you* an empire, Judy," I hiss. "And I don't want any part of it."

"I don't give a shit, Melody! I'm making something here! Something big!"

"On the backs of *lies*, slander, and—"

"Oh, welcome to the world, Melody!" She spits as she lurches to her feet. I stiffen as she storms over to my side of the table, glaring down at me.

"If you want something in this world, it's going to involve breaking some eggs. Do you think I've enjoyed all the things I've done over the years?"

"Yes?"

Her lips purse.

"It wasn't always a party, you know. You think I *wanted* to blow some fucking roadie so that you and I could share a hotel room, and not—"

"I really don't think you want me answering that question—"

I gasp, blinking tears as the slap stings sharply across my cheek. I swallow, my face throbbing as I swivel my gaze lethally to hers.

She just glares at me.

"Do I need Dr. Konrad to start you on your meds again?"

I stiffen.

"So you can shut me up!?"

"So that you stop trying sabotage *our* success!" Her eyes narrow. "Well?"

My eyes drop. My head shakes side to side.

"No."

"What was that?"

"*No*," I hiss thinly. "I don't need to go back on the meds."

"Good!"

She smiles as she turns on her heel and marches back to her seat across from me. When I keep my gaze locked on my plate, she sighs.

"Melody, for the last time. Whatever you think you had with that man?" She lifts a shoulder. "They're all the same, men like Jackson. And life is an exchange, whether you want to pretend otherwise or not. You got something you needed from him. And, obviously, *he* got something from *you*," she smirks.

I resist the urge to throw up.

I know he hates me. After the voicemail I left him? After that article with my name on it? Yeah, he definitely hates me. But if he comes near me, or if I try to go to him, Judy will ruin him.

Irreparably.

The gross lies about him being my father are one thing. But Judy's stacked the deck. Along with Dr. Konrad's fake assault report, she's got some old groupie friends of hers on her payroll willing to lie and claim they had flings with Jackson when they were fourteen.

If I try and reach out to him, or if he tries to come near me, Judy will let it all air out. And they'll burn him at the stake of public opinion.

"Now, eat your dinner. The car will be downstairs in half an hour, and we are not going to be late. We are *going* to be at that production wrap party, and then we will be front and center for Kurt's show, like a happy fucking family."

As if on cue, the door opens behind me, and a now-familiar coldness, and numbness creeps over me.

The footsteps move across the floor behind me—shaking me, making my stomach clench nauseously, turning my skin ashen and cold. And when he drops his hands to my shoulders, I physically flinch as something inside of me curls in on itself to hide, or die.

"Kurt, baby," my mom gushes past me to the man looming behind me. "You should get going!"

He laughs—and it's the same cold, toxic laugh I remember from years ago.

"Alright, I'll see you babes there?"

"You bet!" My mom grins as I die a little more inside.

Kurt chuckles.

"Perfect."

His hands squeeze my shoulders.

"Rock 'n roll, baby."

My vision blurs and dims at the edges. Self-hatred and revulsion curdles inside of me, even after his hands leave me, and his footsteps echo back out the door.

Because the worst part of all of this isn't the invisible prison. It's not being forced to play this horrifying role on Judy's insane reality show gimmick. It's not that my heart has been ripped open and left bleeding for four months. And it's not even knowing that going to the one man who can fix it—ignoring the fact that he definitely hates me—will destroy him.

No.

The worst part is that I'm not alone in this invisible prison.

I'm locked in here with *him*.

The monster who prowled into my bedroom when I was thirteen. The monster my mother forgave, and signed NDAs for, and took *money from*.

Kurt.

The monster is *Kurt*.

And these days, he sleeps right down the hall from me.

"Oh, for the last time, Melody."

My mother eyes me coldly, and I know she sees it all on my face.

"Just get over it already. I have."

I blink numbly.

"And eat your dinner. I don't want to be late."

41

JACKSON

"Sir? Excuse me, *sir?*"

The weasel-looking guy with an iPad and an earpiece stutters as he lurches to step in front of me. I look at him coldly before glancing past him, at the door to the events hall next to the main box office of the Beacon Theatre.

"I'm going inside."

I go to push past him, but the little dickhead plants his feet.

"*Sir!*" He snaps with the attitude of a chihuahua. "Sir, this is a guest-list only event! Now, if you're here for the concert, I believe there are a handful of tickets still available at the box —*sir!*"

This time, when he grabs me, I grab him back. He gasps as my fist takes a handful of his shirt, shoving him away from me.

"Security!" He squeals sharply. "Security!"

People waiting in line outside the concert doors next to us start to turn and murmur. Eyes go wide with recognition, and suddenly, hundreds of phones start flashing and recording me.

"Security!" Clipboard guy screeches into his earpiece. "We have a situation at the events door!"

A huge arm wraps around my chest, making me hiss as it yanks me away from the little guy.

"Alright pal, take a fucking hike or I'll—"

The massive security guard is built like a fucking truck. But when he whirls me around, his eyes widen and his hands drop from me.

"Oh *shit*!"

The guy with the clipboard fumes as he marches up to us.

"Get him out of here! Call the police if you—"

"Mike, you sure he's not on the list?"

The guy with the clipboard—Mike—scowls.

"What? Of course, he's not. Why the hell would he—"

"Because he's Jackson Havoc."

There were a hundred cameras filming me from the concert line a second ago. Now, it's more like a thousand.

Mike's eyes grow wide as his face pales.

"Oh my *God*, Mr. Havoc! I am *so* unbelievably—"

"Can I go inside now?"

"Of course!" He sputters. "Of course! Please!"

I mutter a thanks, turning to give a nod to the crowd outside, which sends them into a frenzy. Then, I duck through the door.

Sometimes, I really do hate fame. Other times, it comes in handy. Like when you're *not* actually on the guest list for the House of Rock production wrap event slash Kurt Harrison album release concert.

I'm obviously not here for the new stinking turd of an album Kurt's decided to shit out onto the chest of the music world. Twenty years later, he's still walking around with the same frosted tips, the same skinny jeans and white belt, and the same litany of terrible, trendy, meaningless tattoos.

He was trash twenty years ago. He's a fucking caricature now.

I'm also *clearly* not here for the House of Rock production wrap party that's being thrown at the Beacon Theatre's events hall right before Kurt's show. In fact, I'm willing to bet if Judy spots me here, shit is going to hit the fan in spectacular fashion.

But fuck it. I'm not here for Judy, or Kurt.

I'm here because…

Well, true to form, I'm actually figuring that part out as I go. Am I here to make a scene? To see if June is right that something is wrong with Melody? Or maybe I'm just finally ready to seek some kind of closure from this whole fucking situation.

All I know is, I'm not leaving here until Melody looks me in the fucking eye and tells me to. And even then, it's a coin toss if I actually will.

I'm not dressed for the event, either. But that's another perk of being a famous rock star. You can go into black-tie events in jeans and a grimy t-shirt, and be praised as some sort of fashion icon instead of schlub thumbing his nose at a dress code.

The production wrap party isn't black-tie, though. And I smirk, rolling my eyes as I look out on what may as well be a John Varvatos commercial. It's like the entire guest list decided to raid Johnny Depp's closet and show up in a sea of all-black suits, leather, and men wearing way too many accessories.

I stick to the perimeter, trying to put off the inevitable recognition for as long as I can as I scan the place for Melody. My eyes narrow lethally as I spot—well, *hear*, first—Judy off on the far side of the events space. She's fawning over a couple of older, square looking guys in suits who must be House of Rock producers.

I ignore her, letting my gaze rake over the crowd of phonies and posers.

Until suddenly, I freeze.

Suddenly, my heart begins to pound like a bass drum in my chest. My jaw grinds, my hands clenching tightly. And I'm not actually sure if it's in fists of anger, or with my body's Pavlovian need to grab her.

But either way, suddenly, as the crowds part in front of me…

There she is.

Melody.

I was prepared for anger. I was prepared to force her to look me in the eye and either admit she stabbed me in the back or else to tell me the fucking truth.

I wasn't prepared to feel my legs go numb. I wasn't prepared for the overwhelming desire to grab her in my arms and bruise the ever-loving fuck out of her lips.

And I'm still trying to process looking at her in the flesh for the first time in four months, when she turns, and our eyes lock.

Yes, I'm still fucking angry. Yes, I still want to scream in her face. But when I march in a straight line, shoving people out of my path as I storm towards her, all I really want is to be near her.

Melody's face pales, her eyes growing wide as saucers as I shove my way through two guys in leather jackets they clearly bought yesterday. But when I'm finally standing right in front of her, glaring down into her heart-stopping face, it's like the crowd of Johnny Depps around us suddenly fades away.

And it's just her and I.

"Jackson…"

Her face drains of even more color as I loom over her.

"You can't—"

"Just walk away."

The words that fall out of my mouth make *me* blink in surprise. Because I just marched over here ready to rip her to pieces, or to demand answers. But now that I'm here, standing inches from her, able to touch her if I wanted to for the first time in months? That all falls away.

And instead, all I want is her.

Without the baggage. Without the war. Without the anger.

Just her.

"Just walk away," I growl quietly.

My hand reaches out, and she jolts, flushing as it lands on her hip.

"Walk away, with me, right now."

She blinks rapidly, swallowing.

"What?"

"Drop all of it, sweetheart. And just leave it."

She slowly shakes her head, her eyes locked onto me.

"I—Jackson I *can't*…"

"Because you don't want to, or because of what—"

"Because if I do…" her eyes squeeze shut with a pain that cuts into me.

"Jackson, if I do, she'll destroy you."

"I don't give a *shit*," I snarl quietly.

"You should."

She opens her eyes, and real fear creeps over her face.

"Jackson, you *should*. Judy has a whole story ready to drop if she even sees you here—"

"All we need," I growl. "All we've ever needed, is right here. Just you and me, Melody," I whisper. "And the island."

"It's not your sanctuary anymore, Jackson," she croaks in a brittle voice. "They'd find us there. The whole world knows about—"

A tear rips down her cheek as her voice breaks.

"*I didn't write it*," she chokes. "That fucking article. I *swear* I didn't—"

"I know."

My hand squeezes her hip, making her flush as I pull her closer.

"I know you didn't."

"Jackson, *please!*" She begs, her face ashen. "You have to leave before Judy—"

"Jackson!"

My face darkens as Melody's pales. Slowly, I drag my eyes from the girl in front of me, to land on the witch that steps up besides us with an evil smile on her face.

"My *my*, isn't this a surprise!" Judy smiles a lifeless, thin smile as her eyes practically shoot daggers at me.

"Why, Jackson, I forgot you were on the guest list!"

"I wasn't."

"No shit."

She keeps smiling in that plastic, surgical way of hers.

"Jackson, honey, before you do anything stupid?"

Her eyes drop to where my hand is still on Melody's hip. Her face darkens before she drags her gaze back to me.

"I'm going to give you one minute to leave, Jackson."

"No thanks. Nice party, by the way."

"Jackson, so help me God. The stories about you I'm prepared to drop will make you *cry*—"

"Go ahead and do that, Judy." I shrug. "Because my lawyer has been *salivating* to fuck you in ways even *you've* never been fucked."

Her face goes ashen.

"How *dare* you—"

"This is *over*, Judy."

"What's over," she snaps.

"Your bullshit. All of this façade. It's done."

"Jackson, I advise you to take your fucking hands off my daughter—"

"*Your daughter*," I hiss, making her flinch as I suddenly whirl on her, my eyes narrowing. "*Your* daughter."

She opens her mouth to say something. But before she can, I grab her wrist and yank her close with my mouth by her ear, so that only she can hear.

"*I know*, Judy," I raps darkly.

"You know *what*—"

"About Iggy."

Judy pales. She goes stiff, her eyes locking with mine and hardening.

"End this shit, now, or—"

"Don't play games with me, Jackson."

I frown as she starts to grin at me.

"You think I'll just take *you* down?" Her eyes blaze as she leans close, putting her mouth by my ear.

"I'll take Iggy down, with you."

I go still, my jaw clenching.

"Think of poor Alice, hearing that her dear Iggy liked touching little girls."

"Fuck you, you toxic piece of—"

"I'll do it," she says smugly, leaning back from me.

"Do what?" Melody hisses.

But Judy just looks at me.

"The truth will ruin—"

"You mean your *lies* will ruin—"

"My lies will be on national news, Jackson," she snaps. "And people *love* to tear down a former idol. Think of poor Alice. Worse, think of poor Eleanor, knowing her daddy was a predator like that?"

Shit.

I was prepared for war, and for Judy to use chemical weapons. I was prepared to walk through fire if I had to.

I'm not prepared to make Alice and Eleanor do it.

I blink, numb as Judy smirks at me. She reaches over, grabbing Melody's hand and yanking her back.

Away from me.

"Jackson!"

"Let's go, Melody," Judy snaps.

My eyes lock onto Mel, my heart ripping open as I watch a tear slide down her face.

"This isn't over," I growl quietly, shaking with rage, pain, and emotion.

"Believe me," Judy hisses. "*It is.*"

All I can do is stand there, my jaw grinding to dust and my eyes lethally locked onto Melody as her mother pulls her away through the crowd to a door at the back of the event space.

Melody turns, and our eyes lock through the sea of strangers.

This isn't over.

But suddenly, another face from my past is slipping in through that doorway. My eyes narrow as Kurt fucking Harrison sees me, grinning that same douchebag smile of his as he flashes devil-horn hands at me like a complete wanker.

But then, something happens.

He nods his chin at me, turns, and puts his fucking hands on Melody's shoulders.

And when he does, she looks like she fucking *dies*.

Right there in front of my eyes, I watch her turn to ash. I watch the light extinguish from her eyes, and her body go rigid and still.

I watch pure trauma play out across her frozen face.

And suddenly, just as they turn and disappear through the security-guarded door, it clicks.

And I see fucking *red*.

42

JACKSON

FAME HAS ITS PRIVILEGES. Plenty of curses, sure. But tonight, it's the privilege of fame that gets me past security into the artists-only backstage area of the Beacon Theatre.

But I'm not here for the show. At the moment, I'm not even here to kidnap Melody or anything like that.

I'm here to slay her fucking monster.

I didn't know. It never even occurred to me. Even knowing somewhere in the back of my mind the random music world trivia that Kurt and Judy once dated. Even knowing from my time on the road with him exactly what a piece of shit he is.

I never put two and two together, until just now. Until I saw him touch her, and watched a piece of her die right there on her face.

And now, I know.

My blood is like acid in my veins as I slink through the backstage hallways. Until suddenly, I'm standing in front of his fucking dressing room door.

I don't knock. I just twist the knob and walk right in. Kurt whirls, his face going white. The girl who looks even younger than Melody gasps as she pulls her mouth away from his pathetic looking dick. Her face turns red as she quickly buttons her top back up. Kurt glances at me, swallowing as he tucks his baby-dick away.

"Fuck, Jackson, man," he laughs nervously, eying me. "I've been meaning to reach out, brother. You're back!"

I say nothing. I just glare death at him before turning to the girl.

"You should go."

Kurt makes a face.

"Naw, c'mon, baby. Stay." He glances at me, grinning. "Shit, tonight might even be your lucky night. Two rock stars all for you? What do you say, Havoc? Want to make this a crowd?"

The girl blushes, grinning salaciously at me.

"Leave. Now."

She blinks, flushing at the lethal tone in my voice. She nods quickly, gathering her bag before she brushes past me and out the door.

I kick it shut behind me. Kurt sighs heavily, reaching for a beer.

"Fuck, man. When did you turn into a cockblock—*fuck!*"

He chokes, spilling his beer as I slam into him. I shove him backwards, knocking him over the couch behind him and sprawling him out on the floor.

"What the *fuck*, man!?" He roars, lunging to his feet and glaring at me. "Are you fucking high? Dude, this is a fucking *custom* shirt—woah, *woah*, Jack—"

He squeals when my fist breaks his nose, splattering blood all over his custom fucking douchebag shirt. He stumbles back, blood pouring down his face as he lands on his ass and looks up at me in horror.

"What the *fuck*—"

"*I know it was you.*"

My voice is pure hatred and vengeance as it rasps from my lips. Kurt frowns, shaking his head.

"I don't know what you—"

"She was thirteen, motherfucker."

He screams when I punch his shattered nose again. And again, and then I hit him in the mouth until he's blubbering and sobbing pure blood and spittle.

"And in the very likely case that *doesn't* narrow it down for you," I snarl. I grab him by the collar, yanking him up as he flinches away from me.

"*I'm talking about Melody.*"

His eyes go wide with abject fear.

"*Jackson, please*," he blubbers. "You don't…it wasn't like that…"

"No?"

I smile as I punch him again, relishing the way he sobs.

"What was it like then, shithead? Tell me the *real* story about a thirty-four-year-old man using touch as a weapon on a fucking *thirteen-year-old kid*."

He trembles in my hands, shaking his head.

"Jackson, you know how these girls get with guys like us. You know the attention they want—"

This time, I don't stop hitting him until part of me wonders if he's actually dead. The man is limp in my arms, shuddering and flinching.

"*Jackson, please!*" He sobs. "Please, man! C'mon, it was years ago! Like you never—"

"*No,*" I snarl. "Because I'm not a monster like you."

"It was just…just rock 'n roll, man…" he mumbles through his shattered teeth. "Just rock 'n—"

"No, it wasn't."

I drop him into the puddle of blood and piss on the floor beneath him. My eyes scan the room, until they land on the guitar propped against his dressing room table.

"Jackson…"

"Oh, don't you worry," I hiss as I march over and grab the guitar. "I'm not leaving just yet."

He whimpers as I march back over, holding the neck of the gleaming gold and silver Fender guitar in my hands.

"You silenced her."

He cries out in pain as I kick his hand to the side and step heavily on his wrist. His eyes widen in horror as he looks up at the way I'm raising the guitar.

Like a hammer.

"*Jackson—!*"

"I'm silencing you."

I'll be honest; the screams as I bash one of his hands, and then other, into pulpy, shattered, nightmarish claws are pretty blood-chilling.

But oh-so-*fucking*-satisfying.

Bones can heal. Skin can be repaired.

The nerves and tendons in his hands will never be the same again, though.

Kurt will never play again.

When I'm done, I actually have to check his pulse, since he blacked out when I started in on his right hand. But he's alive.

Unfortunately.

I should kill him. I *want* to kill him. But I also just got back to the world. Going to prison for murder sounds like kind of a bummer, to be honest.

And so, I leave him there, like the shattered, broken monster he is. I wipe the blood off my shoes and knuckles and head for the door. But when I open it, I flinch as I almost walk right into a familiar redhead.

With a guitar case slung over her shoulder.

Melody's friend June gapes at me. Then she looks past me, and her face turns white.

"*Uhh...*"

"It would probably be for the best if you pretend you didn't see that."

Her eyes narrow.

"Is that Kurt Harrison?"

"It is."

"Is he dead?"

I shake my head. June's mouth thins.

"It's him, isn't it?" Her eyes narrow as she shakes her head. "The guy who…you know."

I don't say anything, but she's glaring pure hate at Kurt's motionless body.

"I've kinda put the pieces together before. He was dating Judy about the same time, and it's kind of an open secret in the music world about the shit he's into."

She pushes past me before I can stop her.

"June—"

She kicks Kurt in the balls, *hard*. Then she does it again, and again, and again, before I finally close the dressing room door, walk over, and put a hand on her shoulder.

She takes a breath, exhaling and then spitting on Kurt's unconscious face.

"Fucking *pig*."

"What were you doing, coming here?"

She turns, eying me.

"I was looking for Melody."

"And you got backstage...how?"

"You mean how because I'm not rich and famous like you?"

"Basically."

"A friend of mine is a sound tech for the theater." She frowns. "What were *you* doing here, aside from taking out the trash?"

"Same story."

She grins.

"So, what now?"

A knock on the door makes June flinch.

"Mr. Harrison!" A voice calls through. "Fifteen minutes, Mr. Harrison!"

It's a terrible idea. Or maybe a great one.

Maybe, the only difference between either of those things is balls and some good ole fashion rock 'n roll shenanigans.

I turn back to June.

"You decent with that guitar?"

"I'm fucking *fantastic* with this guitar, thanks."

I grin.

"Good. Want to do something profoundly stupid with me?"

"Is this about Melody?"

"Yes."

"Then definitely."

I walk over to the rack of Kurt's guitars against the wall and grab the least offensively glittery one I can find.

"You ever play any gigs before?"

June rolls her eyes.

"Dude, I've played like four gigs a week since I was fifteen."

I arch an impressed brow.

"Ever play the Beacon Theatre?"

"Uh, no?"

I grin.

"Well, you're about to."

43

MELODY

Every step down the aisle—with the strangers smiling at me, and the cameras flashing, and Judy's grip on my wrist—feels like my heart is ripping in two. Every beat of my pulse feels like I'm leaving a trail of blood behind me.

So much of me wants to run back through the doors and fall right into his arms. To kiss him and hold him so tightly in my hands.

To tell him I love him.

But if I do any of those things, he'll be ruined. Judy will push the button on her weaponized media lies, and the world will think he's a monster. That he abused me. That he hooked up with girls on the road who were so young.

It doesn't matter if they're lies, and Judy knows it. But her strategy is basically to overwhelm with bullshit. If she floods the news with enough scandalous, horrific things, at least some of it will stick, even if they're lies.

And I won't do that to him.

Because if that happens, there's no place on earth he could go to escape. And if *that* happens, it's the final nail in our coffin.

We'll never be able to be together after that. At least if I go along with Judy, I can hang on to hope.

I can cling to a dream, even if I'm just waiting in tears to wake up.

Judy smiles for the cameras and the sycophant producers of the show as she drags me to the center of the front row. My body clenches nauseously as I stare up at the microphone stand not five feet from me, where *he'll* be standing in just a few minutes.

Leering at me.

Singing at me.

Making me feel like I'm that kid again—cold and motionless and unable to do or say a thing as he puts his hands on me.

"*Mom*," I choke, almost unable to swallow as the anxiety claws at me. "Mom, *please*—"

"Don't make a scene, Melody," she hisses out of the corner of her mouth, still smiling at the cameras around us.

And then, the house lights go down, and the audience begins to cheer.

It feels like they're cheering for my own execution.

Dread swallows me whole as I stare blankly at the stage. An electric guitar starts to play through one of the amps on stage. I flinch, going pale. I glance up, and my eyes follow the trail of the guitar cable leading out of the amp and across the stage into the darkened wings.

The guitar strums again, but suddenly, something ticks in my head. I freeze, my breath choking as the chord blares out again.

My heart begins to swell.

That's not the opening to any Kurt Harrison song.

It's the opening to *our song*.

The lights dim down to blackness as the guitar chord repeats in a rhythm I know too well. My pulse roars in my ears, my skin throbbing with electric current as a dark shape holding a guitar steps from the wings to center stage.

The chord roars out again.

The stage lights come up.

And my heart almost flies out of my mouth as the entire Beacon Theatre loses their fucking *minds*.

Because standing there alone on stage, for the first time in over ten years…

Is Jackson Havoc.

And like magic—like watching an artist touch a brush for the first time in years, or a sports legend pick up a football again—I watch him morph right there in front of my eyes. The brooding, angry, jaded Jackson melts away.

And a fucking rock *god* suddenly looks up and grins that famously roguish, pulse-quickening grin at the audience.

"Been a while, hasn't it?"

He grins wider as the crowd goes apeshit. Judy is gripping her armrests like she might tear them off, a look of pure hatred on her face. But around us, people are surging to their feet. A million phones illuminate the theater as Jackson winks on stage.

"So, I was in the neighborhood, and thought I'd stop by."

A wall of screams and cheers thunders through the audience.

"Which is good," Jackson smiles. "Because, unfortunately, Kurt couldn't make it on stage tonight because he's a child abusing piece of shit who was enabled by *this* piece of shit."

My jaw drops as he points right at Judy, who goes *livid* next to me. She lurches to her feet, her eyes manic and wild and her shoulders heaving with rage.

"*You!*" She screams at Jackson, jabbing a finger at him up on stage.

"I will fucking *destroy—*"

"Yeah, go fuck yourself, Judy."

The crowd erupts in cheers and laugher as Jackson's eyes narrow on my mother.

"By the way, your book has a few typos in it. But don't worry, my lawyer's reaching out tonight to help you go over those."

Judy goes white. Past her, the cabal of producers for House of Rock look equally as pale as they lean their heads together, talking quickly.

"You—! You—!"

"Door's that way, Judy," Jackson smiles thinly, pointing to the exit. "Try not to blow anyone famous on the way out."

Howls of laughter fill the theater as Judy sways on her feet, looking like she's going to be sick. She whirls to me, her face falling.

"Honey, I—"

But when she reaches for me, I jerk my arm away. I don't say anything, because there's nothing left to say. All I do is watch as the realization that she's lost me dawns on her face.

"*Melody—*"

I turn away from her, my eyes locking with Jackson's. And slowly, out of the corner of my eyes, I see her back away, before she turns and flees up the aisle and out the door.

My pulse hums as Jackson begins to strum the guitar.

"This is a new one, so, forgive the roughness."

Yeah, as if the first crowd to hear Jackson Havoc play live in eleven years would care if he played *Happy Birthday* on a fucking kazoo. And predictably, they go *nuts*.

"But it being new and all, I'm going to need some help with it."

He glances off-stage, where the sound of another guitar joins him. I frown as my gaze swivels to the figure stepping out onto the stage.

Immediately, my jaw drops through the floor when *June* locks eyes with me.

She's grinning from ear to ear, staring at me wide-eyed with glee. She drops her hand from the guitar and jabs a finger at Jackson's back, mouthing "*what the FUCK*" at me as I start to laugh. She begins to play again, layering notes on top of Jackson's strums as he looks out over the crowd.

Triumphant.

Relaxed.

Completely in his element.

"Shit," he chuckles, grinning widely. "It really has been too long, hasn't it?"

A million decibels of "yes" hit him back, and he grins.

"Well, like I said, I'm gonna need some help with this new one. What do you say, Melody?"

I go numb. It's like someone else is controlling my body as I slowly rise to my feet, my heart thudding in my chest as I stare at him.

"C'mon up, Mel."

I blink, swallowing the lump that forms in my throat. Fear starts to sink it's claws into me. But it's like he sees right through me. He cups the microphone, pushing the stand aside as he leans down and sticks his hand out.

"It's just you and me, sweetheart," he murmurs quietly, looking right into my eyes. "It's just you and me. But I need you."

The roar of the crowd dulls to a murmur around me. The lights dim away. The earth slows to a crawl.

And then, he's right.

It's just him and I.

My hand slides into his, and everything starts to speed up again, growing louder once more as he lifts me onto the stage. He grins at me, and I just stand there, shaking but so full of happiness as I lose myself in his eyes.

"Turn around," he murmurs.

I do, and it's like a rush I've never once imagined before. A *sea* of faces stretches out in front of me.

Cheering. Screaming. Taking pictures.

Jackson joins June in playing again as he steps up to the mic.

"Ladies and gentlemen, allow me to introduce one of the best songwriters I've ever known."

My face turns to fire as the crowd surges and cheers.

"Who also happens to be the daughter of the best man I ever knew, Iggy Watts."

The floor drops out. I sway, my throat closing as I whirl to stare at him.

Shaking.

Crying.

It feels like I'm about to fall, but suddenly, he's there, right in front of me and steadying me with an arm around my waist and a hand at the small of my back.

"*I'm sorry*," he murmurs, looking into my eyes. "I didn't want to do that publicly. But I'm about to kiss you, and I kinda had to clear up that whole parentage thing before I—"

I grab his collar, yank him down, and I kiss him as hard as I possibly can as the crowd explodes around us.

He groans into my lips, cupping my face with his hand as we forget the world together.

"You ready to sing?" He murmurs against my lips.

"I…."

"Because I'm in love with you, Melody."

My heart skips.

"And right now, I don't want you to sing for me, or for them, or fucking *anyone* but you."

His steely blue eyes stab into mine as he pulls me towards the mic alongside him.

"Sing for you, sweetheart."

I glance at a beaming June. I turn to the roaring crowd.

I grin.

And then, we're off.

The words pour out, and my heart grows ten times bigger than it's ever been before. And then it's over, and the crowd is losing its mind.

A million cameras are flashing

The House of Rock producers are shaking their heads and making a quick exit.

Jackson slides his hand in mine, and we take a bow together. And then he pulls me into him, and kisses me, and tell me he loves me.

Then?

Then it's over.

And it's also just beginning.

EPILOGUE

MELODY

"You ready?"

No. Maybe. I don't know.

But the real answer is "yes". With nerves. With a pit in my stomach. But, it's time, even though I've been putting this off for the last three weeks.

In my defense, though, it's been a *wild* three weeks. I mean where do you even begin?

With Judy, I guess, who by all accounts is having a complete mental breakdown. And my only response to that news is that I'd honestly love to hire the smallest violin in the world to softly play *Cry Me A River* on repeat outside her window for the rest of her life.

Judy can go fuck herself. Because we're officially done, and she's officially out a daughter. Full stop.

She's also out this empire of hers she was so hell bent on building by any means necessary, at any price. Because in the wake of what happened at the Beacon that night, the whole thing has come down in ruins around her.

House of Rock has been shelved indefinitely. First, it was just real shitty PR surrounding everything that came out that night. But as the PR turned into legal battles—like mine, for instance—the producers pulled the plug.

Ten of the absolute *shittiest*, most scripted, most cringe-tastic reality show episodes ever filmed, and they will never see the light of day. Thank God.

With the show went the home-goods line. And the fashion line. And the rest of it. Her book got yanked, too, after Jackson's lawyer went at it with a blowtorch and a tire-iron. Cliff ended up leaking the whole situation to a few media outlets, and Judy's PR disaster went from awful to "change your name, maybe get a surgeon to change your face, and then hide off the map for the rest of your life" bad.

In *The New York Times* piece on the whole saga, their in-house legal expert called the book "the single most egregiously libelous piece of fiction ever penned".

So, there's that.

In further uplifting news as it pertains to journalistic integrity, both Becca Santori and Chuck Garver were summarily fired from Ignition Magazine. Becca for the obvious theft and plagiarism; Chuck for enabling and purposely not fact-checking any of it. Jackson and I even got a published apology letter in the last issue of Ignition from their parent company, Clearsite Publishing.

And that brings us to Kurt; my now-slain monster, who I no longer fear.

Judy's in trouble. Becca and Chuck got what was coming to them.

Kurt is getting royally *fucked* and you can go ahead and pass me the fucking popcorn.

At first, after what Jackson did to him backstage, Kurt tried to sue. What he should have done was slink away into a hole in the ground somewhere, because he would have had a better time doing that than what's happening to him now.

When he decided to go public with his version of Jackson's assault on him, I decided that two could play that game.

I went public, too.

And yeah, it was hard. It was *really* hard, actually. But I've had an amazing man at my side, holding my hand through the whole ordeal of bearing the worst part of my past to the public.

But it's working.

For one, I'm going to be pressing charges. But even better, once my story got legs with the media and started to get spread around, more versions of me came out of the shadows.

Twenty-five versions of me, actually.

Twenty-five incredibly brave, very angry women who'd all been victimized when they were under the age of eighteen by Kurt. Who had been given money, or NDAs, or even just threats to keep quiet.

Forget his reality show and his album being shelved. The piece of shit is looking at prison for the rest of his life.

"You're sure?"

I blink away the bad, smiling as I turn to sink into Jackson's chest.

"I'm sure."

"We can come back another day, Mel. I'm sure—"

"Just ring the bell."

I take a deep breath. I can do this. This'll be fine.

"She's gonna love you!" I can hear June telling me from the other night when I told her about this. *"What are you even worried about? What's not to love?"*

I grin. Jackson being here is helping a lot. But I kinda wish June was too. Though, that'd be hard, given her schedule these days.

Because June Hendrix officially went viral the night she played live on stage with Jackson for his first public performance in more than a decade.

I mean, *obviously* she did. Not just for being there, but because she fucking rocks. After we played our new song that night, Jackson leaned over and asked if June knew how to play *Wreck Me Gently*.

Which, she does. I've seen her cover it in her shows, and it brings the house down. Which it did that night.

About three-thousand people filmed her one-woman, one guitar solo version of the Velvet Guillotine hit. And three weeks later, one of those videos is closing in on eighty *million* plays on YouTube.

Her Spotify plays are through the roof, her email inbox is a disaster, and her phone has been ringing incessantly for three weeks.

I couldn't be happier for her.

Smokey's Joint out on Avenue C was smart enough—and quick enough—to book her as a resident act for two weeks. When that sold out in about eleven seconds, they extended it another month.

It's still sold out. Girl is on *fire*.

"Alright, I'm doing it."

I take a shaky breath as Jackson rings the doorbell of the gorgeous townhouse on Central Park West. My heart thuds like a drum, and every single dread and nagging worry comes out to play.

I mean, Jackson obviously filled me in on the full story of Judy and my father once we had privacy. Once I could cry the tears of loss and those of happiness into his chest.

Is the woman who answers this door going to hate me, because of what I represent? Because I'm the living embodiment of the faults in the man she loved?

The door unlocks, and my heart jumps into my throat. It swings open, and I tense as I lock eyes with Alice Watts.

A second ticks by, my stomach slowly sinking into my feet. But then, she suddenly bursts into tears, while simultaneously smiling widely.

"Alice—"

She throws her arms around me, hugging me fiercely.

"It's so nice to finally meet you, Prudence."

Well fuck me, there I go, too.

The emotional walls in me come crumbling down as tears flood my eyes. I hug her tightly, just losing myself in her embrace as the seconds turn into minutes.

Eventually, we all tumble inside. Where I immediately start to cry all over again when I lay eyes for the first time on my sister, Eleanor.

Eleanor Rigby, meet Dear Prudence.

I think I'm going to really love getting to know who my father was.

Alice makes tea, and we all sit around the kitchen laughing and listening to old Guillotine records as Jackson tells us stories about Iggy from when they were kids.

Eleanor plays her guitar for me, which is…mind-blowing and amazing.

Alice sits down with me on the couch and shows me picture after loving picture of my dad through the years, followed by the letters he never sent.

Yeah, more tears. All the freaking tears.

But even though it's sad, there's also a joy that comes the longer I sit with the woman who loved my father, the sister I can't wait to get to know better, and the man who stole my heart.

As Jackson is oh-so-fond of saying, "the real world isn't a cliched fucking lyric". But that doesn't mean it's not still beautiful. It doesn't mean life can't be a haunted melody, or repeated motif, or a broken line.

Maybe life *is* a song, after all. If we're lucky, we get to keep the chorus going. And if we're *really* lucky, we even get to pick who we sing it with.

"*Okay,*" Alice laughs. "Who needs more tea?"

"Oh, I got it!"

I spring from Jackson's lap before Alice can get off the couch, darting past her to the kitchen. I put the kettle on the burner, and then frown as I glance around looking for the tea itself.

Hmm.

I poke around a few cabinets and then reach for the one above the microwave. I jump, gasping as something falls past my face to land at my feet.

My brow furrows curiously at the postcard with a cartoony cactus drinking a Corona on the front.

Weird.

I go to pick it up, but without really thinking, I glance at the back, which has Alice's townhouse as the "to" address" and what looks like a hotel of some kind in Juarez, Mexico, as the "from" address.

There's just one line written, but when my eyes land on it, I go absolutely still. Not because of *what* it says, which is just "Ally, I made it. Thanks for everything."

No.

I freeze because I'd recognize the handwriting any day, in the dark, with my eyes half closed.

Because it's the same handwriting that's been framed on the wall of my mom's apartment since it was gifted to her by the man who wrote it.

The note on the wall, and this postcard.

The postcard is from Will Cates.

I smile sadly, remembering the man who taught me to play and sing. And I'm about to put it back where I found it and tell myself not to go snooping around other people's things, when my eyes slip to the postage.

I blink, staring at the date, not quite understanding what I'm looking at, until the reality is impossible to ignore.

Until the world tilts a little.

Will Cates died in a motorcycle crash eight years ago.

The postage of the postcard in my hand that he unquestionably wrote is from *seven* years ago.

I stare wide-eyed at the card in my hands.

Ally, I made it. Thanks for everything.

Holy shit.

"Mel!"

I jolt when I hear Alice's voice from the living room.

"Need a hand?"

"Nope!" I almost trip over myself in shoving the postcard back into the cabinet and closing the door.

"I got it!"

The kettle is just beginning to whistle when I turn it off, and then spot the jar of tea bags right there next to the stove. I pour a few mugs, stick them on a tray, and quickly rush back into the living room.

"Sorry, here we go."

Alice grins as I pass her a mug, doing my best not to stare, or just blurt it out and ask her what the *hell* I just saw back in the kitchen.

But I don't do that. Because even if I just met her, I know she's a good person. And whatever the mystery involving Will that I just accidentally looked at is, I'm sure it's been hidden for a reason.

A reason that can wait for another day.

So instead, I settle into Jackson's lap as the afternoon slides into night. And my tears from earlier turn to laughter and smiles as I drown myself in pictures, stories, and the music of the father I never knew. And as I sit there wrapped in Jackson's arms with a smile on my face as Eleanor starts to play old Velvet Guillotine songs, all I feel is lucky.

And loved.

And at peace.

I turn to him, and he grins as he cups my face, leans in, and kisses me softly.

My missing chord.

My killer line.

But most of all, the man I love.

An exclusive extra scene involving Jackson and Melody is available to my VIP readers list! This isn't an epilogue or continuation to *Broken Lines*. But this extra hot "follow-up" story is guaranteed to fog up your Kindle. Sign up now to read. You'll also get a free full-length book when you join!

Get the extra scene!

A WORLD OF BOOKS

Thank you so much for reading! If *Broken Lines* was your first forays into my books, I wanted to let you know that most of my stories all exist in the same "world".

For instance, a young Jackson appears in *The Hunter King*, book 1 in the Hunted Duet. The author Bastian Pierce, mentioned in this book, in fact has his own story in *Forbidden Crown*, part of the Savage Heirs series. And June Hendrix makes an appearance in *The Bratva's Locked Up Love*.

All of my books can be read individually as standalone. You can find complete book lists and suggested reading orders on my website.

www.jaggercolewrites.com

Scroll on for a sneak peek of *The Hunter King*.

THE HUNTER KING PREVIEW

Chapter 1

The darkness of night swirls around me, clawing at my peripherals and snarling at my pounding feet. Branches catch at my hair and ankles, raking my skin and leaving whip-marks I can't feel over the thudding, heaving pressure in my chest.

My breathing is ragged as I race barefoot and naked though the black woods. The thud-thud-thudding of my pulse roaring like a dragon in my ears drowns out everything—the sting of sticks and pine needles under my feet. The branches whipping at my exposed skin. The raised root that slams my shin as I vault over it. The screaming violence of fear, and the dark rush of excitement that comes hand-in-hand with it.

The thudding, pounding sound of heavy, masculine feet on the path behind me grow louder. The low grunt of his breath as he chases me… rhythmically, ceaselessly, sleeplessly. An animalistic, unyielding, utterly driven force inches away from capturing me.

The adrenaline screams through my body as I hear him pull closer. His breath, hot on my neck; his fingertips barely brushing the ends of my long hair, milliseconds away from tangling in my locks and yanking me to the ground like the prey I am.

I scream, my throat haggard and raw, my skin both recoiling and shivering for his touch and that single moment where I'll go from hunted to caught. From fleeing to pinned.

From free to *his*.

The fear spikes through me, shoving energy into my limbs and igniting the last few drops of fuel I have left in the tank. A wrenching sound breaks through my lips as I surge ahead, dodging left and then right through the black trees and swirling shadows. Branches slice at my face, cutting at my nakedness—clawing me back as if the very woods I run through are bent to his bidding, determined to deliver me into his grasp.

Faceless. Furious. Ceaseless.

My venomous fear, and my dark excitement.

The shadow that chases me screaming through the night and leaves me shivering and aching for more when it's over.

I lurch between two trees and jerk to the left, bolting for an opening in the woods. The pounding of his footsteps draws closer, and closer, and *closer*. My heart roars, my muscles scream, and my core clenches as I dig deep for the very last of my reserves, pushing myself to just *get to the clearing*.

If I get to the clearing, I'll be safe. I'll be free from his poisonous, all-consuming need for me.

Until next time.

With a choking, gasping sound from my throat, I surge forward.

Eyes on the prize.

Don't look back.

Swallow the fear.

Run.

Something sharp slices the arch of my bare foot. I scream, stumbling but catching myself. It's only a quarter second… but it's enough.

I feel the ephemeral throb of his power against my back before I feel the very physical grip of his hands circling my neck from behind.

Oh God…

My eyes bulge, my throat closes off the scream. Hot, iron-corded muscles wrap around my body, yanking me against his bare skin before he brings me forward to the ground beneath him, the weight of him pinning me to the dirt and pine needles.

Every molecule in my body explodes. Every nerve ending howls. My breath chokes, my muscles scream, and the horrible ache in my core engulfs me in fire.

Hand on my neck. Skin on my skin. Lips rasping against my ear as he prepares to claim his prey.

"Mine…"

I bolt upright in bed, gasping and choking, my hands flying to my neck as my legs kick and thrash the blankets away.

Silence hums in my ears.

I swallow dryness, and blink at the semi-light of daybreak coming through the window shades. My pulse still screaming in my veins as my eyes dart around the frilly white bedroom.

The woods are gone.

The darkness is faded.

The dream is gone.

The aching throb deep in my core and the shivering fear it leaves teasing over my skin, however, remain.

I swallow again and close my eyes, shivering as my hands slide from my neck to push the fiery tangles back from my face. Sweat slicks across my skin, even in the cool of the air-conditioned bedroom.

Gradually, my racing heart slows. The slick across my skin begins to cool to goosebumps. My clenched throat opens, and the knot throbbing in my core begins to unravel.

In the ephemeral half-light of day creeping over the horizon, my eyes slide to the clock on my nightstand. Four minutes until five in the morning.

Fucking nightmares.

I exhale again, my arms circling as I hug myself. It isn't the first time I've been chased through the woods in my dreams. Though, this is a newer direction than my usual nightmares.

Usually, they're about the accident. Usually, I'm drowning in the water, helpless to stop it. The man, or creature, or devil, or whatever it is that hunts me like prey through the darkness is a recent development.

But, if I'm going to have nightmares almost nightly, at least my brain is keeping things fresh, I suppose.

My brow furrows. My alarm was set for seven this morning—almost two hours from now. But I know from experience that there's no going back to sleep after a dream like the chase through the woods.

A dream that leaves me rattled.

And shivering.

And… *other* physical manifestations that frankly alarm me, considering the content of my nightmare.

The fear is rational.

The arousal is perverse.

I scoot back, leaning my shoulders against the headboard of the large queen-sized bed adorned with lacy frills and elegant details. My gaze sweeps the semi-dark room, slowly tracing over the equally frilly and entirely white aesthetic—like the whole bedroom suite is a white-washed showroom out of a Lillian August or Restoration Hardware catalog. Cold, sanitized, and completely depersonalized.

I have no idea who decided to redo my old bedroom in the two years I've been gone at college. Certainly not my father—interior design is *slightly* outside the purview of running a criminal empire. It could have been my stepmother, Jana—even if only to erase my own personal touches to the bedroom I left behind when I went off to Harvard. Because erasing my history seems to be a pastime of hers.

My musings move on to Senna, my father's head housekeeper and chief of household staff. But then they swing back to Jana.

Painting over the dark blues and ripping down my old punk and indie rock posters was almost certainly Jana's doing.

In the month I've been home, I've been tempted to make it look exactly like it did before, down to the smallest detail—the Sex Pistols and Nick Cave concert posters, the decoupage desk made from Rolling Stone magazine clippings; all of it.

But somehow, the last month has slipped by in a haze of uncertainty and mourning.

Coming back to your father's mansion after he dies unexpectedly will do that, I guess.

We were never close. And I always, *always* knew I came second to his work. I'm not sure he would've even bothered denying that if confronted with it. But still; losing a parent is still a process that takes time.

My gaze flits to the side table again, to the single piece of personalization I've brought back to this showroom of a bedroom. The framed photo of my parents was shot by me, age nine, while we were visiting Paris. In a rare, *rare* occurrence of my father actually appearing in public, he and my mother are standing beside the big glass pyramid that sits in the courtyard of the Louvre. My father, Peter, is unsmiling and cold—nothing outside the usual there. But my mother's smile lights up the photo for the both of them.

That's a loss that still stings four years later.

My phone lights up, yanking my head out of the memories of death. I reach for it, smiling when I see the text from Lyra, my roommate back at Harvard.

Happy birthday, roomie! I hope you enjoy the day. I'm here if you ever need a chat!

My lips curl into a grin.

Well, that's one person who'll remember the occasion today.

Lyra and I were junior year roommates for all of two weeks before the accident—before I had to come home and bury my second parent, and then try and process what comes next. But she's been checking in on me every few days since I left to make sure I'm okay.

Friends are a luxury I'm still getting used to. Or, *was* getting used to, before I was sucked back into this world, and this version of myself.

Not Tatiana Fairist the poli-sci major at Harvard University, lover of quirky indie rock, collector of vintage leather jackets, and drinker of strong black coffee.

No, this version—the version I've tried to bury in two years of college, is a darker version. Here, I'm Tatiana Fairist the Bratva princess. Tatiana who is about to get a deep-end lesson in mafia politics, because as of a month ago, with the death of my father, I am now officially the next in line for Balagula Bratva that was once helmed by my maternal grandfather. Much to the bitterness of my stepmother.

It's not official yet, of course. But it will be, and that's been hanging over me like a prison sentence since I watched them lower my father into the ground. The strict and very old-fashioned "high council" of advisors originally set up by my grandfather is hard at work with what comes next. Technically, pursuant with the laws of the Balagula family, I have to be *married* in order to helm the organization. Or rather, I have to be married so that my—chosen for me—*husband* can helm things.

It's why Peter Fairist, my father, was in charge after my grandfather passed, not Casmir's own daughter, Lisana.

"Bratva" and "old-school sexist patriarchy" are the same word in the Balagula organization. Not that I actually care in this case, since having anything to do with my family's criminal organization, or being forced to marry, or *any* of the current realities of my life are at the very bottom of my list.

I exhale, fully awake now as I smile at the birthday text from Lyra. I'm officially twenty. Though, I won't be celebrating with anyone but myself and maybe some of the household staff, since Jana's been in Paris for the last month on a shopping spree.

Grief works in mysterious ways.

I glance at the book I fell asleep reading last night; a gift from Lyra when I was packing up in a rush to get back home. It's a slightly embellished story of Harriet Quimby, the first female pilot to fly across the Thames river, and honestly, it's not bad.

I open to where I left off, where Harriet is faced with the choice between her aspirations of flying and the advances of the swoony and handsome Lord Buckmiller—that would be the wildly embellished part of the actual history of Harriet

Quimby. But as the room grows lighter with morning, I close the book again.

I might as well get up.

In my closet, I pick out something fun to wear. It's fifty-fifty if anyone else in this house even remembers the day but screw it: it's my birthday and I'll wear what I want. So, my favorite ripped jeans and vintage The Clash t-shirt it is.

I drape them over the back of a chair and sit at the vanity. My eyes drop to the silver ring that sits on a small silver chain necklace—a gift from my father years ago for my sixteenth birthday right after my accident and right after my mom died. There's a little charm of a puzzle piece on it, and my father, in a *rare* blip of sentimentality, told me it was because I was the "final piece of his heart."

I smile wryly as I put it on, clasping it behind my neck and letting it fall across my chest. I exhale, pushing my red tangles back into a messy ponytail as I stand and turn for my clothes.

And that's when I hear the screaming.

I freeze, my pulse jangling as my heart lurches into my throat. A shot rings out, making me flinch as my eyes wrench to the door to my room. More gunshots pound out—a back and forth, closer this time—and I can hear more screaming from the staff.

I drop the clothes I've picked out and bolt for the bathroom door. Inside, my hands shaking and my pulse thudding in my ears, I lock the door behind and move to crank open the window. Barefoot in just sleep shorts and a baggie t-shirt, and ignoring the sounds of gunfire coming closer to my bedroom, I swing a leg over the sill. I find footing it the rose-covered lattice on the outside of the sprawling Tudor brick mansion and swing the other leg over.

Trembling, swallowing back the fear, I climb down as fast as I can, wincing at the sting of thorns and brambles. My feet touch grass, and I whirl to run. It's still barely light out as I bolt for the rose gardens at the back of the house.

There's no more gunshots.

No more screaming.

The only sound is my ragged breathing and my roaring pulse as I run. Just like the dream.

There's a gate at the far end of the property—a service driveway for staff and deliveries. If I can make it there, I can alert the guard on duty. Even if there's no one there, I can escape. I realize I've left my phone back in my room, but if I can get to the gate, I can run the three kilometers into town and—

The scream strangles in my throat as the hard, muscled arm wraps like iron around my neck. Another wraps around my torso, and my entire body spasms with fear. My lungs scream for air and my pulse spikes as I'm yanked back against a man's rock-hard body, his breath hot on my neck.

I'm caught; trapped. Just like my dream.

But I'm not going to wake up from this nightmare.

Keep reading!

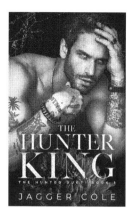

The Hunter King - Exclusively on Amazon and in Kindle Unlimited!

Come hang in my readers-only Facebook group for first glimpses of covers, new books, ARC opportunities, and live readings. See you there!

THE HUNTER KING PREVIEW

ALSO BY JAGGER COLE

Hunted Duet:

The Hunter King

The Hunted Queen

Cinder Duet:

Burned Cinder

Empire of Ash

Savage Heirs:

Savage Heir

Dark Prince

Brutal King

Forbidden Crown

Broken God

Defiant Queen

Bratva's Claim:

Paying The Bratva's Debt

The Bratva's Stolen Bride

Hunted By The Bratva Beast

His Captive Bratva Princess

Owned By The Bratva King

The Bratva's Locked Up Love

The Scaliami Crime Family:

The Hitman's Obsession

The Boss's Temptation

The Bodyguard's Weakness

Standalones:

Broken Lines

Bosshole

Grumpaholic

Stalker of Mine

Power Series:

Tyrant

Outlaw

Warlord

ABOUT THE AUTHOR

Jagger Cole

A reader first and foremost, Jagger Cole cut his romance writing teeth penning various steamy fan-fiction stories years ago. After deciding to hang up his writing boots, Jagger worked in advertising pretending to be Don Draper. It worked enough to convince a woman way out of his league to marry him, though, which is a total win.

Now, Dad to two little princesses and King to a Queen, Jagger is thrilled to be back at the keyboard.

When not writing or reading romance books, he can be found woodworking, enjoying good whiskey, and grilling outside - rain or shine.

You can find all of his books at
www.jaggercolewrites.com

Made in the USA
Columbia, SC
27 October 2022